PRAISE FOR
Within These Lines

"A frightening portrait of how suspicion and fear of Japanese Americans during World War II led to the incarceration of thousands at Manzanar and other camps. Precise in its history, intimate in detail, Stephanie Morrill's sensitively written novel brings to life a shameful era of American injustice, one that echoes events in the present day."

—Janet Taylor Lisle, ALA notable author of Scott O'Dell Award winner *The Art of Keeping Cool* and Newbery Honor book *Afternoon of the Elves*

"A thoughtful and moving story of forbidden love under the dual pressures of wartime and of intolerance, *Within These Lines* grabs you with its mix of fascinating historical fact and heart-melting fiction. Stephanie Morrill keeps you hoping against hope right up to the very last page."

—Caroline Leech, author of *Wait for Me* and *In Another Time*

"*Within These Lines* will steal your breath, your heart, and your thoughts for days after you've finished. An always-timely look at prejudice and the importance of taking action combines with a tale of deepest love and self-sacrifice. Flawless and beautiful."

—Roseanna M. White, bestselling author of the Ladies of the Manor and Shadows Over England series

"Poignant and evocatively relevant, *Within These Lines* is a tale of star-crossed love and heartrending discrimination with characters that leap off the page and challenge us to stand against the injustice in our own time. A gripping read!"

—Lorie Langdon, author of *Olivia Twist* and the Doon series.

"*Within These Lines* will both break your heart and awaken it. Evalina and Taichi's story not only navigates a precarious romance, but it challenges racism, injustice, and the temptation to stay silent. Their boldness and call to action will stick with you long after you turn the last page. I applaud Morrill's storytelling and cannot recommend this book enough—a must-read for all historical fiction fans!"

—Nadine Brandes, author of *Fawkes*

"*Within These Lines* is a moving story of love, hope, and family set against the dark history of Japanese internment in America. This book had me captivated!"

—Maureen McQuerry, YALSA award-winning author of *The Peculiars* and the upcoming *Between Before and After*

"Thought provoking and timely, *Within These Lines* highlights a dark period in history. Through compelling characters, we see the injustice and feel the fears and doubts and dilemmas. But mostly, we see the shimmering ribbon of hope through Evalina and Taichi's unrelenting love. Stephanie Morrill has written a novel to ponder, a novel to cherish."

—Sarah Sundin, bestselling and award-winning author of *The Sea Before Us* and *The Sky Above Us*

"Heartrending and timely, Evalina and Taichi's story leaps off the page. Morrill deftly weaves history and fiction together, shining a light on the realities of America's World War II-era home front through the eyes of her fiery and steadfast protagonists. From start to satisfying finish, historical fiction readers won't want to miss Morrill's latest."

—Hillary Manton Lodge, author of *A Table by the Window*

"In fiercely beautiful prose, Stephanie Morrill delivers a timely new novel that sheds much-needed light on racial conflict and trauma experienced on the home front during World War II. An evocative, impeccably researched story of love, loss, longing, and the necessary hard work of reconciliation, *Within These Lines* offers characters who will inspire readers long into the future. Historical fiction fans, this is a must-read for 2019."

—Karen Halvorsen Schreck, author of *Broken Ground*

ALSO BY STEPHANIE MORRILL

The Lost Girl of Astor Street

within these lines

STEPHANIE MORRILL

BLINK®

BLINK

Within These Lines
Copyright © 2019 by Stephanie Morrill

Requests for information should be addressed to:
Blink, *3900 Sparks Dr. SE, Grand Rapids, Michigan 49546*

Hardcover ISBN 978-0-310-76523-3

Audio ISBN 978-0-310-76863-0

Ebook ISBN 978-0-310-76526-4

Interior design: Denise Froehlich

Printed in the United States of America

19 20 21 22 23 /LSC/ 10 9 8 7 6 5 4 3 2 1

To McKenna, Connor, and Eli.
May you always be brave enough
to care and bold enough to act.

CHAPTER ONE

Evalina

Saturday, March 21, 1942
3 months after the Japanese attacked Pearl Harbor
San Francisco, California

When I jolt awake, the familiar fear smothers my early morning thoughts and thrums through my veins. I gasp for breath, as if there's a shortage of oxygen, until I convince my rhythm to slow.

No light comes into my room—too early—but I draw back a panel of my gingham curtains and peek outside anyway, just to reassure myself that it's all still there—my narrow street, my neighbors' houses, my entire world.

And there it is, the sound that roused me from my fearful slumber. The faint squeak of bicycle pedals as the paperboy pushes himself up our steep hill. When I look closely at the front door of the house across the street, I spot the newspaper lying across the front step like a welcome mat.

The planks of my wooden floor creak as I slip out my door, past Mama and Daddy's quiet bedroom, down the narrow, steep staircase, and out the front door. Even in the dim lighting of the streetlamp, the bold headline of the *San Francisco News* reaches up and grabs at my heart:

First Japanese Ready to Leave Coast

No, no, no. My heart pounds as I reach for the newspaper.

How can you know something is coming, spend every waking moment with it gnawing at you, and still feel a jab of shock when you see it begin?

I devour the article that details how over sixty Japanese Americans living in Los Angeles have voluntarily gone to Manzanar—a place in southern California I had never heard of until earlier this month.

"Evalina?"

I jump at Mama's groggy voice. "Hi. I didn't mean to wake you. I just couldn't sleep."

With her puffy eyes, Mama looks at the newspaper in my hand. Her mouth is set in a grim line. "This obsession is not healthy, Evalina. I know you're worried, but we have nothing to fear. I don't know what it will take for you to believe that."

"Mama, they're going to make *all* the Japanese go." My voice cracks. "Even the ones who were born here like the Hamasakis' children."

"Who?"

I swallow. I shouldn't have mentioned them by name. "One of our produce suppliers at Alessandro's."

"Oh. Yes, of course." Mama stifles a yawn, seeming unaware of how far I tipped my cards. "You're safe, honey. I know sometimes those articles make it sound like Italians are going to be rounded up too, but we're not."

"If the government was being fair, we'd be forced to go too. Especially a family like ours."

"But we're not. Stop seeking trouble. Come inside before somebody sees you looking indecent."

I'm wearing my favorite pajamas, which have long pants

and long sleeves, but Mama hates that I bought them in the men's department. I shuffle back inside the house, and Mama soundlessly closes the door.

She scowls at me in the gray light of the entryway. "I'm going back to bed. I'm tired of these conversations, Evalina. I'm tired of waking up to you crying. Or hearing from your friends that you're distracted and preoccupied by the news. This is not normal behavior for a girl your age."

"Our country is at war." I force my voice to be soft. "How am I supposed to act?"

Mama's mouth opens. I'm wearing away the thread of patience she woke up with—I can see it in her eyes—but I don't know how to lie about this. Why, I'm not sure, because I'm certainly lying about plenty of other things.

"Evalina . . ." Mama takes several thoughtful breaths before saying, "I'm going back to bed. You do the same."

I follow her up the stairs, the newspaper still grasped in my fist behind my back, and I go into my bedroom. But instead of crawling beneath the covers, I ease open my closet door and pull out my green pleated skirt, the one I was wearing when Taichi and I first met.

The words from this morning's article run through my head as I undo the rags in my hair and brush out the curls. "I don't understand how this can be happening."

I clamp my teeth over my bottom lip. I know that's the kind of thing Gia and Tony have been telling Mama, that I'm muttering to myself all the time—that I'm distracted, snappy, and crying easily. Gia should at least understand why, but maybe her "*Carpe Diem!*" kind of personality can't foresee what's going to happen to the Japanese Americans.

I read the entire *San Francisco News* twice before the clock ticks to 6:30 and I can justify leaving. In the last year, Mama and Daddy have grown accustomed to my leaving the house early on Saturday mornings, but since the attack on Pearl Harbor they've requested that I leave notes about where I'll be and what time I'll be home.

I scribble half-truths on a scrap of paper in the kitchen, grab my handbag and a grocery sack, and let myself out the back door where my bicycle is chained in the alley. After tucking my belongings in the front basket and securing the tie on my wool trench coat, I coast downhill toward the bay.

The early morning fog envelops me, and I can feel the dampness soaking into my hair and tightening my curls. The fog is so thick this morning that I can't see the waters of the bay until I'm on the waterfront. I bike along to the soothing *slap, slap, slap* of the water chopping against the docks.

At the park, I find the first of the farm trucks there and unloading, but I don't see the familiar green Chevy of the Hamasakis. Suspicions roar in my head, but I silence them with a look at my watch and common sense. It's not even 7:00 yet. Sometimes they're here by 7:00, but not always. This is nothing to panic about.

My watch ticks to 7:05. Which is barely after seven, and the market doesn't open until eight. Farm truck after farm truck come to a stop, and now it's 7:15. They are *always* here by 7:15. But maybe there was traffic on the bridge. Plenty of obstacles could cause a delay between their farm in Alameda and the waterfront. Just because they have always been here by now doesn't mean that something bad has happened.

I stare at the gap the Hamasakis' table usually occupies. Mr. and Mrs. Ling, who are always in the spot beside them, are nearly done setting up, as are the Carricks on the other side.

I glance at my watch again—7:30—as movement catches my eye. Two Caucasian men carry a folding table and wedge it into the Hamasakis' spot.

Mrs. Ling watches them and then goes back to placing her display signs on the table. Mrs. Carrick notices, and her jaw sets. I'm too far away to hear anything, but she says something to the newcomers. They respond with a shrug and continue with their setup. Mrs. Carrick looks at her own watch and then she looks across the street to where I'm sitting.

Before I can tell my legs they should do otherwise, I push my bicycle across the street to the park. Mrs. Carrick and I have not talked a lot, just warm chatter when I've purchased olives from her or her husband. Even though they're only at the market once a month or so, she's always seemed to know the real reason I come.

"Good morning, Evalina," she says when I draw near to the table. "Where is your friend?"

"I don't know. I hoped you would."

The men are unpacking crates of strawberries and lettuce. One of them sees me watching and offers a polite smile.

Mrs. Carrick shakes her head. "No, but as we set up this morning, I heard some of the other families talking about last week. They said some of the Japanese families were treated poorly. The Akiyamas' little girl was even spat on."

I was here last week, and I didn't see anything like that . . . but I wasn't here as long as usual. Instead of Taichi working their stand with his mother, it had been Taichi with his best friend. Diego had agreed to watch the stand while we took a walk along the shore. He hadn't seemed particularly happy to do it—which is common for Diego—but Taichi and I have so little time alone that I didn't question it.

"I just saw Taichi on Thursday and he didn't say anything about being treated poorly."

Though even as I say it, I know that if Taichi had been threatened or spit upon, he wouldn't have said a word to me. He wouldn't want me getting riled.

Mrs. Carrick's mouth curves downward. "I'm sorry to say, I think this is only the beginning."

I purchase olives, and I can't help glancing at the Caucasian farmers while Mrs. Carrick counts out my change. One of them is arranging bundles of asparagus that are annoyingly beautiful—better looking than the asparagus Taichi brought to the restaurant on Thursday.

"If you see them this week," Mrs. Carrick breaks into my thoughts, "tell them they were missed, won't you?"

"Of course. Thank you."

Despite the temptation of the asparagus, I push my bicycle past to head home. I stop when I see that in addition to her normal signs of prices for produce, Mrs. Ling has hung a new banner from the table that reads WE ARE CHINESE.

As I stare at it, Mrs. Ling notices me and smiles. "Some white people get confused. They think we are the enemy."

"The Hamasakis aren't our enemies."

"Of course not. But I don't know how long that will matter." Mrs. Ling holds out a beautiful navel orange, round and bold. "Share this with your friend. May it bring you both good luck."

The market doesn't officially open for a few more minutes, but San Franciscans already mill about the rows of tables, haggling over prices of the first spring vegetables. The men who stole the Hamasakis' spot chat with customers and the sight makes my chest burn.

I put the orange in my basket and pedal along the street. The fog has thinned, but my thoughts are hazy with anger.

At the ferry ticket booth, I pull coins from my handbag and place them on the counter. "When does the boat leave for Alameda?"

CHAPTER TWO

Taichi

Alameda, California

When the door closes behind the two FBI agents, I take my first full breath in the last thirty minutes. So many Issei men have been whisked away to prison camps, including Uncle Fuji, but my father is still here. All four of us stand here huddled by the front door, blinking at one another.

Their engine kicks to life, and I'm lightheaded from relief. We are still all together. We are still in our home.

"They're spineless men." Aiko's hands clench and her voice is steel. "I detest them."

Mother doesn't even admonish Aiko for speaking hatefully. She doesn't say anything, just keeps looking at my father as though, like me, she can't believe he's still here with us.

"You were right about burning our belongings," Mother says, her words thick.

Father doesn't answer, but his eyes hold tenderness.

The day of the attack on Pearl Harbor, Father had told us we must gather everything in our home that tied us to Japan. Letters, family photographs, kimonos, books in Japanese, records of Japanese music. Mother hadn't argued with him in front of us, until she realized that he intended for her to burn her Japanese dolls too. Even Aiko had cried when Mother fed her childhood treasures to the flames.

All these months it had seemed like we'd burned family heirlooms in vain, but when the agents surprised us with a knock on the door this morning, there had been sweet relief to know they would find nothing worthy of suspicion. They had certainly been thorough in their search of our small home.

"How dare they ask why we are packing, as if we're doing something sinister." Aiko's fists dig into her hip bones. Next, she'll stomp away. "What are we supposed to do when the government is stealing everything from us?"

"They are not stealing." Father sounds tired. "The Medinas will watch everything while we are away. When we come back, it will all be here."

Aiko makes an exasperated noise in the back of her throat, pivots on her bare heel, and storms into the kitchen, where she had been helping Mother pack before the men knocked on the door. After twenty-one years of Aiko's moods, we are all immune to them. With the ground beneath our family constantly shifting these days, her moods are a strange kind of comfort. At least some things have stayed the same.

Father looks to Mother again. *"Shikata ga nai."*

"Shikata ga nai," she says in agreement.

The way they're looking at each other, with the comfort of twenty-three years of marriage stretching between them as they repeat the Japanese mantra—"It cannot be helped, it must be done"—makes me avert my eyes and slip down the short hall to my bedroom.

How long ago did Evalina give up on me being at the market this morning? I should have told her on Thursday during my delivery that we might not be there. Profits had slipped—despite Evalina's best efforts—and that was before the Akiyamas' girl was spat upon. I should have told her that we were moving out of our house, moving in with my aunt. But as usual, we'd had no privacy.

Oddly, Evalina seemed to be at the forefront of Mother's thoughts too when she told me about the decision over breakfast. "Mr. Cassano's daughter who likes the produce so well will have to buy elsewhere. She is such a loyal customer."

I didn't trust myself to respond in case what Diego says is true, that I might as well have throbbing hearts for eyes when I talk about Evalina.

Mother had smiled at me over her teacup. "Strange for a girl her age, to spend Saturday mornings at a market. But it is good for business."

The telephone in the kitchen rings, jolting me out of the remembered conversation—and Aiko answers with a terse, "Hello."

That will be Mrs. Medina, who would've seen the government car outside our home and who is not the type to wait for information to come to her.

I take in the various piles in my room, which I had been sorting before the knock on the door. Almost everything will be packed in boxes or left where it is, under the care of the Medinas. Precious few of my belongings get packed in my suitcase for Aunt Chiyu's.

My baseball bat and glove are on the bed. That's right. When the knock came, I had been considering whether they should stay or go.

I pick up the bat, but instead of the normal comfort of the smooth wood in my hand, I hear Mr. Nielsen shrieking from the stands during my last game, when I went an unusual 0 for 3.

"Hey, coach! Why don't you bench that yellow Jap instead of my son?"

"Taichi?" Aiko's voice is so meek I think she's Mother until I turn and see her. She stands in my bedroom doorway, her face slightly gray while her eyes search mine.

"What is it?" For a fleeting moment, I imagine the men from the FBI have returned and taken Father after all.

"There's a phone call for you." Aiko's words are carefully measured. "She says her name is Evalina Cassano."

I swallow. "Okay. Thank you."

I brush past my watchful sister, and her footsteps stay close to mine as I walk through the living room to the kitchen. The telephone receiver lies on the countertop.

I expect Aiko to give me privacy, but instead she resumes her work in the cupboard closest to the telephone. On our porch, Mother and Father appear deep in conversation with Mr. and Mrs. Medina. How much time do I have before they come back in?

Aiko nods to the telephone. "She's waiting."

I've certainly kept plenty of secrets for Aiko over the years; I shouldn't doubt her willingness to keep this one for me.

I angle away from my sister. "Hi."

"Hi." That one syllable is full of relief. "I'm sorry for calling. I didn't know what else to do when you weren't there."

"I know, I'm sorry. I didn't know for sure until this morning, or I would've told you."

"Was it your sister or your mother who answered?"

I glance at Aiko, who is taking great effort to be nearly silent in her work. "My sister."

"Oh, good. I thought so. If one of your parents answered, I was going to pretend we had an eggplant emergency at the restaurant. Or that I was desperate for blackberries."

I chuckle. "Either would be believable. You have a reputation."

In the background, I hear a car honk. I assumed she was calling from the restaurant, but I guess not. I need to tell her about the farm and Mother and Father's decision about leaving, but the words all stick in my throat. I thought I would have until Monday, when I make my next delivery to Alessandro's, before I had to tell her.

Evalina laughs, high and bright. She's nervous. "So I've done something that you're maybe not going to be happy about."

I grin at the wall. I have no trouble imagining her reaming out whoever took our spot at the market. Or, if she learned about the Johnsons' teenage son spitting on the Akiyama girl, spreading rumors about their produce. "What've you done this time?"

"Well, I was really worried when you weren't there this morning. So I sorta took a ferry to Alameda."

"Evalina . . ." My heart seems to pound right in my ears. "You're in Alameda?"

Beside me, I sense Aiko has stopped packing away dishes and is now unapologetically eavesdropping.

"I could just go home?"

But I hear the pleading in her voice. *Please come get me,* she's really saying. *I took a risk in coming here. I'm hoping you'll take a risk too.*

I don't even care that Aiko is listening, or that I haven't a clue how I'll get out of the house without explaining to Mother and Father. "Don't you dare go home. Of course, I'll come get you."

"Okay. I'll see you soon, then?"

"I'll see you soon." I hang the receiver on the wall and I look into the smirking face of my sister.

"Is it possible that my perfectly behaved, do-everything-he's-told baby brother has been keeping a secret from me? From *all* of us?"

The knowing shine in her eyes makes my chest tighten. "I don't have time to explain right now, but I'll fill you in when I get home."

Aiko withdraws the truck keys from her sweater pocket—*why does she have them?*—and dangles them just out of my reach. "No, you'll explain now. I will even lie to Mother and Father for you, but you have to tell me who Miss Evalina Cassano is."

"As soon as I get home—"

Aiko shakes her head. "I like to be paid up front."

No one can draw a cross look from me like Aiko. "She's waiting for me."

"Then you had better explain fast, little brother."

I suck in a quick breath and exhale. "Her father owns Alessandro's, one of the restaurants we supply. We've gotten to know each other over the last year. That's all."

Aiko raises her eyebrows. "No, I don't think 'that's all.'"

I pitch my voice low. "What do I have to say before you'll give me the keys? That she's my girlfriend? Fine, she's my girlfriend."

Her dark eyes dart over my face. "You *really* like her." It's not a question.

I hold out my palm. "Keys, please."

Aiko's lips purse. "Evalina Cassano doesn't sound very Japanese."

"Because it's Italian."

"Oh, Taichi. This is heartbreak waiting to happen."

I stare at her, stunned. We live in a state that doesn't allow interracial marriage, so it's a natural response. So natural that I had said the same thing to myself over and over as I denied how deeply I had come to care about Evalina. So natural that I had spoken the words out loud just before our first kiss.

This will only lead to heartbreak.

Hearing the word afresh—on the lips of my notoriously rebellious sister, no less—makes me feel as though I've swallowed fire.

I snatch the keys out of her hand. "You wanted to know who she is, and I told you."

"I'm sorry, Taichi," Aiko says. "She sounded really nice."

I don't respond, just barrel out the front door. To Mother and Father's surprised faces, I say, "I'll be right back. Aiko will explain."

If there's anything I can trust Aiko for, it's to come up with a believable cover story. In her first year of college, she hid a Caucasian boyfriend for six months and nearly got away with hiding a miscarriage too.

I drive away much slower than I would like, not wanting to appear too rushed. My teeth grind together as I think of the way Aiko looked at me with such pity. Not that it matters. I don't need her good opinion.

But even after I've left the farm, I find I haven't let go of Aiko's use of the word *sounded*. That Evalina sound*ed* really nice.

As though Evalina is already a piece of my past.

CHAPTER THREE

Evalina

"Evalina, you have flipped your wig." But Gia sounds admiring, not admonishing. "I knew when you finally fell for a boy, you would fall hard, but you seriously took a ferry to Alameda?"

"What else was I supposed to do? He wasn't at the market this morning, plus these articles in the paper . . ." I swallow. "I thought maybe his family had been taken."

"You are so dramatic sometimes. They're not going to be *taken*. It's all voluntary."

"I don't think so, Gia." I twist the cord of the pay phone around my finger. "I think they'll all be made to go."

"I still can't believe you took a ferry to Alameda. What are you going to tell your parents?"

"Hopefully they'll never know. You'll cover for me if they call or stop by, right?"

"Of course. I'm meeting Lorenzo for lunch, but I'll just say you were with us."

Imaginary lunches with Gia's on-again off-again boyfriend are the only kind I can tolerate. "Thank you, Gia. I'll let you know when I'm home."

I hang up and push my bicycle out to the curb. The day has grown warm, but the wind off the bay still bites, so I tighten my coat. Around me, families hurry into line to catch the ferry to San Francisco. The women are dressed in bright spring skirts and sweaters, and many of the men wear their military uniforms. A group of three sailors stand nearby; one winks at me. He reminds me of Gia's boyfriend, so I angle away.

I fold my arms around myself and watch as a seagull grabs hold of a discarded bread crust before flying away. As I track its flight, I spot the familiar green truck pulling into the parking lot. Taichi's black hair is shiny and neat, despite the truck's windows being down. He isn't smiling at me as he pulls up to the curb, but he doesn't look angry either.

The words I want to say—"I was scared. I had to see you."—stick in my throat as Taichi gets out of the truck and walks around to where I stand on the sidewalk.

I want to burst into tears and throw my arms around him, but I can feel the curious and condemning gazes of others.

"I didn't know what else to do," I whisper.

"Let's go somewhere else, okay?"

I nod, and Taichi lifts my bicycle into the back of the truck. As he hoists it, the orange from Mrs. Ling rolls out of the basket and lands in the gutter.

"Of course, you brought fruit," Taichi says with a laugh as I stoop to pick it up.

My heart hammers in my chest as I wipe grit from the orange's peel before dropping it into my handbag. I try to laugh too—I don't truly believe the orange is lucky, right?— but it comes out sounding rusty.

I stand outside the passenger door until I realize Taichi is walking toward the driver's door, not mine. Our eyes connect over the back of the cab, and Taichi winces.

"Sorry, I've never done this before," he says as he jogs around the front.

I stretch the sleeves of my coat to where they cover my hands. "It's fine."

"No, it's not." Taichi jerks the handle, and the door squeals as he yanks it open. Now his laugh sounds nervous. "It's no Chrysler."

The kind of car Tony's family drives. Has Taichi seen their car at the restaurant, or was that comment just a coincidence?

"Taichi, it's fine." I smile in a way that I hope will soothe him. "My family doesn't even own a car."

Taichi waits until I've tucked my skirt underneath me before he shuts the door and jogs back around to his own. Beyond him, the sailors watch with matching disdainful expressions. I look away, shame and anger flooding through me in a strange tangle of emotions. Taichi can't see them, but how would he feel if he knew?

The truck putters away from the dock, and my fingers twist together in my lap. Why is my breathing so shallow? Why are my shoulders scrunched up to my ears? I've been alone with Taichi many times before. I don't need to be so tense.

But it's never been quite like this.

"So . . ." I say as Taichi says, "How long do you—"

Some of the tension between us dissipates as we laugh.

"Ladies first," Taichi says.

But I didn't even know what I was going to say. I just couldn't stand the silence anymore. "No, what were you going to ask?"

"I wondered how long you have. I'm trying to figure out where we should go."

"I shouldn't be gone too long." I smooth the pleats of my skirt so they cover my knees. "The next ferry leaves in an hour, so I guess until then."

Taichi nods. "Okay. If we go up this road a bit, there's a corner of the Medinas' property where I think we could be alone. Being seen in public together . . . just . . . not the best idea."

"I agree." But the admission is still like a heavy blanket over my heart.

I look out the window as we roll by a squat, brick restaurant that has a large black-on-white sign hanging in the window: WE DON'T SERVE JAPS! it says above a caricature of a man with buck teeth, overly slanted eyes, and a sneer.

I sense Taichi shifting, and I look at him, not caring if he sees that I'm on the verge of tears.

He reaches for my hand. "It's fine, Evalina."

As his fingers fold around mine, tears blur my vision. "No, it's not. It's not *at all* fine."

Taichi squeezes my hand but doesn't say anything to combat my statement. I clench my jaw to stop its trembling, and after a few deep inhales, my tears clear. I watch Taichi as he watches the road. I love the angle of his cheekbones and eyes. I love the contrast of colors when our fingers are entwined. And even more, I love his kind heart. How hard he works, how much he respects his family, how determined he is when he wants something. How can anyone look at him and see an enemy?

"Here we are." Taichi withdraws his hand from mine to crank the steering wheel and turn us down a dirt road at the edge of an orchard.

Road might be a bit of an exaggeration, actually. I grab hold of the door handle as the truck bumps and pitches over the rutted earth.

"Diego and I used to play in this creek when we were boys." Taichi speaks loudly over the noise of the engine and tires. "This time of year there's actually some water in it."

My teeth rattle together until Taichi pulls along a grassy bank. I wait for him to open my door, and I take his hand as I climb out even though I don't need assistance.

Taichi reaches under the passenger seat and withdraws a faded, scrappy quilt. He brushes it off. "Not the cleanest, but I think it'll be more comfortable than sitting right on the grass."

The only other boy I've gone out with is Tony Esposito, who I've known all my life. Every date we ever went on was perfectly planned, as if Tony had bought an instruction manual on how to be a good boyfriend and was following it to the letter.

Nothing about this date feels perfect, except for the one piece that really matters.

We settle on the quilt, our legs resting against each other, and watch the dappled sunlight play on the grass. I can think of about a thousand things to say, and yet none of them seem like the right thing to say. The minutes tick by so rapidly it's as though we're sitting inside an hourglass, feeling the sand beneath us shift as it drains away.

"Remember when we used to spend all our time arguing about when and if I would tell my parents I didn't want to be a farmer?" Taichi asks with a wistful air.

"Not *all* our time."

He smiles at me. "Nearly all our time."

I used to think the two of us having a future together was contingent on Taichi being honest with his parents, telling them he wanted to go to college instead of taking over the family farm. Now I would give anything for that to be our biggest struggle.

"Why were you not at the market this morning?"

Taichi stares out at the trickle of water in the creek bed. His jaw is set, and his breathing so steady that I know he's concentrating on keeping it that way. So steady, I know something bad is coming.

"I'm sorry I couldn't tell you ahead of time. I didn't know until I got up this morning that we weren't going." With his free hand, Taichi smooths his jeans over his work boots. "Profits have been down. It doesn't make sense for us to keep going, but the Medina family will continue to send others. They'll be happy to continue sourcing Alessandro's too, obviously."

"Taichi." I blink at him. "I don't care about the restaurant. I care about *you* and your family. Mrs. Carrick said some of the Japanese Americans were treated badly last week. Was that you too?"

Taichi's jaw once again clenches and his breathing is rhythmic, but at least this time he looks at me.

"Yes or no?" My voice has a frantic pitch to it. Why won't he just tell me?

"It's nothing I haven't dealt with before."

The look in his eyes—guarded pain—is enough to make tears well behind my own. "You should've told me."

"It's not pleasant to talk about."

"For me either, but I want to know what's going on."

"I know. I'm trying." His voice is gruff, and I realize he's trying to hold in his own anger and frustration. "We've officially reallocated our farm back to the Medinas."

A gasp escapes from me.

"It's just a formality," Taichi says. "So they can do what they need to do while we're . . . gone."

Gone. The word reverberates in my soul.

"My family is really fortunate," Taichi says thickly. "Yes, our accounts are frozen, but the Medinas are a great family and have been understanding. And the FBI didn't take Father like they did my uncle or the others who had boat licenses."

You don't have to be brave and grateful with me, I want to tell him. But I know if I open my mouth, I'll cry. I don't want to waste our entire visit sobbing.

Right after Pearl Harbor, the FBI swept through Japanese communities and arrested thousands of Issei men, meaning those like Taichi's parents, who live in America legally, but were born in Japan. This move had been praised in the papers, but I've seen how the senseless arrests have hurt families like Taichi's. His uncle was taken away to a prison camp in North Dakota just for having a fishing license.

"Has there been any word on how your uncle is doing?"

"He doesn't say much about what it's like there." Taichi swallows hard. "I know that makes my aunt nervous. It makes us *all* nervous."

I squeeze his hand. "He probably just doesn't want to worry you."

His smile is wry. "Well, it doesn't work. We worry anyway, and we imagine the worst. And Aunt Chiyu is alone and scared in the apartment." Taichi turns and looks at me in a calm, even sort of way, and my heart rate spikes with fear. "The reason we reallocated the farm to the Medinas this week is we're going to move in with my aunt so that when we're evacuated, we're all together."

"But—" I clench my jaw, willing away the tears. "You'll be so close to the bay. The paper says that's where they'll evacuate first."

Taichi nods as he rubs his thumb over the back of my hand. "Yes, but I'll be living much closer to you."

I huff an incredulous laugh. "But for how long?"

"There's no way to know. Maybe a week. Maybe months." He says this all so evenly and unaffected.

My voice comes out squawky. "How can you stay so calm

about this? You *should* know. It's just wrong for no one to tell you when you'll be forced out of your home."

"I know." He squeezes my hand, and his slight smile holds affection. "But at least for the remainder of my time, I get to be near you."

I press my eyes closed and will myself not to cry.

Even before Pearl Harbor, our relationship felt as though all we ever had to get by on was a gas can of fumes. Five-minute conversations in front of our fathers when the Hamasakis delivered produce to Alessandro's on Mondays and Thursdays. And the same on Saturdays during market season. Some weeks we managed to steal extra time, and we almost always slipped letters to each other. We had stayed strong through this because we thought it was temporary. Because we thought this fall we might be at U.C. Berkeley together, if Taichi could get a scholarship too.

The scent of citrus tickles my nose, and I open my eyes to find Taichi peeling the orange from Mrs. Ling. He hands me the generous half.

My fingers curl around it. "How are we going to bear this?"

"We will be fine. We always knew our road would be a rough one. This is a bump."

I snort. "This is more than a bump. This is like a . . . like a . . . canyon or something. I don't know how we get across."

"We'll find a way." Taichi pops a wedge of orange into his mouth. "We can't see it now, and maybe it doesn't exist yet, but we'll find some way through this. Some bridge across this canyon."

"I don't want to wait for someone to build us a bridge," I snap. "I'll do it myself."

Now Taichi's smile is full, as it often is when my temper flares. He leans forward and presses his mouth to mine, melting away the firm, angry line of my lips. His hand threads into my hair, and I try to lean into the moment. Try to not let its inherent joy be stolen by all my fears about what tomorrow or the next day will bring.

"If you intend to build us a bridge, Evalina"—Taichi's forehead touches mine, and his whisper is warm and citrusy— "then I pity whoever gets in your way."

CHAPTER FOUR

Taichi

Wednesday, March 25, 1942

Diego and Ruby, his girlfriend this month, stare at the sky, the ground, the rows of nearly-ripe asparagus—anything that isn't me—while we wait for my parents to come out of the house. Mother and Father are finishing tidying the house, as if it matters. Aiko sits on the porch step with a face of stone.

Ruby pins a smile on her face. "I bet your parents are happy you're not going overseas. At least you'll be safe, right? I think my mother would do just about anything to keep my brothers from enlisting."

A sarcastic response bites at me. *Including the government taking away your right to be on your own property? Sending you away without telling you where you're going?*

But Ruby is a nice girl. She doesn't mean anything insulting by her comments. I just smile back and lean against the truck that's piled with the remains of my family's life. Our suitcases, the produce for tomorrow's deliveries, and thick, puffy jackets that Mother is convinced we'll need. The rest will stay here under the watchful eye of Diego's family.

"But it just isn't right," Diego says. There's an unusual strain in his voice. He looks at me, and then cuts his eyes away.

Ruby gives a small, nervous laugh. "No, of course it isn't right. I didn't mean that. I was just saying . . . you know. At least where Taichi is going, everyone will be Japanese. And that seems like it would be good." She pushes her smile higher. "I mean, because of safety. Not that you aren't safe here, of course. I don't think anyone at school cares that you're Japanese. Except maybe Danny Nielsen. But he's such a dead hoofer anyway. No one cares what he thinks."

She laughs again, clearly nervous, and on any other day I would search for the words to put her at ease. But not today. Because today I unceremoniously graduated from high school when I took my exit exams in the principal's office. Because right now my baseball team—including Danny Nielsen, who definitely cares that I'm Japanese and takes it as a personal insult that my batting average is higher than his—is traveling to play our rival, and I'm not on the bus. Because last night we sat around our family table for a final dinner, and then we walked the farm that we've worked for fifteen years, silently saying goodbye. In light of all that, I'm just too tired to care about the comfort of Diego's current girlfriend.

The front door opens, and my heart plummets to my ankles. Father has his arm around Mother's shoulders. She isn't crying now, but she clutches a handkerchief in her left hand. Father locks the door of our family home, and Mother presses the handkerchief to each eye. Usually they both have so much to do, they are off in separate directions. It's strange to see them completing simple tasks together.

Father offers a slight bow to Diego and hands him the key. "Thank you, Diego. We are grateful for your friendship and your family's friendship."

My father's English is exceptional, considering he came to America when he was nineteen and didn't know how to say much beyond "Hello" and "Are you hiring?" But this morning, my ears catch every bit of his Japanese accent. The way his tongue can't quite produce the *th* sound. The way his Rs have the softness of a W.

The hinges of the truck's passenger door protest as Aiko climbs in. Father doesn't turn and look, and Mother watches with only a vague concern. She has spent so many years worried for Aiko, the concern is like a family member you don't particularly like, but who you have adapted to sharing the table with anyway.

"I understand you will leave for training soon, Diego," Mother says in her quiet, careful way. As though she weighs each word and how to pronounce it before allowing it out of her lips. She has always been self-conscious about her English.

"Yes, ma'am. Just after graduation."

Mother smiles and nods. "We will pray every day for your safe return."

A strange shame washes over me, which is illogical considering I don't have the option to enlist. But I felt the same way right after the attack on Pearl Harbor, as if somehow I had done something wrong. As if somehow I was responsible for all those dead men, just because of my Japanese heritage. Even though I knew it made no sense, I couldn't seem to push away the feeling.

"We must go." Father shakes Diego's hand and offers a slight bow to Ruby. Then he and Mother slip away to give me a small privacy for my own goodbyes.

"Ruby." Diego puts a hand on her back. "Would you give Tai and me a moment?"

"Of course!" she chirps, and she seems relieved to walk away.

Diego sticks his hands in his jean pockets and jingles the coins within.

"Thanks for watching over the place while we're gone." I've said this countless times over the last few days but I don't know what else there is to say.

Diego shrugs. "Of course." He glances at the truck, at its closed doors, before asking, "Will you get to see your girl more? Now that you'll be in the city?"

"I hope so. She's pretty determined when she sets her mind to something."

Diego makes a noise in the back of his throat. If you didn't know him, it would just sound like an acknowledgment. But I can hear the weight of his disapproval.

"If you gave Evalina a chance, you would like her," I say quietly. I don't want to fight about this again. Especially not right now.

"I'm sure she's a peach."

Again, the flat sarcasm. I give Diego a look. "If you really want to help me out while I'm gone, please be nice to her. Talk with her a bit if you make deliveries. Slide her some extra blackberries when our crop is ready. That's her favorite."

My throat involuntarily clenches when I think of the first thing Evalina ever said to me. *You should be charging more for your blackberries.*

"You know, it's not like I'm going to be around here much longer either." Diego's tone is an attempt at sounding light-hearted. "As soon as I graduate, I belong to the U.S. Navy."

I glance toward my house, where Ruby loiters on our porch, trying to look as though she feels comfortable. "What does Ruby think of you enlisting?"

"Oh, you know how girls are. She's worried, but she'll see me in my uniform and won't be able to resist me."

I don't feel like laughing, but I make myself try. If I had been allowed to enlist, what would Evalina have thought?

Diego digs at the ground with the toe of his boot. "Could you write to me once you get where you're going? I don't mean your aunt's. I mean from . . . wherever it is they send you."

"Of course."

Diego rubs at the back of his neck. "It's funny because we were always gonna be saying goodbye in a few months"—his voice has an unfamiliar gruffness—"so it's not like I didn't know this was coming."

I look away as I realize he's blinking funny. As I realize my own eyes have started to pool.

Diego folds his arms around me, clapping me on the back a few times. "I'll miss you, brother."

"I'll miss you too. I'll write as soon as I can."

Diego releases me and takes a step back. He shoves his hands in his pockets. "I've never been much for letter writing. Guess I'll have to learn."

"I guess so."

A smile whispers over his lips, and then trembles away. "See you around, Tai."

"See you around." I clench my jaw for a moment until I'm sure I won't cry, and then add, "Bye, Ruby."

"Goodbye." Her voice breaks, and Diego crosses the scrubby grass to where she stands and fits an arm around her shoulders.

I take one last look at our small, dusty ranch house that I've sometimes despised and sometimes loved, but that has been my home nearly all my life. The window into our kitchen that I once cracked with a baseball. The oak tree that Aiko and I climbed as children. The porch where Mother gave us all haircuts last night.

Just as I'm about to hoist myself into the truck, I look at Diego. His dusky skin gleams in the golden sunshine, and his black hair is styled better than the typical farm kid. Whatever Ruby is saying to Diego causes his smile to flash, and I look away before it vanishes. That's the memory of my best friend that I want to carry away.

CHAPTER FIVE

Evalina

Thursday, March 26, 1942
San Francisco, California

"I just don't understand why he wouldn't have called me." Gia runs her teeth over her bottom lip like she always does when she's thinking hard. "We had a lot of fun on Saturday. We saw that new movie with Ginger Rogers. But he hasn't called since. Why would he not have called?"

I wish she would move a little faster down the stairs toward the door. I have to get to Alessandro's in time to see Taichi during his delivery.

"I don't know, Gia. I wouldn't worry about it."

"The only other times that he has skipped out on calling is when he was about to break up with me." Her lower lip is bright red from all her worrying. "Do you think that's what this means?"

I fight back my urge to say *yes*. Gia and Lorenzo have always been hot and cold, and I thought he was out of our lives forever when he enlisted in the Navy after graduating last year. But then after the attack on Pearl Harbor, Lorenzo apparently "did a lot of thinking" and realized that he had "been in love with Gia the whole time."

Blah, blah, blah.

It's not so bad when he's out to sea, but this last month that he's been back home has been torture. I don't like seeing my best friend agonize over whether she's good enough for a rake like Lorenzo Romano.

"Why don't you call him?" I suggest as I tie a kerchief over my curls. Hopefully my hair won't be a complete wreck by the time I get to Alessandro's.

"Because he always calls me."

I shrug. "Change things up. Maybe he's waiting for you to call."

Gia looks at me like I'm being silly. "I told you. *He* always calls *me*."

"If he truly cares about you, why does it matter who calls who?"

"*If?*" Gia's eyes bulge. "I'm talking to you about this because I'm worried, and *that* is the kind of support you're offering? *If* he cares?"

I try to not let my impatience show, but I don't think I'm doing a good job. "I didn't realize you were looking for support. I thought you just wanted to talk about it or something."

"I don't know why I would even expect you to support me." Gia tears at her bicycle lock. "You've never been able to see Lorenzo's good qualities."

I unwind my lock and try to not yell back at her. I need Gia on my side. She's the only one who knows about Taichi.

"I'm sorry," I force myself to say, despite the hundreds of angry retorts begging to be let out. "I don't want you having to feel this way, is all. You're my best friend, and you're amazing. And I want your boyfriend to make you feel like you're amazing."

Gia's crying now as she tugs at a knot in her lock that she

created with her haste. "I just thought it was really *it* this time, you know?" She wipes at her eyes and smears makeup into her hairline. "I thought being in the Navy had matured him, especially when Pearl Harbor was attacked. And I just didn't think it would be like this anymore. I thought . . ." Her chin quavers as she confesses, "I thought we would get married."

Gia dissolves into sobs against me, and I steal a peek at my wristwatch as I pat her back. *Gee, I hope the Hamasakis are running late today.*

"And maybe you still will," I say, even as I'm praying they won't. "Maybe you just need to tell Lorenzo how you feel. That when you have a date, and he doesn't call for several days after, it worries you."

Tony jogs down the school stairs, sees Gia crying, and makes an abrupt turn back into the building. Typical.

"He's just going to say I'm being needy," Gia blubbers into my shoulder.

"What's so wrong about needing something from the person you love?"

Her crying quiets a bit. "I guess that's true . . ."

"It's completely true." I push her off my shoulder and take hold of hers. "There's nothing wrong with needing each other. If Lorenzo can't handle that, then it's best to know now. Right?"

Her jaw trembles, but she nods. "Right . . ."

"I have to go." I throw my leg over my bicycle. "Daddy's expecting me."

"Okay." Gia sniffles. "Thanks, Evalina."

"I'll stop by your house later, okay?" I call as I push off down the hill.

Ten minutes later, I arrive at Alessandro's with a pounding heart that has nothing to do with the ride and everything to do with the fear that the Hamasakis may have already come and gone.

The bells that hang over the entry jingle as I push open the front door. The restaurant is empty, and I call, "It's me!" immediately so that Daddy and whoever else is here will know they don't need to stop what they're doing to come up front.

"Hello, me!" Daddy calls from the kitchen, the joke he's been making all my life.

I hang my coat and pull my kerchief off my curls, which hang wildly after coasting down the hill. Hopefully I'll have time before Taichi arrives to tidy my appearance.

The air smells strongly of marinara sauce, so Mr. Esposito must be here too. Sometimes that makes it easier to steal a few extra minutes with Taichi, because Mr. Esposito is chattier than my father, and he'll engage Mr. Hamasaki for longer.

I hurry around the deli counter to the back. Daddy is combining ground beef and veal for meatballs and Mr. Esposito slices onions beside a simmering pot.

"How was school, honey?" Daddy asks as there's a knock on the back door.

He starts to pull his hands out of the meat mixture, but I say, "I'll get it!" as I rush for the door.

Daddy shuffles over to the sink to wash his hands. "You're a gem, Evalina."

I whip open the back door and find Taichi holding a crate of eggplant, asparagus, onions, and tomatoes. He has on his flat cap, and he's wearing the blue plaid shirt I gave him for his birthday. Behind him, Mr. Hamasaki pulls another crate out of the back of their truck and turns toward the door.

Taichi's smile is warm and familiar, but he says a very professional sounding, "Hello, Miss Cassano."

My face heats as I open the door wider. "Come on in."

Taichi's elbow brushes against me as he enters, and I smile at Mr. Hamasaki. "Hello, sir."

He nods at me, same as always, but doesn't greet me with words. I want so badly to connect with him, to make him like me, but my small attempts at conversation over the last year have all fallen flat.

Mr. Hamasaki offers a slight bow to my father and Mr. Esposito. "Good day, gentlemen. How are you?"

"We are well, Katsumi." Mr. Esposito dries his hands on his apron. "And you?"

Mr. Hamasaki sweeps his hat off his head. "It is a time of challenge for us, as I've discussed with you before." His voice is as steady and soothing as the sound of the bubbling marinara. "This will be the last delivery my son and I make. Next Monday, there will be others from the farm who bring your order."

Daddy and Mr. Esposito regard Mr. Hamasaki with grave faces.

"We are very sorry to hear that," Daddy says. "You've been wonderful to work with."

"The produce you receive will continue to be high quality from our own farm. Just delivered by different people."

Taichi stands several feet behind his father with his hands clasped behind him. A corner of a folded piece of paper peeks out of his fingers. A letter for me, and a reminder that I have one for him in my coat pocket. And my coat is hanging up front . . .

"We're not as concerned about the produce as we are about what's happening to your family, Katsumi," Daddy says, and I want to throw my arms around him and squeeze. "Are you being evacuated already?"

I lean on the counter near Taichi, where the crate of produce will give us cover for him to slip his letter to me. I only wish I could tell him that I wrote one for him too.

"We do not yet know when we will be evacuated, but we have moved in with my wife's sister. She lives here in the city and has been lonely and scared. She does not speak very good English. However, being by the water, we think we will be asked to leave soon."

It's as though his words have wrapped around my throat and squeezed. A noise emerges that earns me a glance from my father.

"Is there anything we can do to help you?" Mr. Esposito asks, and his face is earnest and caring. So reminiscent of the way his son, Tony, has regarded me when I express a struggle or hardship.

Without looking at me, Taichi pushes the letter into my hand, and for the briefest of moments, our fingers clasp each other in the privacy the crate of produce offers them, and then we must pull away.

I push the letter into my sweater pocket for reading later.

"No, we are very fortunate, but thank you. A good family has taken charge of our farm in our absence, and we know this is the most helpful thing we can do for our government in a time of crisis." Mr. Hamasaki bows his head. "Thank you for your business. Come, Taichi."

The bells on the front door jingle, which isn't necessary because I can hear the raucous chatter of boys from here. Daddy flicks an expectant glance at me. I want to soak up every second I can of Taichi's presence, but lingering will only cause suspicion. I allow myself only a peek at Taichi—he flicks a smile at me—and then I go up front to the counter.

The group of boys is just Tony and his friends, who often

stop by for Coca-Colas. Tony is already behind the counter, helping himself.

"Hey." He offers me a bottle. "What was Gia carrying on about after school?"

I hear the back door close with Taichi and his father's departure.

I scowl at Tony. "You're supposed to let me know that it's you so that I don't stop what I'm doing to come help. I thought you were a customer."

Tony's eyes widen. He makes a show of looking at the empty tables. "Were you busy?"

"And if you cared about why Gia was crying, you should have come over to ask instead of just going back inside school."

Tony only laughs. "I didn't want to get dragged into that mess. Lemme guess. Lorenzo?"

His buddies settle into a table with loads of loud chatter and chairs scraping across linoleum.

"Of course, Lorenzo. Same thing as before. He's not calling. She feels needy. She thought they would get married. What does this mean? Etcetera."

Behind Tony, the Hamasakis' truck rumbles by. I catch a flash of Taichi looking at the restaurant, searching for me through the windows, and then they've passed.

Tony looks over his shoulder and then back at me. He reaches over and pops open my bottle of Coke too. "You okay?"

There's a part of me that wants to break into tears and tell him everything. But this is Tony. My old friend, yes, but also my ex-boyfriend. I can't do that to him.

"Fine." I push a smile onto my face. "Just worried about G, that's all."

Tony clanks the neck of his bottle against mine in a strange sort of commiserating toast, and then he joins his friends at their table. I drink my soda and count the minutes until I'll be home and can read the letter from Taichi.

I push my remaining meatball across my plate, watching the trail of sauce it leaves behind. I just want tonight to be over so that I can wake up tomorrow, go to the market, and then meet Taichi at Lafayette Park.

Beneath the table, Gia kicks my foot. I startle and find the adults at the table—my parents, Mr. and Mrs. LaRocca, and Mr. and Mrs. Esposito—blinking at me with polite smiles.

Mama swoops in. "You'll have to forgive Evalina. She didn't sleep well last night, I'm afraid." She smiles at me. "Mrs. Esposito asked how you think the yearbook will look."

"Oh. I think it will look fine." I offer an apologetic smile to Mrs. Esposito. "We expect it back from the printer any day now."

"I'm sorry you didn't sleep well, honey. Is it end-of-the-year stress?" Mrs. Esposito looks at Tony, who sits on the other side of me. "Tony has been working so hard to prepare for the end of the year. It's a shame that such a momentous time as high school graduation has to be shrouded with stressful exams."

I *wish* my stress was as simple as concerns for my final exams.

"*I'm* not stressed about school," Gia says as she scoops herself another helping of eggplant parmesan.

"I think a little more stress would be good for you, Gia." Mrs. LaRocca shakes her head at Mama and Mrs. Esposito. "I cannot get her to care about her finals. Zola, you are so lucky to have a daughter who has worked hard enough to earn a scholarship. You would never know from Gia's grades that she's so smart."

"A girl as pretty as Gia doesn't need good grades," Mrs. Esposito says as she reaches for a bowl of olives.

Mrs. LaRocca is unsuccessful at hiding her pleasure over this comment. "Still. I never would have dreamed of doing less than my very best in school."

The mothers fall into conversation about their school days, leaving Tony, Gia, and me alone to talk as we please.

From across the table, Gia flashes a wry smile at both of us. "What will they find to talk about at Friday night dinners when we're gone?"

"No Friday night dinners at Alessandro's," Tony says with a sigh. "I can't even imagine it."

Gia checks her watch. "I need to go. I'm meeting Lorenzo." She pauses and then cuts a look across the table at me. "He *did* call me by the way. After school today. Not that you've asked."

"Gia . . ."

But she's already carrying her plate back to the kitchen without a glance over her shoulder.

"She'll be fine," Tony says in his rich, soothing voice. "Easy to injure but quick to heal."

"I know." I eat my last meatball even though there's no room in my stomach for it. "I'm more worried that she'll actually marry Lorenzo. He's not good enough for her."

Tony's smile seems grim. "We rarely want what's good for us."

I feel my face flush, and duck in embarrassment. Dating Tony had seemed like such an obvious next step, like the way our life stories should naturally progress, but I just couldn't get my heart to toe the line. Now I wish more than anything that we had just stayed friends.

"I'm not talking about you, Evalina," Tony says in a rush. "Gee, I didn't even realize . . ." He pulls at the collar of his shirt. "I wasn't talking about me and you. Honest."

"Okay," I say to my lap.

"Actually . . ." Tony winds linguine onto his fork, and then lets it unravel. "I wasn't sure if I should even tell you this, but—"

My ear catches on Mrs. LaRocca's use of the word "Japs," and I turn away from Tony.

"I know *I'll* feel a lot better when they've been cleared out." Mrs. LaRocca pours herself another half-glass of Brunello. "Not that there aren't nice Japs among them, but why risk it?"

How can she even ask that question?

"Because most of them are American citizens, that's why."

I don't realize that it was my voice that spoke with such loud indignation until the eyes of the mothers and Tony fasten on me.

"Evalina!" Mama wields my name like a whip.

I lower my gaze to my plate, but my heart continues to race. This kind of thinking—that the theoretical risk to *our* safety is worth the sacrifice of *their* actual freedom—is why Taichi's uncle was taken away to prison camp for merely being a fisherman. It's why Taichi has been forced out of his home and off their farm. It's why I'll have to say goodbye to him.

Mrs. LaRocca waves away Mama's concern. "No, it's fine, Zola. Evalina has a right to her opinion."

"Well, it should be expressed with respect."

I look up and find Mama's face holds a threat. *Be nice, or else.*

I take a deep breath and hope my voice won't wobble when I speak. "Well, *respectfully*, I disagree that it isn't worth the risk. Frankly, I disagree that there's any risk at all."

"Truly, Evalina?" Mrs. LaRocca leans back in her chair. As much as she seems to loathe Gia's combative tendencies, Gia is an apple and Mrs. LaRocca the proverbial tree. "You think *all* of them are loyal to the United States? You think *none* of them would be tempted to spy for their mother country?"

Beneath the table, my fingers tighten around the hem of my pleated skirt. Is she deaf to the hypocrisy of her own questions?

"Are *you* loyal to the United States?" I try to ask this gently, but I'm not sure I succeed. "Would *you* not be tempted to spy for Italy? See? I could just as easily apply the questions to you, couldn't I?"

"Evalina, that's quite enough." Mama's eyes are wide and her mouth an angry slash. "You will apologize to Mrs. LaRocca, and you will stop this right now."

Even the fathers have ceased their conversation and for the first time in my lifetime of memories, our table is silent.

I swallow. "I know you're loyal, Mrs. LaRocca. I only meant to point out that our situations are similar. You're a second-generation Italian, just like my parents. And just like most of the Japanese Americans who are having everything stripped away from them."

I clench my jaw, but it doesn't quell the trembling. The shocked faces of my parents, the Espositos, and the LaRoccas grow blurry.

I push back from the table—"I'm sorry, excuse me"—and rush out the front door. The bells jangle with my exit.

Outside, I lean against the brick and gulp deep breaths of cool, foggy air. If only they could see the Hamasakis' life up close, then they would understand what Executive Order 9066 is costing loyal Americans who happen to be Japanese.

"I see what you're saying, Zola." Mrs. LaRocca's voice floats to me through the open window. "Are you certain this is just stress about the war? I've never heard her speak so passionately."

"Tony, honey, where are you going?" Mrs. Esposito calls.

"I'm just going to check on her."

I wipe my cheeks with the sleeves of my sweater as Tony emerges from the front door, my trench coat in his hands. He checks to his left, and then spots me to his right.

Tony holds up my coat for me, and I slip my arms into the sleeves. "Thank you," I murmur.

We look at each other a moment. A trolley rolls past us, clanging its bell.

Tony gestures down Broadway. "I'll walk you home."

"Thanks."

The sidewalks on Broadway are busy with couples and families out for Friday night. We pass a rowdy group of sailors just as we turn onto Kearney and start up the steps of the sidewalk.

I don't feel like talking, but I also feel like I should say something. "Are you worried about being drafted?"

"Not especially. The government won't want to interfere with me while I'm getting an engineering degree." His chuckle holds no humor. "I'm sure it'll be the hardest I've ever studied in my life."

When we reach the next block, we wait for a car to pass. I'm always grateful for the chance to catch my breath after so many stairs, but Tony never seems winded.

I open my mouth to comment on this, but Tony has a serious look on his face that makes me swallow the words. Instead, I ask, "Are you okay?"

He looks at me and takes a noticeably deep breath. "What I started to tell you at dinner is that I've been seeing Mary Green. I know you felt guilty about us breaking up. I really don't want you to. It was the best thing for both of us."

I nod, but I still have to clamp my teeth together to keep from apologizing yet again. "I'm . . . happy to hear that. I don't know her well, but Mary seems like a nice girl."

Happy and nice seem like trite words, but I can't find anything that works better.

"She is." Tony's gaze is heavy on me. "Now will you be honest with me about who you've been seeing this last year?"

The car we had waited for is well past us, but we just stand there and stare at each other.

I open my mouth. Close it. Why can't I make the words come out?

"Do your parents know?" Tony pitches his voice low even though we're the only ones on the corner of Kearney and Vallejo.

I shake my head, but still can't seem to make myself speak.

"I won't tell anyone." Tony pushes his hands deep into his coat pockets. "You know that, right?"

I nod.

He holds my gaze a moment longer, and I know Tony well enough to see that he's thinking through what he might say next. He's calculating my potential reactions.

Tony pivots toward the street, takes hold of my arm, and we continue on our way home, the words unspoken.

At my door, I find my voice again. "Thank you for walking me home."

"Of course."

I shift my weight from foot to foot. "I'll apologize to Mrs. LaRocca."

Tony shrugs. "I've always liked that fiery side of you. I wish you would show it more."

A laugh scuffs out of my throat. "When the evacuation finally happens, I think you're going to get your wish."

CHAPTER SIX

Taichi

Saturday, March 28, 1942

The sight of Evalina striding purposefully through the park, her evergreen trench coat cinched tight and her curls springing with each step, makes me smile for the first time in days. I didn't exactly doubt that she would be able to get away, but I had spent the morning reminding myself that she might not be able to make it. I stand from the park bench, and her gaze connects with mine.

"What are all these signs about registration?" Evalina greets me. Worry has drawn a line on the bridge of her nose. "They're on every telephone pole."

I should have expected that question. Yesterday, the government posted signs all over the Japanese neighborhoods that families needed to register.

"Nothing to be alarmed about," I say. "I think they're just trying to get a good estimate of how many they'll be evacuating from each neighborhood."

Her face takes on the pinched expression of one trying to not cry. She swallows hard as she sinks to the bench.

I sit beside her. "We will be fine. Don't let it ruin our time together," I say softly.

She nods and takes a labored breath before saying a tight, "How are things at your aunt's place?"

That question I *did* expect. "Fine. We've been able to help her a lot."

My aunt had done absolutely nothing to prepare for evacuation. The last few days have been spent trying to pack her suitcases, find a place to store her valuable possessions, and unsuccessfully trying to sell whatever we can. But everybody is trying to sell their belongings. Father couldn't get any more than twenty dollars for our truck because of how many vehicles are being sold and decided to just give it to the Medinas.

"Oh, here." Evalina pulls two folded letters from her coat pocket. "I had one of these on Thursday, but I'd left my coat up front. And then the other I wrote in response to yours."

I take them from her, and then let my knee fall against hers.

"I can't stay long." Her voice is husky as she holds in tears. "Daddy asked for my help during the lunch hour."

"A little time is better than no time, right?"

She nods, and I follow her gaze to a nearby telephone pole. To one of the many black-on-white notices about "alien and non-alien" Japanese needing to register. As though even the War Relocation Authority couldn't bear to recognize that I'm a U.S. citizen.

"Does anyone know how much longer you have?"

"The rumor is it won't be long, maybe a week or two, before we receive orders." I try to ignore how Evalina's eyes grow wide and watery. "But they're just rumors. We don't know anything for sure."

"Right." Her voice is solid and her chin raised. "It could also be months."

"Right."

But neither of us believes it. She reaches over and squeezes my fingers. "Still no idea where you'll go?"

"We've heard everything from Northern California to Arkansas. And that maybe we would be in some temporary housing first. No one seems to know." I shrug, as if these details are unimportant. "Lots of questions. No answers yet."

Evalina reaches into her handbag and withdraws a pen and her address book. She uncaps the pen. "This is my home address," she says as she writes. "You have to write to me when you know where you're going. And when you get there."

She rips the paper out of the book and hands it to me. I know I'm gaping, but I don't know how to hide my surprise. "But what will you tell your parents?"

"I don't know. I'm almost always the one who gets the mail. I don't think I'll have to tell them anything."

"But if you do," I press her. "What will you say?"

Her attempt at a laugh is hoarse. "Maybe the truth? If you're not here, what do I care if they lock me in my room?"

I search her face for clues that she's teasing, and I find none. "You would really tell them?"

"If it came to that, yes. I can't handle not hearing from you, Taichi. Not when we don't know how long this—" She gestures vaguely toward the telephone pole "—will go on."

"What do you think they would say if you told them?" I can't bear to look her in the eyes when I ask. I look instead at her pretty fingers threaded through mine, at her nails painted the same shade of red as her lips.

"Daddy likes your family, and they disagree with the evacuation. They're not racist."

I swallow the acidic coating of shame that seems to have filled my mouth. "That's different than learning a Jap has fallen in love with your only daughter." I get brave enough to look up and find that Evalina has lost her battle with her tears. They're rolling down her cheeks one after the other.

"Sorry." She takes in a breath and squeezes my hand. "It's just that when you tell someone for the first time that you love them, it's not supposed to be like this. And don't call yourself that. You're American."

"I've told you before that I love you."

"In letters. Not actual words." She withdraws a hand to wipe her eyes, and I wish I had taken the time to put a handkerchief in my pocket. "I'm supposed to get to feel completely happy."

I squeeze her fingers. "Of course, it's not how it's supposed to be. Because *we* were never supposed to be. Even before the war started we knew this was going to be a hard sell with both our families. But in all this uncertainty, you're still the one thing I'm sure about."

A smile flickers on her face, and she straightens her shoulders. "I'm sure about you too. So we'll just . . . We'll just find a way. I'm a Cassano, after all." Her smile reappears, this time lasting longer. "We don't really talk about it anymore, but both sides of my family have a long, ethically-questionable history of not letting the government push us around."

I grin. "You know, I thought you were making that up the first time you told me."

"Maybe I am."

The combination of her wink, her bright smile, and her hand in mine makes my heart do a somersault in my chest.

The nearby church bells, clanging briefly to usher in 10:30, make Evalina grimace. "I have to go."

"Me too. Aiko is covering for me, and I don't want to wear out her charity."

"Tell her thank you for me."

"I will. And I'm sure . . ." It hits me that maybe this is the last time I'll ever see her. That if the rumors are true—that we're just days away from an evacuation—I don't know that I'll be able to get word to her in time. "I'm sure I'll see you again before I go."

She nods brusquely. "Yes, of course you will. But just in case."

Evalina leans forward for a painfully swift kiss. It's over practically as soon as I realize it's happening. We glance around, but nobody seems to have seen us.

She squeezes my hand, and then she rushes away. Back to her part of town, where her life will go on like normal regardless of what happens in the coming weeks. I feel a throb in my heart as the unbidden thought comes: *It would have been better for her if we'd never met.*

Friday, April 3, 1942

"Evacuees must carry with them on departure for the reception center bedding and linens, no mattress—"

Aiko snorts. "And how do they think we would carry a mattress on our person?"

"They're just being thorough," Mother says. "Read the rest, Katsumi."

Father angles the pamphlet toward the gray light coming in through the window. The side that faces me reads:

Questions and Answers for Evacuees
Information Regarding the Relocation Program
Issued by

THE WAR RELOCATION AUTHORITY
Regional Office
San Francisco, California

Father continues, "Question four. What kind of clothes should I take with me when I am evacuated? Answer. Be prepared for the Relocation Center, which is a pioneer community. So bring clothes suited to pioneer life—"

Aiko snorts from her place on the couch, where she's folding a piece of paper into some shape I can't yet make out. Father ignores her.

"—and in keeping with the climate or climates likely to be involved. Bring work clothes, boots, slacks, and work shirts rather than business suits or street dresses. Bring warm clothes even if you are going to a southern area, because the temperatures may range from freezing in winter to 115 degrees during some periods of the summer. Although you won't want to take many extra clothes to the Assembly Center—"

"Would they make up their minds? Is it a Relocation Center or an Assembly Center?" Another outburst from Aiko. "They don't know what they're doing, do they?"

"Aiko," Mother says wearily.

Father frowns and flips to the back of the pamphlet. "Here it explains the terms. An Assembly Center is 'a convenient gathering point within the military area where evacuees live temporarily while awaiting the opportunity for orderly, planned movement to a Relocation Center outside of the military area.' And then a Relocation Center is 'a pioneer community with basic housing and protective services provided by the Federal Government, for occupancy by evacuees'. So, I suppose there will be some temporary places where we live and some permanent places."

"I wish they would speak straight," Aiko says darkly as she continues folding. "We will be prisoners, not evacuees. And these pioneer communities are concentration camps."

The phrase falls heavy in the room. I glance at Mother and Father, expecting one of them to reprimand Aiko, but instead Mother says, "The newspaper this morning said the first group would be sent to Manzanar, California."

"When I went to register us, nobody there knew where we would go," Father says. "Or if they did, they would not say where."

"Tuesday." Aunt Chiyu speaks the word for at least the tenth time in the last hour, and probably the hundredth since we saw the new notices posted on telephone poles yesterday afternoon. The notices declared that Tuesday was our official departure day. "It is nice to finally know when and to be able to make plans. Katsumi, did you post my letter to Fuji?"

Father nods and says, "Yes, I did," without any hints of irritation that he has already answered this three times.

Aiko stands and wordlessly leaves the room. As the adults lapse into Japanese while discussing what else to pack, I go after her.

She's sitting in the bedroom we currently share with our parents. In the palm of her hand, she holds up what she had been folding. A crane, a Japanese symbol of hope.

She closes her hand around the paper, crushing it.

"What do you think would happen if we just didn't go?" she asks without turning around. "What would they do? Shoot us?"

I settle onto the floor beside her. "I don't know."

"Everybody acts like we don't have a choice, but what if we do?" Aiko's face is set in a fierce expression, calling to mind Father's childhood stories about our samurai ancestors.

"What if we could fight this somehow? This is *America*, Taichi. This kind of stuff isn't supposed to happen."

"I know. You're right. It's not how things are supposed to be—"

"The constitution is supposed to protect us from violations like this." Aiko's voice turns sharp. "Why isn't anybody saying that? Why isn't anyone saying that it's wrong for the FBI to just take our uncle away? To freeze our bank accounts? To give only *us* a curfew?"

She throws the balled-up crane against the wall and it flutters to the floor.

"It *is* wrong." Just speaking that sentence somehow feels dishonoring of America. "I've had the same thoughts, but I keep thinking that if we really did fight the evacuation they would only point to it as proof that we're disloyal. What they are asking us to do is unfair, but ultimately it's the fastest route to regaining our freedom."

"Of course you think that," Aiko snaps, hardly allowing me to finish my sentence. "You always think that if you just do what you're told, everything will work out fine."

She means to insult me, but I shrug. "I find it's generally true."

Aiko slowly releases a breath, like a steam engine releasing the pressure. "And you're probably right about what they would think if we fought back. Even though it's completely racist. But I guess that's why there's that cliché about life not being fair, right?"

"Yeah, I guess."

We sit side-by-side in silence for a while, and then Aiko leans her head against mine. "You should go to Evalina and tell her. She should hear it from you, not the newspaper, that we'll be gone by Tuesday."

I shake my head. The streets of Japantown have been full of stories about unchecked violence against Japanese Americans. Even against some Chinese, who white people mistook for Japanese.

"Mother and Father won't let me out of their sight long enough."

"Tell them why you need to go."

I give her a pointed look. "I can't just tell them."

Aiko blinks at me as though I'm stupid. "Why not? What are they going to do? Lock you up?" She snorts humorlessly. "They don't have to because the President of the United States is doing it for them."

I laugh too, even though the sentence turns my stomach. "They're stressed. Telling them about Evalina will only add stress, and I don't want that."

I tap my foot absently as I think. She should be almost out of school, and she doesn't go to the restaurant on Fridays until dinner. She's said a few times that she's usually home alone after school on Fridays because her mother has some kind of club. Knitting or books or something like that. "Could you cover me for an hour?"

"Fine." Aiko picks up her crane and attempts to uncrumple it. "But you know, Taichi. Sometimes you have to be honest with people, even if you know it's going to hurt them."

CHAPTER SEVEN

Evalina

Gia reverently runs her fingertips along the spines of the books lining the shelves at Cavalli Bookstore as we stroll out the door. "If you're this depressed now—when you saw him less than a week ago—what will you do when he's actually gone?"

"I don't know." I reach into my paper bag from the grocer and withdraw a tangerine. "I suppose the same thing you do when Lorenzo is gone."

"You probably don't even want to go to prom, do you?"

I wrinkle my nose.

Gia smirks. "I figured. That's what I told Tony. He asked me if he should ask you, and I said, 'I would have thought you wanted to have a good time at the dance, Tony.'"

The barb stings more than I would have expected. I brush it away—even I know I'm not particularly fun these days—and pop a wedge of tangerine in my mouth.

"That must have been a few weeks ago." I take care to infuse my voice with a careless tone. "He told me on Friday he's seeing Mary Green."

"Really?" Gia's eyes grow comically wide. "When did he tell you that?"

"After you'd left for your date."

"Before or after you yelled at my mother?" When Gia sees

59

I'm embarrassed, she snorts a laugh. "You know my mother can handle it. I'm honestly surprised she didn't yell right back at you."

We pause our conversation as we skirt around two women walking their dogs.

"Will Lorenzo be in town for prom?" I ask.

"Who knows?" Gia shrugs. "We would probably just fight all the time anyway."

"You're a LaRocca. That's normal."

She giggles and then her smile turns downcast. "I used to feel so proud to be a LaRocca—to be Italian. That's harder these days."

I offer her a wedge of tangerine as stories of Mussolini march through my mind, the invasions, the violence, the palling around with Adolf Hitler.

"I know what you mean. Though I've never felt particularly proud of my family history."

Gia casts a sympathetic look my way. "You can't help who your family is," she says simply, and then pushes open her front door. "See you tomorrow."

I wave and continue the few houses down to my own. I think about the grim line of my mother's face every time we get a phone call from relatives in Chicago, or when she visits one of her older brothers in prison. How as a kid, I would sometimes hear Daddy weeping in the confessional at church. Of the way Mama and Daddy refuse to discuss their lives before we moved to San Francisco. While they've been careful to keep details of our family's mafia roots vague, I know enough to be grateful that they chose something different for me.

The house is usually empty when I get home on Friday afternoons, but I've barely cracked open the door when Mama calls for me. "Evalina?"

"What?"

"In the kitchen, please."

Mama sounds stern. I sigh, slip my shoes off, and trudge toward the kitchen. Did one of my teachers call her again to tell her that I don't seem like myself these days? Or did—

"Taichi!" His name emerges as a squeak, and I clear my throat before speaking again. "This is a surprise."

Mama sits at our small kitchen table, and Taichi sits across from her. What in heaven's name is he doing here? Something terrible must have happened—my throat cinches closed—or he never would've risked coming.

His face is arranged in the polite expression he dons for deliveries and market days. "Hello, Miss Cassano. Nice to see you." He nods to Mama. "I was just telling your mother how sorry I am to drop by unannounced, but it isn't something that could wait. We're letting all our loyal customers, like yourselves, know that we are being evacuated."

The word lands like a punch in my gut, and all the air seems to force itself out of my body. "Evacuated."

From the kitchen stove, the teapot rattles and whistles its high-pitched call. Mama's chair scrapes against the linoleum as she scoots away from the table.

"Have a seat, Evalina. I'll pour us all some tea."

Taichi offers a respectful bow of his head. "Thank you, Mrs. Cassano."

Mama turns her back to us as she strides purposefully to the stovetop. This is the one time of day that sunrays slant through the window at the sink, and they illuminate the steam rising from a pan of cooling lemon bars. Those must be Mama's dessert of choice for our usual Friday night dinner with the Espositos and LaRoccas. In so many ways, this is just an ordinary Friday scene in our kitchen.

I turn my gaze to Taichi as I collapse into the chair Mama vacated. His eyes are fastened on mine, and for a moment we just stare at each other.

"When?" The word wobbles off my tongue. "When will you leave?"

"Tuesday." He says the word quietly, as if that will lessen its blow.

"Tuesday." The word has never tasted so bitter. "That's . . . very quick."

Taichi holds my gaze. "Yes, it is."

"Where will your family be evacuated to?" Mama asks as she carries over three teacups.

"That's still somewhat unclear." Taichi leans back as Mama places a cup in front of him. "Thank you, Mrs. Cassano."

"Do you take sugar or milk?"

"Neither, thank you."

All the polite chatter makes me want to scream, "How can you not yet know where you'll be sent? How can your family be expected to prepare if you're not being told where you'll go?"

I feel Mama's eyes on me, but I can't drag my focus off Taichi, even though it would be wise to do so.

Taichi's gaze flicks to her before returning to me. "When my father registered us, he was given a pamphlet of instructions. We'll be fine." He pauses before adding, "We've heard rumors that the first group will be sent to Manzanar, which is on the other side of the Sierras from Los Angeles. But the pamphlet said most will go somewhere temporary before our permanent homes. Or not *permanent*, but our homes for the duration of the war."

I'm afraid to speak. Afraid that if I open my mouth, I'll be like a volcano, spewing destructive fire. And Mama will be able to see plain on my face that I'm not just heartbroken over losing my favorite supplier of blackberries, or about the injustice of what's being done to Japanese Americans. She'll see I'm heartbroken over losing Taichi.

"The Sierras are quite beautiful down there, I hear." Mama's words curl with doubt, as if even she distrusts her response. "We plan to see Yosemite this summer, though I suppose that's not exactly where you'll be, is it?"

"No, ma'am. But on a map, it looks as though we would be near several other great peaks."

How can they stand to talk about sightseeing at a time like this?

"What will happen to all your belongings?" I ask.

"Much of it is still at our house. You've met Diego Medina at the market, I believe? They will look out for our home and continue to provide the same great produce and service your family has always received."

Taichi's smile doesn't reach his eyes, and he looks away from me as he takes a noiseless sip of his tea.

Mama glances at me and then back at Taichi. "My husband speaks so highly of your family. And Evalina is very picky about her produce, as I'm sure you know. She always wants to be first at the market so she'll have the best selection." Mama forces a strange sort of chuckle at my expense. "Thank you for the kindness of telling us about the changes in person. We're . . . we're very sorry for the evacuation. It seems like an unnecessary step to us."

Air huffs out my nose. "Unnecessary *and* cruel."

"Yes." Mama nods. "And cruel."

"And blatantly racist. I don't see Germans or Italians being forced out of their homes and businesses."

Mama's hand lands on my shoulder. "Evalina, we should

let Mr. Hamasaki get on with his day. I imagine you have many more customers to visit."

Taichi stands. "Thank you for your hospitality, Mrs. Cassano." He nods to me. "Miss Cassano."

"I'll walk you to the door." In my haste, I stumble over my chair.

Mama catches me by the elbow. "Are you okay, Evalina?"

"I'm fine." My laugh rings high. Too high. "Just clumsy."

I don't look at Taichi, just pivot toward the door.

Mama says, "Thank you, again. We'll be praying for your family during this difficult time."

To my great relief, she stays in the kitchen. Does she realize we're the only customers Taichi is visiting? That Taichi isn't merely a boy from whom I buy produce? What will she say to me when it's just the two of us?

The worries clip at my heels as I guide Taichi the short distance to the front door. I step outside with him, even though there isn't much more privacy out here where anyone in my nosy, Italian neighborhood can notice Taichi.

"I'm sorry for the surprise," Taichi murmurs. "I thought you were home alone on Friday afternoons."

"I usually am. But it sounds like you handled it well. If Mama suspects anything, it's because I couldn't keep my blasted emotions in check."

A smile plays with the corners of Taichi's mouth. "I like your emotions."

He has on a red plaid shirt beneath his brown work coat, and one of the points of his collar is flipped funny. My fingers itch to adjust it. I push them deep into my trench coat pockets.

"What time do you leave on Tuesday?"

His smile vanishes. "We're supposed to be there by noon."

"Be where?"

"The civic control station is what they called it. I don't know when the buses leave."

"Where is it? What's the address?"

Taichi gives me a look of caution. "You have school, Evalina."

I squeeze my eyes shut, trying to hold back the tears that press against my eyelids. In a matter of days, Taichi is going to load onto a bus and be taken to an unknown location until the end of the war. How can he think I care about school?

"I already have my scholarship and acceptance to Berkeley. What's the address?"

"Evalina, you can't."

I open my eyes and take in his handsome face. The angle of his brown eyes. The sharpness of his cheekbones. His thick black hair. Near his right eyebrow, there's a small scar I've never noticed before. His face is one I've spent more time with in my thoughts and hopes than in actual reality. "I'm not asking you, Taichi. I'm informing you I will be there. We'll tell your family . . . I don't know. Something. But I'm going to be there."

I glare up at him, anticipating how he'll argue.

But instead he releases a breath, and that faint smile returns. "2020 Van Ness," he whispers. "You should get back inside."

My toes wriggle in my shoes, longing to push up closer to Taichi. "I'll see you Tuesday."

"See you Tuesday."

Taichi's fingertips brush over my arm, and then he turns and strolls down the hill, back toward his borrowed corner of our city.

I linger until I lose sight of him, and then I turn back toward my front door. Is Mama on the other side, fists on her hips, waiting to badger me about the true nature of my friendship with Taichi? She realized before I did that Tony liked me, and I only figured it out because of the way she tried to hide her smile as she asked about why he had walked me home from school or stopped by the house. I don't think she'll be smiling about Taichi.

But Mama isn't waiting for me just inside the door. Instead, I hear her at the kitchen sink. My feet want to carry me up to my room, where I can throw myself on my bed and weep, but I know if I do that, I might as well flat out tell her who Taichi is to me.

Instead, I go to the kitchen and refill my teacup. "I'm so sad for them."

Mama turns to me, and her eyes are red. She's been crying. "I'm sad for all of us. This is a bad path for our country to travel down." She places the teacup she had washed on a towel to dry. "He seems like a really nice boy."

My throat is dry, and I take a gulp of tea. "He is."

"You have become friends this last year." Mama looks at me as she says this, and her expression is so open and kind, a piece of me longs to confess it all. Every last ounce of my feelings for Taichi.

I just nod.

"You have seemed so distraught since the attack on Pearl Harbor. More so than I might expect. I couldn't figure out why. I hadn't put together that you had built a friendship with a family that is personally impacted."

Again, I nod.

Mama crosses our tiny kitchen and hugs me. "I love your tender heart, my Evalina. If we could all feel the empathy that you do, our world would be a much more beautiful place."

"Thank you," I say into her shoulder. All other words are choked out by guilt over not telling my mother the truth.

Mama smiles at me and cups my face, tears glistening in her own eyes. Then she releases me, and I turn back to my tea. "I'm glad I had a chance to meet your friend before he left. He's very kind and respectful. And quite handsome, don't you think?"

I feel myself stiffen and can only hope that she didn't notice. "Yes." I sip at my tea. "I suppose he is."

Mama finishes wiping off the counter, and then leaves me alone in the kitchen, wondering if I only imagined the pointed nature of her questions.

CHAPTER EIGHT

Taichi

Tuesday, April 7, 1942

Father turns the alarm clock off within several seconds of it sounding. We have all been staring up at the ceiling for hours, even Aiko, who normally doesn't allow her sleep to be disrupted for anything.

Even though I'm not tired, I stay under the blanket and continue to stare at the old water stain that no one ever got around to painting over. When I wake up tomorrow morning, what will I see when I open my eyes?

Mother rises first. I hear the sounds of her wrapping her bathrobe over her nightgown and slipping out of the room. Minutes later, water runs in the kitchen sink, and Father's feet hit the floor too. Aiko and I wordlessly rise as well, tidying our makeshift bed before going to the kitchen.

Aunt Chiyu is there, wiping already-clean counters with a damp cloth, her mouth set in a grim line. Mother has the tea steeping as she lays out *mochi* on a plate for our breakfast. We sit around the small table, silent except for our chewing and drinking. Even though the sun is up, the fog outside keeps Aunt Chiyu's apartment dark and silent.

How many other families in the neighborhood are eating

silently and warily? We're to be at the civic center at noon, which feels both far too soon and far too far away. Other than packing my toothbrush, there's nothing left to do except sit and wait. Our suitcases are crowded around the door, two for each of us. I had wanted to bring my letters from Evalina, but instead I made myself burn them before we even left Alameda. The only memento I allowed myself to keep was her senior portrait, which I have buttoned into my breast pocket.

I glance at the clock. Seven a.m. Just a few miles away, Evalina might be eating breakfast too and getting ready for school. How is she planning to sneak away to come see us off? What am I going to tell my family when she arrives?

A soft rain patters against the window, and we all watch.

"It's like heaven is crying for us," Mother murmurs in the quiet, gray kitchen.

Aiko speaks the very words I think: "At least someone is."

At 11:30, after a morning of fidgeting and tidying, we pick up our suitcases and walk out of the apartment. Aunt Chiyu locks the door, and then stares at the key in her hand. "I suppose I bring it with me?"

Father nods. "Let's put it somewhere secure."

Aunt Chiyu zips the key into her pocketbook, and then bends to pick up her suitcase once more. Around us, other families are leaving their apartments as well. The adults exchange murmured greetings and pleasantries as we all descend the stairs.

The walk is not much more than a mile, but that feels very far when you're carrying everything you think you'll need for the foreseeable future. When you keep passing Caucasian men and women, many of whom turn away from you, but some who openly glare.

We're not far from the civic center when I hear clapping.

I look up from my shoes for the first time in a while to see a man about the age of my parents, standing in the open door of a doughnut shop. His eyes are narrowed at the group of us, and his smile is triumphant as he claps enthusiastically.

"The neighborhood is looking better already," he shouts above his own clapping. "That's right, keep walking!"

Father and I immediately move Mother, Aunt Chiyu, and Aiko to the other side of us, and the same shift happens in the other families.

The man's voice is loud in my ears as I walk by. "Get outta here, you Japs!"

I try not to look, but my gaze catches on the poster he's hung in his store window. The text reads JAPANESE HUNTING LICENSE: OPEN SEASON, NO LIMIT! above a buck-toothed, slant-eyed caricature of what I can only assume is supposed to be a Japanese man.

I quickly avert my eyes to Father's shoulders and try to keep my own as squared and strong as his. My underarms are suddenly damp with sweat, my heart racing in my chest, and my mouth full of bitterness, the taste of shame.

Our silence continues the rest of the way to the civic center, where we join the line of Japanese American families that stretches along the sidewalk. I rest my suitcases on the cement and bend my aching arms. My gaze is still cast down, my mind still ringing with the man's clapping.

How can I be sweaty and cold all at once?

I look to Mother and Father, hoping for some kind of comfort from them. I find they are already looking at Aiko and me. We stare at each other for a moment, and then Father speaks.

"It is good that the rain stopped."

Mother nods. "Yes. The weather is quite beautiful today."

We are not going to talk about the man. We are just going to carry on. *Shikata ga nai.*

I swallow away the words I want to speak—*why does he hate us so much?*—and they scrape down my throat. "The breeze is nice."

Aiko flexes her fingers several times, and I imagine they're just as sore and stiff as mine. "I will go see how long the line is."

And then she's disappearing along the sidewalk, into the sea of black-haired heads. Never in my life have I seen so many Japanese in one location. The men all have freshly clipped hair beneath their hats, and all the women took the time to curl theirs. The faces around me shine from the exertion of the day so far, and we haven't even begun our trip.

The line shuffles forward, and we heave our suitcases several steps.

"We should have left the house sooner." Aunt Chiyu pushes up on her toes, as if there is anything to see up ahead, other than a line that curls around the corner. "What a line!"

"But how eager are we to get to where we are going?" Mother asks.

Aunt Chiyu considers this. "I am at least eager to be done with the unknown."

Yes. About that, I agree.

Aiko returns, her eyes wide and her face pale.

"How long is the line?" Aunt Chiyu greets her.

"There are guards," Aiko says on a trembling exhale. "When we get around this corner, you'll see them." She swallows hard and fusses with a curl on her shoulder. "And they have these long guns with bayonets fixed to the ends."

Aiko has now attracted the attention of the families on either side of us, one of which has a girl of about eight. She's watching Aiko with round eyes.

"What are the guards doing?" I ask.

Aiko shakes her head. "Standing and watching. There's nothing else for them to do. Everyone is just in line waiting, talking quietly."

Aiko helps to push our luggage forward as the line shuffles again.

"How long is the line?" Aunt Chiyu asks again as Mother says, "Did you learn where we are going?"

"No. The line is very long. There are Caucasian women who are taking down everybody's names and making us wear a tag with a number. As if we're cattle."

Aiko's voice has risen, and Mother shoots a nervous look at those around us. "There are so many families. I'm sure the tags are just to keep everything organized."

Aiko presses on. "And then after you get your tag, you stand around waiting for a bus, while the guards stare at you. Some people said these buses were going to Fresno, but others said Arizona. Nobody knows a thing."

Several families behind us, a baby lets out a shrill cry. The mother is trying to hastily change the baby's diaper on top of one of the suitcases. An older child holds the soiled diaper with a look of disgust.

"What do I do with this, Mama?" she asks.

But the mother is holding a diaper pin with her teeth and cannot yet respond. I realize I'm staring, waiting for the answer as well. What *will* she do with the used diapers?

Aiko tugs on my sleeve so I'll help with pushing our luggage up again.

"At least we don't have any children," Aiko says through gritted teeth as we push our suitcases forward again. "That mother's suitcase is probably full of baby clothes and diapers. She probably has no room for her own things."

Surely Aiko's thoughts go to where mine are. That if she hadn't lost the baby, we would have a three-year-old child in tow.

We shuffle forward in line for another ten minutes before turning the corner and spotting the guards of whom Aiko had warned us. Even knowing about them, the sight of their long weapons, the bayonets glinting in the sunlight, make me feel as though I swallowed a block of ice. Their uniforms are a drab olive color, but I can't tell what branch of the military they are. I try to not look at them overly long.

Instead, I look toward the crowd near a bus. Most are Japanese, but I'm surprised by the number of Caucasian faces I see. Some appear to be journalists, taking notes on the scene with a photographer trailing behind them, but others are speaking with familiarity to the families. They seem to be here for the same reason as Evalina will be. Just to say goodbye.

"Would you like a sandwich?"

I blink at a middle-aged woman wearing bright yellow and holding out a tray of sandwiches like we're at a party. She could have been a severe looking woman, with her long face and sharp nose, but the yellow of her dress and her bright, dimpled smile prevent that.

When we seem hesitant, she adds, "The women of the First Congregational Church made these for you folks. Waiting in line is bad enough. No need to do so on an empty stomach. This side of the tray is chicken salad, and this side is egg salad."

She beams a delighted smile as the adults take the sandwiches, and then she offers them to Aiko and me. "My daughter, Grace, will be here soon with water. We ran out of cups."

"Do you know how much longer until we reach the desk?" Aiko asks after we thank her.

"I hope not much longer. I know you've been waiting a

long time already." She turns a smile to the next family in line. "Yes, please take a sandwich. These are chicken salad and these are egg salad." She looks back to Aiko. "Maybe twenty or so minutes? We are trying to make the process as smooth as we possibly can."

She moves on down the line, and Aiko and I exchange confused looks.

"When she said 'we,' do you think she meant it's the church that's handling the registration?"

"That's sure what it sounded like," Aiko says as she sinks her teeth into her sandwich.

The sandwich is dry and tastes hastily made, but I make myself eat all of it. There's no sign of anyone bringing water, and the sun is hot on my neck. I almost hope Evalina doesn't come. I must smell terrible.

Thirty more minutes pass before we are next in line at the desk, and as we approach, I think the sandwich woman really did mean that her church is handling the registration. There are three Caucasian women sitting there, all in bright dresses, without any kind of badge or anything to give them an air of officiality.

A girl about my age rushes up to the desk with a tower of paper cups in one hand and a water pitcher in the other. There's a sheen of sweat on her forehead as she plops it all down at a folding table and begins to pour.

"Sir? I can help you."

The woman speaking to my father has a friendly but frayed smile. She takes down our information, verifies our evacuation orders, and begins to write 2413 on a stack of tags like those I've seen dangling from the coats and luggage of others.

"Do you know where we're being sent?" Aiko asks, as I'm sure everyone has.

The woman gives a regretful shake of her head. "No, I'm not with the War Relocation Authority. Many of us are just volunteers from a church around the corner." She gestures to the other women, as well as a group of Caucasian men who are moving and sorting luggage.

"We enjoyed the sandwiches very much," Father says with a slight bow. "Thank you."

"It isn't much, I know," the woman says with a shrug. "We thought we could at least be friendly faces who helped today go smoother. Now, you'll want to loop your tag through the buttonhole of your coat because the guards will ask to see them before you get on the bus."

We tag our bags as well as ourselves, then we leave our possessions with the men from the church. For a moment, we stand huddled together, surveying the crowd.

"Strange that it is so many volunteers," my mother murmurs. "How are we supposed to know what bus to get on?"

My elbow is bumped by the girl passing out waters. "Oh, I'm so sorry!" She has a high, clear voice that rings excessively loud. "There's just so little space in here!"

She holds out the tray of small paper cups, which we gratefully take.

"How do we know where to go?" Aiko asks her.

"I'm really not sure there is a place you're supposed to go." The girl flutters a hand toward the buses. "There's a lot of families just standing alongside the sidewalks out there. It should get a little less crowded now that the buses are arriving. Sorry I can't be more help."

And then she's gone, carrying her tray of cups to a line of people who are happy to see her.

"Let's go this way," Father says, and we nudge our way through the crowd, back out into the fresh air.

Several guards bearing bayonetted rifles stand at the end of the sidewalk, clearly marking a line we're not to cross. A bus has just filled up, leaving a few vacated spaces where we can stand. I scour the sprinkling of Caucasian faces for Evalina. I thought she would be here by now. What if she is, but she just can't find me?

"It seems like nobody is in charge here," Aiko says through gritted teeth. "*He* is the closest I've seen."

I follow her gaze to a Caucasian man wearing the same uniform as the guards, only he's holding a clipboard instead of a gun. He steps off the bus that just finished loading, and the doors shut behind him.

Inside the bus, a young boy waves out the window to someone. "See you soon!"

An elderly man leaning on a cane waves back at him. "See you soon!" he echoes.

Aiko snorts in my ear. "Yes, it's sure a good thing all these guards are holding guns. We certainly want to keep this situation under control."

I think of the man at the doughnut shop, his sneer and the poster. "Maybe they're here for *our* protection."

Aiko flashes me a dirty look. "You're naivete is insufferable at times like this. I'm going to try and find a drinking fountain."

I want to call to her to keep an eye out for Evalina, but she disappears into the crowd before I can.

With the sun directly overhead, the sky is a washed-out shade of blue. There's not even an interesting building or a glimpse of the bay to suggest that we're in San Francisco. What will it look like wherever they let us off?

The bus pulls away from the curb, and as another pulls up, the guard with the clipboard yells, "Numbers 2200 through 2350, line up in an orderly fashion!"

I check my tag—not us—and rub at a rough edge on my

thumbnail as I half-listen to the conversation my parents are having with the family next to us. I know some Japanese, of course, but Mother and Father hardly ever speak it to us. With the noise of the crowd and their rapid speech, I can only pick out a few words. Sounds like this family has heard Manzanar as a possibility, but more likely Santa Anita or Tanforan.

My father's brow creases at this. "Where they race the horses?"

The man shrugs. In Japanese he says, "It is not race season now."

My father chuckles. "Even still. I do not wish to sleep in a horse stall."

Another family pushes past us—a mother, father, and five stair-step children—in search of their own space on the sidewalk. My gaze follows them, and a heaviness drapes around my shoulders. We all need seats on a bus, a bed, and three meals a day. And we're just a fraction of the people who are being evacuated. If the government is relying on church volunteers just to get us fed and sorted onto the buses, what's waiting for us on the other end of the ride?

"Taichi!"

I open my eyes to the sight of Aiko's face—which looks much more cheerful than the expression she left with—but my attention snaps to who she has with her: Evalina.

Aiko pulls Evalina until she's standing right in front of me. Her eyes are red, and her forehead is pinched as if she's holding in more tears.

"I saw the bus pulling away," she says on an exhale. "I thought . . ."

Her face crumples, and Aiko chimes in, "Luckily, I spotted her."

"Yes." Evalina takes a deep, wobbling breath. "Luckily."

Evalina looks up at me through her tear-soaked lashes. Her smile is weak, but it makes my breath hitch all the same. She's here. She somehow got out of school and made it here. All to see me tagged and loaded up like livestock. I probably smell like cattle now too.

"Miss Cassano." Mother has appeared at my elbow, and she reaches out to clasp one of Evalina's hands in a warm handshake. If only I were free to do the same. "This is a nice surprise. Are you here with the church group?"

Evalina blinks and then, "Yes. Of course. I saw you all over here and wanted to say hello."

"No school today, then?"

"It's . . . I received special permission."

"Very good of you." Mother smiles and nods. "There are many of us to organize. You are good to help out."

"I wish there was no reason for helping out, Mrs. Hamasaki." Evalina's chin trembles for a moment. "This is an injustice. An embarrassment for a country that prides itself on freedom and equality—"

"No, no," Mother smiles kindly as she shakes her head. "Our government is doing what they think is best. We will be fine. Taichi, you see who it is?"

As if I haven't been standing here the entire time. "Yes, of course. Nice to see you, Miss Cassano."

"You will still find good Hamasaki produce at the Medinas' stand at the market," Mother says. "Maybe you have met Diego already? Young like Taichi, but taller and broader."

"Yes, I've met Diego. I imagine I will see him most Saturdays now."

This sentence causes a twist in my heart. While I'm scratching out a new life at . . . wherever it is I'm going, Evalina and Diego will still be at the market on Saturday mornings. Their lives get to continue as normal.

"Do we know yet where you'll be going?" Evalina's question draws me back into the moment. Which is where I should be. As it is, it'll be over far before I'm ready.

"No. That is a great mystery, it seems. Did you learn anything new, Aiko?"

"Still nothing certain." Aiko turns her back to Evalina and me as she answers Mother's question. "Most say Manzanar is the only camp that's ready for residents . . ."

Her voice drops lower, and her body angles more. I'm about to lean in so I can hear when I realize that Aiko is doing her best to give Evalina and me a moment of privacy.

I glance at Evalina, and we slip around the corner, back to the chaos of the tagging and the luggage. There's so much commotion—luggage being moved on dollies, families herding children, a girl crying as her mother pries a cat from her arms—no one is paying attention to us.

"I thought maybe I was too late. I stayed longer than I wanted to, to take an English test, and I saw that bus pull away, and . . ." Her jaw trembles.

I decide no one is looking at us—or that if they are, I'll accept the consequences—and I put a hand on her arm. "I know, but it's fine."

I hear the distinct squeal of brakes as another bus arrives.

"I'm just glad Aiko noticed me because I couldn't see anything, I was crying so hard. How much longer do you have?"

The bus that just braked is likely ours. "I don't know. I think we're one of the next groups, but nobody is keen on giving us information."

Evalina's humph speaks her annoyance. "What church

group was your mother talking about? I feel terrible about lying, but I didn't know what else to do."

"Oh." I gesture toward the table where more families are getting their tags. "I guess they're from a church around the corner and volunteered."

One of the men rolls by with a dolly, headed toward the curb. My heart seems to jump up to my throat when I spot one of our suitcases on it. My time with Evalina is nearly up.

Evalina's gaze latches onto my tag, and a rush of shame sweeps over me. I cover the numbers with my hand. "It's fine, Evalina. It's not like they tattooed us."

"It's not fine." Evalina says through a clenched jaw. "Maybe they didn't tattoo it on, but it's not like this will just wash away either."

I take hold of her hand. "It's going to be fine."

Her glare is full of fire. "'Fine.' You keep saying that, but you don't know. Maybe it's *not* going to be fine, Taichi."

I know she's angry on my behalf, not at me, but I really don't want to spend our remaining minutes fighting.

"Because what other choice do I have, Evalina?" I grip her hand. "I have to believe it's going to be fine. That though you're not physically getting on the bus, you're still with me. *That's* why I can feel this will all turn out fine. Because I believe that someday in the future, I'm going to leave wherever it is that I'm going. And that when I step off *that* bus, you'll be there waiting for me."

Evalina's teeth are clenched to the point of trembling, and she nods at me as the fire in her eyes melts away. "I will." Evalina's tears break through. She wipes them with the palms of her hand. "I promise."

I can feel the crowd shifting around us, can sense that I'm about to be pulled away, but even though I think I should tell her bye, should walk away, I instead put my arms around her waist and pull her close to me.

Her eyes widen as she realizes that I'm about to kiss her. Maybe she too has all the reasons why we shouldn't pounding through her head. The guards with the bayonets, my parents who could see us at any moment, and all the Japanese around us who are just as likely to disapprove of Evalina as her family is to disapprove of me.

But I'm not going to let all of those should-nots rob me of this. This one moment where all that matters is this girl in front of me, and that she knows without a doubt everything I feel for her. I kiss Evalina, and for a blip of a moment, everything really does feel like it's going to be fine.

"Taichi." Aiko stands beside us with round, apologetic eyes. "They're asking us to line up."

I'm lightheaded as I blink at Aiko, as I take in the pulse of the crowd around us.

Evalina blinks too, and then yanks open her schoolbag with a panicked, "Food!" She withdraws a paper sack. "I didn't know what they would have for you, or how long you might be traveling, so I packed things that don't need to be refrigerated. It's almost all Italian food, so I don't know if you'll like it or not, but I . . . I just wanted to do something."

I take the bag from her, making sure my fingers touch hers. "That's really thoughtful of you."

Aiko's smile holds a rare warmth. "If you really want to be helpful then write to my brother frequently or he'll be depressed all the time."

"Of course." Evalina looks up at me, all strength now that the time has come. "Every day."

"Every day." I squeeze her hand and make myself say the last word I want to speak. "Goodbye."

CHAPTER NINE

Evalina

As Taichi mounts the bus steps, he turns and searches for me in the crowd. I make myself smile. I don't want him carrying away any more memories of me bawling on the San Francisco sidewalks.

"Goodbye! See you soon!" call several other Japanese families, many of whom are not yet wearing tags. Maybe they haven't received their evacuation orders?

Those being evacuated file onto the bus in an orderly fashion, even the young children. They're so quiet and polite, the guards must feel ridiculous holding those bayonetted guns.

A young woman not much older than me crouches to tie the saddle shoe of her toddler while also cradling a newborn. Somehow she does so with efficient pulls and loops, and then she holds her daughter's hand as her stout legs attempt the steep bus steps.

Fury blazes in my chest. Oh, yes, I'm *so* thankful that these dangerous people are being removed from my city. Thanks ever-so-much, Mr. President.

I've been so absorbed with the young woman and her children, I lost track of Taichi. Panic claws at me as I scan the silhouettes of passengers filing deeper into the bus. Even though Taichi stands several inches taller than many of the others, it's impossible to make out a difference like that through the windows. Foolishly, I had counted on one more smile. One more wave. Only now—

Aiko's delicate features appear in an open window toward the middle of the bus. She waves to me and says something, but with the idling bus and the chatter around me, I can't hear her.

I cup my ear. She mouths TAICHI and points to the other side of the bus.

He must be on the other side.

I don't think, I just move. I skirt my way around the Caucasian men loading the luggage, dash through the exhaust, and search for Taichi's face in the windows. When I find him, he raises his window and reaches out a hand.

I reach back, pushing up on my tiptoes. Even still, I can't quite grasp his fingers. "I should've been born taller," I shout through the window.

Taichi laughs, but his grin evaporates as a guard closes a hand around my arm. His grip isn't overly firm, but it's not gentle either.

"Sir, your entire body must remain in the bus." The guard turns his steely gaze on me. "Miss, this is an unsafe place for you to stand. The bus is about to depart."

"We're just saying goodbye," I say, but the guard is already pulling me away.

I look back up at Taichi's window and find he's tracking me as best he can while keeping his head inside the bus. We're still close enough that he could hear me if I shouted to him, but my voice is suffocated by fear as I allow myself to be led back to the sidewalk.

The guard releases me. "Stay here, or I'll have to remove you from the loading zone."

I don't meet his eye.

When I do look up, I find the Japanese American families around me are angled away, as if to offer me a moment of privacy after a public embarrassment. But one of the Caucasian men loading the buses watches me openly. His gaze holds no condemnation, only curiosity and perhaps sympathy.

I seek out Aiko's face once more in the window and find her looking at me as though she's been struck. She must have seen the guard escort me back to the sidewalk.

I flash a thumb's up.

She nods, but her face still looks ashen.

The bus must be full by now. There are many standing in the aisle. They must not be going too far if they're expected to stand for the journey, right?

No, they're still letting people on. An elderly man, leaning heavily on his cane and being helped by a middle-aged son, struggles up the first step.

The woman behind them watches with a stricken expression similar to Aiko's, as if she can't quite process what's happening in front of her. When the elderly man stumbles— and is caught by the man helping him—her jaw trembles. She releases a sob so loud, I can hear it from where I'm standing.

The woman boards, crying into her hands, and somehow a few more behind her are squeezed on. Then the bus door swings shut, as does the luggage compartment. Aiko faces forward, her jaw locked tight.

The woman's cries are still echoing in my ears as I stand there waiting. Minutes tick by. Another bus comes and idles behind this one, and the families who have tags begin to organize into a line.

The brakes pop as they're released, and the bus lurches. Aiko raises her hand in a farewell to me, and I've barely raised mine in return when the bus chugs away from the curb.

They're gone.

All this waiting, all this agonizing over when it would happen and how it would happen and if it would happen. And now, it's happened.

I know I need to be getting home, but I can't seem to move.

"You had friends aboard?"

I look up and find the man who'd been loading luggage standing near me. He looks as though he's about my parents' age, with silver strands threading his auburn hair and creases around his mouth from years of smiling. He's not smiling now, though.

"Yes." The syllable is coated in tears, and I clear my throat. "Yes, I did."

His gaze flicks to my arm. "Did the guard hurt you?"

"No." Not physically, anyway. "Are you with War Relocation? Do you know where their bus is going?"

"I'm sorry, I'm just a volunteer."

"You're with the church group, then?"

He nods.

"Your help has been greatly appreciated. My friends"—I gesture to where Taichi's bus disappeared—"spoke of the kindness of the church volunteers."

"We're not able to do much, unfortunately. You're welcome to stay and help, if you like."

I look at my wristwatch and grimace. The school day is gone, and Mama will expect me to come home from Gia's—my cover story—in time to help with dinner. "I wish I could, but I'm expected at home. Will your church help with other evacuations? If so, who could I leave my name and phone number with?"

"My wife, Mrs. Bishop." He points down the crowd. "She's the one dressed in yellow."

I dig in my school bag for paper and a pen. "Can you give her my name and number, please?"

"Of course."

I scribble my information as fast as I can. Mr. Bishop looks at the paper before tucking it into his breast pocket. "Nice meeting you, Miss Cassano."

"You too, Mr. Bishop."

He flicks a polite smile at me, and then turns toward the cart of luggage that's been wheeled to the curb, ready for the process to start all over again.

I weave my way through people, heading back toward the block where I can catch a trolley. Is that woman still crying on the bus? Or is she sitting there stoically, crying in her heart, as I am in mine?

At the fringe of the loading area, I allow several feet between me and a guard as I pass him. Something draws my gaze to his face, though, and I'm shocked by how he glares at me.

He spits at my feet, hitting the sidewalk beside them. "Jap lover."

His hatred cracks open something in my soul, as if a seed had been planted there long ago awaiting the nourishment of his glare, the woman's tears, and the look on Taichi's face as the guard grabbed hold of me.

I stop and match him with a nasty look of my own. When I spit back, it lands square on the toe of his polished black boot.

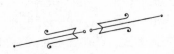

When I arrive, Mrs. LaRocca directs me to Gia's room. I slip off my school shoes and trot upstairs in my bobby socks. My head is loud with stories and outrage from the afternoon, and I don't know what to share with my best friend first.

I find Gia sprawled on her bedroom floor with her left

hand splayed over a sheet of newspaper. A bottle of crimson nail polish sits open beside her, and she whistles something jaunty as she strokes the tiny brush over her fingernails.

Gia grins. "Perfect timing! You can paint my right hand. I'm atrocious."

I stare at the scene before me. Gia's face is glossy from makeup she wasn't wearing at school and framed in precise cordovan curls. Even with the open bottle of nail polish, I can smell the hot curling iron. Her bed is covered with skirts and sweaters.

I think of the young Japanese American mother. The woman brave enough to sob as she climbed onto that wretched bus. The harried church ladies passing out sandwiches. How can all that be happening at the same time as this?

"You look like you've been busy."

Gia nudges the bottle of polish closer to me. "I read this inspiring article in a magazine about how now more than ever it's important for us to look our best."

"Why 'now more than ever'?" My question has a starched, stiff sound to it.

Maybe Gia hears it, because her smile falters. "I think they just mean during times of war. You know how they say the wife is the heart of the home? Well, women are the heart of the *country*. So, when our men go off and fight for us, we don't want to be sitting around at home looking dowdy. That doesn't help their spirits any."

"So, this—" I gesture to the chaos of her room as I sit on the floor "—is you doing your patriotic duty?"

Gia's lashes flutter against her cheeks. "I wouldn't phrase it like *that*."

I pick up the bottle of polish and rattle the brush around inside. "Keep your hand still so I can serve my country by painting your nails."

Gia flashes me an annoyed look. "You don't have to poke fun, Evalina. If you disagree, fine. But you don't have to be mean."

"I just watched Taichi and his family load onto a bus with no idea where they're going. They tagged them all with numbers, like they're a shipment leaving a warehouse. And there were all these armed guards standing around. After watching that, I really don't care how I look."

Gia stares at the floor. Her heavy rouge makes her look as though she's blushing. "I'm sorry."

The waver of her voice takes the edge off my anger. It's not as though what's happening to Taichi and his family is Gia's fault. "Sorry, G. I'm not very good company right now."

"I know you're just sad."

Sad. What I feel is far greater, far deeper, than sad. "Thanks for covering for me today so I could be there."

"Of course. Evalina, don't," she says as I press her right hand onto the newspaper.

"I can't in good conscience leave you with only half your nails painted. Think of how it would impact the morale of our troops."

I make myself smile, and Gia giggles. The sound is soothing after this afternoon, and my muscles relax.

But when I catch myself, I tense again. How could I let myself do that?

How easy it would be to get used to this new reality. Right now the heartache of saying goodbye is fresh, but as weeks and months and maybe even years pass, it could be easy to forget to fight. To forget that an entire race of Americans is being robbed of everything they've worked for because they happen to look like our overseas enemies.

If Italians could be so easily spotted, I have no doubts that I would be sent to a concentration camp too.

I finish Gia's hand, and I take the tiny brush and stroke lines of the red paint onto my left thumbnail. Then I close the bottle, set it aside, and blow on it to speed the drying.

She blinks at my red thumbnail and then at me. "You're just painting one?"

"Yes." I blow again and watch the polish harden, feel my resolve do the same. "So I'll remember that this isn't normal."

CHAPTER TEN

Evalina

I awake the next morning gasping for breath and grasping among my bedsheets for a gas mask. When my hands find only fistfuls of cotton sheets, I realize the bombs had been a dream. I take several drags of clean, cool air.

My shoulders and legs ache, as if the muscles have been clenched for hours. I unfold my body and stretch my arms above my head. My lips are dry, and my mouth is too. My cheeks and eyelashes are crusty from dried tears.

After coming home from Gia's yesterday, I helped Mama prepare gnocchi, participated in the conversation at dinner, and did a pretty great job of acting like it was a totally normal Tuesday.

Or so I thought.

While I dried dishes, Mama asked, "Are you all right, Evalina?"

I continued to rub the pot dry in even, circular motions. My one red nail reflected back at me in the shine of the stainless steel. "I am, thank you."

Mama scrubbed at a stubborn bit of dried potato. "The Hamasaki family left today, right?"

"Yes, that's been on my mind tonight." I was impressed that my voice sounded so steady. "I do feel rather down about that."

90

I crouched to return the pot to the cabinet. Where was Taichi? What was he doing? Where was he going? How long until I heard from him?

"Understandably so." Mama left it at that and didn't press me when I said I felt extra tired and was going to bed early.

As I mounted the stairs to my room, I felt as though Mama's unasked questions followed me. Or maybe I had imagined her curiosity, because it wasn't in her nature to keep silent.

I look at my clock now—5:30. If he were home, Taichi would be up doing farm chores before going to school. Where is he waking up this morning?

A familiar and welcome sound enters my room. The faint whine of the paper boy's bicycle.

My body groans and pops when I ease out of bed. The floorboards are cool beneath my bare feet as I slip out my bedroom door and down the stairs, with only a couple of squeaks to give me away. The newspaper awaits on our front step, so fresh the ink clings to my fingers when I touch it.

I find what I'm looking for buried within the *San Francisco News*.

"Goodbye! Write Soon!"
Alien Exodus Like an Outing

With a few courteous bows, lots of promises to "write soon" and many sturdy American-type handshakes, the first Japanese involved in military evacuation orders yesterday said farewell to San Francisco.

The elders, steeped in their native traditions, displayed few emotions. School-age youngsters romped and played among the piles of household goods strewn in front of the control stations of the

Wartime Civil Control Administration, 2020 and 1701
Van Ness Avenue.
  College-age boys and girls and their slightly older
friends and relatives, most of them American citizens, still laughed, wise-cracked in the latest slang,
and gave the scene the air of an outing—

The edges of the paper crumple beneath my tightened
grasp. "The air of an outing"? Who wrote this piece of delu-
sional garbage?

Armed military police patrolled the sidewalk in
front of the station, watched over personal proper-
ties, kept motorists and gawkers on the move.

Oh, is *that* what they were doing? Because I recall them
being turned *toward* the Japanese Americans, as if keeping the
rest of the city protected from *them*. I recall being spat upon
by one of them! Or would've been, if his aim had been truer.

As the buses rolled away, friends remaining
waved goodbye, raised their thumbs in the air, made
the victory V signal in final tribute. The younger
Japanese responded, broad smiles on their faces;
heads bobbed up and down in affirmation.

Was I at the same place as this moronic journalist? Because
I saw no victory signals. No broad smiles. No bobbing heads.
And the only raised thumb was *mine* to reassure my friend
that I was okay. What a load of propaganda. In America! In
my own newspaper!
  How many San Franciscans will read this article and

think, "That doesn't sound so bad." Or, "Wow, those Japanese American families sure are having fun." He made having your property seized and being loaded onto a bus while surrounded by military police sound like heading off for some kind of vacation!

I mash the newspaper shut and throw it onto the front step. The ink is all over my hands, and I stare at them, as appalled as if it were blood. I stop just short of slamming the front door when I re-enter the house. My soul is so loud, it's hard to keep the rest of me quiet.

I march to the desk shoved in the corner of our living room, yank out a piece of writing paper, and I throw down a scathing letter to the editor of the *San Francisco News*. At the end, I press the pen to sign my name, only to hesitate. How seriously would they take a girl named Evalina Cassano?

After a moment's consideration, I sign it simply, "A Concerned Citizen."

Taichi

Air. Fresh air. I need fresh air.

That's all I can think about as I shuffle down the aisle of the hot, rank bus. Standing on my legs is both agonizing and amazing all at once. Every muscle in my body is sore from over twenty-four hours of being squashed onto a bus seat, then squashed into a train seat, and then squashed onto another bus seat.

The newborn starts his now-familiar furious cry for food,

and his mother bobs up and down as she seeks to comfort him while simultaneously herding her young daughter off the bus.

Many have it much worse than me. I would be wise to not lose sight of that.

A high-pitched whistling sound fills the air, and the bus sways as wind pushes against it. During our fifteen-minute ride from the train station in Lone Pine, California—wherever that is—I had noticed a few times that something seemed to push against the bus as we drove. As though the bus were a large sail.

Somebody slow must have gotten off because the line resumes moving. I angle for a view out the windows but I don't have enough room to bend. I catch glimpses of brown earth, and the black boots of a guard.

"Single-file line, folks. You can collect your bags after you've been processed. Keep your tags out where they can be seen."

Finally, I'm on the deep stairs, stepping out onto solid ground. The sun is unbearably bright; I shade my eyes and squint.

All the breath in my lungs clears at the sight of the mountain peaks. I've never been this close to the Sierras, never seen mountains so tall, so strong. Or perhaps their majesty is an illusion because of the sharp contrast to the flat and dusty valley, pockmarked with squat, rectangular houses, all painted black.

Or "house" might be too glorified of a name for them; they look more like crude barracks, all lined up in orderly rows, as if a guard commanded them to be in single file and uniform.

"Bags can be collected after you've been processed," a military policeman calls as he strolls along our quiet line, a bayonetted gun held firmly at his side. Why the weapon? Who among us has the energy to fight after twenty-four hours of travel? "Stay in a single-file line. Single-file line, folks. Ma'am, your number is hidden. You need to keep your tags out where we can see them."

Aiko pokes me in the back. When I turn, she points to a sign on our left.

Owens Valley Reception Area
Manzanar, California

So, the rumors were true after all. Our family had pulled out a roadmap several weeks ago—though it feels like several lifetimes ago—to see where Owens Valley was because that was the only evacuation camp the newspapers had mentioned. We finally spotted the valley between the Sierra Nevada and Inyo Mountain ranges.

"It will be cold at night," Mother said as we looked at the altitude. "I should buy us winter jackets and boots."

Father removed his eyeglasses and rubbed them clean with a handkerchief. "Maybe. We do not know if we will go there."

"We do not know that we will *not,* either."

But Mother had made a special trip into the city just to find jackets and boots she deemed sturdy enough. As I stand in the valley now, the sun cooking my face, that puffy winter jacket and clunky pair of boots stealing so much room in my suitcase seem ridiculous. As ridiculous as my baseball bat and glove. Who did I think I would be playing baseball with?

The line inches forward toward a building, also black like the houses. But not painted black, as I'd originally thought. Rather the structure is wrapped in some sort of black paper like I've seen used on rooftops. It rustles when the wind blows.

Another whistling sound fills the air, and I feel as though a handful of dust has been thrown into my face. I cover my eyes, coughing and exhaling out my nose to try and clear the dirt.

"That wind." Aiko's words are sharp, as if swearing. "My eyes are full of sand."

I mop my face with my handkerchief, and it comes away an ashy brown.

Mother keeps turning to check on us and fusses several times with our yellow tags. Father and Aunt Chiyu are quiet, their jaws clenched, as we take shuffling steps.

Several guards are posted on either side of the building door. They wear helmets and hold bayonets as if this is a war zone. Their hard faces remind me of the guard who grabbed Evalina's arm at the bus. The thought of his hand closing around her, pulling her away from me, makes my fists clench as a flush of anger rolls over me.

"Where's your tag, miss?"

One of the guards has snapped to attention, his focus drilling into someone behind me. I turn and see a teenage girl who had been several rows behind me on the bus from Lone Pine. She's holding her young sister—maybe two years old?—who's asleep on her shoulder. Her eyes are full of fear as she realizes the guard is speaking to her.

"I . . . I don't know." She looks down, patting at her chest. "I had it on when I got off the bus . . ."

"Step aside, miss, until you find it."

"Is that really necessary?" I don't realize I've said it out loud until the gazes of everyone around me swing my way. I swallow and continue, "Why else would she be here if she wasn't supposed to be?"

"Taichi," Mother admonishes under her breath.

The guard ignores me, but snaps, "Get out of line," to the girl.

She obeys. One hand is occupied by supporting the weight of her sister, and her other hand trembles as it digs into the pockets of her sweater, then her trousers. "I don't know. I just don't know. I swear I had it when I got on the bus." She scans the ground, her voice climbing higher as she calls down the back of the line, "Has anybody seen my number?"

Aiko lingers with me, even though the line in front of us has moved. "Try your handbag."

"I did." The girl's eyes swell with tears. "Where could it be?" To the guard's shoes she says, "My name is Rose Ogawa. I'm from Terminal Island. My number is 2453. My mother is already here. She was on the first bus with my brothers. You can ask them."

The guard's jaw is tight. "Everyone must have a tag, miss. No exceptions."

Aiko steps out of line and holds out her hands for the sleeping toddler. "I can hold her while you look."

"Aiko," Mother says sharply. And then, surprised, "Taichi," when I step out too.

"What am I going to do?" Rose's voice climbs higher as she passes her sister to Aiko. "What happens if I can't find my tag?"

The flash of yellow catches my eye as Aiko fits her arms around the toddler. I reach into the pocket of the sleeping girl's sweater. "Here it is."

Rose smiles at me through her flowing tears. "Oh, God bless you."

"She found it," Aiko says to the guard, her voice cool. "Satisfied?"

I grimace at Aiko's attitude, but the guard just says a dry, "Tags need to be affixed to the front of the shirt."

The tremor in Rose's hands is so great that she can't even take the tag from me.

"Here, let me." I loop the string through the buttonhole of her sweater and pull it tight.

"Thank you," she whispers. "Taichi and—" she looks to Aiko's tag. "Aiko. I'm very appreciative."

Aiko passes the sleeping toddler back to Rose. "Let's find our place back in line."

Mother, Father, and Aunt Chiyu are inside the building now, nearing a long table of Caucasian women. All three of them have been watching the doorway, and their relief over spotting us is clear. The room is warm, but it's nice to be out of the dusty wind.

I expect a scolding, but instead Father just says, "We are being assigned apartments and given shots."

He nods to the chaos on the other side of the room where Caucasian nurses have trays of medical supplies. Parents put on brave faces and hold their crying children steady.

Aiko narrows her eyes. "What kind of shots are those?"

The floor creaks beneath me. It's made only of planks of wood, and the knotholes reveal there's no foundation, only dirt. Which explains the crunch of sandy grit beneath my shoes. The walls are constructed from the same type of knotty lumber. Even if there weren't natural holes in the boards, there are still gaps between the planks, evidence of how hastily they were nailed up. Is the black paper supposed to help keep out dust?

Mother waves me forward, and I realize my family is being assisted. I step out of line to join them.

After providing our names and former addresses to a woman at the desk, she counts out a stack of ten thin, green blankets and plops them on the table, disturbing the coating of dust that had gathered there. "You're in block four, barrack eleven, apartment one. Step over here to get your inoculations, and they'll show you where to stuff your mattresses." She leans out over the table. "Next in line!"

"Stuff our mattresses?" Father says, but the next family is already edging us out of the way.

Mother's face turns pale as we stand in line watching others receive their shots. One nurse in particular really jabs the needle in, and Mother looks away as if she'll be sick. She happens to be the nurse who barks, "Next!" when it's Mother's turn.

I step around Mother, taking her place.

The nurse doesn't even glance at me as she reaches for a set of shots. "Take your sweater off."

Aiko, who's only a few feet away, asks, "What kind of shots are these?"

"Just standard shots."

"Next!" calls another nurse, and this time I cannot protect Mother. Thankfully this is one of the two gentler nurses. Even still, my mother looks like she might faint before she gets to the table.

"Standard shots?" Aiko echoes. I don't need to look at my sister to know she's scowling. "And what are 'standard shots' for prisoners?"

The nurse flicks Aiko an annoyed look. "Standard inoculations." She speaks in a slow, loud, insulting voice. "Typhoid, diphtheria, tetanus, and small pox."

"Are you sterilizing those needles that you're about to poke in my brother's arm?"

"Next!" another nurse calls.

My nurse arches her eyebrows at Aiko. "That's you. And of course we're sterilizing them. Cleanliness is very important to us here in America."

By the time I understand the implications of her statement, the nurse holds my arm steady with a hand that feels as though it's made of steel. I clamp my mouth shut so I won't cry out from the burn of the first shot.

I take a deep breath as she reaches for the next. "Should I expect any side effects from these?"

"No."

As we exit through the door the nurses pointed us to, a hot, dusty wind tries to slap us back into the building. Aunt Chiyu supports some of Mother's weight and murmurs comfort to her in Japanese.

Aiko's facial expression makes me think of a hornet that's been poked with a stick. "We're all going to be sick as dogs from those stinking shots."

I rub at my arm, which is more sore from the nurse's grasp than the shots themselves. "She said we wouldn't."

Aiko makes a scoffing noise. Before dropping out of school, Aiko was on track to become a nurse. She learned just enough to scare us all with horror stories.

We enter the doorway of the next building and wait for our eyes to adjust. Inside, there are two piles. One of hay and one of large, empty sacks. Japanese Americans of all ages hold a sack in one hand and use the other to shovel in straw.

"What are they . . . ?" Aiko's voice curls with disbelief as she realizes what's going on. She looks at me, and the indignation on her face reminds me of when she crushed her paper crane in her hands. "They don't even have beds for us."

Her sentence is like a suitcase stuffed with thousands of corresponding thoughts to be unpacked. That the pamphlet about what we would have at camp was wrong. That the government can't even be bothered to give us something as basic as a bed. And if they can't provide us with beds, what else have they not provided for us? Should we expect a roof? Food? Toilets?

I pick up one of the sacks and hand it to her. "I don't think Manzanar is any more ready for us than we are for it."

CHAPTER ELEVEN

Taichi

We step outside the building, juggling our mattresses and suit-cases. I stare out at the bleak valley, the soaring peaks, and my mind is curiously blank.

"Hi."

I jump at the greeting.

The man—in his mid-twenties, maybe?—sticks out his hand to my father. "I'm Ted Kamei. I'm going to show you where your apartment is."

"Thank you." Father sets down his suitcase and, while balancing his stuffed mattress over his shoulder, fumbles in his trouser pocket for the paper we were given with our new address.

Mr. Kamei smiles when he sees it. "How funny! We'll be neighbors. I thought our block was full. I'm in 4-7-2 with my wife and parents. I'm not your official block leader—that's Karl—but I've been here since the beginning, so I can usu-ally help if you have questions. Oh, excuse me a moment." He waves to another family who's gazing about the barracks with dazed expressions and luggage puddled around their feet. "Hi, I'm Ted. I'm going to show you to your apartment. I'm just waiting for a few more to join us."

I shield my eyes from a gritty blast of wind and watch a group of men work together to hang the black paper on a newly constructed house. We all watch them silently for a few minutes.

Then Aunt Chiyu turns her back to the construction. "The mountains make me think of Fujiyama."

Mother nods and turns her back as well. "Yes. They are very majestic."

After a moment, Father, Aiko, and I follow their lead and fix our focus on the dramatic snow-topped range of the Sierras.

"I look forward to telling Fuji in my next letter. He has missed living near great mountains." Aunt Chiyu looks back toward the entrance and scans the few buildings. "I did not see a post office, did you?"

I had been looking as well. "No."

Without realizing, my hand has found its way to my breast pocket, where Evalina's photograph is still secure. How long will it be before I can get a letter sent to her?

Mr. Kamei has greeted several other families, and now calls for us to follow him. He walks backward as though a docent in a museum. "As you can see, there is much still to be done here at Manzanar. Your help will be critical to getting our community up and running. Each of the blocks are numbered, but it's easy to get lost. Don't be embarrassed when it happens to you; we're all finding our way around. Those of us who have been here the longest arrived three weeks ago." He chuckles, but the sound holds an edge of anger to it. "That first number on your card is your block number, the second is your barrack number, and the third is which entrance to the barrack is yours. Unfortunately, none of the barracks have interior walls yet, but Mr. Campbell, the assistant camp manager, told us partitions are coming."

They have no interior walls? I stare at the ugly black

barracks. They're maybe one hundred feet long and twenty feet deep, with a door on either end, and small windows. Are we really expected to share one of these with complete strangers without so much as a wall between us? Heat rises up the back of my neck. How could they ask that of us?

At block two, the first block we come to, Mr. Kamei stands in the middle of our group. He points down the far row of barracks and says, "Each block is arranged the same. These buildings down the center are men's and women's latrines and showers, the laundry room, and then the mess hall and the recreation hall on either side at the end. Meals are served three times a day. You'll hear the bells."

"There are no bathrooms *in* the houses?"

I don't know if Aiko intended her question to be directed to Mr. Kamei, but he gives her a soft, "No," all the same.

She does something she hasn't done since we were little kids: she reaches out and takes my hand. I want to tell her it'll be fine, but the words stick in my throat. Instead, I squeeze her fingers and attempt a reassuring smile.

As Mr. Kamei shows several men to their apartments, I try to catch a glimpse of the interior. It's too dark for me to make out much, though. A wave of homesickness hits me for the bright sunshine that filled our home in Alameda, and I clench my teeth to ward off the overwhelming desire to cry.

I don't have to wait much longer to satisfy my curiosity, however, because block four is next. As we pass by his barrack, Mr. Kamei points out his door to us. "My wife, Lillian, and I live here, and you're always welcome—"

The wind swirls, and a stench hits us like a punch. Even Mr. Kamei covers his nose and mouth. "Sorry, the latrines in four have been down all day. We have men working on it."

As we draw closer to the building, I see men wearing

masks as they work in an open trench. The brown muck is up to their knees.

"Where do we go, then, if we need to . . ." Aiko swallows, "use the facilities?"

"The toilets in block ten should be working again. That's just one block west. And I know the pipes have just been repaired in block twelve." Mr. Kamei points toward the mountain range. "That's about two city blocks south."

Aiko's grip on my arm has grown increasingly tighter, and I put one of my hands over hers.

Mr. Kamei surveys us all. "I know. Believe me, I know. When I arrived, we didn't even have toilets. And with new residents showing up every day, we need help with everything. The more we all pitch in, the better this experience will be. Job openings are posted at the administration building. Please help us by signing up." Mr. Kamei has a wide-eyed, expectant look on his face, perhaps waiting for us to grab a shovel and hop into the trench. I get the feeling that's what he would do, fatigued or not. "Once you've settled in, of course. Now, Hamasaki family, this one is yours."

Mother, Aunt Chiyu, and Aiko are all still staring at the open trench. Father nods to Mr. Kamei. "Thank you for your assistance."

Mr. Kamei takes hold of the lever and pushes open the door. He casts us a sympathetic smile as we cross the threshold.

Once I'm inside and my eyes have adjusted from the bright sunlight, I see why.

Just like in the room where we registered, the floors are bare planks, coated in a layer of sand that's blown up and in. The only thing separating us from the other families already living in the barrack are the olive-colored blankets like those we're holding in our hands draped from the roof beams. One bare lightbulb dangles over each apartment, which I can see because of the open rafters.

All five of us stand there, looking at our designated space—twenty-five feet by ten feet—that is to house the five of us for an undetermined amount of time.

My heart feels like a fist as it pounds in my chest. This is too much. Too much to take in. Too much to be asked of us. Too much dignity to lose all in twenty-four hours. How can this be real?

One of the blankets is yanked aside, and a young boy grins and yelps, "Hi!"

We all stare at him. After a few seconds, the blanket falls to the ground, revealing his family's apartment in one dramatic swoop. Their crudely stuffed mattresses are piled on one army cot, and their luggage on another. The boy's parents are nailing tin can lids over knotholes.

"Norman." His mother's reprimand makes even me jump. "I told you not to touch the blanket." She glares at us, and I get it. Because I senselessly find myself wanting to glare back. Shame has given birth to anger inside my chest, and there are precious few safe places for us to show our anger. To one another is the only one we have left.

I expect Aiko to growl fiery words at the boy, but instead she turns away. Turns against me, her shoulders shaking as she sobs silently.

When I awake in the night, the wind whistles through the gaps and knotholes of the pine boards. Even in my sweater, socks, and flannel pants, I shiver and grasp for the edge of the army blanket to be sure it's secured around me.

My bladder aches.

I open my eyes. The apartment is still illuminated intermittently by searchlights, which had given me an uneasy feeling as I dozed off hours ago. Do they keep those on all night? I suppose that's a good thing, considering I'm about to have to wander out onto the block to use the restroom, and I'd rather not do it in the black night of the Owens Valley.

Beside me on the floor, Aiko grinds her teeth in her sleep. In another apartment, a man snores. I hope I can get out of here without waking anyone.

I step gingerly through the apartment, conscious of every creak and pop of the hastily constructed floors. Everyone is so exhausted from our journey, they sleep right through my sneaking out the door.

I stand in the doorway a moment to get my bearings. The men's latrine is the building right outside our barrack . . . but have those been repaired? Or should I try to find block ten in the—

I'm blinded by a sharp light. I clap my hands over my eyes to shield them from the searchlight that's fixed upon me. I wait for it to pass over, but it doesn't.

I stumble down the steps to get out of its accusing glare, only for it to follow me. My heart pounds as I attempt to make my way toward the men's latrine, but it's hard with the burn of the light in my eyes. Even when I manage to find the door and get inside the bathroom, my vision is clouded from when the searchlight hit my eyes directly.

I'm not sure my heart has ever beaten so fast. After a few minutes, I can make out the two rows of toilets and the urinal trough. There are no partitions, but I'm alone anyway. And I no longer care if the plumbing is operational; there's no way I'm wandering over to another block with a searchlight tracking me the whole way.

Even with the sharp ache of my too-full bladder, I stand at the trough for minutes before I'm able to pee. The sink doesn't work, but I forgot my bar of soap anyway.

I open the door and find the light fixed on the staircase. Waiting.

The light follows me back to my door before resuming its oscillating scan of the camp. I lie on my lumpy mattress, hot with shame as the cold Manzanar wind continues through the night.

When I awaken the next time, it's because a piece of straw tickles my ear.

The morning light that filters into the apartment is gray and dusty. Aiko is still beside me. Everything from her nose below is tucked beneath her blanket, like a turtle snug in its shell. What I can see of her face and hair looks as though she's powdered herself. Her eyelashes are like miniature ash-gray fans on her cheeks.

When I stir, a cloud of fine dust billows into the air.

Without opening her eyes, Aiko says, "I've never been so cold in all my life."

"It'll be better once we get cots. I'll ask Mr. Kamei about them today."

"The brochure said the cots would be here when we arrived." Even muffled by her blanket, Aiko's raw sarcasm comes through loud and clear. "I'm starting to believe the government isn't 100 percent prepared for us."

Mother, Father, and Aunt Chiyu stand in the middle of the barrack as a middle-aged man demonstrates how to light the fire in the oil-burning stove. "You will get the hang of it quickly. The hardest part is venting without letting sparks escape. I won't be surprised if half these barracks have burned down by Christmas."

"That's comforting," I murmur to Aiko.

Her eyes crinkle, hinting at her hidden smile.

I sit up, cringing against the cold and tightening the blanket around me. Dust clouds form with every movement. The only thing around me not covered in dust is where I slept. There's an outline of my body on the mattress. By the time I get back from the latrines, that will probably be covered too.

My face flushes as I recall the glare of the searchlight during my last bathroom trip.

"I hope the toilets are fixed." Aiko sits up and finger-combs the dust from her hair. "The latrines you went to the next block over, did they . . . ¿ I mean, were they . . . ¿ Was there any privacy¿"

My heart plummets at Aiko's expression. Even in block ten where the toilets supposedly worked, two of them had been bubbling, spewing sticky brown waste over their rims and making the bathroom floor slick, and there had been no dividers of any kind. I had hoped more care had been taken with the women's bathrooms.

I shake my head at Aiko.

She blinks away tears. "That's what I assumed. A few of the women had boxes that they use to shield themselves, but . . ."

She stands, presses a hand to her abdomen, and winces.

"Good morning," Mother greets us. "This is Mr. Abe. These are our children, Aiko and Taichi."

We offer slight bows in response to his. Mr. Abe continues his demonstration, and Mother adds, "The facilities in our block are still broken. Do not forget your paper," before turning back to watch.

Aiko pats her coat pocket where a small roll of toilet paper is wedged.

When I undo the latch on the door, the wind grabs hold and slaps it against the barrack. Aiko stretches her coat to shield her face from the blast, which feels as though it's made of the mountaintop snow.

We trudge between the barracks, toward block ten. Aiko now clutches at her stomach with both arms.

"Are you okay?"

"No, I . . ." Her face is grim, and tears glint in the corners of her eyes. "I need the latrine."

She remains bent for the rest of our walk, and we find a line stretching out the door. I count twelve women ahead of Aiko, and I know there must be more inside. Aiko stands with her legs crossed, and she stoops further. I can't just leave her here.

"Of course there's a line, right?" My chuckle is wooden. "What else do we do these days but stand in line?"

She doesn't answer. Her face scrunches, and her legs twist tighter together. I long for Mother or Aunt Chiyu, but it's just me and a long line of strange women. Several others have lined up behind us, their faces resigned and stoic.

Aiko emits a low groan and bends deeper at the waist.

I tap the shoulder of the woman in front of us. "I'm sorry, but my sister really needs to use the facilities. Can she—"

"We *all* need to use the facilities." Her no-nonsense tone matches the no-nonsense bun on the back of her head.

"But she—"

"Taichi." My name is a strangled sound on Aiko's lips, and her nails bite into my arm. She leans against me, hides her face in my sleeve, and sobs.

The other women back away from us, their eyes on the ground, and I know what I'll see even before I confirm it with my eyes.

Aiko and I are now standing in a watery puddle of diarrhea.

CHAPTER TWELVE

Evalina

Thursday, April 9, 1942

As I lock my bike outside of Alessandro's after school, I'm trying to ignore that it's Thursday—a day I would normally be racing here for the chance to see Taichi. I'm not going to fixate on this, though. I'm going to—

"Evalina!"

I look up to find a pickup truck idling alongside the curb. Diego Medina leans across the passenger seat to call my name out the window.

I drop my lock and run to the open window. I should probably start with a hello or how are you doing. Instead what comes out is, "Have you heard from him?"

Diego blinks several times. "I was going to ask you the same thing. Is he still in the city?"

I thought I had cried all I could, but as I shake my head no, tears bubble up inside me.

Diego's smile slips off his face. "When did he leave? Where did he go?"

"Tuesday. And I don't know. Some people at the center were saying Manzanar, but others said the camps aren't ready, and they would be going to temporary housing at Santa Anita. I guess that's a horse racing track by L.A."

Diego shuts off the engine, pulls the parking brake, and gets out of the truck to stand on the sidewalk with me. "What do you mean 'the center'? Who was saying that?"

"The War Relocation Authority Center. That's where the buses picked them up. But they weren't being told where they were going. I asked everybody I could."

"You were there?"

I can't read his expression. Is he mad about that? "Of course I was."

Diego's arms are like strong tree branches around me, and my shock has me as unyielding as a tree trunk in his embrace.

"I'm so glad you were with him." Diego breathes the words into my ear. "You have no idea."

"It was selfish. I wanted to be there."

He releases me, only to clasp his hands on my shoulders and make searing eye contact. Our comparative sizes leave me feeling like a little kid, even though I know I'm only a few months younger than him. I make myself stare back.

"You really love him," Diego finally says.

My laugh is a surprised bark. "You didn't know that already?"

He releases my shoulders and looks away, breaking the tension of the moment. "I hoped you did, but . . . You've gotta understand that I've known Tai my whole life. He had never broken a rule, and then you came along. And he was risking so much, and I just . . . I mean, he's my best friend, I . . ."

Diego seems incapable of articulating the rest, but what he's said is sufficient.

"My best friend, Gia, says, 'You barely get any time together. How can you possibly be sure about him?'" I shrug.

"And I ask her the same kinds of things about her boyfriend. That's a best friend's job, right?"

Diego flashes a smile at me. "Must be. Tai never really likes my girls either." His smile turns serious. "Whether he said it or not, I'm sure Tai was glad to have you there on Tuesday. And *I'm* glad to know you were there."

"If you read any details about the evacuation in the paper, you should know that journalist was dead wrong about what he wrote in the piece."

"We don't get the city newspaper, and ours didn't say a thing about it."

"If you're going to be at the market on Saturday, I'll bring the article." Already I can feel my blood thrumming faster through my veins. "He made it sound like the government was throwing a big party for the Japanese Americans and sending them all away on a paid vacation. He didn't say a single thing about how the guards were all armed and glaring at us like we were guilty of some heinous crime. I wrote a letter to the editor that I'm sure they won't print because it was practically on fire, I was so angry."

Diego shakes his head. "I've heard that kind of stuff is happening in Germany. But I wouldn't have expected it to happen here. Oh, I need to go, but . . ." He reaches through the open window of the truck and pulls out a small box of blackberries. They're rather puny, but a beautiful inky purple color. "I brought these in case I saw you today. They're not our best, not yet. But Tai asked me to bring you some when they were ready."

I long for a letter from Taichi just as much as I did ten minutes ago, but as I reach for the box, my heart feels more tethered to Taichi than ever before.

Gia plops a large scoop of linguine in white clam sauce onto her plate. "You seem like you're in a bad mood tonight."

I glance down the length of our usual Friday night table to be sure our parents are engaged in their own conversations. "Is that unusual these days⸮"

Gia flashes me a smile that has a mischievous edge to it. "You seem particularly blue tonight." She arches her dark, freshly-plucked eyebrows. "Does it have something to do with Tony being out on a date instead of being here with us⸮"

Annoyance flares within me. Considering Taichi boarded a bus three days ago, how can she even imagine that bothers me⸮

"I'm quite happy about that, actually. Tony moving on makes me feel less guilty."

"That's good. You could do with feeling less these days rather than more."

I push an olive into my mouth before I snap a retort.

The adults laugh about something, and Daddy pours more wine into Mama's glass. Even their good cheer rubs at something raw inside me, like when you get burrs in your socks.

Maybe I need to limit how many complaint letters I write each day to government officials, because I've been in a sour mood since finishing those. My last one was to General DeWitt, or General Halfwit as I wish I could address him. He's leading the charge against the Japanese Americans, and I had to write my letter three times because I kept ripping a hole in the paper from pressing down so hard with my pen.

I had also written several letters to the editors both in

San Francisco and in Los Angeles, because the San Francisco papers had reprinted a few propaganda-like articles from the *Los Angeles Times*. I imagine, like the *San Francisco News*, my letters won't be printed. Briefly, I wondered if signing my name would increase the chances, but I had noticed several other Letters to The Editor had been signed in a similar anonymous fashion.

I snap back into the moment and find Mrs. Esposito smiling expectantly at me. I realize she asked me a question.

"Your trip to Yosemite?" Mrs. Esposito glances across the table at my mother. "You're still planning to go in June, right?"

"Yes." Mama smiles at me, but her eyes scan my face. "We're all really looking forward to it. Right?"

I nod. "Right."

Mrs. Esposito slices her asparagus into dainty bites. Did Taichi pick that stalk? "I've always wanted to go. I hear that nothing is quite as breathtaking as being in the valley with El Capitan and Half Dome. But Frank says, 'Mountains are mountains. We don't need to drive four hours to see specific ones.'"

I shake my head. "No disrespect intended to Mr. Esposito, but I wholeheartedly disagree. That's like saying, 'People are people. No need to meet any others.'"

"I'm with you, Evalina. Perhaps I can ride along with you." Mrs. Esposito gives me a teasing nudge with her elbow. "You won't mind me joining in on your graduation trip, will you?"

"The more the merrier."

Gia raises her fork. "Then count me in. I've always longed to go on a good, honest vacation."

"Agreed. The last trip Alessandro and I took that was more than a few nights long was our honeymoon." Mama won't say it at the table with our guests, but she was already pregnant with me at the time and could barely keep any food down. "I'm excited about Yosemite Valley, but I'm actually most excited about seeing Mono Lake. Evalina brought home a travel brochure that had the most interesting pictures of it. Do you have it with you, honey?"

"I think it's in my schoolbag in the kitchen."

"Run and get it, won't you?" To Mrs. Esposito, she says, "The lake is on the other side of the national park, practically in Nevada. But it looks like another planet. There are all these salts in the water, and over hundreds of thousands of years, they've built up these deposits . . ."

Mama's voice fades as I duck back into the kitchen of Alessandro's for my schoolbag. With all the stress of the evacuation this last week, I haven't thought about my graduation at all. The brochures and maps are buried under newspapers and the list of addresses for congressmen and representatives that I gathered at the library before coming to our Friday night dinner.

I smooth the crumpled pamphlet on Mono Lake and take a moment to stare at the strange pictures. I hadn't been sure Mama and Daddy would be open to venturing to the east side of the Sierras, but fortunately the strange rocks in the pictures had incited their curiosity and sense of adventure as well.

When I hand the brochure to Mrs. Esposito, her gaze catches on my hand. "Thank you, dear. Perhaps by the time you go, you will have had time to finish painting your nails."

Heat rushes to my cheeks, and I make myself laugh airily. "Maybe."

"I hadn't even noticed." Mama blinks at my red thumbnail, and then up at me. "Is this a new style?"

"Evalina is making a political statement," Gia chimes in.

I don't bother to hide my annoyed look at her.

"Ah." Mama smiles. "Yes, she's very upset about what is happening to the Japanese."

I almost don't say it, almost let it go. "They're Americans, actually."

"Of course they are. I only meant to specify what heritage of people we're speaking about."

Gia gives a careless shrug. "Aren't both equally true, though? Same as we're Italian and American?"

"No. Because you're not a *citizen* of Italy. You can't vote there. You've never even been there. And it's the same for the majority of the Japanese Americans who are being evacuated. They've done nothing except be born to parents who have Japanese heritage. And most of their parents would have become citizens long ago, except that our government has denied them that option since the 1920s."

I take a deep breath and lower my gaze when I realize all conversation has stopped. That all eyes are on me.

"Evalina, I love and admire your passion." Mrs. Esposito beams at me. "How wonderful that you care about what's going on in our country, even when it doesn't directly impact you."

CHAPTER THIRTEEN

Taichi

Tuesday, April 14, 1942

As I cut across the block toward the shower room, footsteps pound closer to me. I glance over my shoulder to see James Kanito looking as filthy as I do but wearing a huge smile.

"You know what I heard?" As usual, James doesn't wait for me to answer. "We have a baseball field."

"Where'd you hear that?"

"I was in the trenches with Woody today, and he heard they put one in by block nineteen. There are already a few teams playing regularly."

I have no idea who Woody is, but I really hope he knows what he's talking about.

Most of our block is lined up for dinner already, but a shower isn't exactly optional considering where we've spent our day. The good thing about it being dinnertime is that no one else is in the shower when we arrive. And I can tell, because the shower room is just one big room with shower heads fixed to the walls. There's no hiding in here.

Our conversation pauses while we shower—an unspoken rule at Manzanar—and we manage to get dressed without the door ever opening. Once we've dropped off our dirty clothes at our barracks and picked up the mess kits we were issued, we join the chow line and resume our talking.

The whole time, my mind is on the baseball field. Even though I tell myself it's unwise to feel too hopeful, just having the chance to think about doing something I love, something that isn't standing in line or working down in a trench, has my heart feeling as though it sprouted tiny wings.

"Playing baseball again would be swell," I let myself say to James.

"Did you play on a team back home?"

"I played for the school team. I was supposed to be captain this spring, but some of the parents complained." I shift my weight from foot to foot. "Coach kept me on, but not as captain."

"And he expected you to be grateful for that, did he?"

I turn to the man behind us in line, who interjected himself into our conversation. He appears to be in his early twenties, with a long face and a dusting of a mustache.

"Probably." I feel an uneasiness in agreeing with him. Doing so feels like a betrayal to my coach, who I always really liked. "He was nice about it, though."

The man grunts in response as the line shuffles forward.

James rocks back on his heels, then forward, then back again. "You a ballplayer? They put in a field on block nineteen."

In my few days of knowing James, I've learned he can make conversation with just about anybody. Even Aiko.

The fellow just shakes his head. "And they expect us to write thank-you cards to General DeWitt himself, yes?"

James just shrugs. "I know I'll be happy to have a ball field. What's your name? Where you from?"

The look he gives James is cold and criticizing. "Raymond. Los Angeles."

Raymond from Los Angeles looks away, as if making a point. An I-don't-want-to-continue-talking-to-you point.

James goes on undeterred. "Me too. What's your last name? You live in four?"

"Yamishi. And, no, but your cook is better. Our cook used to be a gardener."

"I tip my hat to the man for trying. Even if you're a professional, it can't be easy trying to cook three meals a day for three hundred people. Plus those who jump over from another block, no offense. I don't even know how to make dinner for myself."

James chuckles at his own expense, but Raymond Yamishi from Los Angeles just gives him a bland look.

James is unfazed by the lack of response. "What neighborhood are you from? Where'd you go to school?"

Again, Raymond casts a cold look at James. "You ask a lot of questions. You should be careful about that or people will think you work for the FBI."

Raymond Yamishi's combative nature makes me want to drop out of the chow line and go find another.

"I'm pretty sure the FBI already knows where you lived and went to school," James says flippantly. He angles his shoulder away from Raymond and back toward the front of the line. "Think we're having Vienna sausages again for dinner? I could eat those every meal."

Raymond turns to the timid-looking woman standing behind him and speaks to her in Japanese, too low for me to understand. He seems content to ignore us, and that suits me fine.

My stomach groans at the thought of more sausages. I hope it's something bland that Aiko will eat. She's hardly touched food these last few days, nor has she gotten out of bed.

The first few days here in Manzanar, Caucasian staff

prepared the food. They didn't seem to know what to feed us and we wound up with strange combinations of American style and Japanese style food. Like bologna sandwiches and a side of rice with canned peaches poured on top. As if the rice was supposed to be some kind of dessert. The last few days, as more Japanese Americans have arrived and jumped in to help with cooking, meals haven't been quite so strange.

Dinner is chicken, thankfully, with some kind of brown sauce. I get an extra helping of rice to take to Aiko after I finish. James and I spot Margaret, a girl who lives in barrack eight, eating with a friend. As we draw closer, I realize it's Rose, the girl whose tag had fallen off the day we arrived.

James plops his mess kit across from Margaret's. "Did you know we have a baseball field on block nineteen?"

Margaret smiles at us. "Hi, boys. Have you met Rose? She's from Terminal Island."

Rose's smile is shy, but her eyes light with recognition when she sees me. "Taichi. I wondered when I would see you."

"If you haven't been in the drainage trenches, you wouldn't have seen him," James says, and a discomfort stirs in me. The trenches don't seem like something we should be discussing at dinner with two girls. "I'm James."

Rose smiles into her plate. "Nice to meet you."

James attacks his chicken with his fork and knife. "So, do either of you play baseball? Softball?"

Rose shakes her head, and Margaret says, "I'm better at basketball. Think we'll get a court anytime?"

"Maybe around the time they build us a school?" James laughs, but it has a bite to it.

My heart feels as though it's beating right in my ears as I ask, "When do you think we'll get a post office?"

"We have one already." Rose is just pushing her chicken

around rather than eating it. "You can send mail, but it's hard to receive anything yet. They aren't very organized."

James snorts. "What a surprise."

Rose's lips flicker with a smile. "Our names confuse them. They're having trouble sorting."

But at least I could send Evalina a letter. I know she must be frantic about where I am and what it's like. Only, what am I going to tell her? That we had to stuff our own mattresses once we arrived? How I wake up every morning in a house that was built in an hour, shivering and covered in dust? How sick Aiko has been since day one? How my time has been spent mucking about in drainage ditches just trying to get toilets working so my poor sister doesn't have to humiliate herself in line?

I can't tell her any of that, can I? She'll only be more worried and angrier than she already is.

"Taichi, is something wrong?"

I blink and find Rose looking at me, head tilted slightly in concern.

I've been sitting here rubbing at the spot over my heart. The pocket where I keep Evalina's photograph.

I pick my fork up and scoop rice. "I'm fine."

"Do any of you know who that Caucasian woman is?" Margaret asks. "I'm so curious about her."

For a moment, I'm sure Evalina's photograph somehow tumbled out of my pocket. But Margaret's gaze is fixed over my shoulder.

I turn and see that across the mess hall, taking a seat next to a thirty-something man I've seen on our block, is a small Caucasian woman with hair as dark as Evalina's.

"Oh, that's Elaine." Of course James knows who she is. "She's married to our block leader, Karl Yoneda. They live in the barrack next to me."

Married.

I can't seem to breathe. They're married. He's Japanese and she's Caucasian and somehow they're married.

Margaret frowns. "Are you sure?"

"Yep. They have a little boy."

I thought all the air was out of my lungs, but somehow more whooshes out when Karl Yoneda scoops a young boy onto his lap. The rows of crowded tables between us make it difficult for me to get a good look at the boy, just snatches of cocoa skin, a bowl cut of black hair, and round eyes.

Mother would scold me for staring, but I can't tear my gaze away.

"In Washington you can be married even if you're different races." Rose has pitched her voice quiet, as though discussing something scandalous. "Maybe they're from there?"

"Why would she be *here*, though?" Margaret pokes at her fruit cocktail. "That's kind of weird, right?"

I have to force myself to turn my back to the Yoneda family.

"Mrs. Yoneda told my mother that she didn't have to come, and that the administration fought her on it," James says around a large bite of chicken. "But Tommy, that's their boy, had to go and she didn't want to be apart from him."

Evalina would have done the exact same thing. Had this all happened a few years from now when we were married, she would have boarded that bus with me. She would have taken the hot, airless journey to Manzanar. She would have stuffed her own mattress and stoically used the community showers and commodes.

And she would've done it all because of me.

"Taichi, are you sure you're okay?" Rose's inquisitive eyes are fastened on me.

Again my hand has found its way to the pocket with Evalina's picture. Beneath her smiling face, my heart aches.

I put on a smile for Rose. "I'm fine."

And I'm going to tell Evalina the exact same thing.

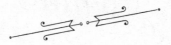

Dear Evalina,

I'm sorry for how delayed this letter is. Getting oriented in our new home has taken a few days. As you can see from the address, we're in Manzanar, California. I've never been this far south before, and it's really beautiful. We can see Mt. Williamson from our front door, and there's another mountain range, the Inyo, on the other side.

Many new families arrive each day so there has been a lot of work to do. Aiko will be helping at the hospital, and she is excited for the chance to use some of her nursing skills. Mother and Father have been talking with other farmers about an old orchard that's here and how to revive it. I think the camp is open to them planting new crops too. I'm not sure yet how I will help out.

A new friend of mine, James, is organizing a baseball team. Many of the boys have never had a chance to play on their school teams, so this is very exciting.

We don't get much news from the world outside of camp, and we would be grateful for any news or papers you could pass along. I miss you and look forward to hearing from you. I keep your picture with me at all times, and you're never far from my thoughts.

With love,
Taichi

CHAPTER FOURTEEN

Evalina

Saturday, April 18, 1942

With Taichi's letter in hand, I zip back to the market, praying all the way that Diego hasn't left yet. Sweet relief fills me when I find him loading the truck.

"Manzanar," I greet him between gasps for breath.

Diego whirls at the sound of my voice.

I hop off my bicycle and hold up the letter. "He's in Manzanar. He's okay. Look!" I push the envelope into his hands and jab at the Manzanar address.

"What does it say?" Diego's words are clipped with eagerness. "How is he?"

"He's good. You can read it if you want." I pant for breath. "I read it real fast and thought if I hurried I could catch you." Diego is already pulling the letter from the envelope.

While he reads, I take in deep breaths and wait for my heart to slow. The park looks brighter than it did this morning when I was here to make my purchases. The morning fog has burned off, and the bay winks in the late morning sunlight. Gulls call cheerfully to each other, as do children who are reclaiming the stretch of green grass now that the farmers have cleared out.

"You're right. He sounds pretty good."

My soaring heart snags on Diego's frown. "What's wrong?"

"Nothing." Diego folds the letter and returns it to the envelope. When he hands it back to me, his smile looks forced. "I just hoped for more details. He's very vague."

I roll my bottom lip in and pull Taichi's letter back out. "Maybe he was just short on time? He wanted to get the letter sent out before the post left for the day?"

My eyes skim the words. Diego is absolutely right. With the exception of the close to the letter, which had caused me to swoon, this could just as easily have been written to a distant aunt. Scenery, baseball, farming. The only vague detail that's missing is the weather.

Diego secures another crate in the back of the truck, and then hoists himself inside the bed. "Maybe their mail is being read. That happens in the military, right? They make sure they aren't giving away locations or top-secret information. Maybe Tai was being vague because he knew others would censor it."

"Yeah, maybe . . ."

But now I can't stop seeing everything that's *not* there. What was the trip like? What kind of house are they in? Are they being fed well?

After another reading, I fold the letter back into my pocket. "He sounds upbeat, at least."

Diego grunts as he pulls the rope tight around the crates. "And maybe if you ask in your letter, he'll tell you more about what it's like."

"That's a good thought. I'll do that."

"I wasn't trying to worry you, Evalina. It's great knowing where he is, isn't it?" Diego hops down from the truck and scans my face. "I bet you're right, he was just in a hurry. The next letter will be longer."

Yes, Diego is surely right. There will be more details next time.

"Thank you for coming all the way back." Diego's smile is warm now. "My week will be much better knowing where he is. You want a ride home?"

Not having to ride back uphill to my house sounds too good to pass up. "Sure. Thanks."

Diego loads my bicycle into the truck, holds the door open for me, and I climb in. I pull Taichi's letter back out of my pocket and reread it, my mind spinning with all the ways I want to respond.

"I hate driving in the city," Diego says as he looks over his shoulder, waiting for a break in traffic. "Everyone is so rude."

"I don't think I would like it either. My family doesn't even own a car. We're taking our first vacation ever this summer, and we're renting one. My father was joking about how he's not sure he remembers how to drive."

Diego smirks. "Where are you going?"

"Yosemite National Park." I rearrange my plaid skirt to drape nicer over my knees. "It's kind of a silly time to be going on a vacation, with the war and all. But we've been talking about it for years, so we didn't really want to cancel."

"You shouldn't," Diego says. "That's why I enlisted. I don't want our people so worried that they can't enjoy something like a once-in-a-lifetime vacation."

The heaviness of what he's signed up for weighs on me. In this morning's paper, in addition to an article about how 3,000 Japanese Americans from Los Angeles were being sent to Manzanar, there had been a story about General Doolittle. That his raids on Tokyo, Kobe, and several other Japanese cities had begun.

A shiver rips through me when I think of a few weeks ago

when the ship carrying those B-25 bombers sailed under the Golden Gate Bridge.

"Are you nervous?" My question doesn't rise above a whisper.

Maybe that's why Diego's Adam's apple slides down and back up before he says, "Yes."

"Oh, turn here!"

Diego makes a jarring right turn.

"Sorry," I say. "I forgot I needed to direct you."

"I forgot we weren't going to the restaurant," Diego says with a laugh. "Sorry about that."

"You can just drop me off in a couple blocks at Kearney. You don't need to take me all the way to my door."

We ride in silence for the next block. I feel a similar discomfort on the occasions that I'm left alone with Gia's boyfriend. That strange sensation where you know a lot about a person, but you don't really know the person.

"When do you leave for basic training?"

"Right after graduation."

I try to imagine having something like that—shipping off for training to fight in a war—looming over my high school graduation date. "What does your girlfriend think?"

Diego doesn't answer right away. "Well . . . we aren't together anymore."

I should've asked about his parents, not his girlfriend. "Oh, I'm sorry."

"It's fine. It's not like it's my first breakup or anything." Diego's smile looks overly cheerful. "Really, Evalina. Don't worry about it."

The truck idles as an old woman shuffles across the street, leaning heavily on her cane. This drive cannot end fast enough.

Even over the engine, I can hear Diego's sigh. "She was

probably right to end it. She said it doesn't make sense for us to stay together when I'm leaving so soon. That a long-distance relationship was a bad idea, they never last. That kind of thing. It's all very practical." His snort sounds harsh. "Which I didn't really expect from Ruby, but I guess you never can tell."

The truck lurches forward. I grip my seatbelt, trying to not look too nervous about how quickly he sped up.

"And she's probably right," Diego continues. "It's just kind of fresh right now."

I shouldn't feel injured by Ruby's words to Diego—after all, I don't even know her—but her sentiment about long distance relationships feels like a thorn jabbed into my heart. "*I* think relationships can work long distance. Just think of all the married people who have to be apart right now because of the war."

Diego looks startled. "Of course it can work, Evalina. Sorry, it didn't occur to me how that would hit you. Ruby is completely wrong about that. I mean, she was right that she and I wouldn't have worked long distance. But we aren't like you and Tai."

It's a nice thing for him to say. "Still, I know breakups are painful, no matter what the circumstance. This is my street."

Diego pulls the truck over to the side of the road. "You had a boyfriend before Tai?"

I don't know why I say it, to Diego of all people, but I do. "We were supposed to marry each other. That's what everyone thought would happen, anyway. Our parents had been dreaming of it since we were in elementary school."

Diego puts on the brake. "Tai said he's a real nice guy."

I feel a twinge of guilt. "He is. We're good friends. We probably would've had a fine marriage."

"Why did you break up?"

"Because I fell in love with Taichi." I pull the door handle. "Thanks for the ride."

"Anytime." He gets out of the truck as well and lifts my bike out of the back. "I'll see you at Monday's delivery?"

"See you then."

I walk my bike up my street, feeling as though the weight of all the hard stuff around me—Taichi and the evacuation, boys like Diego being sent off to war—is trying to push me back down the hill.

When I get home, the telephone is ringing.

"Mama?" I call out, but she doesn't respond. I jog into the kitchen to answer it. "Hello?"

"I'm calling for Evalina Cassano?" The woman's voice is brisk.

"This is Evalina."

"My name is Karen Bishop. I'm with the First Congregational Church. I believe you met my husband at the evacuation last week? He said you were interested in volunteering with us."

"Yes." I wrap the telephone cord around my wrist. "I'm extremely interested."

"Wonderful. Many of our families have been sent to Tanforan Assembly Center. Are you familiar with it?"

"No, I'm not."

"It's a horse race track in San Bruno. About forty-five minutes from the church. The conditions are appalling." Her words become even more clipped. "We are putting together some care packages the morning of Sunday, May 3rd, and then we will deliver them that afternoon. We would love to have your help."

The conditions are appalling. The words reverberate in my

ears, like a bad song that's stuck in my head. *Appalling. The conditions are appalling.*

"Absolutely. I'll be there."

"I look forward to meeting you. Good day."

"Good day," I echo to the dial tone.

For a moment, I just stand there in the kitchen. Taichi's letter, full of descriptions of beautiful mountains and baseball teams, is gripped in my hand. *The conditions are appalling.*

I thunder upstairs to my room, where my desk is littered in newspaper articles and drafts of letters. I pull out a fresh sheet to write to Taichi, but after writing *Dear Taichi*, I just stare at it, wondering the best way to put my question into words: *What aren't you telling me?*

Taichi

Friday, April 24, 1942

Dear Evalina,

Thanks so much for the letter and the news. I'm glad you told Diego. Right now I'm short on stamps, so it's nice to know he's being kept updated.

Yes, my last letter was written in a hurry so I wasn't able to tell you many details about life here. Sorry that caused concern for you and Diego. I assure you, there's no need.

Manzanar is very beautiful. The valley can be dusty sometimes, and I imagine it will be a bit hot here in the summers, but right now the weather is very mild during the day.

There is a lot of building going on to make Manzanar home, and every day we have a little bit more. The school still needs to be built, but since my principal was kind enough to help me graduate before leaving Alameda, that won't impact me directly. Not everyone was so lucky to make such an arrangement, so I'm thankful.

I'm meeting lots of interesting people, and we always have plenty going on. Everyone is determined for Manzanar to feel like our home, and we are all working together to make that happen. Already I've seen people organizing dances, game nights, and art classes, in addition to the many baseball and softball teams that are recruiting players. We do not have a phone yet, but maybe in the future. And there is plenty of food for all of us. I think Mother enjoys not having to cook all the time.

I'm glad to hear you're going to help Mrs. Bishop. I met her, and she's very nice. I'm so sorry to hear conditions at the temporary centers are not good. I'm sure your care packages will be welcome there.

With love,
Taichi

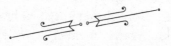

My feet protest every step I take toward the post office. After spending the last four days either curled up in bed or running for the toilets, my body is exhausted.

The guilt doesn't help either. I wince as I drop the letter to Evalina into the box of outgoing mail. I've never lied to her so blatantly before.

An honest letter would have read like this:

Dear Evalina,

On Sunday, the refrigeration in our block's kitchen lost power, so nearly everyone on our block ate stew made with spoiled meat. I've never thrown up so much in my life and haven't left my block in days. It's terrible to be experiencing it all in a place where your bed is full of hay that pokes you all night long, and where you have to wait in line for the bathroom or laundry facilities. And when the only privacy between you and the people you live with—many of whom you met only a few days ago—is a blanket hung on a rope.

To make matters even worse, the six-year-old boy in our barrack was the only one who didn't get even a smidge of food poisoning. He's occupied himself by climbing up on the rafters so he can peek in on us over the blanket. Once he laughed at Aiko when she was throwing up. She threw a shoe at him, which missed, but nevertheless his mother was furious since Norman is just a "helpless boy trying to find some entertainment." Aiko snapped back that watching her vomit wasn't an option for entertaining him, and next time she would aim for his head. As you can imagine, the two of them now refuse to speak to each other.

There is no dignity here.

Love,
Taichi

But how would knowing these details benefit Evalina? She would pity me, and my pride can't take that on top of everything else. For the first time, I understand why Uncle Fuji's letters have been vague. If life here in Manzanar is this bad, how much worse is it for the prisoners in North Dakota?

By the time I get back to the block and through the chow line, I feel like I will pass out if I have to stand any longer. I find James, Margaret, and Rose at our usual table and collapse onto a seat. Their plates look similar to mine, only rice and fruit cocktail.

"You look like death," James greets me.

"You too."

His smile is wry. "The girls were talking about the co-op store being started. Have you heard about this? Some community members are asking families to chip in so they can start a store."

"I heard they're going to have soda pop." Margaret beams. "I've been wanting a Coca-Cola so badly."

My head is too fuzzy to pay close attention to the conversation. I finish my water quickly and get up to refill my cup. As I navigate my way back to our table, I spot Aiko several tables over with her new friends. She's laughing, and for a second, it's like being back at school again, when I would pass her in the halls or at lunch and see her socializing.

Mother and Father are on the other end of the mess hall. They're at the same table, but not by each other. Mother converses with the women and Father with the men.

My heart aches for the table in our farmhouse. It had been left behind by the family who lived there before us, and Mother had worked to buff out scratches and stain it so that it looked new. And while there was the occasional night that one of us was out, most nights we sat around that table and ate together.

A rush of hatred for this place comes over me. Hatred for this place where I've been not only ripped away from my home, Diego, and Evalina, but also where the foundation of our family is crumbling away. What will we look like when we come out on the other side of this?

CHAPTER FIFTEEN

Evalina

Sunday, May 3, 1942

Mrs. Bishop fusses with the road map on her lap. "We're going to be late."

"Just relax, Karen," Mr. Bishop says in his deep, soothing voice.

Beside me, their daughter, Grace, flashes me a smile. Piled around us and in the trunk are shoeboxes full of fruit, candy, toiletries, stationery, and stamps for the evacuees at Tanforan Assembly Center.

Mrs. Bishop glances at her wristwatch. "We should have left fifteen minutes earlier."

She's a serious-looking woman with a high forehead, stiff hairstyle, and sharply angled nose. But she also has a dimpled smile that flashes frequently, and a heart that bleeds for others.

"What do you think will happen if we miss our time slot?" she asks.

"This is our turn," Mr. Bishop points at the traffic light ahead. "We won't."

Mr. Bishop turns at the next street, and in the distance I see the high grandstands of a racetrack. We must be very close, though there's something else in the area that requires high-security. Along the road is a tall fence with three strands of barbed wire running along the top.

And then I see the reason for the barbed wire.

A group of Japanese American schoolgirls jump rope on the other side of the fence. The car engine is too loud for the others to hear me gasp.

"Despicable." Mrs. Bishop spits the word, and wipes at her eyes with a handkerchief. "How can they stand themselves, keeping innocent people fenced in like that?"

Within the fence, Japanese Americans mill about, stand in lines, or carry bags of some sort. There are rows of rectangular buildings, black and ugly, that have been built right on the racetrack parking lot. What are those? Is this what I would see if we were to pull up to Manzanar?

As Mr. Bishop turns into the parking lot, I catch sight of the tall guard tower, of the silhouettes of guards holding guns just like I saw during the evacuation. I can't seem to take in a full breath. The barbed wire isn't enough? They have guards here too?

"They'll probably want to search the boxes." Mrs. Bishop's voice has snapped out of its watery sorrow and into the brisk tone I'm accustomed to after a morning of working alongside her. "I'll go speak to the guard, show him our pass, and see what the most efficient way is to get all the boxes inside."

Mr. Bishop has hardly put on the parking brake when Mrs. Bishop opens her door and strides across the lot. She looks formidable in her tailored jacket with squared shoulders, and her hat at a sharp angle.

I want to be just like her.

"What pass is she talking about?" I ask Grace and Mr. Bishop as we restack boxes that toppled during the drive.

Grace's gaze is latched to the guard towers. She looks as unsettled as I feel.

Mr. Bishop says, "You have to have a visitor's pass to get in. They only allow you to visit for thirty minutes."

"I didn't even know there'd be a gate." I swallow. "I thought it would be like an emergency shelter. That we would just pull up and walk in with the boxes."

Mr. Bishop's face is grim. "That would be nice. Unfortunately, they're seen as prisoners. Not evacuees. Per the memos I see at work, anyway."

Mr. Bishop, I've learned, is with the Navy. I'm not clear on what he does for them, only that he's at no risk of being sent overseas.

"Is it like this at all the camps?" The words tremble as they emerge from me. "The barbed wire? The guards?"

"I don't know. Since this is still the military zone, I'm guessing security is tighter here than places out of the zone."

"What are those black buildings?" Grace asks. "Houses?"

"I'm not sure. When your mother and I speak to Jeanine, we'll ask."

Mrs. Bishop marches back to us with a sour expression. "We have to bring all the boxes in for inspection. The guards said they can search them while you and I meet with Jeanine. I asked about the girls coming in, but the guards are adamant that they can't since their names aren't on the pass."

Mr. Bishop frowns. "I'll show them my military I.D. I'm sure that will—"

"It's okay." Grace interrupts, her tone short and business-like, just like both her parents. "Evalina and I will take care of the boxes. Give Jeanine my love."

Mr. and Mrs. Bishop have a brief, silent conversation with their eyes, and then tell us they'll be back out in thirty minutes.

Grace releases a breath and begins stacking the boxes. "I'm afraid to go in there. I don't like guns. Especially ones with big knives on the end of them."

I nod in agreement as I lift a stack of shoeboxes. I square my shoulders, just like Mrs. Bishop, and approach the guard stand. I brace myself for the cool hatred in the eyes of the guard, like the one who called me a Jap lover. If we want these boxes delivered, I can't spit on anyone.

I take a quick, fortifying breath, look up into the eyes of the guard on the other side of the window, and say a curt, "Hi."

He grins and tips his hat at me. "Hello, doll. Did you bring me a present?"

"I . . ." I wasn't expecting that. "No. Mrs. Bishop said—"

"I'm just pulling your leg, doll," he says as he stands. He rubs his hands together. "Let's see what we have in here."

He flips open one of the lids as Grace approaches, and he pokes around the items. He holds up a bag of cookies. "You know we feed the inmates, right?"

His eyes sparkle with humor, but I find nothing about this situation funny.

I keep my voice dry and my mouth unsmiling. "That's awfully generous of you all."

He slides the box aside and flips open the next. "If I thought you ladies would come visit me, I sure wouldn't mind being fenced in here."

The guard whistles as he pokes around. He has bright red hair and a youthful face. If I saw him on the streets, I would have guessed he was no more than sixteen.

"What are the black buildings in there? Houses?"

"Yep." He moves onto the next box. "They put up two of those an hour, if you can believe it. Hard workers, the Japs are."

"Americans," I correct in a hard voice. "They're Americans."

He raises his eyebrows at me and looks amused rather than shamed. It only stokes the fire of outrage that constantly smolders in my chest.

"Evalina, why don't you get another load of boxes?" Grace says in a gentle voice.

I stalk back to her family's car and pound a stack of boxes together. What kind of person works here and isn't sickened by the sight of little girls jumping rope inside a barbed wire fence? Of people living inside buildings that are built on a parking lot at the rate of two each hour? How can he smile and joke?

I close my eyes as they burn with building tears. This is wrong. This is *so* wrong.

"I'll take those up."

I startle at Grace's voice—I hadn't heard her approach—and I hastily wipe at my wet cheeks. "No, I'm fine."

Her steady, blue gaze is evaluating. "Are you sure?"

"Yes." Without waiting for more discussion, I grab the stack of shoeboxes and turn. If Taichi can board that bus with a straight face and dry eyes, then I can withstand the guard's carelessness.

"You girls have sure been busy," he says, the same broad smile on his face.

I decide this doesn't merit a direct response and look away instead, to inside the fence. "Have you been in there?"

"Nah. Us MPs stick to the guard towers and the sentry."

"MPs?"

"Military police."

My teeth dig into my lip as my eyes prickle dangerously. "Are there MPs at the camps like Manzanar? Or just the temporary residences, like Tanforan?"

He now just flicks open the lid of each box before sliding it aside. "Dunno. I think at all of them. Otherwise, why would the inmates stay inside the fence?"

I swallow hard as my mind flits back to watching the buses load a month ago. Not a single Japanese American had looked to me as if disobeying government orders had been on their mind. Taichi had certainly never talked like they would do anything less than what was asked of them, and that was before the guards.

There are boys nearby. I can't see them, but I hear one say to another, "Here's a good rock."

"This rock is better," the other responds. "You use that rock, and I'll use this rock."

As they pass by my field of vision, I see they're young. Maybe six or seven. The taller of the boys grabs the other's sleeve and tugs him away from the fence. "Don't get too close."

They both look up at the guard tower as they back away, their eyes round and their feet clumsy with haste.

I turn and look at the guard. I find him already watching me, his expression markedly different than before. "When I'm up there, I try to smile at the kids." His voice is quiet as he says this. Earnest. "They can't help it."

I want to push him on this. What does he mean by "it," because if it's their race, none of them can help it. Same as he had no say in his red hair or his blue eyes.

Grace arrives at that moment with a cheerful, "This is the last of them," and it's probably good that we were interrupted.

After the guard gives all the boxes his stamp of approval, there's nothing to do but lean against the car and wait for Mr. and Mrs. Bishop to return. This morning at church, Grace and I found a lot to talk about, because Grace is a freshman at U.C. Berkeley this year, so we'll be seeing each other on campus next fall. But now I don't feel like chatting about the campus or extracurriculars. I can't get the frightened faces of those boys out of my head.

"You know," Grace says in a slow and careful voice, "I saw you at that first evacuation."

I turn to her. My face feels hot from the memory of Taichi's kiss. I'm not sure what to say.

She has many of the same sharp features as her mother, but fortunately she also has Mrs. Bishop's kindness, and it shines in her eyes now. "Have you heard from him?"

I nod. "He's in Manzanar."

"What's it like there?"

My thoughts are a tangle of Taichi's upbeat but vague letters, the strands of barbed wire around Tanforan, and the boys' scared faces just now. "I don't know," I finally say. "I don't think he likes to talk about it."

"What's his name?"

I haven't spoken it in so long, and it tastes sweet on my tongue. "Taichi."

"You're in love." Grace is not asking a question.

I answer anyway. "Yes."

She sighs. "I'm so sorry."

Dear Taichi,

I've had the most awful day.

I think I mentioned a few letters ago that I was going to help that church with care packages for Tanforan Assembly Center? We delivered them today, and I was shocked by the conditions there. Barbed wire around the whole place, and as if that wasn't enough, they had armed guards.

You had to have a pass to get into the visiting room, which I didn't, so I waited outside with Grace Bishop, the daughter of Mr. and Mrs. Bishop. We could see all these rectangular buildings in the parking lot of the racetrack, and it turned out they were houses. When I asked about them, the guard said they can build two an hour. The Bishops' friend said they call them barracks, and that there are four families sharing each one. They couldn't have been any bigger than a hundred feet or so.

She said they have no privacy other than if they hang blankets between the "apartments," but that it's better than the people who have to live in the old horse stalls, which still smell like horses. She said they wait in lines for everything, even the toilets. And that the food is mostly bread and hot dogs and canned fruit.

We were all so mad on the way home that we couldn't speak. Mrs. Bishop and I both kept crying. I was so distraught, I even told them about you and your family being sent away. Nobody seems to know how long the temporary centers will be needed. Hopefully soon they'll be sent somewhere like Manzanar where life is more bearable. I'm grateful you're not suffering like they are, but it still makes me miserable to think of the families I saw within the fence.

Sorry I don't have anything cheery to say. I love you.

Evalina

I spritz the letter with perfume like I always do, and then I dissolve into tears, allowing my forehead to fall hard onto my desk. How can thousands of Japanese Americans, most of whom are American citizens same as me, be living in a place so degrading and carelessly thrown together? This is 1942, for heaven's sake!

I pull myself together and fold Taichi's letter. My gaze catches on the stack of brochures for my trip to Yosemite with Mama and Daddy. How can I even consider indulging in something as frivolous as a vacation when there are problems like this going on around me? When little kids are playing within barbed wire fences and families are sleeping in horse stalls that smell like urine?

In a swell of fury, I swipe at the colorful brochures with the back of my hand and send them fluttering to the floor of my room.

That wasn't nearly as satisfying as I thought it would be.

I sigh and gather them back up, arranging them into a tidy stack. As I do, one of the topography labels on the map to Mono Lake catches my eye: Inyo Mountains.

I scramble down the stairs for the atlas I used several months ago when the newspaper started talking about Owens Valley being picked for a relocation camp. Yes, there it is! Mono Lake is close enough to Manzanar that they're shown on the same page of the atlas.

Heart pounding, I grab a ruler from the kitchen junk drawer and measure out the distance. There's around 110 miles between our hotel and where Taichi is if we take the road through the valley. We could be there in two-and-a-half hours, maybe faster if Daddy didn't insist on driving 45 miles per hour the whole way, we didn't have any flat tires, and I could get a visitor's pass. And if my parents said yes …

My heart deflates. They're never going to say yes to visiting Taichi. That would cost almost an entire day of our vacation, plus gas. And if visiting restrictions are similar to those at Tanforan, we would drive all that way just so I could have thirty minutes with Taichi. Who's supposedly nothing more to me than the son of our produce supplier at the restaurant.

I put one finger on Mono Lake and the other on Owens Valley. They look so close together, and yet the distance feels insurmountable.

Taichi

Monday, May 11, 1942

I tuck the bat under my arm so I can clap for James as he crosses home plate with a flourish of dust. "Atta boy, James!"

We slap high fives before he joins the rest of our teammates, and I return to practicing swings on deck. With my fingers curled around the smooth wood of the bat, I feel as though my heart has come home after far too many days away.

I stand within the circle I drew in the dust and throw my strength into a practice swing.

Baseball in Manzanar is everything pure and fun that I love about the game, probably because it's in such sharp contrast to everything else I do here. And there are no bitter Caucasian fathers like Danny Nielsen's watching in the stands, hoping I give Coach a reason to bench me so his son can take my spot.

My gaze sweeps over the crowd as I take another swing. I try not to count how many are here to watch our pickup game. The audience is mostly younger boys and teenage girls, including Margaret and Rose. Margaret grins, something she does far more than the other girls, and waves.

Our player grounds out, and I offer him a few claps of encouragement as he jogs past me. "You'll get it next time."

I step up to the plate and dig my shoes in. I should ask Diego if he can mail my cleats.

I swing mightily at the first pitch, and feel a flush come over my face when I nearly fall down. Yes, I should *definitely* ask Diego for my cleats.

"Thanks, Taichi. The breeze is nice," calls the third baseman.

I straighten my hat and squint down the line to find Raymond Yamishi, the rude fellow from Los Angeles, sneering at me. Hot words are on the tip of my tongue, but I swallow them before they escape. This is just for fun. I don't need to prove anything.

But when the next pitch barrels in, I swing with even more gusto, and, thankfully, more accuracy. The ball sails over the heads of the infielders, and my foot is secure on second base before it's thrown back in.

I glance at Raymond, but he's watching the next batter, seeming content to ignore my hit.

Our next batter, Yosuke, looks surprised when the bat connects with the ball. From the bench, James yells at him, "Run! Run!" and Yosuke scuttles to first while I make it easily to third.

I sense Raymond taking up his position behind me. "I have been meaning to talk to you."

I shuffle a few steps away from the flour sack that marks third base. "What about?"

"My cousin works in the mail room." Raymond speaks English well, but doesn't seem very comfortable speaking it. "He says you receive many letters from a Caucasian female."

This is so far from what I expected—not that I had any clue about what he would say—that at first I can't seem to do anything but turn and look at him.

My heart thumps wildly. I turn away as quickly as I can, hoping he can't see whatever emotion might be playing across my face. I've lost track of how many pitches have been thrown to Woody.

I try to keep my voice light. "You and your cousin don't have anything better to talk about?"

Woody swings and misses.

As I jog back to touch the base, Raymond says, "We are looking for traitors. I suggested he keep an eye on you and your friend."

I swivel my head toward him. Is that some kind of joke? The line of his mouth and the clench of his jaw tell me no, but how can he possibly think that?

"You're serious?"

Raymond's only response is a flat look.

There's a loud crack as the bat connects with the ball, and I turn to run—Coach would have my head for having my back to the batter—but Woody had just fouled it off.

As a young boy from the stands throws the ball back in, I return to the base, feeling hot from the embarrassment of running. From the accusation.

"I'm not a traitor." I take a breath and try to smooth the indignation out of my voice. "I sure didn't think I'd have to say that to anyone in here."

I can almost understand Caucasians being suspicious of Japanese—*almost*—but to be suspected that I'm not 100-percent loyal to my country by a fellow Japanese American?

Raymond's laugh scrapes out, as if rusty. "You think I mean you are a traitor to the United States? Of course not. I mean to the empire."

My chest goes cold as I look at him. As my brain churns away at the implications of his statement. Raymond Yamishi is close to my age and is likely an American citizen. His stiff use of English makes me think he is a Kibei—born here but sent to Japan for his education—but even still. It hadn't occurred to me that there might be people here who considered themselves more Japanese than American. Certainly not of my generation.

There's the distinct, perfect crack of when the ball hits the sweet spot of the bat, and I scramble into action, taking off as it arches well over the infield. Some applaud and some groan as I cross home plate.

James is off the bench, jumping and pointing and waving. "Back to third! Back to third!"

I turn to see the right fielder throwing the ball in to the cut-off man. Still reeling from Raymond's words, I didn't even think to check if the outfielder caught Woody's hit. I hustle back toward third, but Raymond catches the ball cleanly. He grins as he plants his glove into my chest.

Leaning closer, he says, "The Black Dragons are watching you."

The Black Dragons are watching me? What does that even mean?

I try to laugh, but instead it comes out as a pathetic squeak. I watch as he drops the glove onto third base for one of us to use, and then jogs off the field.

The Black Dragons. Is it a club here in Manzanar? Every day it seems like there are more clubs being formed. Would the administration really allow a club for those who side with Japan?

"At our next practice, do we need to review the basic rules of baseball?" James asks as I jog past him on my way to first base. He smiles at me, but I can tell he's miffed about my error ending the inning.

I tip my baseball cap. "Just a little out of practice is all. Sorry about that."

I glance at the bench of boys from Los Angeles. Raymond chats with a fellow in his early twenties, who's short and thick. Is that his cousin? How many of those guys are "Black Dragons"? Or did Raymond just say that to mess with me?

From the pitcher's mound, James tosses me the ball. "You okay, Taichi?"

"Of course." I throw the ball down the line to second, and I try to imagine throwing away Raymond's words with it. This is the last inning, and no good can come from dwelling on what he said.

But that doesn't keep my eyes from drifting over to Raymond during the next ten minutes. Or nearly dropping a routine catch because I had been trying to figure out if Raymond knowing about Evalina could mean my parents would soon know. Or from following Raymond's retreating figure after the game and keeping an eye on which fellows walk with him.

James rests his bat over his shoulder and makes a show of turning to follow my eyeline. "Are you scoping the crowd for options for tonight?"

"Tonight?"

James laughs, and then realizes I'm not joking. "The dance. Didn't you say you were coming tonight? Because I know last time when you didn't come, there were quite a few ladies who were disappointed."

I shake my head and try to make a scoffing kind of laugh. "I'm working in the mess hall now, remember? I have the dinner shift tonight."

"The dance is after dinner."

"Even so. Dances aren't really my scene."

Should I suggest to Evalina that she just put her initials on her return address? Not her full, very Italian name? Though if I did that, she would want to know why . . .

"I know you don't have anything else going on tonight," James says. And my mind is so preoccupied that at first, I can't remember what he's talking about. "You don't have to dance to have fun, you know. Lots of squares come and just watch."

Woody joins us, and thankfully the conversation shifts to organizing a baseball game tomorrow too. My gaze finds Raymond as he heads away with his teammates. Or, possibly, fellow Black Dragons.

I think of cheerful Mr. Kamei who showed us to our block that first day and who is always happy to answer questions. He seems to be involved in a bit of everything here in Manzanar; would he knows anything about a group that goes by that name? If there's anti-American activity in the camps, the administration should know.

Yet another piece of camp life that I won't be sharing with Evalina.

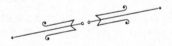

Mr. Kamei is the last person to come through the line for dinner that evening, arriving as I'm putting food away. He merely flicks a distracted smile my way instead of his usual friendly greeting and passes me his tin plate. "Just rice and fruit tonight."

"The stew is actually pretty good," I say. "George made it."

"Okay, then. Some of that too."

I scoop a helping onto his plate, then offer it back to him. Mr. Kamei is staring off, lost in thought. "Here, Mr. Kamei."

He blinks rapidly and puts on a smile. "Thank you, Taichi."

I watch him walk to an empty table, set down his plate, and then pull out several folders. I hastily put away leftover food and wipe a few tables that have already cleared. As I draw closer to Mr. Kamei, I see he's going through notes from some kind of meeting.

When I approach, he looks up and smiles. "You were right about the stew. Thank you."

"Sure." I linger a moment. "Something happened to me today that I'd like to talk to you about. Is now an okay time?"

"Of course. I certainly don't mind taking a break from this." Mr. Kamei punctuates this with a slow and heavy sigh.

"You seem upset."

He shuffles the papers together in a methodical way. "I'm disappointed. It was one thing to face discrimination when I lived and worked among Caucasians. It's another to feel it from one's own people."

I take a seat. "That's oddly what I wanted to talk to you about."

His eyes narrow on me. "What's happening, Taichi?"

"Well, Mr. Kamei—"

"You can call me Ted."

"Ted." I flinch at the sound of an adult's first name on my lips. "I had a strange conversation today."

I recount for him what I can remember of my conversations with Raymond Yamishi, beginning with James chatting him up in the chow line, to today at the baseball game and his talk about the Black Dragons.

"Have you heard of a group that calls itself that?"

A swell of wind pushes dust through the cracks of the nearby window. Ted watches for a moment and then says, "Given the conversations I've been having this afternoon, I wouldn't be surprised if a group of young Kibei have officially or unofficially banded together and started calling themselves something that sounds threatening."

Ted seems to be thinking something through, and I try to wait patiently. My knee bounces beneath the table, and I can hear the *creak, creak, creak* of the floorboard my foot is on.

"I think I can ask some of the Isseis about this." Ted speaks this sentence slow and measured. "After today's meeting . . . Well, I'll just be frank with you about what I've seen going on."

Ted gives me an evaluating look, and I nod.

"Many are very hurt and bitter over the evacuation. I suppose I don't need to tell you that. Some believe the best thing we can do is follow the government's orders and prove our loyalty that way. Specifically, those like Fred Tayama, and others involved in the Japanese American Citizens League. They feel our government has made a mistake, but we can show our loyalty by being good citizens." Ted evaluates me a moment longer.

"Not everyone feels that way," I prompt.

"Some feel that by doing this we are making ourselves doormats. They fought for the United States during the Great War and now are being imprisoned like they've done something wrong. If I were a veteran, perhaps I would feel the same way as Joe and Harry." Ted digs trenches in his hair with his fingers. "I don't know. I just don't know. I'm a Nisei, and they sometimes seem suspicious of me. Like I'm going to report them to the FBI."

"Who are Joe and Harry?"

"Harry Ueno is a cook in block twenty-two. A great cook, actually. He deep fries rice and rolls it in sugar for the kids." Ted's smile is tinged with sadness. "I like Harry, even if we disagree politically. Joe is fine too, really. He'll have somewhat reasonable conversations."

"I don't think I know either of them."

"There's no reason you would. Joe is a veteran, and he feels deeply betrayed. He's from Terminal Island, and the evacuation was particularly bad there. Joe has been very vocal about how he wants to be sent back to Japan if this is how America is going to treat war veterans, that he's not going to disgrace himself by holding a job here in Manzanar. That it only helps the government holding us as prisoners."

Ted makes a rolling motion with his hand, indicating that he could go on for a while about Joe's philosophies.

"Anyway, Joe made a comment in our meeting about how he's had conversations with many of the young Kibei from Los Angeles and Terminal Island. He says they all think we need to take more action against the administration if we want change and respect. When you mentioned the 'Black Dragons' it just sounded like something Joe would know about, that's all. I'll see what I can learn. In the meantime, try not to worry."

"Okay. Thanks, Ted."

"Taichi . . ." Ted looks at his hands for a moment as he debates. "You said Raymond brought up that you exchange letters with a Caucasian girl. It's none of my business, and you've a right to correspond with whomever you wish, but if the correspondence continues, Raymond and his friends might only antagonize you further."

For a moment, I consider telling Ted about Evalina. Several times I've seen him talking to Karl Yoneda and his wife. Once I even saw him playing with their son.

But while I don't think he would be too scandalized, he's also on friendly terms with my parents. What if he doesn't feel comfortable keeping secrets from them?

"I'm going to keep corresponding with her," I say to my hands. "Regardless of what Raymond said."

When I look up, Ted's gaze moves about my face, as if he's searching for more information. "I felt the same way about a Caucasian girl once," he says quietly. "Long ago, before Lillian. So I understand."

My mind pulses with questions, but his wife approaches the table before I can ask any of them.

"Ah, here she is. Lillian, have you met Taichi Hamasaki? He's in barrack eleven."

I stand and offer my hand. "Nice to meet you, Mrs. Kamei."

Even by Japanese standards, Lillian is short. Her hair is straighter than most of the girls, and she's thinner than most as well. I feel like a giant next to her.

"It's nice to meet you too." Her voice is surprisingly low for how tiny she is in every other sense. "You can call me Lillian."

I take a step back toward the kitchen. "I need to finish cleaning up. Thank you for the talk, Ted. And nice to meet you, Lillian."

As I finish putting away food, I can't help glancing at the Kameis several times. Lillian is angled toward Ted, attentive as he speaks in a private voice. When they leave, he has the folder grasped in one hand, and his other hand holds Lillian's.

Their contentment with each other should be a pleasant sight, but I can't get my mind off the Caucasian girl he alluded to. A girl he'd once cared deeply about, it sounds like. Instead, his happiness with Lillian only causes my chest to tighten with questions and confusion.

CHAPTER SEVENTEEN

Evalina

Saturday, May 30, 1942

When I come out the front door, Daddy chuckles. "Are you trying to scare everyone away? You look more like you're going to a funeral than a Memorial Day picnic."

I glance down at my gray sweater and black skirt. "I'm not going to parade around in red, white, and blue as if I'm so proud."

"You're not proud of our country?" Daddy's tone is light, inviting conversation. He shifts the weight of the picnic basket he's holding, and hands me a bag with a jug of lemonade.

"I'm not proud of everything our country does, no."

"Countries are run by men. Men are fallible."

"Currently, I find the men who run our country extremely fallible."

Daddy chuckles as Mama comes out the door at last. She struggles under the weight of three bags full of food we've been preparing all week for the picnic. Even though everyone contributes, each family brings so much, you would think they're solely responsible for feeding the neighborhood.

"Alessandro, did you get the picnic basket, because . . ." Mama's words trail off as she takes in my less-than-festive ensemble. I can almost hear the debate going on in her mind as she tries to figure out what to say to me. "Evalina . . ."

I square my shoulders.

"This is some sort of political statement, I gather?"

"Yes, it is."

Mama looks to Daddy. Daddy shrugs.

She looks back to me and hesitates a moment before saying, "Would you carry one of these bags, please?"

We join other Italian families heading to the park for our annual Memorial Day picnic. Many families look different than they did this time last year, with sons or fathers or both gone to war or away at training. Several wear black bands of mourning around their sleeves.

Mrs. Esposito arranges her food on the table as my family approaches. "Hello, Cassano family." She gives my outfit a once-over but makes no remarks. "I had to bring extra food this year because we've brought a guest. Evalina, have you met Tony's new girlfriend?"

"We had P.E. class together last year, just after she moved here. She's very nice."

To my parents, she says, "She's the one over there with the beautiful blonde curls. They're getting a game of volleyball going, if you'd like to join them, Evalina. Mary is wonderfully athletic." Mrs. Esposito takes a knife and drags the blade down her pan of lasagna, drawing precise lines. "I've never seen Tony so excited about a girl. It's wonderful."

She possibly intends the words to slice me, considering I'm the one who ended things with Tony. And they do, a bit. A papercut to my ego. A sharp sting, but one that fades quickly. "I'll go join them. Excuse me."

I set off toward the volleyball net. In the sea of dark haired and olive skinned Italian Americans, Mary is easy to spot. Her blonde curls are held out of her face with a red headband that sports a navy bow. Her skirt is red plaid, her blouse white, and her sweater navy blue. She looks like an advertisement for the American way, all the way down to her navy-blue saddle shoes.

About halfway to them, my pace slows. I feel suddenly ridiculous in my statement outfit and one red thumbnail. Just as I'm about to veer away, Tony spots me. He waves enthusiastically and gestures me closer to them. I wave, smile, and—what else can I do?—resume my walk to them. I can see his mouth moving, and Mary's eyes find me in the crowd.

"I hoped you would be here," Tony says. "Mary, do you know Evalina, my oldest and dearest friend?"

Mary offers her slim hand. All her fingernails gleam patriotic red. "Yes, I think we've had a couple classes together. And now I feel like I know you because it seems every childhood story of Tony's stars you."

Mary doesn't have a face of stunning beauty, but there's an endearing sweetness there. Especially when she beams up at Tony.

"Yes, I was always trying to keep Tony out of trouble."

Tony shakes his head. "A complete lie. Both of us were always trying to keep Gia out of trouble. Where is she, by the way?"

I scan the crowd and wince when I see Gia talking to Lorenzo. Why hasn't he shipped out yet? Isn't he needed for the war effort?

Tony follows my gaze. "They looked like they were fighting at prom. I thought maybe they had called it quits."

"She told me she thinks they should either break up or get married."

Tony grunts his disapproval. His dislike of Lorenzo has

always made me feel better about my own. Tony usually likes everybody.

I make small talk with Mary—where she lived before here, what her plans are for next fall—until the lunch buffet opens. We load up our plates, and Tony steers us to a sunny patch of grass.

Mary has just said to me, "Tony says you plan to study political science at U.C. Berkeley," when Gia arrives, Lorenzo in tow.

"Hello, all." She plops beside me. Gia is also dressed like the American flag threw up on her, and Lorenzo has on his uniform. "Lorenzo, you know Tony and Evalina, of course. This is Tony's friend, Mary."

Mary takes in Lorenzo's uniform. "Nice to meet you. Thank you for serving our country."

"Yeah, I'll be shipping out soon," Lorenzo says, as if he was asked. To me, he adds, "I ate this afternoon at your family's restaurant. Best homemade pastas in all of San Francisco, I say."

"Thank you. I agree, but I'm biased."

Gia beams at the two of us, clearly pleased by Lorenzo's efforts to compliment my family. "Their meatball sandwich is my favorite. Anything with their mozzarella, really. You know, Tony's dad is the one who makes it. I love watching."

"Do you know where you're being sent, Lorenzo?" Mary asks.

"Dunno. Probably Asia." With a grin, Lorenzo adds, "I'm hoping so, anyway. I'm dying to hunt me some Japs."

I feel my heart pause, and then break into a gallop. I look up at Gia. Her eyes are wide, and she shakes her head at me. As if that's going to stop me.

I snap a carrot stick with my teeth. "That seems like a

rather crude way to refer to taking the life of fellow human beings."

Lorenzo startles at my cold voice. His gaze scrapes down the length of me, sizing up my stark, black attire. "They killed friends of mine at Pearl Harbor. Unprovoked."

"I'm aware of that. It's terrible. But there's still a more respectful way—"

Lorenzo barks a laugh. "Gia said you've turned into quite the Jap lover. I just didn't realize you were rooting for them over your own boys."

My mouth falls open. Gia's cheeks burn scarlet, and she's suddenly captivated by her plate. How could she have told Lorenzo about Taichi? In an instant my anger turns from ice cold to boiling.

"That is not at all true—"

"The Japanese are swallowing up every country they can, preying on the weak. Do you know what those men would do to you if they were ever to land on our shores? I don't want to give you nightmares, so I'll just say that you would be begging me to kill them if that happened."

"Lorenzo, you've crossed a line," Tony says in a quiet, gentle voice.

Lorenzo turns his glare from me to Tony. "I'm not surprised to hear you say that. Considering you don't even have the guts to enlist."

Poor Mary looks like she would rather be anywhere but here, and I don't blame her.

"You guys." Gia's tone is light and playful. "This is supposed to be a party."

A beat of uncomfortable silence falls. I keep my teeth clamped over my lower lip so I don't yell at Lorenzo anymore and try to corral the wild galloping of my heart.

"Sorry," Lorenzo says—to Gia, not to us.

"We're all grateful, Lorenzo, that you're serving our country." Gia looks to me and bobs her head, as if encouraging me to second her words. "Right?"

I scowl at her. "I have a headache."

I stalk all the way home.

When Mama and Daddy return from the picnic that evening, they're only home a few minutes before Mama comes up to check on me.

"Hi, honey." Mama sinks onto my bed and presses her wrist against my forehead. "How are you feeling?"

"It was just a headache. I'm better now."

Mama doesn't say anything for a moment. "Gia thought maybe you left because you were upset. Not because of a headache."

Gia should keep her mouth shut.

"Lorenzo is insufferable."

Mama frowns. "He's serving our country, Evalina. He deserves our respect."

"Does he? He's the same boy who took Mrs. Rando's car for a joyride and crashed it."

"Technically, yes." Mama smooths my hair out of my face like she used to when I was a young girl and needed soothing. "But in many ways, he's not the same boy. Just because you were troubled in your youth, it doesn't mean you're troubled forever. Don't you think our family heritage proves that, Evalina?"

I don't like thinking about our family heritage.

"He called the Japanese 'Japs.'"

"Ah." She sounds satisfied, as though she's solved the puzzle. "Was he speaking of Japanese Americans?"

"No. The Japanese military, specifically. But it's still not a nice way to talk about other people."

"You've always been very tenderhearted, Evalina. We love that about you."

I wait for her to say more, but she doesn't, so I sit up. "You think I shouldn't have argued with Lorenzo because he's serving our country?"

"I wasn't there, Evalina. I don't know."

"He was rude to Tony too. And he was speaking about very crass matters."

"Then I'm glad you didn't continue to converse with him, but you didn't have to let him ruin the whole party for you." Mama rests a hand on my shoulder. "Though I'm not sure you were in a mindset to enjoy it, were you?"

"Not really."

"I think our vacation is coming at an excellent time. All three of us are feeling so worn out right now, and we will really be able to enjoy getting away, I think."

Especially if I can maybe see Taichi. My heart kicks up a notch as I consider asking Mama.

Mama sighs. "There's still so much to be done. We'll have your graduation next week, and I have to get the house clean."

"So it can gather dust while we're gone?"

"Mrs. LaRocca will be coming by the house to water my plants and keep an eye on things. I don't want her having to deal with a messy house. Oh, and I have to visit my brother before I go." She wrinkles her nose at me. "I never look forward to that."

I take a bracing breath. "Speaking of visiting people in prison—"

Mama laughs. "I'm very curious to hear where *this* leads."

My stomach pitches on a sea of nervousness. "I was looking at a map, and I saw that Mono Lake is really not that far from Manzanar, California. Which I've heard is where the Hamasaki family is living right now."

Mama's smile fades from her face. "That's not really speaking of visiting people in prison, Evalina. They're not incarcerated, they're . . . evacuated. For safety purposes."

Bitterness slicks my throat. Safety purposes. What a lie.

"Do you remember what I told you about Tanforan? The barbed wire? The soldiers with guns? It sure looked like prison to me."

"I know, and it's awful, but that's not a permanent location. And they probably have the fence up to protect the Japanese. You know as well as I do that there are many who would harm them if they thought they could get away with it. I'm sure the permanent communities where they've been evacuated to don't feel like actual prisons."

I make myself swallow the combative words sitting on my tongue. I need Mama on my side.

"Regardless, I saw we'll be quite close to Manzanar—"

"How close?"

I swallow again. "About a hundred miles."

Mama huffs an amused laugh. "I don't call that 'quite close.'"

My dream of seeing Taichi slips through my fingers as though I'd been trying to hold a handful of water. "Yes, but . . ."

But what? What is there to say, really?

Mama's gaze latches on me. I look away.

"Evalina," she says softly. "The Hamasakis are a lovely family, and we were sorry to lose them as suppliers. But considering we never knew them as friends, it seems like a lot of effort to take a day of our vacation just to go see them."

I nod, but I keep my eyes focused on my hands. I fear if I look at her, she will know everything.

"Evalina, are you . . . ?" She lowers her voice to just a notch above a whisper. "Did you have, well, *feelings* for the Hamasaki boy?"

I cannot seem to speak or even breathe. What would she say if I answered yes? If I said we'd been seeing each other for the last year? That six months ago, I went to the library to research which states allowed interracial marriage?

Mama's breathing becomes loud and even, the way it sounds when you're focused on calming yourself. "I see." She folds her hands on her lap. "He seemed like a lovely young man, but I'm sure you already know that encouraging such feelings is . . . unwise."

My anger flares at her words, yet I know this is nothing compared to what Taichi and I will face from the rest of the world. I know if I can't keep my head together for my mother's mild discouragement, then we have no chance of making this work.

Mama stands. I'm eager for her to be gone, to leave me to my stewing, but she lingers in the doorway. "He really did seem very nice, Evalina."

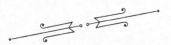

Dear Taichi,

Do you remember me telling you about the trip my family is making to Yosemite in June? One of the places we're visiting, Mono Lake, is actually on the east side of the Sierras, and I happened to notice that it's not too far from Manzanar! I am trying to figure out how I can get down to see you.

Ordinarily I might try and surprise you, but at Tanforan guests needed special passes to be able to visit. I know you've said Manzanar is very different, but I would hate to get there and not be able to see you just because I had hoped to keep my visit a surprise.

We are in Mono Lake on June 18 and 19, so if I'm able to come, it will be one of those days. Please write back as soon as you can to let me know if those dates will work. I'm hoping there is enough time for your response to reach me before we leave.

And pray that I'm able to talk my parents into this!

Love always,
Evalina

CHAPTER EIGHTEEN

Taichi

Saturday, June 6, 1942

I can't stop reading Evalina's letter.

What is she thinking, asking her parents if they can come visit here? Isn't it going to be just a little obvious that I'm not simply the guy she buys blackberries from if she asks to come visit me?

They'll say no, of course. There's no way they want to give up vacation time to come see me here, and I don't blame them one bit. Why would she have even asked?

And what if . . . ?

My eyes slide closed with the horror of the thought. What if she came here? What if she saw how we live? Seeing Tanforan horrified her so much. What if she saw *our* barbed wire fences that they've begun to stretch around the camp, *our* guard towers that seem to double each day, and *our* military police? How could she ever have any respect for me again? How could I ever expect her parents to approve of us being together if they saw what I've been reduced to in Manzanar?

I make myself take a few breaths.

"Hi, Taichi."

At Rose's greeting, I jam Evalina's letter into the pocket of my pants. "Hi. What are you doing here?"

"Mailing a letter to my father." Rose holds up the letter as if displaying evidence. "He's in North Dakota."

I flinch. I hadn't realized her father was a prisoner. "I'm sorry. My uncle is too. He was a fisherman."

"Same. They took my father just a few days after Pearl Harbor. We didn't know what had happened to him until we got a letter from North Dakota. You?"

I swallow as I remember those terrifying days that were so similar for our family. Three days had passed before Aunt Chiyu telephoned to tell us that she had received a letter from him, that he was being held in North Dakota for an undetermined amount of time.

"Yes. Us too," I say to Rose as she drops the letter into the box. "I'm so sorry."

She gestures to the bat and glove I'm carrying, clearly ready for a subject change. "Are you playing now?"

"I am." I'm probably late. I had intended to just stop by the post office, not stand here for minute after minute rereading Evalina's letter.

"I'll walk with you. If you don't mind."

"Sure."

We start along the dusty road toward the baseball fields. The sounds of hammering fill the air as another guard tower goes up. I'm prepared for a quiet walk, but Rose says, "Six months tomorrow. Doesn't it feel like longer?"

I nod, my chest suddenly tight. "Where were you when you heard the news?"

"I was standing on the dock watching my father's fishing boat go out, along with some other families. And then we realized that the boats were coming back. That had never happened. We were standing there trying to think of why, and then this man we didn't know came running by shouting that the Japanese had bombed Pearl Harbor." Rose laughs a small, humorless laugh. "I didn't even know what that was. *Where* it was. And he just kept running, spreading the news. Like a Japanese Paul Revere." She turns to me. "Where were you?"

In an instant, I'm there in my tiny kitchen. It feels like another life, Sunday morning, December seventh. We were home from church and working together to put lunch on the table before Father and I would head out to take care of the rest of the farm chores. I had been at the sink, working away stubborn grit under my fingernails. My thoughts had been on Evalina, on the city boys that she went to school and church with, who always had clean hands.

"It was a completely ordinary Sunday." I shove my hands in my pockets, and Evalina's letter crunches. "I was helping get lunch ready when they announced it on the radio. My parents seemed to understand right away what this could mean for us. That night we started burning anything Japanese. I thought they were overreacting."

"Me too." Rose's voice is small.

We're silent for a bit. Tumbleweeds beat against the new fence as the wind blows, as if desperate to break into camp.

"I wonder if my father and your uncle know each other." Rose's smile is soft. "Wouldn't that be something?"

"I hope they're here soon."

Rose nods. "Here is better than there, I'm guessing."

What a sorry thing to think about.

"Have a good game, Taichi." Rose seems embarrassed or shy or something as she waves goodbye and splits off to join the other spectators.

I jog over to my team and start my routine of stretches. The hard corners of Evalina's letter poke into my thigh.

I don't want to hurt her feelings by acting like I don't want her here. But it's not like I need to worry, because surely her parents will never agree to the visit. I'll write back with an enthusiastic yes, I'll get the guest passes for the days she mentioned, and then I'll pray they go unused.

The barrack door swings open, and Aiko stomps inside before yanking the door shut. Her nurse's uniform has smears of blood on the skirt and sleeve, and her shoes are thick with dust. Something about the gray lighting of the room, or the fierce expression on her face, calls attention to how sharp her cheekbones have become since our arrival.

I lay down the issue of the *Manzanar Free Press* that I had been reading. "Bad day?"

"Just frustrating." Aiko plops onto her cot, sending up a puff of dust, and digs underneath for her towel and soap. "Sometimes at work I just feel so *stupid*."

"You're not stupid."

"Tell that to the patient who I thought was having stomach cramps from food poisoning, and it turned out to be appendicitis." Aiko rips off her nurse's cap and flings it against the wall. "In front of Ichiro, of course. What are you reading that for?"

The subject change is so abrupt that it takes me a moment to realize she's talking about the newspaper. "Just seeing what's going on in camp, that's all."

Aiko makes a sour face. "It's just a mouthpiece for the administration, Taichi."

"No, it's all residents who put it together."

"I'm not disputing that. It's still a mouthpiece for the administration. Did you do something with my soap?"

"Why would I have done something with your soap?"

"I don't know, but I swear I put it—There it is. Never mind." Aiko sits upright. "I stopped trusting the paper when they didn't say a word about Hikoji getting shot by that guard."

A zip of fear races through me, the way it does anytime I hear Hikoji's name. No one witnessed it, but the story zoomed all over camp that after going through a scrap lumber pile around the edge of camp—like all the families do—Hikoji was headed back toward his barrack when an MP fired his rifle for no reason. The MP claimed Hikoji was trying to run off, but none of us believe it.

"How is he?" I ask. "Is he still at the hospital?"

"Released, finally. He screamed so much in his sleep." She shudders. "And the newspaper doesn't even have the dignity to report it. Or maybe they tried, but the administration took it out. Either way, I'm not touching another issue."

With that, Aiko stalks out of the barrack and toward the shower room.

"Norman, get down from there!"

I look up to find Norman in the rafters, looking down at me with a bright grin. I make myself smile back. He's just a kid. What else is he going to do but turn this place into a big playground?

I chuck the newspaper onto the table that Father built with scrap wood. Everyone goes through the piles to get what they need to make hooks for their walls, tables, or chairs. What happened to Hikoji could have happened to any one of us, and as far as I know, whoever shot him is still walking the boundary lines or up in the new towers.

And there's nothing for us to do but sit here and take it.

Evalina

Tuesday, June 16, 1942

Daddy fits his arm around Mama's shoulders as we watch the sun turn the iconic Half Dome a blazing orange, and then he puts his other arm around me. "I have everything I need right here."

I make myself smile back at his beaming face, guilt twisting at my heart for not being able to echo the sentiment. For not feeling capable of freely giving myself to this moment, to this blessing of a vacation. But how can my heart not be fragmented at a time like this? How can I feel joy when Taichi's family has been stripped of everything that belonged to them? When Diego is away at basic training, preparing to go to war? When families on our street are losing people they love?

Before we left town, Gia had grabbed hold of my hand and scrubbed nail polish remover on my lone red nail. "This is a once-in-a-lifetime experience, Evalina," she had said when I struggled. "You're not going to throw it away by obsessing over everything that's wrong in the world."

"I don't know if I can do that. How can I just ignore that Taichi—"

"Stop it," Gia snapped. "Stop acting like you're the only one who's hurting."

"I'm not acting like—"

"Yes, you are. You don't see me moping about or wearing black to parties."

"But Lorenzo actually had a choice when he enlisted. Taichi's life has been stolen from him."

"It's terrible. I agree with you. But you spoiling your own vacation isn't going to solve anything. Just be grateful."

I stopped fighting and let her scrub away the crimson polish. Then I repainted my nail at home. As I stare up at the same mountain range that Taichi can see from Manzanar, I offer up a prayer of protection and rub at my thumb like rosary beads.

"What a gift, to be able to capture beauty like this." Mama nods at a painter who's also watching the sunset and transferring it to his canvas. "Alessandro, are you okay?"

I swing my gaze to Daddy in time to see a pained expression fade from his face.

"Yes, I'm fine." His smile seems strained.

"No, what is it?"

"Nothing serious. My throat feels a bit scratchy is all. And I have a slight headache. But I'm sure all I need is a good night of sleep."

A shuttle bus pulls up to the stop near our viewpoint. With a *schhh*, the doors open and out spill other tourists who have come to watch the sunset at Half Dome. The empty spaces around us fill in with others who gaze in wonder or set up their tripods to take a photograph.

A man standing at my elbow says, "Yep. Looks just like it did this afternoon. Like a big rock."

"Arthur," says a woman, her tone suggesting the well-practiced eye roll of a wife.

I glance their way and find two couples who look to be about ten years older than my parents. The men are both in slacks and sweaters with excessive pomade in their hair and shoes that are a bit too nice to be hiking trails. The women wear stylish, jaunty hats over coifed hair and earrings that dangle. One of them has on pumps.

"You want to see a nice sunset?" the other man says to no one in particular. "Hawaii is the place for that."

One of the women rests a hand on her heart, as if overcome. "Hawaii is divine."

"Too many Japs in Hawaii," Arthur says with a sniff.

Daddy's arm stiffens around my shoulders, and I feel Mama's sidelong glance.

"Speaking of Japs, you know what I heard? I was talking to my cousin John in Bakersfield. He said the Japs who farmed the strawberries there had cut arrows into their fields, pointing toward the cities on the coast."

"Chuck, we don't *know* that," says the woman who thinks Hawaii is divine.

"John saw them for himself," Chuck says. "Said the arrows were pointing toward Santa Barbara, and sure enough that's where that oil refinery was blown up."

I try to keep the words locked in my mouth. Nope, they're coming out. "By submarines." The two couples have turned to look at me, but I'm too furious to feel the embarrassment I probably ought. "That refinery was hit by Japanese submarines, not airplanes."

They all blink at me, as if in disbelief that I spoke. As if they didn't realize others could hear them.

One of the women puts on a smile. "Let's all just enjoy the beauty of the sunset, why don't we? Let's not ruin it with discussing politics."

"This isn't politics, it's people." But I'm now talking to the backs of their heads.

"Evalina," Daddy says quietly. "Just let it go."

That seems to be what everybody wants me to do these days. Stop talking about it. Stay quiet. Don't point out inconvenient facts or question the fairness. *Just let it go.*

Yet everything within me wants to grab hold tighter. Wants to yell louder. Wants to ask every question, push down every wall.

"Alessandro, are you okay? You feel feverish." Mama frowns up at Daddy. "We should leave now."

Daddy grimaces when he swallows. "The sunset will only last a few more minutes. I'm fine."

I fix my eyes on Half Dome and watch. As the brilliant sunset cools to gray, I vow my anger over blatant discrimination will *not* cool. As these rocks stay steady through season changes and time, so I will remain steady.

I will not be silent. I will not let this go.

CHAPTER NINETEEN

Taichi

Friday, June 19, 1942

I can tell Margaret is trying to catch my eye as I wipe up tables after dinner. Finally, she says, "Hey, Taichi. Can I talk to you a minute?"

I like Margaret, but I don't think I want to discuss what she came here to talk about. "Of course."

Margaret twists her fingers together and smiles without showing her teeth. "I know you aren't a big fan of dancing, but I wondered if you were coming tonight anyway? The music is going to be swell."

I slop my washrag onto a table I've already cleaned. "I'll be there. Aiko said she would only go if I went, and she loves to dance. So, *that* is why I'm going."

Please let that be enough. Please don't let her bring up—

"Rose will be really happy to hear that. You know, tomorrow is Rose's seventeenth birthday." Margaret twirls a clump of hair around her finger. "I know it would mean a lot to her if you asked her to . . . I mean, if you decide you want to dance, I know Rose would be happy to dance with you."

My laugh sounds tight. "That's only because she hasn't seen me dance before."

Margaret releases the lock of hair. "I'm sure you're a fine dancer. Even if you're not, Rose would still be happy."

I rub the washcloth over the table again. I've practiced this response for the last few weeks now, ever since I began to suspect that I might have to have this conversation. "I'm not going to ask Rose to dance, because I have a girlfriend."

This doesn't seem to surprise Margaret. "James told us. She knows it would just be a dance, Taichi."

"Still, it doesn't seem very honorable to either of them. So, I'll be there, but I won't dance."

Margaret twists her hair again and releases it. "That's really not helpful. If I tell Rose why, she'll only like you more."

Her smile shows she's teasing, and I don't know what to say to that, so I just smile back.

Margaret rocks on her heels. "Did you see they have Coca-Cola stocked at the store again?"

The tension leaks away from our conversation as we chat for a few minutes, and then Margaret heads off to get ready for the dance, and I put away my cleaning supplies for the night.

I suppose it's time to admit that Evalina is not going to pay me a visit. Yesterday was the first day she thought she might come, but all that arrived was a postcard from Yosemite. And now that dinner is over, and the sun is slipping closer to the mountains, I know she's not coming today either.

Not that I really expected her, or that I even wanted her to see me here. Still there's an aching disappointment in my chest.

When I step out the door of the mess hall, I find Ted hurrying by. "Are you okay, Ted?"

He looks up, and it's clear I've jolted him out of his thoughts. "Sorry, I wasn't paying attention. I'm coming back from the hospital."

"Lillian again?"

Ted nods. "Dr. Goto says it's this dust that keeps aggravating her lungs. She's had problems before, but never like this."

"Could you get transferred to another camp? One with less dust?"

"Lillian wouldn't want that. She feels like we're needed here. Plus my parents are here. Though if she keeps having trouble . . ." He cocks his head to the side, listening.

I hear it too, the rumbling that grows increasingly louder. Almost like—

Ted grabs me by the shirt and pushes me against the wall as the Manzanar garbage truck comes careening around the corner. Hitting the wall knocks the breath out of me, but it's better than being knocked flat by the truck.

"Hey, watch it!" Ted yells after the truck.

The boys in the cab of the truck are laughing, and Raymond Yamishi leans out the window and yells something at us in Japanese that I can't make out. Two flags have been affixed to the top of the truck, and they whip violently in the wind.

"Raymond is going to kill someone with that stupid truck." Ted pulls me away from the wall. "Are you okay? I didn't mean to push you so hard."

"I'm glad you did. I would rather not be carted off to the hospital." My hands tremble as I wipe off my shirt. "I haven't seen the flags on there before. Could you tell what they said?"

Ted's face is grim. "Manzanar Black Dragons Association. They're idiots, every one of them. They had a meeting last week, and that Raymond Yamishi talked nonstop about how Japan will win the war, how Japan will be landing in California soon. I spoke up against him, which is probably why he nearly mowed us over just now. Sorry about that."

I take a step and feel the shakiness of my knees. "I can't believe the administration would let them keep those flags up."

"They can't read them. They don't know a lick of Japanese. Still. It's on my list of items to discuss with Ned Campbell tomorrow. He's the assistant camp director. Do you want to come with me? Corroborate my story about the truck nearly running us down?"

I'm not sure that my word will mean much, but, "Sure."

When we say farewell, I duck into my barrack intending to change into my nicer clothes and head over to the dance. But I find myself just sitting on the edge of my cot, staring at the ugly walls, reliving the careening garbage truck over and over.

Then I'm lying on my cot, a headache blossoming as I stare up at the single lightbulb. Other lights are on in the rest of the barrack, but in our apartment, the light is off. Who made the decision that one bare lightbulb was all each family needed? What happens when it burns out? Is there a supply somewhere, or will we just live in the dark for days?

The beam from the searchlights crosses over our wall, alerting me to how late it is. I'm not going to the dance, apparently. My hand finds my breast pocket and withdraws the photograph of Evalina.

She's beautiful in her senior portrait, but it's a sterilized beauty with every curl in place and a practiced smile. I close my eyes and think about the way she looks when she arrives at the market—her curls windblown, her cheeks pink, and her smile warm and personal.

I knew it would be best if she didn't come. If she didn't see how we live, or that I've been less-than-truthful about our conditions, but the less rational part of me wanted more than anything for her to show up. For the chance to see her, smell her, touch her.

I tuck the picture back into my pocket, where her image is safe from prying eyes, and I watch the searchlights cross over the ceiling.

It really is for the best that she didn't come.

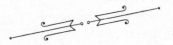

Ned Campbell has a round face, like a boy's, and he pats at his temples every few minutes with a handkerchief even though to me it feels nice and cool in here with the fan.

"See, now, we had some of your people consult us on what kind of food to buy so they could make meals y'all would eat. Are you saying the food still isn't satisfactory?"

"There's very little protein," Ted says, gently but firmly. "And very little variety. Some blocks have cooks who were in the food industry before coming to Manzanar, and they're able to do more than most. But, sir, in block nine, the cook used to be a gardener. In block two, the cook who just quit was a janitor, and the one who took his place was a tailor. They're each being asked to cook breakfast, lunch, and dinner for three hundred people."

Mr. Campbell dabs at his red face again. "We're all doing our best, Ted. I commend those men for stepping up to the challenge of feeding their blocks."

The two men look at each other.

Ted speaks slowly. "I do too, sir. But that doesn't change the lack of satisfactory food."

"The refrigeration isn't very stable either." My stomach churns just thinking about that week all of us on block four had been running to and from the bathroom.

Ted nods at me and looks back to Mr. Campbell, who's

regarding me with a bit of skepticism. "Taichi's right," Ted says. "The administration needs to pay for more reliable refrigerators, or they're going to be spending more money than they'd like on food."

Mr. Campbell leans onto his desk with his elbows. "I'll see if I can get a bit more money in the budget for protein. But I can't promise anything. Is there anything else?"

"Yes." Ted straightens his shoulders. "Yesterday, Taichi and I were standing just outside the mess hall in block four when we were nearly run over by the garbage truck. I had to throw poor Taichi against the wall just to avoid it." Ted glances at me before continuing. "I've told you about the Black Dragons. It's mostly youth, particularly younger Kibei—"

"Those are the alien residents?"

"No, sir. Issei are the first generation, and Kibei are the citizens born here, but educated in Japan. Anyway, the garbage truck is driven by a group of young Kibei, one in particular, who Taichi has had words with before. Taichi said that he was threatened by them. Now they have flags hanging from the garbage truck that say Manzanar Black Dragons."

Mr. Campbell frowns and considers this. Then, "Where did they get the flags?"

Ted takes in a breath, and I can tell he didn't anticipate this being the first question. "I'm not sure, sir. I imagine they made them."

Mr. Campbell continues to frown. "Well, the administration can't handle every little detail. That's why there's the Manzanar police force, to help with disagreements among your own kind."

"Sir, right now it's a small percentage of the Manzanar population that's stirring up Anti-American sentiment. I'm afraid if it's not taken care of, and if all these other issues like poor food, open showers, and no privacy for families continues, this anger is just going to fester and grow. And it might become uncontainable."

Mr. Campbell looks at Ted with bored tolerance. "You're all Japanese. You'll have to figure out a way to get along."

His chair scrapes against the carpet of his office—my eyes haven't seen a carpeted floor in over two months—and he holds out his hand to Ted. "As always, thanks for coming, Ted. You and the rest of the community councilmen are doing fine work." He offers his hand to me too and winks. "Don't walk in the middle of the road anymore, okay, son?"

We walk through the door to the sound of him still chuckling at his own wit.

Ted shields his eyes as a gust of dusty wind smacks us when we walk out the door. "I don't even understand why we have a council if he won't listen to what we're saying. 'You are all Japanese. You'll have to get along.' That makes no sense. I could just as easily say to him, 'Americans and Germans are all Caucasians. You'll just have to get along.'"

My eyes water from invading grit. "I don't know."

Ted makes a growling noise in his throat. "Sometimes I just feel so frustrated I don't know what to do with myself. Is this where I have to raise my child? To go to a makeshift school, never eating a home-cooked meal?"

Through my streaming eyes, I can barely make out Ted's face, but I can hear the darkness in his voice.

"Lillian is with child, by the way," he mutters. "If you didn't guess it from my statement. Sorry, that's not the way I intended to share that news."

My, "Congratulations," has a dull ring to it, even though it's sincere.

Ted doesn't speak. I'm not used to this discouraged side of him.

"We'll just keep pushing, Ted. We're only a few months into this. Things are bound to get better. Especially with people like you fighting for change."

"I'm already fighting the Ned Campbells of the world. I didn't realize I would have to fight the Black Dragons too. They think I'm just some stool pigeon."

Our conversation fizzles when we run into my mother and Mrs. Kanito, James's mother, standing outside chatting about gardens. Ted tucks away his frustration to greet them, and I stand there, looking around for James, but not seeing him. Maybe he's sleeping? He's started working at the police station in the dispatch room, and they've given him the really boring overnight shift.

When there's a break in the conversation, I ask Mrs. Kanito, "Is James around?"

Mrs. Kanito opens her mouth to respond, just as someone walking by says, "Taichi Hamasaki?"

I turn to find a boy close to my age, who I think plays baseball. "Yes?"

He grins. "I thought so. You play a bang up second base."

"Thank you."

"That play you made in Wednesday's game, where you jumped over the batter as he slid, and threw to first? That was amazing."

My feelings of flattery have shifted into embarrassment. "Thanks."

The boy grins at me a moment longer, and then startles. "Oh, right! I came here to fetch you. Your visitor is here."

Everything seems to stop. Except for my heart, which might as well be pounding directly in my ears, it's so loud.

"My visitor," I echo.

The boy nods. "Yep. She's waiting in a front office. I'll show you where."

I don't intend to look at my mother, but I can't seem to stop myself. I expect her eyes to be full of questions or curiosity, but instead I see something far more perceptive.

"Who is here, Taichi?" she asks quietly.

I put on a smile that I hope looks reassuring. "I'll explain as soon as I return."

And I hope by then I've thought of a satisfactory answer that doesn't involve Evalina.

CHAPTER TWENTY

Evalina

Dust.

Tar-papered buildings.

Tall fences with five strands of barbed wire snaking around the top.

The echo of hammering as another guard tower is erected.

The soaring beauty of the Sierras overlooking all the ugly dustiness of this prison.

I cannot decide which detail is the most shocking as I stand in the administration building at Manzanar War Relocation Center and stare out the window.

The guard lumbers over to me and looks out the window as well. "Sorry to make you wait, miss. The camp is a big place. It can be hard to track down residents."

My jaw has been clenched tight as I hold in tears and fury. Somehow I manage to say in a light, conversational tone, "How big is Manzanar, exactly?"

He hitches his thumbs in his pockets. "One square mile."

"Is it fenced all the way around?"

"We hope it will be by the end of July, miss. It's extremely secure."

My throat seems to close off at that statement. The door swings open, but it's a middle-aged couple who comes in, not

Taichi. They smile and bow to the Caucasian husband and wife who have also been sitting here waiting.

"Good afternoon, folks," the guard greets them. "Visits are restricted to forty-five minutes today, and I'm unable to let you leave the room."

The Japanese American couple bow in acknowledgment, which makes my stomach tighten, and then they sit at a small, round table with their friends. Their voices are low and warm, and something about the pitch of them makes me want to burst into tears.

The guard turns his attention back to me. "We only have the restrictions sometimes. I'm not sure why, but they've been stricter this week. Unless you're visiting one of the Caucasian families inside the fence, of course."

"There are Caucasian families here too?"

"Sure. The administration and all their families. Eventually there will be Caucasian teachers too, but we don't got the school built yet. We—the MPs—don't live inside the fence. We're out south of the entrance."

He nods southward. He doesn't look old enough to be military police, with his round face and short stature. I imagine he tires of hearing that.

"Do you interact with the residents much?"

"Only if they're too close to the fence or something." The guard shrugs. "They kinda keep to themselves."

My head whirls with angry retorts. *Gee, really? What options do they have besides keeping to themselves, considering they've been fenced in and you're holding a gun?*

The door squeals on its dry hinges, and a boy calls a gleeful, "Found him!"

My gaze zooms to Taichi, and the breath whooshes out of my lungs as his eyes meet mine. These last twenty minutes,

I've paced this room feeling fury and outrage and hurt over Taichi not telling me the truth. All of those thoughts slip away at the sight of him.

"Good afternoon," the guard says to Taichi. "I already told your friend, but visits are forty-five minutes today, and you can't leave the room."

Taichi's gaze slips over to the guard—"Thank you"—and then finds me again.

I had thought when I saw Taichi, I would run and jump into his open arms, but with the guard watching us, I feel like we're fish in a bowl. My skirt is creased from the drive here, and my curls are a mess from the windy walk from the sentry post, where I left my mother, to this building.

Taichi recovers first. He gestures to a table near the window. "Here."

I sit in the chair he pulled out for me, and I smooth my skirt over my crossed legs. Taichi takes the chair next to me, and beneath the table, his knee bumps mine. We look at each other, and I swear I can hear the seconds ticking away, faster and faster.

His face is several shades darker and thinner. His hair longer than I've ever seen it.

"I can't believe you're really here." His voice holds awe.

I can't get mine to go above a whisper. "Me neither."

"When you didn't come yesterday, I thought I wouldn't see you."

"I know. I didn't think so either. My mother is the one who made it happen." I realize I'm fidgeting with a curl, and I clasp my hands in my lap. "My father hasn't been feeling well. Starting yesterday, he didn't have much energy and couldn't keep food down, so we stayed around the cabin. He wanted one more day to recover, but said he didn't want us just sitting there staring at him all day today. Said he was just going to be reading, and that we should get out and enjoy the scenery."

My fingers are in my hair again—why am I such a nervous wreck?—and I again knit my fingers together in my lap. "I had talked to Mama before we left about how close we would be to you, and she said to Daddy this morning, 'Evalina noticed that we're pretty close to where the Hamasaki family is living now. If it's fine with you, I think we'll drive over and pay them a visit.' He said that was a fine idea, and he sends his love."

Taichi just looks at me. Why doesn't he say anything?

I have to again take my hands out of my hair. "He would have liked to see you too, but didn't feel up to travel, of course."

"I'm sorry he isn't feeling well. Especially on a rare vacation. But Evalina . . ." His face is strangely blank of emotion as he says, "You couldn't have been close enough for it to truly make sense to drive all this way."

That's classic Taichi. It's okay for him to inconvenience himself for me, but never the other way around.

I press my knee tighter against his. "You don't get to make those kinds of decisions for me."

His mouth flickers into a warm smile, the first I've seen since April. "So your mother is here too?"

I nod. "They wouldn't let her come in because her name isn't on the guest pass. The guard acted like he was doing me a favor by letting me come in, even though the pass expired yesterday."

"Yes, I'm a little surprised they let you in. They like their rules."

My throat tries to close, and I swallow. "I didn't realize it would be like this."

Guilt shows in Taichi's eyes. He seems to consider a moment before saying simply, "I know."

"How could you . . . ?" Tears prick my eyes. I stop short of accusing him of lying. I don't want to spend our precious minutes fighting.

Beneath the table, he holds one of my hands between his. "I didn't want you to worry."

Again, it's okay for him to worry about me, but heaven forbid my thoughts be preoccupied with the suffering of him and his family. "I understand. But, Taichi, I want to know what your life is *really* like. I want you to trust me with that."

"Of course I trust you, I just . . ." Taichi trails off, but grips my hand harder. His shirt is one I've seen before, but now it's fraying at the collar. What state are his shoes in? Is there a place to buy clothes here? Should I send him some?

"It's really not so bad here, Evalina. We get along fine."

If we were at home, that would be enough to send me into a fit of yelling. *Stop lying to me! People who love each other are honest. I want you to confide in me, not push me away!*

But we're not at home. I pitch my voice low. "Just the view from the window is enough. This looks just like it did at Tanforan."

My brain ticks through the list of horrible things the Bishops had reported from their friends who had been sent there. Toilets and showers with no partitions. Living in poorly constructed houses with strangers, and nothing but blankets to hang between you. Long waits for every meal, every load of laundry, every shirt ironed.

"We only have a short while together," Taichi says. "Let's talk about more pleasant things. Tell me about Yosemite."

"I can tell you that stuff in letters. It doesn't matter."

"It matters to me. It makes the outside world seem not so far away."

The silence that falls between us is thick with the pressure to make the words count, to make the visit meaningful. But every word I speak feels clumsy, knocking into topics and sensitivities that I don't intend.

I swallow away my accusations and questions. He's right. We don't have to have that conversation right now. "Yosemite is really beautiful. I knew the mountains would be big, I just didn't expect them to be *so* big. Kinda like here."

We both look out the window at Mount Williamson and her neighbors. Dust swirls by.

"Is it always this windy?"

He hesitates. "Yes."

Had he been considering telling me no? I've always thought of Taichi as being someone whom I can totally trust. I hate that our conversation is shrouded in questions about whether he's telling me the truth or not.

I blink away the tears that are trying to gather. "I had a letter from Diego before I left."

Taichi's gaze slides over to me. "Oh?"

"You probably did too. It didn't say much. That he misses home but is doing okay at basic training. It's hard, but he likes it. That sort of thing." I fidget with the hem of my skirt. "He probably told you that he and Ruby split?"

"He did." Taichi sounds as though he's choosing his words carefully. "Said she didn't want to continue long distance."

"That's what he told me too."

"What do you think of that?"

I blink at him, caught off guard by the question. "Well, it's not exactly easy, is it? But nothing worthwhile ever is."

Taichi is silent as he continues to stare out the window.

There's a tension between us that I can't decode. That I don't have *time* to decode. I steal a glance at the clock. How have twenty minutes ticked away already?

"How is Aiko doing?" I ask.

"As strange as it may sound, she seems better here than she did at home." Taichi's gaze loses its far away quality, and he again looks directly at me. "She likes her work at the hospital, and she's pretty popular at the dances. She's been seeing this fellow who works with her. He's her first boyfriend my parents have approved of. That's a nice change."

Something inside me twinges. "There are dances?"

"Yep. Much as I try, I can't seem to escape them." Taichi's smile is wry. "Back home, I could skip and people assumed you had other stuff going on. But here they know that you don't. My buddy, James, would go to a dance every night if he could."

I try to scrub away the image of Taichi dancing with cute Japanese American girls. I don't want to say anything that makes me sound completely jealous. "And do you dance with lots of girls?"

Well, that failed.

Taichi blinks at me. "Of course not. I go sometimes, but I don't dance." He studies my face for a beat of silence and pitches his voice low, "How can you not know that I would never do that to you?"

I'm pleased . . . but hasn't he been asked to give up enough? Should he really have to give up a simple pleasure like dancing just because I'm being silly and jealous? I shift on the hard chair. "It's just a dance, Taichi. I would understand."

His smile is tender. "I hate dancing. I certainly don't mind using you as an excuse."

My heart warms even more. "You use me as an excuse?"

He squeezes my hand. "I do. I tell them my girl is vicious, and it would be dangerous for anyone to dance with me."

A giggle escapes me, and Taichi grins back. For a smidge of a moment, everything feels blissfully normal and happy.

"Five minutes," the guard says, and I jump. To us he adds, "For them. Ten for you."

I grip Taichi's hand. In ten minutes this will just be a memory. What do I say to ensure that it's a *good* memory? That we used our time the best we possibly could?

We look at each other. Will we ever be able to communicate the way my parents do, with just their facial expressions? Will there ever be children of ours to be mystified and annoyed by it? That there could ever be anything besides this—Taichi stuck within these lines our government has drawn for him, and me stuck outside—feels impossible in this moment.

The other friends are saying their goodbyes. Deep bows and hugs. I can't start crying because my handkerchief is in my handbag, which is with my mother. My jaw trembles from how hard I clench my teeth.

"How long until you get home?" Taichi asks conversationally, but his voice wavers.

"We drive back across the park tomorrow, and then set off for home after that."

Taichi's gaze tracks the families, who exit through separate doors, and he crushes my hand. "Who's running the restaurant while you're gone? Mr. Esposito?"

"Yes. My father has never been away this long. The first few days of our trip, he kept saying things like, 'The lunch rush should be starting now. I hope Franco remembered to slice the mozz.' But he seems to have stopped thinking about it so much."

"I'm sorry he had to spend vacation time in bed."

With the other families gone, I feel as though the guard

is sitting at the table with us. "Today is the only day it really altered plans, and . . . well. That's not so bad."

Taichi's smile seems self-conscious. "Tell your mother thank you for me. This was incredibly kind of her."

"If we'd known we were coming, we would have brought something. Can we send you anything?"

"No." He drops his voice even lower. "Seeing you was more than enough."

I look at him, words eluding me.

Taichi stares back. He opens his mouth.

"Sorry, you two." The guard calls from behind his desk. "Time's up."

We stand, and Taichi offers me a slight bow of his head, the way he used to back when I was just the restaurant owner's daughter and he was the farmer delivering our produce. "Thank you for coming."

The same generic phrase I say to all our guests after they've dined at Alessandro's. Not exactly the parting words I want from Taichi.

The guard approaches with my yellow visitor's pass in hand. This is it.

I throw my arms around Taichi's neck and squeeze. He hesitates a moment, and then his hands fall light on my waist. "I love you," I whisper fiercely into his ear. The words tumble out again as I squeeze him one more time. "I love you."

We release each other. The guard and Taichi are both blurry, and when I wipe the tears from my eyes, I wish I hadn't. The guard looks stunned, and Taichi looks embarrassed.

I embarrassed him. My own face burns.

The guard clears his throat. "You go this way." He points to Taichi's door, and then shoves my pass into my hand. "The sentry will need to see this."

"Travel safely, Evalina." Taichi offers a polite smile, and then turns and walks straight to the door the guard pointed him toward.

"Tell your family I say hello," I call. "I'll . . . I'll write."

At the doorway, I turn for one more glimpse of Taichi, but he's already gone.

CHAPTER TWENTY-ONE

Taichi

She drove all the way here for *that*.

I drag my feet—Mother would scold me for stirring up so much dust, like it can be avoided here—as I meander along the fence near the entrance. Is Mrs. Cassano in one of those cars in the parking lot? Is she in another building? What must she be thinking as she looks around? Surely she no longer buys that Evalina and I are just friends. Did Evalina tell her parents about us? After seeing how far my family has fallen, how could they ever approve of the match?

And what am *I* going to say to *my* family? That it was a case of mistaken identity? That the visitor was really here for someone else? My mother would see through that in an instant. Not only that, but Manzanar is too small a place to keep a secret. I was seen with Evalina. I will have to tell the truth.

I look through the fence just in time to catch a glimpse of Mrs. Cassano and Evalina in the parking lot. Her navy-blue skirt shimmies in the wind, and she leans heavily on her mother, who has an arm around her shoulders.

That's what time with me does. It burdens Evalina with sadness.

I loiter until their vehicle has pulled away, and then I dawdle back to my block. There's an aching hollowness inside like

I haven't felt since that guard pulled her away from the bus back in April. I had forgotten how much being away from her hurts.

When I open the door to our apartment, I find Mother and Father seated on stools built from scrap lumber. Their heads are bent toward each other in quiet conversation.

Father pats the edge of my cot. "Come have a seat, Taichi."

I do as I'm told. I've *always* done what I'm told, with one giant exception.

I look at them, and they look back. With the sun high in the sky, the barrack is dark and unusually quiet. A rare moment when all the other families are out.

"Who came to visit you?" Father asks.

I had hoped to lie. The truth pours out. "Evalina Cassano. She was . . . in the area."

Mother and Father look at me with steady, unsurprised expressions.

"She was at the station to tell us goodbye, and now she came here to visit you." Father speaks slow and soft. "And why did she do this, son?"

They've both already guessed. I can see them bracing for the confirmation.

"Because we've been seeing each other."

Mother's gaze drops to her lap. Father winces.

The barrack creaks under a gust of wind while I wait for them to respond.

"This is not like you, Taichi." Father's voice sounds bruised with disappointment. "From Aiko, I might have expected this, but you . . . You have always been our good boy."

"I'm sorry I lied." I bow my head low. "Please, forgive me."

"Miss Cassano is a nice girl," Mother says. "You cannot do this to her."

The words are a punch. Even to my own parents, I'm something bad for Evalina.

"I really care about her." I can easily imagine the panic that would strike their faces if I used the word 'love' to describe what I feel for Evalina. "This isn't like it was with Aiko and Dennis."

Mother flinches at his name. We never use it.

"That does not make this okay, son." Father rubs at his arthritic knuckles. "You know it is unfair to both of you to stay in a relationship that cannot lead to marriage."

I could argue that the laws against me marrying Evalina are morally wrong. Or that if we lived in another state, our marriage would *not* be against the law. Just against societal expectations.

"What about the Yoneda family?" I say to my hands.

"You are just a boy," Father says. "You do not understand what that choice involves."

That's unfair. Boys my age are fighting in battles all over the world.

Mother bends to catch my eye. "Mr. and Mrs. Yoneda were already married before the evacuation. Surely, my son, after what has happened to our people, you would not want this for Miss Cassano."

Shame burns bitter in my throat. This is true, I don't want this for her. And we have no idea how long we'll be held here, or if we'll ever be released. Even when we are, am I really so selfish that I would saddle her with a life of scraping by and making do? She's so smart, she's the first in her family to go to college. With an academic scholarship, no less. The fellows she'll meet there could offer her so much more, and I'll just be some "Jap" nobody without a cent to my name.

"You're right," I say thickly to my dust-covered shoes. "I'll end it."

Aiko rolls her eyes at me. "Don't be an idiot, Taichi. You don't have to listen to Mother and Father. You should make your own decisions."

I should have predicted this response. "But what if I think they're right?"

"But you *don't* think they're right."

"Maybe I do."

"No, you don't." She jams her nurse's cap onto her head with more force than necessary. "Not really."

"Would you keep your voice down?"

We're in the barrack getting ready for our shifts, me for dinner, and her for an overnight at the hospital. Unlike when I had my conversation with Mother and Father this afternoon, we can hear the other families moving around on their sides of the blankets.

Aiko purses her lips as she fusses with her hatpins. "Protest if you wish, but I know you never thought you and Evalina were headed 'nowhere.'"

That's true. I had been intrigued by her since that first conversation—*you should charge more for your blackberries, you know*—and had spent several months pushing away my attraction to her. There were many reasons to not pursue Evalina, including that neither of our families would approve, and the reality that she was dating the son of her father's business partner.

I did my best to ignore that Evalina started coming alone on Saturday mornings to the market. That while she had sometimes been present during Monday and Thursday deliveries at Alessandro's, soon she was always there. And how sometimes I would glance at her, and find she was already looking at me.

One Saturday morning, a few months after we met, Evalina was already at the market when I arrived. For the first time, it was just me and Diego who had come, not my mother. And, of course, Diego put on his most charming smile and flirted fruitlessly.

Evalina left her purchases with us to pick up later—was I imagining that this was yet another way she'd found to steal more time together?—and went to take care of the rest of her shopping.

Diego's eyes followed her as she walked away. "I'm not sure I've ever met a girl who's less interested in me."

The look he gave me was pointed, and I felt heat crawling up the back of my neck. "I guess it was bound to happen one of these days."

Diego smirked. "I think it was less about my charm and more about her being preoccupied with someone else."

"I think she has a boyfriend," was all I had time to say before we both had to help approaching customers.

Customers came so steadily Diego and I didn't get another chance to talk. Half an hour later, I spotted Evalina approaching the stand again. I smiled at her, but the woman I was helping was very indecisive about her spinach purchase.

My hopeful heart deflated when Diego finished with his customer first, and he began chatting with Evalina. I would probably still be assisting this woman by the time they wrapped up their polite conversation. Maybe I wouldn't even get to say goodbye to her.

"Is there any more spinach that I can look through?" the woman asked, peering behind the table, as though we hid the best of our crops back there.

I hoped my smile would mask my impatience. Just as I was about to respond, Diego stepped between us. "Ma'am, spinach happens to be my expertise. Let me see if I can help you." He glanced at me and gave a sharp nod toward Evalina.

Her smile made me feel like fireworks were going off inside my chest.

"How was the rest of your shopping, Miss Cassano?" I asked.

"Fine." From within her shopping bag, she pulled a blackberry she had purchased from us earlier and popped it into her mouth. "The Johnson family has strawberries that aren't nearly as pretty as yours, and they're selling them for a dime more a basket. It's outrageous."

I wanted to say something witty or at least mildly interesting. All I could think of was, "That's a lot."

Evalina swallowed. "You know, you could call me Evalina." She dropped her gaze to her saddle shoes. "If you'd like."

I had thought her name hundreds of times in my head, but I had not yet spoken it. "Evalina. You may call me Taichi."

She pulled at one of her windblown curls. "Taichi." Then she glanced at Diego. "Your friend said that you were wanting to take a walk down by the bay."

My throat went dry. I felt both deeply grateful for and deeply embarrassed by Diego.

I couldn't bring myself to say it was true, to lie to Evalina, even about something so small. "I would enjoy a walk if . . ." The words almost stayed in, almost remained suffocated by my fear. "If you would go with me."

When Evalina beamed at me, I knew I hadn't been imagining the clues these last weeks. That what I had been feeling for her was not one-sided. Only . . .

"Though, if your boyfriend wouldn't like that, I understand."

I could hardly stand to look her in the eyes as I said it, but her smile dimmed only slightly. "Tony and I have been broken up for over a month. So, a walk would be fine."

I tried to not smile too broadly as we strolled away, and I ignored Diego's cheerful, "See you later, Tai!"

From that first walk, I had known two things with absolute certainty:

This was a hard road we were starting down.

And Evalina Cassano was worth every bump and twist.

But we could never have imagined Pearl Harbor. Or the executive order that had me living inside barbed wire. How could I keep her chained to me through something like this?

To Aiko, I gesture to our sparse corner of the barrack. "What if we're still here in five years? In ten? It's just not fair for me to ask Evalina to wait for me, especially when she could marry someone else."

Aiko's scowl deepens. "Evalina doesn't want to marry someone else."

"Oh, really?" I pull my shoelaces with such force, I'm surprised they don't break. "She told you that during one of your many conversations?"

Aiko sighs. "She doesn't have to tell me. I've seen the way she looks at you. And the way you look at her. That's enough for me to know."

Aiko rummages for her shoes under her bed. While our heads are bent together, she says quietly, "I think you're so tired of having everything taken away from you, that you're just trying to beat her to the punch. But I don't think that punch is going to come, Taichi. She loves you."

Was it really just hours ago that Evalina was brave enough to hug me in front of the guard? To tell me she loved me? And I had just stood there like an idiot, feeling ashamed of how my clothes were coated in dust, of how I must smell, of how we had an armed guard in the room with us because I'm Japanese.

"I'm not asking for your opinion, Aiko." The words come out cold. "You asked what happened with Mother and Father, and I'm telling you."

Aiko's face turns stony. "Excuse me for caring about you. I think you're really good for each other, and I hate to see you throw it away because you're trying to make this"—she gestures to our surroundings—"easier. Because this is temporary."

"We don't know that."

Aiko gives a huffy sigh. "Fine. Throw away everything you've worked for. Break Evalina's heart. I don't care."

She slams the door behind her when she leaves. Several minutes later, I do too.

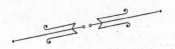

Dear Evalina,

There's no easy way to write this, but after your visit, it was clear to me that it's not fair to continue this relationship. We don't know how long this war will last, or who we will be when it's over. I just wish I had realized this before you took the trouble to visit.

I'm sorry to have to do this through a letter. I know you'll be very upset, but I hope that once you've given it some thought you'll realize that this is the best thing for both of us.

Sincerely,
Taichi Hamasaki

Evalina

We've been on the road for at least thirty minutes, my mind numb from the noise of the tires against the blacktop, before Mama speaks.

"I think that's the saddest place I've ever been."

I turn away from the repetitive landscape—dust and sagebrush and tumbleweeds—and look at her. Her cheeks are wet.

"I guess I knew they probably hadn't been sent anywhere real nice. But I didn't think . . ." Mama trails off. "I couldn't see much from where I was, but there were so many guards. And I could hear these young Japanese girls playing hopscotch and singing one of those songs that you and Gia used to sing when you were little."

"Thank you for coming." Even though right now I'm wishing we hadn't. There's a part of me—a part of me that I'm ashamed of—that wishes I still believed the glossy stories Taichi had told in his letters.

"It was a worthwhile journey," Mama says. "Just a very hard one."

We drive past the café where we'd stopped for lunch several hours ago, even though I had been too nervous to eat much. What kind of food is Taichi served? He had been noticeably thinner when I hugged him.

"Evalina." Mama's voice has turned firm. "Will you please

203

trust me enough to tell me the truth about you and Taichi? I know you're . . . interested in him."

I take a bracing breath. "I am."

What will she say? Will she lecture? Will she cry?

"Thank you," Mama says. "And is he interested in you?"

I should tell her we've been together for a year now. After what she did today, making it possible for me to see Taichi, she deserves the truth.

But I'm too chicken to give it to her.

I swallow. "I think so."

Seconds tick by without any more words. Then minutes. Does she know I'm lying?

"We've always hoped that you and Tony might find your way back to each other," Mama says. "I suppose now that he is seeing someone else, we really should give up on that."

That's really not the direction I expected the conversation to go. "Tony and I are good friends, but that's all."

She has nothing to say about my admission? No admonishment?

"I understand. Tony is good for you, but if you don't feel that way about him, you can't help it."

I bite my lip. Why are we talking about Tony? I should be grateful, though. It's not like I want her grilling me about Taichi. I'll just let the subject drop . . .

"So, you're not going to lecture me about having feelings for Taichi?"

"Would you like me to?"

"Well, no . . ."

"Would it change how you feel?"

"Probably not."

Mama shrugs. "Okay, then."

She must feel my gaze on her, because she looks at me

after a bit and smiles. "I'm not so old that I've forgotten what it's like to be young, Evalina. We don't always want what's best for us, and being told we can't have it—or shouldn't want it—never makes it better. You'll find your way. I'm sure of it."

The implication is clear. She's decided my interest in Taichi is a passing fancy, and she's not going to expend the energy to fight with me about a boy whom she believes I'll be over before too long.

My nails bite crescents into my palms. "What if that doesn't happen?"

"We will cross that bridge if we get there, Evalina." Mama's sentence is a clear punctuation mark on the conversation.

Less than two hours later, we pull up to our rented cabin. My head is still a mess of fiery arguments about why Taichi is good for me, guilt over not being more truthful with Mama, and anger from what I saw at Manzanar.

When we let ourselves in, it's clear Daddy had been asleep. He cracks open his eyes and smiles at us. "There's my two favorite girls."

Mama drops her handbag onto a chair and sits on the bed beside Daddy. "How are you, dear?" Without waiting for an answer, she presses her wrist to his forehead. "You're much cooler."

"I told you I thought my fever broke overnight."

Mama smiles. "I shouldn't have doubted."

Daddy pushes himself to sit up, disturbing the book that had been fanned across his chest. "How was the visit?"

He looks from Mama to me, but I feel as though my tongue is glued to the roof of my mouth. How do I answer that? I don't know how the visit was, really.

"It was good that we went," Mama says when I don't speak. "But it was hard to see."

Yes, that's a good way to put it. And it was especially hard to see how much Taichi didn't want me there.

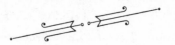

Friday, June 26, 1942

Mama has just turned on the stove to make coffee when there's a characteristic rapid-fire knock on the door.

Mama arches her eyebrows at me. "Gia must've missed you. Don't go outside in those pajamas."

I pat my hair, which doesn't know what to do with itself now that we're back in the humid San Francisco air, and open the door wider than Mama would like.

Gia beams at me from the doorstep. "Here's-your-mail-and-I'm-engaged!"

Before I've even processed what she's said, she's pushed the stack of mail into my arms and raised her hand so I can see the diamond chip gleaming on her finger.

I grab her hand. "No . . ."

"Yes! We're getting married in two weeks before he's deployed, and I've been dying to tell you!" She throws her arms around my neck, and the mail crumples between us. "I'm engaged!"

Mama must have heard the commotion, because she has materialized in the entryway, asking to see the ring and offering her congratulations. I force myself to smile, to echo her words. Nothing good could come from any other kind of response. Not at this point.

Mama hurries back to the kitchen to take the coffee off the burner.

"You will be my maid of honor, obviously," Gia says as we move into the living room. "My mother is still a wreck over not having time for our family from New York to come, but the Navy isn't very flexible . . ."

I flip through the mail quickly, finding only one letter from Taichi. Postmarked the Monday after my visit so that I would have something waiting for me when I got home. How sweet.

I tuck it into the pocket of my pajamas and return my attention to Gia, who hasn't let up the conversation.

". . . just as legal in a courthouse, you know? But of course our families would never go for that. Oh!" Gia flutters her hands. "I have to tell you how he proposed! We were going to one of the Navy dances, and he says to me, 'Lots of people here tonight think we're getting married.' And I said to him, 'Why is that?' And he said—this is so romantic, Evalina, you're just going to die—'Because I told them we are,' and then he pulled out the ring and put it on my finger! Can you believe it?"

That Lorenzo didn't even wait for her to say yes? Why, yes, I can. But, again, I've already expressed every concern about Lorenzo. Not celebrating with Gia is only going to wedge us even further apart.

"Two weeks, huh?" I say with the brightest smile I can muster. "We'll have a lot to do."

"Yes, we will! What are you doing today? Do you want to come dress shopping with me? I'll have to buy off-the-rack, but I know with your help, we can find something great."

Barely two months ago, we went shopping for Gia's prom dress. How is it time to shop for a wedding dress *now*?

"Of course. I'll just need to get dressed."

"Great!" Gia springs up from the couch. "I promised

Mother that I would help with cleaning this morning, so I'll run home and do that, and then we can go! I'll ring you when I'm done!"

Her exuberance seems to prevent her from realizing my lack thereof, and I'm grateful. In a few hours, the shock will have worn off, and I'll be able to fake enthusiasm with much more ease.

Back in the kitchen, Mama raises her eyebrows at me.

I shrug. "It's not like it's a total surprise."

"Isabella will no doubt be delighted as well." Mama's heavy sigh reveals that her feelings are not so different from my own. "I need to wash up so I can get to the market. There's no food in this house."

She drops a kiss on my head as she walks by. "Take my advice, Evalina. Do not make strife with your friend over this. I think she's going to need you in the years to come."

I unfortunately agree. I sit at the table with my cup of coffee, ruminating on what life will look like in two weeks when Gia is a married woman, and I'm still just me. Though if Lorenzo is shipping out soon, I guess it may not look very different at all. She would still be at home, living up in her room. How strange.

My pocket crinkles as I take a sip of coffee, and I remember Taichi's letter. I can hear the creaking of Mama moving about in her room upstairs, so I pull it from my pocket and tear into the envelope.

As soon as I see the letter only takes up half a page, I know my day is going to get worse.

Dear Taichi,

I have been in shock over your letter for days. Every response I have attempted has been long and wretched.

What I've decided is this isn't a decision you get to make for me. I think you're trying to protect me, same as when you lied to me in your letters about what life is like for you. I don't need to be protected, Taichi.

You said before you left that we could get through this if you knew that when you got on the bus to come home, I would be waiting on the other end for you. I told you then that I would be, and that's not a vow I'm going to break.

I refuse to choose something else simply because it could be easier for now. I will continue to write to you, and I will continue to be faithful to our commitment, and you cannot force me to do otherwise.

I love you,
Evalina

CHAPTER TWENTY-THREE

Taichi

Friday, September 5, 1942

There's clearly something wrong with me, because every other person in my generation is smiling and having a great time here at the dance. But the pulsing of the music and the rising temperature of the mess hall only make my head hurt.

I move over to a window, hoping for a bit of fresh air. How can people stand to dance when it's so hot? I shouldn't have let Aiko's words bother me so much. When I said I wasn't coming tonight, she'd scoffed, "What are you going to do? Sit on your cot and stare at Evalina's picture? Read her letters again and think about how stupid you've been?"

Back home, when she was sullen and reclusive, I had left her alone. Why couldn't she return the favor?

"Hey, there you are." James materializes at the window. He holds hands with Margaret, and Rose trails behind them. Like always, the girls took special care with their appearance for tonight, curling their hair and wearing their nicest skirts.

I tug at my collar. "It's warm in here."

Margaret fans herself with her free hand. "It's warm everywhere. But the band is swell tonight, don't you think?

Last Friday the guitar was out of tune, and it ruined Rose's entire night."

Rose plays with one of her curls, just like Evalina does when she's nervous. "How can I be expected to keep rhythm if Tetsuno can't manage to hit the right notes?"

"You should be able to dance with no problems tonight, Rose." James punctuates his statement by drilling me with eye contact.

I try not to notice. I never should've told him that I broke up with Evalina, but at the time it had felt easier than pretending everything was okay. He had assumed that whoever my girlfriend was, she was Japanese and had been sent to another camp. I hadn't corrected him.

"Well, Margaret and I are off to dance." James cuts a not-so-subtle look at Rose before returning an unblinking stare to me.

My breath hitches in my chest, and my gaze flies to the exit. How did I let it get so far away from me?

Rose directs her focus on her saddle shoes, and it's clear she appreciates James's hint about as much as I do. My conscience nags at me to not let her wallow in a pit of embarrassment when I have the power to reach down my hand and help.

But I detest dancing.

I unclench my teeth. "Rose, would you like to dance?"

Her gaze meets mine before diving back to the safety of her shoes. "Okay."

Despite how sweaty I am, I feel cold as I survey the dance floor. Why couldn't a slower song be playing? "Okay . . ."

Rose looks up and giggles shyly. "It doesn't look like *you* want to, Taichi."

"It's not that." It's totally that. "I just . . . I've never been very good at this."

Or I assume I'm not. The only place I've ever danced is in

the privacy of my room, when I practiced because I thought there might be a chance to take Evalina to dances at college.

"It's easier than it looks." Rose takes a tentative step toward the dance floor.

I'm not sure I believe her, but I also don't know how to back out now.

On the edge of the floor, Rose pivots toward me. I glance at the other boys, and then with a hard swallow, I mimic their stance. Regret stirs inside me as I entwine my fingers through Rose's, and let my left hand fall as lightly as possible on her waist. My hands remember touching Evalina when she was bold enough to hug me goodbye in the visiting room, and how I responded by breaking things off.

"I think you're supposed to move when you dance," Rose says in a teasing whisper.

Around us, couples whirl and laugh; I'm just standing here like an idiot. My face grows hotter every second, and I want to punch James for manipulating me into this situation.

"I'm sorry, I told you I'm not a good dancer."

I pull my hand off Rose's waist and open my fingers to release her hand, but her fingers crush mine, and her arm clamps, smashing the careful space I had left between us.

"You are not leaving me here on the floor." Her words are steel and her expression so fierce, she reminds me of Evalina. "That would be humiliating."

"Okay." I swallow. "I won't."

We're still up against each other. The other couples are foxtrotting. I can do that. Not in the fluid style that James is, leading Margaret around the floor with ease, but I can make do for a couple minutes until the song is over.

I move my left foot forward as she moves her right back, and I breathe a bit easier now that we aren't mashed up against each other. How do people carry on conversations while they dance? My brain is absorbed with counting off steps and not crushing Evalina's toes. I mean, *Rose's* toes.

It's September fifth. Evalina will move into her dorm room this weekend, per the letter I received yesterday. Her letters have continued with the same frequency and devotion as when I first left, with only a bit of detectable frostiness since June. Every day I think about writing her back, but for what purpose outside of my own selfish desire? Nothing has changed in our circumstances.

"When your face looks like that, where is it you go?"

I blink and find Rose staring up at me inquisitively. I step on her foot, and she winces. "Sorry. What do you mean?"

"I often see you looking sad and far away like that. What are you thinking about?"

How unforgivably rude is it to talk about another girl while you're dancing?

"Home," I say. "What would've been."

"That's what I guessed." Rose's eyelashes flutter against her cheeks as she looks down again. "Margaret has also mentioned you used to have a sweetheart at another camp. I thought you might be thinking of her."

Again, I feel her foot beneath mine. "Good grief, I'm sorry. I can't seem to think about the steps when I talk."

"If you stop focusing on getting the steps just right, you might enjoy dancing more."

My face burns. "I told you I'm a bad dancer."

Rose's fingers are stiff inside mine. "I know you didn't even want to ask me, but James made you."

"James didn't make me."

"He did. He knew you would be too polite to not ask. This whole thing was a mistake."

We turn about the floor in mutual silence for another minute. I'm still reciting the steps in my head, and I'm sure I look like I'm dancing with a coat hanger in my collared shirt, but at least I'm not stepping on her toes. And at least the song must be close to over.

"Why were you and your girlfriend sent to different places?"

I hesitate. "We lived in different communities."

"Where is she now? Ouch!"

I've landed on her foot again, just as the song has come to a close. "Sorry," I mutter. "I'll see you later."

I flee the dance floor that I never should have stepped foot on, and I leave behind the suffocating heat of the room for the waning heat of outdoors.

That was mortifying. It'll be so uncomfortable when I see Rose tomorrow at breakfast. I know James is just trying to help me move on, but I don't want to. If anything, I want to move backward. I want to go back to the time before the evacuation. Before Pearl Harbor. I want it to be Thanksgiving 1941, when Evalina and I stole our first kiss at Golden Gate Park.

This will only lead to heartbreak. That's what I'd said just before my lips touched hers. I'd so wanted to be wrong.

My tangle of thoughts is interrupted by the clatter of applause and rumble of feet stomping. I look about. What block am I even on?

The clapping and stomping dies down, and from a nearby mess hall, Japanese rings out. This must be an Issei or Kibei meeting, because all the Nisei prefer to speak English.

I draw close enough to peek in the door. Hundreds are packed into the mess hall to hear the speaker, who yells in high-pitched, agitated Japanese. I wedge myself into the back. At 5-foot-seven, I'm one of the tallest in the room, but there's still such a mass of people, mostly men, that I can't see who the speaker is.

My brain was once slow at translating Japanese, but it's improved with practice over the last few months. Even still, everyone is already applauding when I've translated his shouts:

"August's food was even worse! I lost many pounds, and I know many of you did too. We must demand more meat! More eggs and butter!"

Well, I'll applaud to that. Despite the meeting Ted and I had with the assistant camp director, the amount of meat the kitchens have been allotted to serve per day was reduced even more due to "budget cuts."

"The administration has no sympathy for anyone who is Japanese! Nash is a dictator like Stalin."

Everyone around me bursts into applause, but the mention of Roy Nash, the camp director, in the same sentence as the Russian dictator leaves me feeling as though all the blood has drained from my face. Can you truly say a thing like that with no consequences?

"Heil Hitler!" The call goes up from a man toward the back. I can't make out who it is.

That's some kind of joke, right? But several more call out, "Heil Hitler!"

I take a step back, only to discover I'm already flat against the rough pine of the mess hall wall.

The person in front of me shifts, and I finally see the man who's yelling. From his balding head, I would guess he's in his forties, maybe fifties. His face is round, pudgy even, and that might make him look younger if it wasn't for his unshaven face.

With both hands, he holds a piece of paper over his head. "I am circulating a petition to oust Nash! To oust the Stalin of Manzanar!"

There's more feet stomping and applause.

"Signing the petition shows you have Japanese national spirit! It says, 'I am 100-percent Japanese!'"

"I am, Joe!" yells an exuberant audience member. "I am 100-percent Japanese!"

Joe. This must be the Joe Kurihara whom Ted has spoken of. I angle for a view of those around the stage, searching for Raymond Yamishi and the Black Dragons, but I'm so far back, I can't see well enough.

"We are Japanese!" many in the audience chant. "We are Japanese!"

A fear like I've never known before crawls across my skin. What if somebody sees me here and believes I'm betraying my country? I look toward the door, but find even the bits of space that had been available when I came in are now gone.

"Those Nisei who claim they are Americans are fools!" yells Joe from the stage, his voice rising high. "They think they're American citizens? Let me see them walk out that front gate without getting a bullet to the back! Then maybe I will believe that they are citizens!"

I'm surrounded by more applause and more chants of "We are Japanese! We are Japanese!"

Joe allows the crowd's energy to bubble for a few seconds, and then he raises his hands in a bid for their silence. "I have heard—his voice is solemn—there are Nisei spies among us."

Boos rise up among the crowd, and my face goes hot at the accusation. At the memory of Raymond Yamishi accusing me of just that. I sense several heads turning my way—I appear to be the only Nisei here in the back—and I let out a loud, "Boo" with the rest of the crowd.

"And they are sending reports outside!" Joe's voice rises

loud above the booing. "They're sending them to the JACL! They're sending them to the FBI!"

"Down with those rats!" many yell, along with, "Strike them down!"

Somewhere around me, a man yells, "Cut their heads off!"

Those who had been by the door must have decided this wasn't the place for them, because my escape route is again clear. I want to sprint away from the room and leave Joe and his angry mob behind, but as a Nisei, what would happen if the crowd took notice of me fleeing? Would they chase me down and beat me? Or worse?

"Even if the army or the FBI take me into custody, I will remain Japanese! I will continue to fight for the rights of our people in this country that claims belief in democracy!" Joe yells from the stage as I inch toward the exit. "Don't get scared! Look to our brothers in Japan who are making a great sacrifice in their fight of the enemy. Let us follow suit!"

Chants of "We are Japanese!" follow me out the door.

My breath comes in bursts as I run for my barrack. With every footfall, their patriotic chants seem to echo in my head. I swear I can still hear them hours later as I lie in bed, watching the crisscross of searchlights out the window while sleep eludes me.

Evalina

Tuesday, September 8, 1942

It isn't a very mature thought to have on my first day of college, but I desperately miss mornings at home. I miss coming downstairs to the sound of Mama stirring oatmeal on the stove, of Daddy getting coffee prepared. I miss the cheerful, "Good morning, sweetheart," greeting, and the creak of the wooden chair I've always sat in.

But Grace Bishop is practically glowing on the other side of the table. She smiles so big, she can hardly manage to take a drink of her milk.

I pierce the peel of my orange with my thumbnail. An orange for good luck. "Aren't you nervous?"

"Maybe a little, but mostly I'm excited. Aren't you excited?"

My stomach flutters. "I'm too nervous to know."

"You should be even more excited than I am. This is the first day of the life that *you* are choosing. Have you thought about it that way? Don't you think that's exciting?"

"I guess so." I peel off a wedge of orange. My stomach feels too tight to accept food.

Grace digs into her oatmeal with gusto. "Who picked the

classes you're taking? You did! It's not like high school where you had to take everything that everybody else took."

"Comparative Politics is the only political science class I get to take this semester. The rest are all general education requirements."

Grace raises her eyebrows at me. "Why are you determined to not be excited?"

"I'm excited, I'm just . . ."

Homesick. Achingly homesick for my life a year ago. When I was at the same school with the same kids I had known all my life. When Taichi and I were still untainted by Pearl Harbor and the evacuation. When my off-beat plans to major in political science and go to law school felt exciting because it was still so far away. When I *knew* I belonged.

The clock ticks ever closer to my first college class, which happens to be the one I'm most nervous about. "What if I'm the only girl in Comparative Politics?"

Grace shrugs. "What if you are?"

"I'll feel uncomfortable."

"But you'll survive." Grace's no-nonsense tone makes me think of her mother.

"I know I will, I just wish I was headed to Crocheting Potholders 101 or something."

Grace hoots so loudly with laughter, others turn and look at us. "That's because it's easier to not care. You don't care about potholders, but you do care about politics. To care means to be brave." Grace points her spoon at my plate. "Eat your food, or you'll wish you had in about an hour."

I make myself eat all my orange, and I take three bites of cereal before declaring myself done. Grace gives me a disapproving kind of look that I imagine her mother wears on occasion, but says nothing as I throw the rest away.

"Have you heard from Taichi recently?" Grace asks as we walk along the bustling pathway from our dormitory cafeteria toward our first classes.

I hesitate. "Not since coming to school."

"We don't hear from our friends as much now that they're at their final place in Utah." Grace's mouth is set in a grim line, like it always is when we discuss the camps. "I don't know if they're busier, or if there just isn't much to say. The last letter we got talked about how much monotony there is in their days. They have some family in Baltimore, and they're trying to get released to go there."

My heart stutters in my chest. "That can happen?"

"Daddy says the camps are costing the government a fortune." Grace's voice takes on a superior tone of being in-the-know, but I don't mind one bit. Mr. Bishop is a Lieutenant Colonel in Navy Intelligence, which has nothing to do with the camps, but his perspective is still very interesting to me. "He says he doesn't know how the government can continue to pay for both a war and the camps. We've already seen the WRA releasing some Japanese Americans to help out with the labor shortage on farms. It doesn't seem outrageous to think they would let them resettle away from the west coast."

Taichi's family has a lifetime of farming experience. Surely it would be easy to get them released to a farm. I'll have to mention the idea in today's letter. Maybe Mr. Bishop could help somehow?

"Evalina." Grace points to the sidewalk veering off our path. "You're that way."

"Oh, right. See you this afternoon."

"See you. Good luck!" she calls after me, and my stomach swirls with the reminder of my anxiety.

Nobody else around me looks like they're going to throw up, which is completely unfair. I've walked the campus several times since moving in on Saturday, so I know exactly where my class is, but that's not as comforting as I hoped it would be. Especially when I open the door and see a room that looks like it could seat my entire high school.

I'm early, but several other students have beat me here. All boys. They're flipping through a packet of papers, and they stare when I enter.

"Miss, this is Comparative Politics."

The professor stands at the chalkboard, drawing some sort of diagram. He has curly gray hair, round glasses, and a stern expression.

There's a part of me that wants to pretend I'm lost. To turn and walk away.

I swallow down my fear. "Yes, I know."

His mouth sets in a line that's unreadable. Does he disapprove of me being in his class? Am I just paranoid? "Ah. The syllabus is on the desk."

"Thank you." I feel as though the entire room watches me cross to the desk. I tell my hand not to tremble as I reach for the top packet. My red thumbnail glints in the overhead light.

"What is your name?"

I freeze and look up. The professor stands a few feet away, one hand holding chalk and the other resting on the edge of the desk.

"Evalina." For some reason my throat clenches tight, and it takes me a moment to get out my last name. "Cassano."

"Mmm. Italian."

My face feels as though he just struck a match and threw it at me. "Yes." I try for a lighthearted tone. "That's right."

His gaze skims over me in a cool, calculating kind of way.

"I expect you'll bring a different slant to our discussions in here, Miss Cassano."

I manage a weak smile and a murmured thank you—though he didn't sound particularly pleased—before turning and finding a seat. I feel as though there's a spotlight on me, and a flashing sign reading that I don't belong. That no one in my family has ever gone to college. That I don't know what I'm doing.

So much for blending in. And so much for this being the start of the life *I* choose. The ghost of my heritage has already arrived, and my first class hasn't even begun.

I watch the party from the edge of the hallway, trying to not glance at the clock too many times. After surviving my first week away at college, my first week of living with someone besides my parents, all I really want is to be curled up in bed, tackling my mountain of reading and essays, and speaking to no one. But when Diego asked me to his farewell party tonight, I couldn't say no.

I allow myself to look at the clock. I need to stay at least fifteen more minutes, and then I'll excuse myself so I can get back to the train before dark.

Diego materializes with bottles of Coca-Cola in each hand. He passes one to me with a grin. "You're allowed in the room with the rest of the party guests, you know."

I return his cheeky smile. "Thanks. How generous of you."

"Tai hates parties too. If he could, he would be holding up this wall with you."

"Yeah." I try to ignore the slice of pain his name causes.

"I'll have to do it for him." Diego makes a show of planting his hand against the wall, then relaxes. "Speaking of Tai, I had a letter from him today."

The pain cuts even deeper. "Really? What'd he say?"

"All stuff you already know, I'm sure. He's playing lots of baseball, working in the mess hall, that kind of thing. I think it's funny they call everything by military names."

I look at my shoes. "Yeah, it is."

"You okay?"

"Of course. It's just sad to think about him."

"I know. For me too. I sure wish I could visit him. I know your visit really lifted his spirits."

The party chatter is too loud for Diego to hear my snort. "How is school?" he asks.

"I don't know. Mostly good. My roommate is really quiet. I have a teacher, Professor Blake, who seems to hate me already."

"Hate you?" Diego raises his eyebrows. "How is that possible?"

"Diego," Mr. Medina blessedly interrupts. "Abuela is going home. Come say goodnight."

"Yes, sir." Diego straightens. He clinks the neck of his bottle against mine. "I'll come back, and we can finish this conversation."

I loiter at the wall a bit longer and then attempt conversing with a wife of one of the field-workers, whom I've met at the market before. Her minimal English and my abysmal Spanish make for very little that can be said. Diego has been pulled into a group of some high school chums, and I'm not particularly eager to conclude our talk about Professor Blake, so I thank Mrs. Medina for her hospitality and tell her I need to get back to campus.

"Diego can drive you," Mrs. Medina says. "No need to ride bicycle."

"Thank you, Mrs. Medina, but it really is—"

"Diego," Mrs. Medina calls above the volume of the party. "Miss Cassano must go. You can drive her to train station?"

Diego's gaze connects with mine. "Yes, of course. Let me get the keys."

"It's really not necessary. I don't want you to leave your own party."

Diego waves away these concerns as he leaves in search of the keys. He returns a moment later, jingling them from his fingers, and I have little choice but to follow him out the door and into the air that's losing its warmth as the sun sinks.

"This is very nice, thank you."

"I'm happy to." Diego grabs hold of my bicycle, which I'd rested against their fence post, and loads it in the back of the truck. "It was nice of you to come."

Once we're on our way, we immediately pass the Hamasakis' house, looking dark and lonely.

I avert my eyes. "What time do you leave tomorrow?"

"0-700." Diego winks at me. "That's sailor-talk for seven a.m."

"I'll be thinking of you and your family at that time." In an attempt at humor, I add, "If I'm awake, that is."

"Very kind of you, Evalina."

The silence that follows leaves me fidgety and fearful of what Diego might say next. I had been shocked when we spoke a few weeks ago and I realized he didn't know Taichi had broken up with me. I took it as a hopeful sign. A sign that Taichi was as uncommitted to the break up as I thought, but nothing has changed.

Diego clears his throat. "I'm sorry for how I used to act around you."

I startle. "It's fine."

"It was just that Tai liked you so much, and I was worried about him getting his heart broken." Diego casts a glance at me, looking worried about my response.

"Diego, you've already apologized. I told you, it's fine."

His laugh sounds tighter than normal. "I think also . . ." Diego shifts in his seat. "I think I was a bit jealous. I mean, Tai tried to play it cool, but he was so enamored with you. I had never seen him like that before."

I look out the window when I feel a familiar prickle in my eyes. He's not so enamored with me now. Not if he can stand to not write to me.

"I'm sorry, am I upsetting you? I'm not good at serious stuff. I was just trying to apologize for how I acted for a while when you and Tai were dating. I know there were times that I wasn't as friendly to you as I should've been." His laugh is tight. "I guess when a man is heading off to war, he wants to go with a clean conscience."

The statement sends a zap of fear through me, and when I try to smile, tears come out instead.

Diego groans. "I was *not* trying to make you cry."

I dig through my handbag for a handkerchief. "It's not your fault. I cry easily these days. Especially since Taichi left."

Diego shifts more than normal in his seat and clears his throat. "I know everything that's happened with Tai has been really hard on you. I'm amazed you made a way to visit him. I know he really appreciated it."

I have to settle for wiping my eyes with the sleeve of my sweater. Diego is too blurry for me to read his expression. "You said that earlier. Did he tell you that?"

"That he appreciated you visiting?"

"Yes. Did he say those words?"

"He didn't have to. I just know he did. Oh, Evalina . . ."

I'm bawling. I can't seem to make myself stop. Of course he didn't tell Diego that he appreciated my visit, because he didn't! The break-up letter he had sent to me was postmarked within days; obviously my visit was a huge mistake.

The truck stops, and I find we're at the station already. Diego peers at me from the driver's side, his back against the door as if wanting as much space between us as possible.

His expression is full of caution. "Evalina, what's wrong? Really?"

I dab at my eyes. My sleeve is black from mascara. "I don't think our visit went very well."

"But when you wrote to me at training, you said it did."

"I know." I wring my hands in my lap. "When I wrote to you, I hadn't come home yet. So I thought it had . . ."

"What happened?"

I look up at Diego and make myself admit the truth. "Taichi broke up with me."

"No," Diego says flatly, as though I've just said something highly inappropriate. "That doesn't make sense."

"He did. When I came home from vacation, there was a letter waiting. He said it wasn't fair to either of us to stay together." Tears press against my eyes again, but I manage to keep them away. "And that was the last letter he sent me."

Diego's skepticism is all over his face. As if I would make this up.

"He hasn't said a word of that to me in his letters."

"He's probably embarrassed or something." I wipe under my eyes, hoping to clear away any flakes of eye makeup. I don't want to get on the train looking like a racoon. "You're the only person I've told."

"Evalina." Diego's voice has gone soft, consoling. "I have to think Tai is just stressed about the evacuation, and is trying to do what he thinks is best for you. He loves you, I know it."

"That's what I keep telling myself," I say to my soiled sleeve. "But I send him letters every few days, same as always, and he never writes back."

"I'll talk to him."

"Diego, no—"

"Yes. I think he's just trying to protect you, but he needs to be told that he's acting like an idiot. That's my job as his best friend." Diego looks down the track and grimaces. "I think your train will be here soon."

We get out, and he lifts my bicycle out of the back of the truck.

"Don't give up on him," Diego says. "Please."

"Never." I fix my hands on my handlebars. "Good luck, Diego."

His smile hangs crooked. "I'm leaving to fight for our country, and I don't even get a handshake?"

I roll my eyes, rest my bicycle against the truck, and hug him. I shouldn't have told him about Taichi's letter, because now he's going to write to him about it, and their friendship will be strained at a time when they both need each other, and . . .

"Evalina." Diego squeezes me tightly. "It's going to be okay."

That's when I realize I'm crying hard enough for Diego to feel my shoulders shaking against him. "Maybe it isn't."

"Yes, it is. You and Tai are going to get through this, and a few years from now when we're old and married, our kids will play together, and we'll tell them stories about what it was like when it seemed like the whole world had gone mad. Okay?" Diego holds me at arm's length, his grasp strong on my shoulders. "That's what I'm holding onto. Can you hold onto that too?"

I nod.

"I need a verbal response, soldier."

A smile sneaks out. "I can hold onto that."

The commuter train approaches on the tracks. I push up on my toes and press a swift kiss to his cheek. "Good luck, Diego. I'll pray for your safety."

"Thank you." His face flickers, and I catch a glimpse of his fear before he tucks it away. "I'll need it."

CHAPTER TWENTY-FIVE

Taichi

Wednesday, September 16, 1942

As I wipe off a lunch table, I see Ted and Lillian Kamei in what looks like an intense conversation with Aunt Chiyu. Lillian's hands rest on her bubble of a pregnant stomach.

As I approach the table, Lillian stops speaking and smiles at me. "Hello, Taichi. How are you?"

"I'm well. How are you?"

"Good, thank you." But her face is wan. I know from Ted that the pregnancy has taken a toll on her.

Aunt Chiyu looks from me back to the Kameis. "It's fine to discuss this in front of Taichi." To me she adds, "Have a seat. I was telling them about the letter from Fuji. That we think he'll be here next Monday."

Ted's gaze seems to be purposefully focused out the window. Lillian's smile shows strain that maybe isn't about pregnancy, as I'd first thought.

Despite having work to finish, I sit. "Is there something about Uncle Fuji being released that's upsetting?"

Aunt Chiyu twists at the band on her finger. "Because he's being released earlier than other prisoners, Mr. and Mrs.

Kamei are concerned this might cause distrust among those whose husbands and fathers are still away."

I look to Ted. "I don't understand why."

Ted folds his hands together on the table. "Because the others might suspect he made some sort of deal with the government or turned someone in to the FBI."

I laugh a single, dry huff. "But he's innocent, just like the other men being held. Why *shouldn't* he be released?"

Ted's smile holds sympathy. "You know I agree, but I don't think all at Manzanar will see the situation the same way."

The meeting I stumbled into a few weeks ago flares to the front of my memory. "But Uncle Fuji is an Issei. Won't that count for something?"

Ted holds my gaze for a moment. "I hope so."

"What can we do?" Aunt Chiyu's meek voice is full of worry.

Ted regards her for a moment before admitting, "I don't know. Some men in the camp won't listen no matter what we do. Unless you fully agree with their perspective, it doesn't matter what you say, or what generation you are."

Lillian turns her gaze from Ted to my aunt and me. "Ted was invited to speak at one of the meetings, but when they realized he believed in cooperating with the administration, they booed him off the stage. Raymond Yamishi had that group whipped into such a frenzy, they wouldn't listen to a word Ted said. And Joe Kurihara doesn't help."

That's easy for me to imagine.

Ted shrugs. "Joe cares a lot about the residents here, and he's doing what he thinks is best. Besides, as a veteran of the Great War I don't blame him for being bitter." Ted's gaze sweeps around the room. "I don't blame anyone who's bitter about being here."

"That doesn't make it okay for him to disregard every other point of view," Lillian says with a huff. "The things they were saying about Ted, that he's a stool pigeon. Grown men yelling at him to shut up and get out of there. Why must disagreement so often reduce us to childish behaviors?"

Ted's smile holds affection. "Imagine if you'd fought for your country during a nasty, ugly war. And then twenty-five years later, because of your race and your race alone, your country forces you into a prison camp and treats you like an enemy. Don't you think you might be prone to strong rhetoric now and again?"

Lillian gives Ted a flat, unimpressed look, then turns to Aunt Chiyu and me. "Ted will take the opposing side in any discussion. If *I* had been the one to say that Joe has a right to his bitterness, Ted would say Joe is being as intolerant of other viewpoints as the men he's angry with."

Ted grins at his wife. "I can't resist a good discussion, you're right."

Lillian looks about the emptying mess hall. "I suppose we should let Taichi do his job, shouldn't we?" She smiles at me as she stands. "We'll be at your game today. I'm hoping the wind lets up long enough for me to stay the whole time."

"My game is certainly not worth you having to go back into the hospital. I'll see you guys there."

On my way back to the kitchen, I nearly trip over young Tommy Yoneda, who gives me a bashful smile before scuttling away. He's such a unique blend of his two parents, with his round eyes and Japanese coloring. I wish I could take his photograph and send it to Evalina.

As I wipe off the newly vacated table, my mind drifts to the one time we dared to talk about our potential children. Evalina had twisted a curl around her finger and confessed,

"Everybody I know is just one thing. Just Italian, or just Greek, or whatever. Do you think . . . ¿ Do you think they would fit in anywhere¿"

I squeezed her hand. "Of course."

It had been the first lie I ever told her.

"Is George still here¿"

I startle at the Japanese words and look up into the face of an Issei man. I glance toward the kitchen where our block's cook normally is at this time. My Japanese sounds rusty as I say, "I think George already left, but you are welcome to check."

The man buzzes toward the kitchen without another word. I've just finished wiping down the last table when he comes back, clearly agitated. "He isn't here. Has he spoken of your sugar¿"

I'm still translating his question into English, when he says, "Your sugar. Do you normally have more sugar¿"

"I don't know. I don't do . . ." What's Japanese for inventory¿ Hopefully he knows the word in English, "Inventory."

"When you see George, tell him Harry Ueno from twenty-two came and that I want to know if he's missing a bag of sugar. Because we certainly are." His gaze flicks over me, as if wondering how much of that I caught. He points to himself. "Harry Ueno. Block twenty-two. Missing sugar."

I nod to show I understand, and Mr. Ueno turns on his heel and disappears out the door before I have a chance to reply.

Not until a few minutes later, when I'm scribbling a note for George, do I remember why Harry's name sounded familiar. I've seen the children flocking around him because he's known for deep-frying rice, rolling it in sugar, and setting it out as a snack for the children. Ted has also mentioned him and his friendship with Joe Kurihara.

I hang my apron and head out the door, where I'm met with a blast of wind and a face full of sand. I cover my face and feel an increasingly familiar flash of anger at being here, where even in September the wind feels like having a furnace blow on you. Where you never feel clean, and you always feel trapped.

I flip my collar against the wind in meager protection. "*Shikata ga nai,*" I mutter to myself. *It cannot be helped.* I must endure. Must push through. Must make the best of a troubling situation. I repeat the Japanese phrase all the way back to the barrack, hoping the words sink into my increasingly rebellious soul.

"It's okay, Taichi!" Margaret shouts encouragement from the fence as I walk away from the plate having struck out. "You'll get 'em next time!"

I acknowledge her with the slightest wave I can—I wish she would be a bit quieter—but she's already turned her focus to cheering for James as he steps up to the plate. Rose continues to look at me, though. I offer a flick of a smile and turn away.

Since our extremely awkward dance together, all our interactions have been intensely polite. The only good that has come from it is that she must realize now that I'm a waste of time, and she should look elsewhere for a dance partner.

Ted stands near the team bench. "Ken really throws fire. I'm impressed you even fouled one off."

A crack interrupts our conversation, and we cheer as James's hit bounces between the left and center fielders.

"Atta boy, James!" Ted yells through cupped hands. Then

to me, "I hope your aunt isn't too discouraged over the conversation at lunch today. That wasn't my intention. I just wanted her to be prepared for possible pushback. The Wakatsuki family just got their father back from North Dakota, and they've faced great distrust from their neighbors. It's awful when we suspect the worst of each other. Like we don't have enough troubles in here."

"I'm glad you told us. My aunt . . ." Voicing that she isn't a very strong person sounds far too disrespectful. "It's a good thing for her to know." I look toward the stands, but don't see Lillian anywhere. "Was the wind too much for Lillian?"

"And the heat. I finally convinced her to go back home and rest."

"I'm glad."

"Since we have a moment to talk, just the two of us, I want to let you know that I'll be leaving camp soon. I'm heading off to help in Idaho with the sugar beet harvest."

Idaho. What's it like there? Green? Dust-free? Fence-free? Toilets with doors? I would harvest anything they want if I can get out of here for a bit. "Really?"

Ted must see my thoughts playing out on my face, because he says, "I already tried with your parents, but they don't want you to leave camp."

"What?" Anger slashes through me. "They didn't even talk to me about it. What about what *I* want?"

Ted hesitates. "Their fear is understandable. We're being given a military escort, because the administration is worried about violence against us. Honestly, I'm not sure that what we face out there will be any better than what we deal with in here, Taichi."

"But *you're* going." I wince at how childish I sound.

"Because this is how I can best serve right now. I tried

enlisting right after Pearl Harbor, but obviously they denied me. This is finally something I can do."

"What does Lillian think?"

Ted considers this. "She may seem slight, but Lillian has a backbone of steel. She'll be fine. My parents are here. And I know your family will help too, should she need it."

"Of course we would," I say. "But I'm going to talk to my parents again. I want to come with you."

"There will be other opportunities to serve if this one doesn't work out. Don't be too hard on your parents, especially when your uncle is about to be released. We need good men here inside the fence, Taichi."

I stew on this while Yosuke fouls off several fastballs. I can see Ted's point . . . but I'm itching to get outside the square-mile of Manzanar.

"How are things with Raymond Yamishi?" Ted asks in a quiet voice. "Have there been any other developments?"

"Nothing more than a snide comment or two when our teams play." I shrug. "I can handle him."

"He hasn't continued to harass you over correspondence from your sweetheart?"

My heart twists at the mention of Evalina. Sweet, devoted Evalina who has sent me three to four letters each week despite my silence.

"No, he hasn't."

Ted turns his gaze to me. "And how are the two of you faring?"

I should say we're good, just so we can move on from this conversation. I swallow, and the lie slides down my throat. "I don't know. Not great."

Ted exhales slowly. "I think I told you once before that I used to care for a Caucasian girl?"

I nod.

"We were in high school. She was a lovely girl. If either of our families had approved, then maybe …" Ted shrugs. "We went to different colleges and tried to stay in touch, but we got busy with our separate lives. She met a Caucasian boy, I met Lillian. We learned we could be just as happy—if not happier—with other people, and that was that."

My heart pounds in my chest. I don't want Evalina to find she can be happier with someone else, and I know I couldn't be.

"I'm not trying to discourage you, Taichi, but I thought maybe it would be good for you to know that even if it doesn't work out like you want it to, you can be okay." He claps a hand to my shoulder just as the inning ends. "Don't misunderstand, it's painful. But that's just love in general. Sometimes loving another person feels like the most painful thing there is."

CHAPTER TWENTY-SIX

Evalina

Thursday, September 24, 1942

Around me, classmates stream out the door, and I try to keep my knees from buckling as I approach Professor Blake at the front of the class. Praying my voice comes out steady and strong, I say, "Professor? Do you have a moment?"

He looks up from the briefcase he'd been loading and peers at me over the top of his glasses. "I have *a* moment. What is it, Miss Cassano?"

"I want to discuss my paper. And the grade you gave me."

He continues to look at me. "Okay. Discuss."

I swallow. "Well, I don't think the grade was very fair—"

"This isn't high school, Miss Cassano. You can't turn in poorly researched papers and expect a decent grade." Professor Blake snaps his briefcase shut.

It's all I can do to keep my volume from rising. "My paper is *not* poorly researched."

"You were asked to write a paper on the role of the press in politics in several countries. What you handed in was your own personal conspiracies about the evacuation of the Japanese. I'm sorry if you don't like it, but you handed in a D paper."

"I did *not* hand in a D paper."

"As your professor, I'm telling you that you did." Professor Blake slides his briefcase off the desk and strides out of the classroom without another word. Was that supposed to be the end of the discussion?

I follow, taking several steps for each one of his.

"Professor Blake, I've been to the Japanese American camps," I say between huffs of breath. "Two of them, in fact, and I can tell you without a doubt that the way the newspapers cover them—when they deign to cover them at all—is not accurate. How is that poorly researched? I have seen the camps with my own eyes."

Professor Blake turns and gives me a cold look. "Miss Cassano, if you don't like your grade, you are free to drop my class. But if you continue to turn in papers that sympathize with our country's enemies, then you will continue to be marked low. Good day."

He marches through the exit, and the door swings shut behind him. I watch him go, feeling like a riled bull in the ring baited with a red flag. I want to charge after him and knock those stupid words right out of his mouth.

Believing the Japanese Americans have been treated unfairly means I sympathize with our country's enemies?

You are free to drop my class.

That's what he wants, isn't it?

Professor Blake probably thinks it's silly for a girl to major in political science, or to have any interest in politics whatsoever. Maybe he's right, that I should drop it. A bad grade would cost me my scholarship, and my family can't afford for me to go to college without it. Is there a chance I could drop the class and take it with a different professor next semester . . . ?

But if I go into law or politics, this is something I'll face for the rest of my life. I'll always be discriminated against because of my gender, or because I'm Italian, or because my family has roots in the mafia, or—*please, God*—because my husband is Japanese American and my kids are biracial.

If I tuck tail now, when I'm up against a skinny, scruffy-faced, know-it-all windbag of a professor, how can I expect to be strong enough to push back when the battle is public?

I will think of Professor Blake's class like studying for a final exam or training for a big game. I'm *not* going to back down. And I'll just have to find a way to be so convincing, he can't do anything but give me a passing grade on every other paper.

As soon as the waitress leaves with our dinner order, Mrs. Bishop offers us the bread basket. "Tell us how your studies are going, girls."

Grace's roommate, Sally, is a journalism major like Grace, and very outspoken. She launches into a list of assignments they've had, including her opinions on what would have been more worthwhile assignments, and how she's done on them.

The table is a rectangle, with Mr. and Mrs. Bishop on one side, and Grace sitting in between Sally and me. As Sally rambles, with Grace putting in a few details here and there, it becomes more of a conversation between Grace, Sally, and Mrs. Bishop.

Eventually, Mr. Bishop glances across the table at me and smiles. He passes the butter and says a quiet, "How about you, Evalina? Are you enjoying your classes?"

"I . . . am." That sounded less-than-convincing. "Yes, I am."

Mr. Bishop arches his eyebrows. "Are you sure?"

I spread butter across my bread with a self-conscious laugh. "Yes, I'm enjoying them . . ."

"But?"

"I'm taking one political science class this semester, and my professor has different political beliefs than me. It's reflected in the way he grades."

Mr. Bishop frowns. "You should speak to the counselor about that."

I tear off a bite of bread, but I don't eat it. I hate feeling so ignorant about how college works. "What would they do?"

"Evaluate the situation. Help mediate between you and your professor."

My insides squirm at the thought. "I did okay on the first two papers. But on the one he returned this week, I got a D. He claimed it was because it was poorly researched, but I think he just didn't like my view of the evacuation."

Mr. Bishop's mouth quirks. "I wondered if that was involved."

"To claim it wasn't researched well was just stupid. I told him I've been to two of the camps and read every newspaper article I can get my hands on. Not that the press is covering the story much anymore. And what they *are* saying is completely off base and makes it sound like living in the camps is akin to a holiday in Hawaii." I shove bread in my mouth, hoping to prevent the rest of my rant.

It comes out anyway. "I just don't understand how anyone can argue that locking up the Japanese Americans isn't about race. Why not Germans? Why not my family?"

Mr. Bishop's expression is thoughtful, but he chews and swallows before speaking. "There are some Italians and Germans who have been detained, but you're right. There hasn't been the widescale evacuation like with the Japanese.

Germans and Italians are spread all over the country, while the majority of the Japanese were still on the west coast. And, yes." He winces. "They're more noticeable."

I look at the other ladies at the table and find they're still locked in conversation. "What really makes me think Professor Blake is just biased against me is that on the first day of class, he commented that I'm Italian. That I would bring a different 'slant' to our class discussions. Can you imagine if he knew that both my grandfathers were in the mafia?" My laugh comes out high and self-deprecating.

The waitress arrives with our entrees, thankfully breaking up the conversations. If only she'd arrived before I decided to air my family's blood-stained laundry. Fortunately, Mr. Bishop is a kind, understanding soul.

The rest of dinner passes in casual group conversation, and I try to forget about Professor Blake and join in.

Loneliness surrounds me as dinner ends and we walk back to campus. I had so looked forward to tonight, to dinner away from the school cafeteria and my overly-quiet roommate. To enjoying time with the Bishops, whom I admire so much. And now it's time to head back to my room and write a paper that hopefully Professor Blake will approve of.

"Evalina."

I startle from my downward spiral of thoughts to find that Mr. Bishop has lagged behind the group, slowing his pace to match mine.

"May I ask you about your Japanese American friends? How are they faring?"

"Okay." What else can I say? "They're making the best of a bad situation, I think."

He nods. "I was speaking to Grace about them. She said your friends are farmers?"

"Yes. Wonderful farmers."

"Has Grace told you that her older brother is a cattle rancher in Kansas?"

I'm not quite sure where this is going, but . . . "Yes. Jeremy, right? She said that growing up, he always wanted to be a cowboy."

Mr. Bishop grins. "Yes, that's my boy. With the war on, they're increasingly short on help. Jeremy is going to talk to his boss about having a few Japanese Americans come help. More and more, the WRA is open to that."

I tell my hopes not to soar too high. That cattle are not crops. That Kansas is very far away. That Mr. Bishop may not even be thinking of the Hamasaki family, just making conversation with me about subjects he knows I'm interested in.

"How does it work?" I ask, sounding breathless. "Getting a family released?"

"We're trying to figure that out. I'm not even sure we can ask for the release of specific families. But would you mind giving me your friend's information? In case we're able to?"

"Of course." I tear off a page from the back of my address book and scribble the names of Taichi's family and his aunt and uncle, as well as their address in Manzanar. "Thank you so much for thinking of them."

Mr. Bishop tucks the paper into the breast pocket of his suit. "It may come to nothing," he warns. "I'll be in touch."

With my head light from hope, I thank Mr. and Mrs. Bishop for dinner, and then say goodbye so I can be alone to think. Kansas. If Taichi got released to there, could I go too? They have universities, same as California. Maybe even more affordable. Or maybe I could get a scholarship there.

After I've said goodbye to Grace and Sally, I peek in my mailbox. My heart leaps into my throat when I spot the envelope, but it's from Tony. I'm grateful that he's such a faithful letter writer, even with his intense load of engineering classes, but right now I feel only disappointment. I close the square metal door, and the hollow sound echoes how my heart feels now that yet another day has gone by with no word from Taichi.

CHAPTER TWENTY-SEVEN

Taichi

Monday, September 28, 1942

Dear Tai,

    I don't know how to write this letter. I've been try-
ing to ever since I saw Evalina, but you know I've never
been good with serious conversations.

I cram Diego's letter into my pocket. Judging by the opening lines, I'm guessing I don't want to read it here in the post
office.

Squinting against the late afternoon sun, I slip through
the crowds of dusty Japanese faces until I happen to come
alongside a face that isn't Japanese. Mrs. Yoneda is also
headed toward our block, walking with Lillian, only not with
her usual efficient gait, but rather with a limp as she favors
her right foot.

As I'm about to say hello, Mrs. Yoneda waves to Lillian
and hobbles into her own apartment.

"Hi, Lillian."

Her face is serious and pinched, but she smiles at me.
"Hello, Taichi. Are you headed home?"

"Yes. You?"

"Just trying to get some exercise while the wind is somewhat calm."

"Did I see Mrs. Yoneda limping?"

"Yes." Lillian grimaces. "She's been working at the camouflage net factory, and not everyone cares for the work the women do there."

My teeth grind together as I think of the careening garbage truck and the flapping flags. "Black Dragons?"

Lillian nods, and the anger that seems much closer to the surface these days flares inside me. "They were throwing rocks today, Mrs. Yoneda said. I have another friend who used to work in there, but her husband made her quit because of being harassed. Her husband was put on some 'death list' because of their involvement. What a load of hooey."

How is nothing being done about this? "Someone needs to tell Mr. Campbell."

"Oh, he's been told. Karl Yoneda is off harvesting sugar beets with Ted, of course, but Mrs. Yoneda took it up with him, it sounds like."

She's white. Surely he listened to her. "And?"

"He told her she didn't have to be at camp. That she chose to come here and could choose to leave whenever she liked."

I snort a laugh. "Never mind her husband and son being here?"

"I guess." Lillian's cough has a wheezy tinge to it. "Of course she won't quit, either. I've never met a more determined woman."

That's because she hasn't met Evalina. I coddle the memory of her reaching up to me on the bus. Of her fierce expression when she hugged me goodbye at the end of our visit. My dried-out sinuses prickle when I remember Diego's letter in my pocket. She probably told him what I did, and he's going to ream me out for it.

Lillian coughs again, this time even wheezier. "How is your uncle doing? I've been meaning to come by, but the wind has been so bad."

I hesitate. Lillian notices.

I can't un-hesitate, so I say, "He's fine. He's adjusting."

I think both of these are true statements.

"And your aunt?"

"The same. She's fine. She's adjusting."

Lillian frowns at this. "Okay. If I can help in any way, let me know."

"I will. Thank you."

When she coughs once more, she smiles, "I suppose it's good that we're at my place. I think it's time for me to head indoors."

"Tell Ted I say hello next time you write."

"Of course."

I dawdle the remaining yards to my barrack and find Uncle Fuji is outside, puttering about his garden. He offers me something reminiscent of a smile but doesn't say anything as I head inside.

When he first limped off the bus two weeks ago, a cane aiding him down the steep steps, I hadn't been able to move. Uncle Fuji had never been a large man, but he'd been as strong as well-woven rope, always quick with a grin and a funny, if crass, comment. The man who got off the bus looked twenty years older than my father, rather than just two. His voice had a grainy quality to it, and his shoulders a stoop.

Aunt Chiyu had just stared at him, her eyes wide and welling, her teeth clenched tight. When Uncle Fuji looked at her, his face softened, and he spoke her name in his new graveled voice. "Chiyu."

My aunt choked on a sob as she wrapped her arms around him, a shocking display of affection for the two of them. In his two weeks at Manzanar, he's done little else but fiddle with the Japanese garden and eat the meals Aunt Chiyu brings to the barrack for him.

Though the barrack provides relief from the beating sun and wind, inside is airless and stuffy. I crack open a window, tuck myself into the modest privacy of my cot, and withdraw Diego's letter.

Dear Tai,

I don't know how to write this letter. I've been trying to ever since I saw Evalina, but you know I've never been good with serious conversations.

Evalina came to my farewell party, and I was shocked to hear that you broke up with her. I thought it was some weird joke at first, honestly. I wish you could have seen how much she cried when she told me. I think then you would know—if you don't already—what a mistake this is, but if not, hopefully I can make that clear in my letter right now.

I know you love her. I'm guessing you're scared. You don't know how long you'll be there, or what life will be like when the war is over. You don't want to be a burden to her. Maybe your pride stings a bit too, after having her see you there in the camp.

If this is an accurate description at all, it's only because that's the way I think I would feel if I were in your shoes. And if I were in your shoes, and you were in mine, here's what I would need to hear: letting fear and pride make your decisions is only going to lead to regret.

She loves you, and you love her. I think there will be rewards for persevering.

You can thank me by naming your first child after me.

Diego

I stare at the letter, cycling through a range of emotions. Convicted. Shamed. Indignant. Thankful. Lonely. Regretful.

But Diego only has half the story. He doesn't know that I'm saving Evalina from a life like Mrs. Yoneda's. From a life of being married to someone who looks like our country's enemy. From the pain of trying to raise children who aren't Japanese enough or Caucasian enough to belong anywhere.

This isn't about my pride or my willingness to persevere. This is about protecting Evalina.

Right?

CHAPTER TWENTY-EIGHT

Evalina

Saturday, October 3, 1942

"We figured we would lose you to the market this morning." Mama scoops scrambled eggs onto my plate. "I'm surprised you're still here."

"Surprised, but grateful," Daddy says as Mama adds eggs to his plate as well. "Thank you, Zola."

I didn't know just how much I love my mama's cooking until I had to go without it for a month. Poor Taichi hasn't had home cooking since April. The thought lands like an unexpected punch. If I'm homesick after just a few weeks at a university that I chose to go away to, how much worse must it be for Taichi?

"Are you okay, Evalina?" Mama frowns at me from across the table.

"Yes." I shake away the clouds of my thoughts. "I was just thinking about my plans for the day. I'm going to the market this morning—"

"Shocking."

I raise my eyebrows at my father. "I was about to ask if you need anything while I'm there, but maybe I won't."

Daddy grins. "Fennel and tomatoes. Oh, and lemons. I forgot to order those from the Medinas on Thursday."

The clock in the living room chimes eight o'clock. I push my last bite of eggs into my mouth. "They'll be scraping the bottom of the barrels by the time I get there if I don't leave now. Mama, you want anything for dinner?"

Mama reaches into the pocket of her robe and hands me a neatly written list. "What time will you be back home?"

"Probably mid-afternoon. I'm meeting Gia at the restaurant for an early lunch."

"Have fun, honey," Daddy says as I drop a kiss onto his thinning hair.

My heart soars as I tighten my wool trench coat and coast down the hills toward the choppy, gray bay. Even though I arrived last night and slept in my own bed for the first time in over a month, *now* it feels like I'm home.

I lock my bike and head into the bustle of the market. The Medinas are in the middle of multiple transactions, so I go to Mrs. Ling first. She's no longer hanging the WE ARE CHINESE banner on their stand. I suppose because everyone knows the Japanese are all gone.

Mrs. Ling bustles around the table to give me a hug. "Miss Evalina, I am so happy to see you! How is school?"

I hate that the first thing I think of is Professor Blake, because there are so many wonderful things about school. "Mostly good. I'm adjusting. How has business been?"

"Our tomato crop is very good. Your mother came to buy from us last week."

"Today she sent me. Do you mind if I choose my own?"

"Of course not. We are always happy to do anything for our Evalina." Mrs. Ling hurries around the table and pushes the large crate of tomatoes my way. "Here you are, my dear. Oh, this is a nice one."

She takes one from the top, places it in the bag, and then steps back to let me take over selections.

"Have you been in touch with the Hamasakis recently? How are they?"

I swallow. "I haven't heard from them recently, Mrs. Ling."

Her sunny smile falters. "No?"

I shake my head. "Not since June. The Medinas will have more current information for you, I'm sure."

I can feel Mrs. Ling looking at me as I pick through the tomatoes for the ripest ones. I'm so self-conscious, I nearly add a subpar selection to my bag.

"I imagine they are very busy in their new community." Mrs. Ling kindly offers me an excuse.

"They are." I should leave it at that, but Mrs. Ling watched me hang around the market for a year so I could be close to Taichi. I'm embarrassed to think she might assume the affection was all one-sided. "Taichi and I wrote some. But . . ."

I don't know how to finish the thought. I never should've started it. Stupid pride.

"Such a difficult time for the Japanese Americans. And those who care about them." She nods and smiles, as if to encourage. "They are strong, and so are you. You will both endure."

I roll shut the paper bag of tomatoes. "Thank you, Mrs. Ling."

I hand her the money, and she offers me an orange. "For luck."

"Thank you." I push away memories of the last orange she gave me for luck, which I enjoyed with Taichi. "Why are oranges considered lucky?"

"I'm not sure," Mrs. Ling says. "I have always thought they were the perfect fruit because they are the easiest to share. There's something lovely about that."

Another potential customer is browsing tomatoes, and I step away. "Thank you, Mrs. Ling."

"Always a pleasure, Miss Evalina. Thank you for your business."

I turn toward the Medinas' stand and find Mrs. Medina has been anticipating me. Her smile has the same breadth and warmth as Diego's, and my heart lifts up a prayer for his protection.

Mrs. Medina grasps my hands between hers. "You are home this weekend?"

"I am. How are you, Mrs. Medina?"

"I am good. Very busy. Always very busy. What can I get for you today?"

"Daddy needs fennel and lemons to tide him over until Monday's delivery."

Mrs. Medina pulls out a paper sack to fill. "You want to choose your own?"

"Yes, please. Have you had any news from Diego?"

"News is slow. Some weeks we get no letters. Other days, three arrive." She laughs at this, despite the way concern flits over her face.

"I imagine the inconsistency is normal."

"He is being sent to help in Guadalcanal." She says the word slowly and purposefully. "We had to look on a map. My geography . . ." Mrs. Medina shakes her head and laughs in a self-conscious way. "But he seems happy."

I smile and hold out the money. "Diego always seems to be happy."

"He is my good boy. Came into the world laughing, that one." Mrs. Medina counts out my change. "Thank you for your business."

"Of course. How are . . ." I swallow as a flutter of nerves

takes over me. "Have you heard from the Hamasakis at all? Do you know if they're doing okay?"

"*Si, si.* I had a letter from Mitsuno yesterday. She says they are all very good. Much to keep them busy."

"I'm happy to hear that." I make myself smile. "Has there been any mischief at their house?"

"Not one bit. We keep a close eye on it."

We exchange several more niceties about the weather and business at Alessandro's, and then I pedal over to the restaurant to meet Gia.

Mr. Esposito is there when I come in the back door, working his magic with the mozzarella and whistling off-key. "*Buongiorno*, Evalina. How are you this morning?"

He angles his face for me to kiss him on the cheek.

"Good, but busy." I settle the two bags onto the counter. "How are you? How is Mrs. Esposito?"

"We don't know what to do with ourselves now that our nest is empty. At night, we just stare at each other. It's terrible. I don't know why all my children insisted on growing up." He winks at me. "Gia is up front waiting for you."

"Okay, thank you." I glance at the door that will take me out of the kitchen, but I don't move. Ever since Gia got married, she's been in such a blissful, lighthearted mood, I've struggled to not pull away from her. Conversing with her has felt like trying to drink the bubbles of a Coca-Cola; there's nothing of substance to enjoy.

Maybe today, with the space we've had from each other, will feel different.

I put on a smile and head out to the seating area, where several tables are occupied and my father is making sandwiches.

When Gia spots me, she squeals, runs, and throws her arms around my neck. "I'm so happy to see you! I'm pregnant!"

"... and then it turned out that she was just mad because she thought I had never sent a thank you card for the wedding gift. I said, 'Aunt Brunella, you know me. How could you think I had forgotten a thank you card? Obviously it was just lost in the mail.' Since then she's talked much more kindly about the baby."

Gia runs a hand over her stomach as if there's any indicator that she's three months pregnant. She beams at me across the table. "I think that's everything going on with me. How's school? How's you-know-who?"

She gives an exaggerated wink.

My laugh sounds forced to my own ears. I glance toward the counter, where my father and Mr. Esposito work hard to keep up with the lunch line that's formed.

"School is fine. I'm one of three girls in my Comparative Politics class. That's a bit uncomfortable."

"Lorenzo thought I was joking when I said you're majoring in political science." Gia laughs brightly. Pregnancy really seems to agree with her. "He doesn't understand that with all the men away at war, we need women to step up and work."

"Does he not think you should work?"

"He was fine with the idea until we found out I was pregnant. You know how protective he is. He doesn't want me doing anything that might be remotely stressful. Are you having any fun at college, or just studying?"

"I'm not just studying."

Gia arches her eyebrows expectantly.

I tweak my water glass. "I've joined a Future Leaders of America club. We work on creating opportunities at school for those who are marginalized."

"Well, then. I stand corrected. You're definitely having some fun." Gia grins at me. "And how's your boyfriend?"

"Fine." The word pops out easily, just like it did the few times over the summer when Gia thought to ask about Taichi through the haze of her newly wedded bliss. "The camps are still terrible of course, but he's enduring."

Her smile morphs to the no-teeth, sympathetic variety. "The separation is awful, isn't it?"

The diamond chip on her ring happens to glint in the light, and I swallow the jealousy that rises up bitter in my throat.

"It's the worst."

"I lie awake at night wondering if Lorenzo will come home." Gia's hands settle on her stomach as her eyes grow misty. "At least you know Taichi is safe."

With a shudder, I think of all those guards and all those guns. "Yeah." My words come out as an unintentional whisper, "At least, I hope he is."

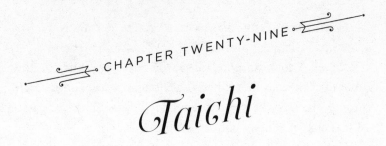

CHAPTER TWENTY-NINE

Taichi

Wednesday, October 14, 1942

The secretary, who looks as dried up as the Manzanar ground in the middle of summer, speaks in firm, efficient sentences. "Mr. Campbell cares very much about the concerns of individual camp residents. That's why you have block leaders. Just take your concerns to your block council, and he will bring them to Mr. Campbell."

"Most of my block council is gone to harvest sugar beets, and they've already discussed the issues with Mr. Campbell—"

"There you have it, then." Her smile is thin. "It's practically resolved."

"But that was weeks ago. And there's still flags on the garbage trucks. There's still rumors about camp sugar being stolen."

Her thin smile presses into an even thinner line. "We have very little control over rumors. And even if someone were to steal something, where would they go? Even if they somehow managed to get through the fence, we're in the middle of the desert."

Does she think this is comforting to me, to be reminded of how trapped I am?

The angry words I flung at the Kitchen Workers meeting

this morning, about being a U.S. citizen, suddenly seem naïve and foolish.

Harry Ueno had called the meeting to discuss the benefits of organizing a union of mess hall workers. "After all, whoever controls the kitchens"—I had been close enough to the front to see his wink—"controls Manzanar."

Apparently, Mr. Ueno had found that many other block kitchens were short on sugar, and at the meeting publicly accused Ned Campbell and the mess hall Chief Steward of the theft. I didn't particularly like Mr. Campbell when I met with him and Ted, but the evidence presented against him didn't seem convincing enough.

Not everyone agreed with me, though. Many other kitchen workers spoke with frightening intensity about what they would do if they ever got their hands on Mr. Campbell.

About halfway through the meeting, James materialized in the seat beside me, already dressed for our baseball game.

"What are you doing here?" I asked. "You don't work in the kitchens."

He shrugged. "You know me. I can't resist a crowd."

A few times, he joined the others with some boos and hissing, but then punctuated them with a wink at me.

"You should be careful," I said in a low voice as the meeting broke up. "I think they're really serious. And it can't be good for your job in the dispatch office, right? If they find out you're encouraging those who are pro-Japan?"

"I'm not pro-Japan. I'm pro-deep-fried rice rolled in sugar." James's gaze skimmed my blue jeans and collared shirt. "Why aren't you in your uniform? Our game starts in forty-five minutes."

"Go on without me. I just want to speak to Mr. Ueno real quick."

I elbowed my way up front where Mr. Ueno spoke in a high, excited voice to another cook about the need for all the kitchens to stand together, that it didn't matter if sugar had been stolen from each one or not. As I waited, the back of my neck prickled, and I turned to find Raymond Yamishi standing beside me, along with another boy I had seen playing baseball on their team. I didn't know his name, but I often saw the two of them together.

"Hello, Taichi. I'm surprised to find you here."

"Why? I work in one of the mess halls."

Raymond Yamishi just smirked and turned to speak to his friend in low Japanese. I caught the phrase *inu* paired with Ted Kamei.

"Ted Kamei isn't a traitor."

Raymond's eyebrows raised. "I'm pleased that your parents at least taught you the language of your home country. A sad number of Nisei know Japanese."

"I know some Japanese, but we spoke English in our home. And Ted Kamei isn't a traitor."

"Ted is a stool pigeon with confused politics." Raymond spoke this casually, as though he just told me the most obvious of facts. "You should be careful what you share with him. He does not care for the people of Manzanar the way Mr. Kurihara does. Those like Ted care only for themselves."

"That's not true." I heard my voice rising, but couldn't seem to stop it. "He's trying to work with the administration for change. To benefit all of us."

Raymond glanced at his friend and snorted. "Oh, he's certainly working with the administration. No one disputes that." His eyes shined as he turned his gaze back to me. "Do you believe you are American, Taichi?"

"I know I'm American."

"Excellent." Raymond crossed his arms over his narrow chest. "My friend and I will come with you to the entrance and watch you walk through the gate. If you are not shot on sight, then we will believe you are American."

And now, standing in front of Mr. Campbell's secretary, hearing her explain why it's ridiculous to think anyone would bother stealing sugar when it would be impossible to leave the camp with it, it feels that Raymond is more right than I would like.

I take a deep breath. Appearing angry and unstable won't win me any points with this woman. "Could I please leave a message for Mr. Campbell?"

She regards me a moment. "A short one."

But she makes no movement toward pen or paper.

"May I have something to write with?"

She hands me a square of paper and a dull pencil. I consider my words for a few seconds before writing:

Dear Mr. Campbell,

Please address the concerns about missing sugar and the pro-Japanese flags on the garbage trucks. I am a loyal U.S. citizen. That feels like an increasingly dangerous thing to be inside Manzanar.

T

I write the first letter of my name and stop the pencil as my mind flits to Raymond's garbage truck careening around the corner, to the way he'd threatened me on the baseball field. I put down the pencil without finishing my name, thank the secretary, and leave.

I shield my eyes to orient myself—the post office is to the left—and then I shuffle down the dusty path with my letter to Diego in my pocket. Hopefully I'll have one waiting for me from Evalina too.

I pull the post office door open, and I'm about to let the door close when I realize there's a girl right behind me. "Oh, sorry, I didn't see you."

It's Rose. She looks like she's in a bad mood.

I hold open the door for her. "I didn't realize you were right behind me."

"Yes, I know," she mutters as she walks through the door.

Rose stands in the short line with crossed arms and rigid shoulders. She appears to have zero interest in talking to me.

I take my spot in line behind her. "Hot out there today."

Nothing.

"Is something bothering you?"

She throws a glare over her shoulder. "I'm not interested in discussing anything with you."

I stare at the back of her head. Evalina would just yell at me, and we'd be able to move on. Same with Aiko.

It's Rose's turn in line. She purchases a stamp for her letter, and then marches back out the door without another word.

I pay to mail Diego's letter, collect a newly arrived letter from Evalina, and take off after Rose. She's walking fast toward block nine, but I run her down. "Hey, Rose, wait."

"I said I don't want to talk to you."

"I know. But I want to know why. What did I do?"

"Why don't you talk to your uncle about it?"

"My uncle?" I search my memory for any possible time Uncle Fuji and Rose would've been in the same room, but I'm coming up blank. Fuji still rarely takes his meals in the mess hall. "What does he have to do with anything?"

She turns so I can see her roll her eyes. "My father is still in North Dakota, you know. He didn't make up lies about the other men just so he could get released. He has honor."

I blink rapidly in the face of Rose's accusations. "My uncle didn't do that."

"Of course he did. That's why he was released and others weren't."

A gust of wind kicks up with such force, it feels like a hand is trying to shove us backward.

"That's just gossip, Rose," I say. "You can't believe everything that everybody says."

"So you think I'm stupid."

"Of course not. I think you're rightfully sad and angry that your father is still—"

"I don't care!" Rose stops so abruptly that I barely keep from crashing into her. "I don't care what you think. You're a rat just like your uncle, writing letters about what goes on at camp to your stupid white girlfriend. Or are you going to tell me *that's* a rumor too?"

I stare at her, baffled about where to start.

"Just leave me alone, Taichi." Rose marches away.

Don't we have enough problems in Manzanar without us turning on each other? Without stirring up crazy rumors about those who get released and those who are still wrongfully imprisoned?

I trudge back toward the barrack, where my uncle is cutting squares of the linoleum the administration delivered. Instead of just laying them how they are, he's gathered several different colors, cut them into squares, and is arranging them in a pattern.

"The floor looks good, Uncle Fuji."

He bows his acknowledgment, but doesn't look up from his scissors.

If my father had owned a fishing boat instead of being a farmer, he also would've been taken to North Dakota in the days after Pearl Harbor. After the horrors of being wrongfully imprisoned for ten months, only to be released to a place like Manzanar, it seems horrible to me that those who should understand better than anyone have also turned suspicious.

I sit beside him on the steps.

He sets down the scissors and rubs at his knuckles. We sit there for a minute, watching those who pass by, and then I eye the scissors and roll of black linoleum.

"Could I help?"

Uncle Fuji looks at me a moment and smiles. "Yes, Taichi."

A few minutes later when I've started on my third square, my uncle exhales and says, "Thank you," in a sad, soft voice.

"Rose is just upset that you don't carry a torch for her," Aiko says in a flippant voice as she rolls bandages, sitting beside me on the empty hospital bed. "Ignore her."

I'm here to sit with Lillian, whose asthma has flared again, while Ted's parents go eat dinner. Fortunately, she's sleeping comfortably now.

Or maybe unfortunately, because I don't know that Aiko is going to say anything that I want to hear.

"I don't think that's it—"

"That's because you're naïve. She's hurt because she found out about Evalina—"

"How *did* she find out?"

"I assume James, but I don't know. What I *do* know is that Rose was crying in the co-op yesterday because she'd just found out. When Margaret and Rose realized I was standing right there, I told them Evalina was the best kind of girl and that she would be my sister-in-law someday. So ignore her. It's just bruised pride." Aiko pushes a basket of clean linens my way. "Make yourself useful while you sit here. Fold these into thirds."

I do what's asked of me. Like Aiko knew I would. After I add three cloths to her stack, I grumble, "You could've been kinder about it, you know."

Aiko gives me a wide-eyed look. "I was as kind as the situation deserved. Margaret was telling Rose that it surely wouldn't last, and that she just needed to be patient. Those girls didn't need false hope, Taichi. They needed to know the truth."

I squirm in my chair, sweating, as I think of the girls talking about me like that. Back home, none of the girls ever seemed interested in me.

"I've never done anything to encourage Rose."

"You really think you need to tell me that? Of course you haven't. I only told you because I didn't want you thinking this is a problem you need to solve. Just leave this one alone."

Several beats of silence fall before Aiko asks quietly, "Have you heard from her recently?"

I swallow and meticulously fold a towel. "Of course."

"But you're still pretending she isn't worth fighting for?"

If she'd said it with her usual tone of judgment and hostility, I might have come back swinging. Instead, her tone is soft. Inviting.

"I know it doesn't seem like it to you, but I *am* fighting for her. I'm fighting for her to have the life she deserves. I don't want her stuck here like Mrs. Yoneda."

"Do you think that's how Mrs. Yoneda sees it?" Aiko

arches her eyebrows at me. "From what I've heard, she fought to be here with her family."

"It's different, because they're married. I can still save Evalina from this."

"No, you can't. Because she *is* going through this, through the evacuation, even though she isn't literally here in the fence. You can't save her from that."

"I don't want to talk about it," I snap. Then I remember where we are, glance at Lillian, and lower my voice, "And I *can* save her from it. Yes, she's hurting now, but she'll meet someone else. Someone who can eat at any restaurant. Someone who all her friends will accept."

For a moment, Aiko just rolls bandages in silence. And then, very quietly, "But think about if it was reversed, Taichi. If she were Japanese and you were Caucasian. Would you want to eat at restaurants that refuse to serve her? Would you want friendships with people who looked down on her? Of course not." She waits until I look her in the eyes before saying, "Evalina being with you doesn't cost her anything more than what her own principles already demand."

Lillian stirs, but doesn't wake. I finish my assigned folding and immediately wish there was still more to do. Still more to occupy me.

Aiko gathers the last of the folded linens in a basket and stands. "I'm going to put these away, and then I'm done for the day." She sets it against her hip. "Ichiro already left, but Peggy is here if you need anything."

Aiko looks at me a moment longer, and then leaves. I'm certainly not sorry she is going, but her words continue to needle at me in her absence. Poking holes in all my good intentions.

"So thankful you would sit here while we eat." A soft

voice startles me out of my thoughts, and I look up to see Ted's mother smiling at me. "Did she sleep the whole time?"

I stand, knees stiff even after less than an hour of sitting with Lillian. "She did."

"It's that good medicine they give her." Mrs. Kamei covers a yawn with her hand. "I wish I could have some. Then maybe I sleep better at night."

"You are not sleeping well, Mrs. Kamei?"

"Last two nights, I wake up thinking someone is trying to get into apartment. That I hear man voices outside." She laughs at my concern and shakes her head. "No need to worry, Taichi. Just dreams. Once in August, some angry men came to talk to my Ted. But just talk. I am just jittery, as Lillian says." She laughs again, as if to drive the point home to me.

"Mr. Kamei and Lillian haven't heard anything, though?"

"No, no." She straightens Lillian's already-tidy bedding. "Just my wild imagination."

There's no real reason to doubt her. The three weeks that Ted and the others have been gone to Idaho, camp has been quiet. Residents have all been excited to have linoleum arrive for the apartment floors, and the temperatures and winds have been milder. The general attitude at camp feels upbeat.

"Well, you know where to find me, should you need anything, Mrs. Kamei."

"Yes, yes." Mrs. Kamei grips my hand between hers, squeezes, and smiles up at me. "Thank you for sitting with Lillian. Hurry now or you will miss your own supper."

"I'm heading to the post office first. Do you need anything?"

"Oh!" She reaches into her bag. "I forget earlier. Lillian had a letter for Ted, and I forgot to mail it. Already stamped."

"Any word yet on when he'll be home?"

"Early November, he says. Weather depending."

"I'm glad he'll be home for Thanksgiving."

"Us too." From her bag, she pulls out her knitting needles, settling in for the evening. "Thank you, Taichi."

Outside, the air is dry and growing chilly with the setting sun. Many Manzanar residents are enjoying the cooler temperatures out in their gardens or chatting outside their front doors.

When I cut through block twenty-two to get on course for the post office, my gaze catches on Raymond Yamishi. He sits on the front steps of a barrack with a few other Black Dragons who I know only by sight. They have a stack of papers on a table and appear to be discussing something as a group.

Raymond sees me passing by, and when his gaze lands on me, a shiver races up my spine. I smile, trying to seem casual, but hurry my footsteps.

Evalina

Saturday, November 7, 1942

"If you're upset about the way American citizens of Japanese heritage are being treated, come to our meeting tomorrow night!" I make my voice rise high so it will reach those who are purposefully skirting around me and the other students from the Future Leaders of America club as we pass out fliers in the courtyard. "Two-thirds of those locked away in camps are American citizens! If you think that's unacceptable and you want to take action, come to our meeting!"

Several boys gathered around a nearby bench look at me and snicker. A girl who took the flier I gave her chucks it into the closest wastebasket without breaking her stride.

I take a deep, bracing breath. "If you think it's wrong to hold people prisoner without due process, come to our meeting tomorrow night!" I offer a flier to a passing blond girl. I try to soften my voice as I add, "We'll be discussing the unfair treatment of Japanese Americans."

Her face twists into an angry scowl. "My best friend's brother was killed over the summer in Japan. The government should send every last one of those Japs back to where they came from."

"*America* is where most of them come from. They have nothing to do with—"

"They're raised by Japs." She's walking backward now, so she can continue to yell at me as she walks away. "Once a Jap, always a Jap."

Anger zips up my spine and shoots out my mouth. "Congratulations, that's the dumbest thing I've heard today! What country are *your* parents from?"

"Evalina," Grace admonishes from behind me. "That's out of line."

"Sorry." My anger roars in my ears, like a sea throwing itself against the cliffs. "I just don't understand how people can choose to not care."

"I know your passion is coming from a good place, but when is the last time somebody yelled at you and, in doing so, changed your mind about something? My mother is always saying, 'When someone yells, we cover our ears. But when someone whispers, we strain to hear them.'"

"How am I supposed to get people to our meeting by whispering at them?"

"It's not meant to be taken literally."

"Hi, girls. How is the social activist work going?"

We turn to find Jack, the boy Grace has gone out with these last few Friday nights, grinning at us. He's a soft, cheerful sort of fellow who nicely complements Grace's harsher edges.

I put on a big smile. "Ducky. Grace had to remind me to not yell at people."

Grace laughs. "Just one person. Otherwise I think it's gone really well."

"Glad to hear it." Jack taps his wristwatch. "Grace, we need to go. I told everyone we'd meet them at six."

"Oh, right. I'll just run up and change real quick." Grace smooths her sweater and turns to me. "Are you sure you don't want to come?"

"You really should," Jack adds. "I've got a buddy who knows how to cut a rug, and you're just his type."

Taichi always told me he's a terrible dancer, but I never had the chance to find out. "Thanks, but no. I have a bit of a headache and loads of homework. Including a paper for Professor Blake."

Grace makes a sour face. "If you change your mind, come on over. It's okay to have fun now and again, you know."

Jack fits his arm around Grace, and the way he smiles down at her leaves my heart feeling achy and empty. How silly to not simply be happy for my friend.

"Enjoy yourselves," I say with a wave, and I turn toward my dorm.

I pitch the last of the fliers into the wastebasket—where many that I passed out earlier ended up anyway—and try to push away the whispers that I failed. That I didn't move a single person to action today.

I try not to notice the mailboxes as I walk into my building. I shouldn't stop. It's just going to be an empty box. One more way I've failed. One more disappointment.

I fit my key into the lock, turn, and then slam it shut.

Of course it's empty. What had I expected? That today of all days is when Taichi finally writes back?

Maybe Diego never sent Taichi an angry letter after all. Or maybe he did, and it just didn't have the impact I thought it would. Maybe I really do need to take a hint and give up.

I stare in disbelief at the posted grade. How did I possibly get a D on my mid-term paper for Professor Blake⸮ I peek through his cracked office door and find he's inside. I say a quick prayer for strength and knock.

"Come in," Professor Blake calls. His face grows stonier when he sees me. "Ah, Miss Cassano. I suspect you are dissatisfied with your grade⸮"

I sit in a wooden chair near his desk. I try to keep my voice soft as I say, "I would like to understand, professor. I felt as though I turned in a quality paper."

Professor Blake pulls open a drawer with a metallic whoosh, withdraws a file folder, and flips through the papers. Then he hands one across the desk to me. "My comments are in the margins. You may read those on your own time, as I'm currently working on—"

"I cited all my sources." I angle the essay toward him and jab at the first cardinal red comment scribbled in the margins. "There isn't a sentence in here that I didn't research."

"If that's true, your paper did not—"

"Of course it's true."

"Do *not* interrupt me, Miss Cassano." Professor Blake's voice is dark. "You came in here for answers, you said. You're not going to find them by interrupting me."

I curl my lips between my teeth and clamp down. Indignant anger boils in my chest.

"As I was saying, *if* it's true that you thoroughly researched your topic, I did not see evidence of it in your paper. I saw evidence that you thoroughly researched one side—the side you agree with, I suspect—but not the other. For example, nowhere in here do you talk about how immigration has hurt these countries."

"I see." I struggle to keep my voice quiet and steady. I flip several pages. "But I do talk about it some—"

"A cursory mention. Nothing substantial enough to show that you really understand the issue."

I make myself inhale and exhale deeply before responding. "I didn't understand from the assignment that our paper was meant to be an exhaustive discussion of all the views—"

"Clearly."

Hot tears build behind my eyes. Through clenched teeth, I say, "Professor, I *need* a good grade in this class. Otherwise, I'll lose my scholarship."

"You will need the highest of marks for the rest of the semester if you want a passing grade, but I believe you can achieve this if you put your mind to it. You did very well on your last few papers."

That's because I had picked topics I didn't care about. Because I had taken care to strip away any traces of my voice. I hadn't been so careful with this one, and yet I know this is a superior paper to those other two.

I stand and turn toward the exit. "Thank you for explaining."

"You are clearly a very bright, passionate girl. Just misguided."

I freeze in the doorway. "Respectfully, sir, I think I just view the world differently than you do. That doesn't make me misguided."

"Good day, Miss Cassano." His voice is clear and cold.

I leave before I can say anything else that I might later regret.

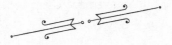

Back in my dorm room, I stare blankly at my desk. Before heading out to check my posted grade, I had been working on final edits for the article Grace asked me to submit about the treatment of the Japanese Americans. I stare at the byline: A Concerned Citizen.

That's what I had told Grace when she asked if I would write a piece. I said I would write the article, but only if I could be anonymous, same as I have been for my letters to the big newspapers and the congressmen. I had told myself that I would be taken more seriously if they didn't know I was an Italian American teenage girl, but for the first time I actually admit what I feel when I think of using my name:

Afraid.

I have felt afraid of people knowing that it was me, Evalina Cassano, who wrote those angry words. Afraid of being laughed at, ridiculed, told that I should just be quiet and feel grateful. Told that I'm too young to understand or too Italian to be a real American.

I feel afraid of people knowing that this fight I'm fighting isn't just about the evils of racism, but that it's personal to me.

From my handbag, I pull out my compact and fix myself with a hard stare.

"Here is the deal, Evalina. You may write papers you don't care about for Professor Blake's class. You may say what you need to say in private so that you can get the grades you need to keep your scholarship. But you are not allowed to write anonymously anymore. You must use your name."

I snap shut the compact.

With my pen, I draw a single, bold line through the words A Concerned Citizen and replace them with the three most terrifying words I've ever written.

By Evalina Cassano

CHAPTER THIRTY-ONE

Taichi

Thursday, November 26, 1942

"I have never seen you in a bad mood before, Taichi." George reaches across me to refill the slices of turkey. "It is Thanksgiving! You should feel happy!"

But that's precisely what I'm in a bad mood about.

George whistles as he saunters back to the kitchen.

Last year for Thanksgiving, we'd stayed in the city for several days with Uncle Fuji and Aunt Chiyu. There had been fish, cranberries, rice pudding, and competitive games of Go.

And then I claimed I wanted to go for a walk, and I met Evalina at Golden Gate Park. That had been our first time spending several hours alone together, and the first time I gathered the courage to kiss her. Two weeks later, I had still been flying high from the stolen, blissful moment.

I fell hard back into reality when Japan attacked Pearl Harbor. Sometimes it feels like I've been falling ever since, and now we're coming up on the one-year anniversary. I can't imagine life improving anytime soon.

I leave my lunch shift a bit early after spilling gravy down the front of my pants, and when I hurry back to the barrack to change, I find my parents, my aunt and uncle, and Ted standing on our steps, talking. Their faces are all grave.

As I approach, Father is saying, "It isn't that I don't believe you, Ted. It just seems that if such a list exists, the administration will put a stop to it."

Ted's gaze connects with mine. "Hello, Taichi. I'm glad you're arriving in time for this discussion."

Their heads swing to look at me. My mother stands closest; she puts her arms around me.

"Mitsuno, you'll scare him," Father says.

Even if Mother hadn't touched me, their faces alone have me scared. "What's going on?"

Everyone looks to Ted, whose gaze falls heavy on me. His face is a shade darker than all of ours after all his weeks away harvesting sugar beets. "Joe Kurihara and his followers have put together a list of names. They claim it's a death list, but I don't know how seriously to take it. As big and brave as he talks, and as the Black Dragons talk, I'm not convinced any of them could actually go through with killing someone. I don't think so, anyway."

I think of that night when I stumbled into the meeting. Of the man who yelled, "Cut their heads off!" Maybe Ted is right if we're talking about individual men, but when they get together as a group . . .

"You are on the list." I mean for the words to curl with question, but they lie flat instead.

Ted nods.

"So are you and Fuji," Aunt Chiyu says before clapping a handkerchief over her mouth, as if to hold in tears.

My mind flips through individual moments. Raymond razzing me about Evalina, about being disloyal to Japan. The garbage truck flying around the corner, nearly crushing Ted and me.

Raymond questioning if I could walk out the front gates without getting a bullet in the back. The way he watched me cross block twenty-two that night when I had left Lillian at the hospital. Like one of those flip-books for children, the isolated memories add up to something greater.

"You and Fuji are on the list, yes." Ted says in an even, measured voice. "I was telling your family before you arrived, Taichi, that this is all information given to Lillian by Fred Tayama, so I don't know anything firsthand. Fred is gone now for the JACL convention in Salt Lake City, but he's, of course, number one on the list."

My family nods, as though this makes perfect sense.

"I feel a bit stupid saying this, but I don't know who that is."

"Fred used to be the leader of the Japanese American Citizens League chapter in Los Angeles. He believed and promoted the idea that if we evacuated peacefully, it would show our loyalty to the U.S. Many of the Issei, especially those from Terminal Island where the evacuation was particularly cruel, blame him personally for us being here. That's nonsense, of course, because we would've been sent here no matter what he did, but he's become something of a scapegoat."

"I want to know who these people think they are, putting together such a list." Aunt Chiyu's voice warbles.

"There's nothing in particular that gives them authority. Joe was an accountant and lived on Terminal Island, so he carries some weight with the boys from there. He is a fine enough speaker, though I'm surprised that so many follow him. But they do."

Joe doesn't worry me nearly as much as those like Raymond who follow him. "You said Fred is number one. What number are you?"

Ted offers me a wry smile. "Four. Tokie Slocum is second, since he likes to speak very loudly about how close he is with the FBI, and then Karl Yoneda. You and Fuji are so low, you don't have a number."

"Well," I say dryly. "We will have to exert more effort in the future."

Ted snorts a laugh, but my aunt snaps, "This isn't funny, Taichi."

I bow an apology. "I'm sorry, Aunt Chiyu. You're right."

Ted bows too. "That's my fault, I'm afraid. My wife has always said I find the oddest things funny."

"Have you already spoken with the administration?" Father asks. "Has the new camp director come yet?"

"Not that I know of. I have an appointment with Mr. Campbell tomorrow morning. I came to tell you all about the death list business because I thought you deserved to know, but I don't think you're in any *real* danger. Some of the same men got angry with me back in August and showed up at my house in the middle of the night, but it was just angry words that were thrown about. Not even fists. Certainly bar your door and perhaps keep Taichi's baseball bat handy, but I don't think it will turn into anything."

"Ted." Uncle Fuji clears his throat, but his voice remains gravelly. "We are not like you. We have always kept our heads down, so we don't have any experience with a situation like this."

Ted considers this. "I know, sir. But now it seems as if we must all fight, regardless of whether it is our nature or desire. I'm sorry for that." He offers a slight bow. "I'll let you know how my meeting with Mr. Campbell goes. I hope he will give this matter the respect and attention it deserves. Taichi, will you walk with me for a moment?"

I glance at my family, whose faces are still etched with worry. Father nods at me to go on.

When we're out of hearing range, Ted claps me on the shoulder. "How's your Japanese, my young friend?"

That's not the direction I expected the conversation to take. "Passable," I say. "Why?"

Ted's eyes shine. "Because the military has finally seen our value, and I've been asked to gather a group of men willing to serve our country as translators."

My stomach does a strange flip-flop, part excitement, part terror. "Oh. I don't know what my parents—"

"I already spoke to them. Right now, they think anything that gets you out of camp is a good idea."

"Two months ago, they wouldn't let me harvest sugar beets in Idaho. But being sent to war is okay with them?"

"Two months ago, you weren't on a death list. And this wouldn't be a combat situation. We would be in linguistics intelligence. Code breaking, that kind of thing. The military is finally recognizing the value in having some people around who speak the same language as their enemy."

I consider this. "You are going?"

"Yes."

"You barely got home two weeks ago. What about the baby?"

"This is a time of war. Sacrifices must be made." But his duty-filled words don't match the regret in his eyes.

"We would be paid?"

"Of course."

"And we would be considered soldiers?"

"Yes, sir."

If I could earn a decent living *and* serve as a soldier, that would put me back on the right path for being able to court Evalina. "Okay, what do I do?"

"First, you'll have to pass a language test four days from now. Those who pass the test will take a bus the next day to training in Minnesota."

That means by this time next week, I could be gone. Not only that, but I could be on a journey—however indirect—to get me back to the life I'd once imagined with Evalina.

My heart soars at the possibility.

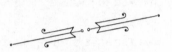

The last three days are the hardest I've ever studied. As I stop by the post office on my way to take my test, I try to make myself think in Japanese the entire way.

Kywa samui desu. It is cold today.

Sanpo wa nagai. The walk is long.

Of course, thinking in Japanese isn't where I struggle. I can understand it okay when I hear it, but I'm still very clunky with speaking, and my writing is abysmal.

There's a dusting of snow on the ground that I can feel in my bones. Especially the bones of my feet. I need to order myself new shoes. Or maybe, if I pass this test today, there will be shoes issued to me with my uniform. Do you get a uniform when you arrive at training?

Doa o akeru. Open the door.

"Hello, Taichi," the clerk at the post office says as she disappears into the back room. "Give me just a moment."

Watashi wa gamandzuyoi. I am patient.

She returns with a smile and two letters. One is from Diego with a month-old postmark. It appears to have traveled around the world to get here. Maybe twice. There's even a boot print or two on there. The other, oddly, is from Mr. and Mrs. Medina, mailed just a few days ago from home.

On my way to the testing room in the administration building, I tear into Diego's and find that it's surprisingly long, considering how much Diego loathes writing letters. I don't have time to read much before my test, which begins in ten minutes. I skim enough to see that he's happy and healthy, and that he calls me an idiot at least three times for pushing Evalina away.

When I write him back, maybe I'll be able to tell him that I'm no longer a prisoner of the U.S. government, but rather in training to be a linguistic specialist for the military. And that I've already written to Evalina and begged her forgiveness.

I refold the letter and stick it in my back pocket. I intend to tuck away the missive from the Medinas, assuming it's addressed to my parents, but rather it's *my* name that is printed on the front. I'm at the door to go into the office building, but I linger outside a moment longer. Why would they write specifically to me? The envelope feels thin. I pull open the flap so I can satisfy my curiosity before I walk into the room and sit for my test.

The single sheet of paper contains only a few lines.

Dear Taichi,

I am writing to share the sorrowful news that we've learned Diego is missing in action and assumed to be a prisoner of war. We knew you would want to know. Please tell us if you hear from him, and please pray for his safety.

Mrs. Medina

CHAPTER THIRTY-TWO

Taichi

December 1, 1942

When I awake, my eyes are crusted shut, as though even in my dreams I cried for Diego. It's dark enough that the search-lights still scan the blocks, occasionally illuminating a part of my wall. Who is in charge of the lights? Have they ever seen anything that made all that watching worthwhile? What's he supposed to be looking for, since the administration doesn't seem to care about the concerns we bring to them?

Through the grimy window, I see clear, starry skies. I pull the blanket as tight around me as possible to ward off the cold. Is Diego somewhere cold as well? At least the govern-ment in charge of my prison feels somewhat responsible for and benevolent toward me. Does Diego get a bed? A toilet? A meal each day?

Is he even alive?

Tears roll down my temples and into my hair as I gaze up at the single lightbulb, which swings lightly from the occa-sional gust whistling through the barrack. I watch shadows move in the room as memories spin through my mind. Diego whooping and hollering as he swung from the rope into the creek. The spectacle he made of himself when he had his first crush. The fierceness in his eyes when we learned about the impending evacuation.

As quietly as I can, I reach under my cot for the box where I keep my stationery. While the sky lightens from inky black to steel, and the searchlights shut off, I let my pen ramble to Evalina without bothering to censor or sterilize. About Diego. About the what-ifs circling my head.

And about Manzanar. Raymond Yamishi at the baseball game. The garbage truck. How the searchlights follow you to the latrines in the middle of the night. That I haven't eaten a meal with anyone in my family since April. The meeting I accidentally found myself in. How some of the residents have put me on a death list.

About how I'm sorry for putting space between us, because it was really the last thing I wanted.

I shove the letter into an envelope, slap a stamp onto it, and slip out of the barrack.

Outside of the Kameis' and Yonedas' apartments are two Caucasian MPs, their guns at their sides and their faces grim as they watch me walk by. I pass as far away from the MPs as I can, my thoughts on the summer, when Hikoji Takeuchi was shot for no reason, and our newspaper couldn't even report on it.

Are these MPs part of the entourage that will help the fifteen recruits get to their training? After reading Mrs. Medina's letter, I had been a shell of myself during and after the test yesterday. I can't remember everything that was said, but I have a foggy memory of protection being offered to those who passed the test and would be leaving.

The administration is apparently smart enough to realize protection is needed . . . they just don't care enough to try and fix the problems.

My heart sags with disappointment that there was no need for MPs to guard my barrack last night. Nearly everyone who did pass the language exam had spent years in Japanese schools. Ted had encouraged me to keep at it, that he'd heard the recruiters would make another round in a few months, and if I continued to study hard, I could be joining him in Minnesota soon.

The thought of a second chance buoyed me, but it didn't prevent me from feeling crushing disappointment as the life I had imagined for myself—outside of Manzanar, earning a living that could someday support Evalina and me—evaporated.

At the post office, I stare at my letter to Evalina for a moment, debating putting it back in my pocket for editing. I'm confident I've never written anything so raw. But I'm equally confident that I can trust Evalina with my uncensored self. Before I can change my mind, I drop the letter into the box.

When I get back to the block, Ted is outside his barrack with a suitcase at his feet. He's chatting with James, who has just returned home from his night shift in the dispatch office. The MPs are nearby, but don't seem particularly interested in what's going on.

Ted waves me over, and as I approach, James is saying, "I had to go every Saturday, but I hated it and never did very well. I couldn't figure out why I would need to know Japanese. Now I wish I had been a better pupil."

Ted smiles at James. "There will be other opportunities for you to serve. Your turn is coming, I'm sure."

James's smile is rueful. "I wish it would hurry up."

"Soon they'll realize that there are thousands and thousands of able-bodied men in these camps, and they'll change their minds," Ted says. "You'll see. There'll be a place for men like you, even if you don't speak fluent Japanese."

James nods to the MPs. "Why do you have bodyguards?"

Ted glances at the MPs with a grimace. "Not everyone at Manzanar thinks us helping the government that locked us up is such a great idea. I finally got Campbell to realize the threat is strong enough, that he needed to give us all police protection overnight."

I pitch my voice low. "What about when you're gone? What about Lillian and the baby?"

Ted hesitates. "I couldn't get Campbell to agree to anything as far as that goes, but he pointed out that my wife and parents are probably safer when I'm *away* from camp—"

"He *said* that?"

"He is likely right." If the assistant camp director's comment hurt Ted's feelings, he's not letting it show. "Though I still don't think anything will come of this death list business. While Joe and I differ on how to best go about creating change for our people, I don't think he would hurt Lillian. And young pups like Raymond Yamishi will follow his lead."

I hope he's right.

"Besides," James says through a yawn. "Me and Taichi will keep an eye on them."

"I know you will. And Fred and the others will be back from the JACL meeting before too long; they'll watch out for Lillian too."

James snorts. "The JACL are like lightning rods for Joe and the Dragons. Nobody is going to be thinking about Lillian if they're back."

Ted flinches. "I've made Campbell aware of the trouble, and the rumors going around about lists. He's a smart enough guy, I think. He'll keep the place in check." Ted sounds as though he's giving himself a pep talk. "The Manzanar Police too. Right, James?"

"Definitely. We'll keep this place buttoned down."

Lillian and Ted's parents come out of the apartment then. Lillian is shined up for the occasion, with her hair curled and her dress fresh, but her eyes are swollen.

Ted swallows as he watches her. "Sometimes I feel like me doing what I think is best only lands my family in more trouble."

They join us, and after a few pleasantries, it's time for them to meet the others at the entrance.

Ted picks up his suitcase, and then rests a hand on my shoulder. "Keep your chin up, Taichi. I know you're disappointed, but I'm comforted to think there's a good man like you inside the fence."

I didn't realize I needed the encouragement, but something inside me lightens with his words. James and I wave goodbye. We watch them join the Yoneda family and walk as a group to the entrance, the MPs trailing them.

"I'm dog-tired." James removes his hat, rubs at his rumpled hair, and puts it back on his head. "I think I'll skip breakfast and just go right to bed."

"I work lunch today," I say. "I'll be sure to set aside extra for you."

"Especially if George is making that stew again." James frowns and shields his eyes from the bite of the dusty wind. "I've never seen *them* building anything before."

I follow his gaze to a group of young men, including Raymond Yamishi, walking by with armloads of mangled two-by-fours. Wayward nails glint in the sunlight.

"I can't imagine they're building anything great with boards like that."

"They're odd ducks, aren't they?" James rubs at an eye. "I've got to get some sleep. I'll see you at lunch."

I watch Raymond Yamishi and his friends until they can't be seen from our block. When I get back to our apartment, my hand instinctively reaches to bar the door.

Evalina

December 2, 1942

The library has always been the place I concentrate the best, but today my brain is intent on wandering. Despite my efforts to focus on my notes from American Literature in preparation for my final exam, my mind instead wants to stay fixed on my article that was published in Monday's newspaper.

In yesterday's issue, there were multiple letters to the editor about it. One praising my point of view, and the other three protesting. One of them pointed out that I'm "obviously Italian" and should be grateful for the country I live in. As if having grandparents that were born in another country somehow strips away my right to question the decisions my government is making.

I have to stop dwelling on it. I redirect my focus to the textbook in front of me, but I struggle to really care about the symbolism in *The Scarlet Letter*.

Can't it be both? Can't I feel grateful for the freedoms of my country, as well as voice my opinion about errors in judgment that I see? Isn't my right to do so part of what makes our country great?

Focus, Evalina.

I bend deeper over my notebook and clasp both hands on top of my head, as if this will keep my focus on my scribblings from the semester.

Grace drops into the seat across from me and slings her bag onto the table with a *thump*. "You look like you're afraid your brain is going to explode."

"I am, though unfortunately not because of all the information I'm retaining about Nathaniel Hawthorne." My sigh is gusty, but it doesn't leave me feeling any lighter. "I'm really struggling to care right now."

Grace gives me a frank look. "This is about the angry letters to the editor, isn't it?"

I tap my pencil against my notebook. "Maybe."

A noise of frustration uncurls from Grace's throat. "What you wrote moved people, Evalina. That's amazing."

"But not really in the way I hoped people would be moved."

"We don't know that. Not everyone who's changed will write in. Some people may not even realize that you affected their view of the issue. And those who are deeply offended? They still stopped what they were doing to consider your viewpoint and respond. That's incredible."

"I don't know, Grace." I flip the page of my notebook. Hopefully the macabre Edgar Allen Poe will hold my interest better. "Maybe it's unrealistic, but I was really hoping that at least one student would read it, and then understand the evacuation in a completely different way. That I would overthrow their old way of thinking."

"We all hope for that when we write, but how often are you completely persuaded to a new way of thought within a six-hundred-word article? Change is a gradual thing. We have to chip away at the hard-heartedness of others and ourselves.

We have to gradually open eyes, not just grab eyelids and yank them open."

I giggle at the imagery. "Okay."

Grace sets about spreading notes across the table. "I think Monday's vigil is going to be swell, don't you? Jack had some really great ideas for how to best organize everything."

On Monday, it will have been one year since the attack on Pearl Harbor. It feels more like centuries ago with everything that's happened. At our last few meetings, the Future Leaders club has been planning a schoolwide vigil to honor those who died.

Grace taps her pencil against the library table with a quick *rap, rap, rap.* "Jack isn't very political. But I suppose that's okay. He doesn't need to be, right?"

"Right." I stare at my textbook, but my thoughts have drifted to a small ranch house on a farm in Alameda, like they often have as the anniversary of Pearl Harbor has drawn closer. But I'm not going to say anything now, because I need to study.

I turn the page. Okay, yes, I am. "I think on Sunday, I'm going to go to Taichi's house. He's not there, of course. But just . . . to see it. Like my own private kind of vigil."

Grace blinks at me a moment, looking stunned. "Evalina, I'm so stupid. I completely forgot to tell you. Over Thanksgiving, my father said he'd been in touch with Manzanar War Relocation Center about Taichi's family and he wanted me to tell you. How did I possibly not bring that up the moment I saw you?"

I didn't know my heart could go from normal to racing in such a short amount of time. "What did he say? Are they out?"

"He said it took him several weeks to get in touch with the director at Manzanar. I guess they're getting a new one or something. He finally got all the paperwork, and now he's waiting for the man in charge of transfers to get the work release in order. There's a lot of red tape, it sounds like." Grace smacks her palm against her forehead. "That was the very first thing I was going to tell you when I saw you at the FLOA meeting last night, but then we were talking about the vigil, and I got so excited . . . I'm so sorry."

"Stop apologizing, it's fine." I close my textbook. Studying is out of the question now. "Did your father say how quickly he thought it might happen?"

Grace shakes her head. "That's everything he said, I swear. Has Taichi said anything to you in his letters?"

The question lands like a kick in the stomach. I haven't wanted to admit to Grace how one-sided my relationship with Taichi is these days.

Or maybe I haven't wanted to admit it to myself.

If his family gets released on a work permit, will Taichi even write to tell me the news? It's been just short of six months since he sent me a letter. Why should I think that he'll give me his new address?

"No," I say. "He hasn't said a thing."

CHAPTER THIRTY-THREE

Taichi

Saturday, December 5, 1942

The mess hall is decorated festively with garlands and red ribbons and other items that look wonderfully out of place here in Manzanar. The band plays Christmas music that's upbeat enough for dancing, and those who are inclined cut up the dance floor, including James and Margaret, and Aiko and Ichiro.

Aiko is usually glowing when Ichiro shows up for these events, but tonight she seems a bit more sluggish out there. A bit more grim. Maybe they've been fighting?

"Hi, Taichi."

I turn to find Rose standing beside me. "Oh, hi . . ."

I instinctively look toward the door, as if I could somehow hide. But this is Manzanar. There's nowhere to hide.

"How are you?" There's a softness in the words that wasn't there the last time we spoke.

"I'm fine." I put on a polite smile. "And you?"

"Honestly, I feel really stupid." She blows out a puff of air. "I was downright awful to you the last time we spoke, and I'm really sorry about that. I don't know if you heard, but my father was released to Manzanar earlier this week."

"James told me. I was really glad to hear it."

Rose is no longer looking at me, but rather her hands, which she twists together in front of her. "Thank you. I'm so sorry for the awful accusations I made about your uncle—"

"It's fine."

"It's not. I was stupid for listening to gossip. My father . . ." Rose's eyes grow watery, and I look away. "He's not himself. Not yet."

I reach into my pocket and shove my handkerchief into her hand. "My uncle gets better with each week that passes. I hope the same will be true for your father."

Rose wipes at her eyes. "He used to be embarrassingly patriotic about America. He was so reverent about the flag, the National Anthem, everything. If the government ever opened up doors for Japanese nationals to be citizens, he would have camped outside the office for a week just to be first in line." Rose's wistful smile dies on her lips. "But last night I heard him and my mother talking about how there's no life for us here. How we should just go back to Japan when we get the chance."

It's strange to stand so close to her when she's crying, yet to keep my arms crossed over my chest. Any kind of affection seems awkward, though. Especially considering what Aiko told me. "He's been hurt and betrayed. Don't we all feel that way, if we're being honest? And the majority of us weren't sent to North Dakota."

"I suppose." Rose sniffles. Her tears glitter when the light catches them. "Taichi, I think Aiko needs you."

The change of her tone—watery to urgent—makes my heartbeat kick up a notch. I follow her eyeline to see Aiko shuffling off the dance floor with her arms crossed over her stomach. Her face is blank, but I've seen my sister mask pain enough times to recognize it for what it is.

"I'll see you later, Rose." I skirt around the dancers to where Aiko is easing into a chair. "Aiko, what's going on?"

"Probably nothing. Maybe just really bad"—her face twists briefly before she can slide the mask back over it—"cramps? I don't know."

"Where's Ichiro?"

"Getting me a drink. It's been so dry. I might be dehydrated." She winces again, and her breathing becomes even more labored. "Or maybe it's my monthly cycle."

"But I've never seen you in this much pain."

Aiko groans and leans forward. "Food poisoning?"

Ichiro materializes with a cup of water and a deep frown. "She's worse."

"I think she needs to go to the hospital."

"I don't need to go"—she gasps for air—"to the hospital."

Ichiro is as inclined to ignore her as I am. He takes one side, and I take the other. Despite Aiko's initial protest, she does nothing to prevent us from helping her out of the room. Ichiro thinks to grab coats from the pile, which is good because the temperature has plummeted to the thirties with the setting sun, and the hospital is several blocks away.

When Aiko cries out in pain and her legs collapse beneath her, Ichiro scoops her up and carries her the final block to the hospital. I jog alongside him to keep up, and then hold the door open so he can run through.

"Ichiro!" A nurse rises from behind a desk. "Aiko! What's wrong?"

"I don't know for sure," Ichiro pants. "But I think Aiko's appendix is about to burst."

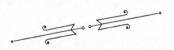

Dr. Goto briefly examines feverish, vomiting, and moaning Aiko before agreeing with Ichiro.

"Prepare her for surgery," he says to the nurses.

Horror rises up in me as the nurses spring into action, as I think of my sister being sliced open and possibly losing her life here.

Dr. Goto turns to Ichiro and then me. "Are you family?"

I try to speak, but can't seem to find my voice.

"Taichi is her brother, doctor. Should I go get her parents, or do you need me in surgery?"

"I have Peggy. Please go get her parents." To me, Dr. Goto adds, "Do you know where they'll be, son?"

"Playing Go with the Kanitos and Kameis, I think. Maybe in the rec room on block four?"

Ichiro races off, and Dr. Goto and I both watch as Aiko retches into a pail one of the nurses holds for her.

"Hopefully we've caught this early enough that her appendix isn't leaking or ruptured. When that happens, there's a high risk of infect—"

"Help me!" A yell from outside the room cuts into our conversation. The desperation infused in that voice makes my blood freeze in my veins. "Someone, please help me!"

"Get Aiko moved and the room prepped," Dr. Goto orders the nurses over his shoulder as he jogs out of the room. "I'll meet you in surgery."

"Help me!" The voice calls again from the direction of the front doors. "Is anyone here?"

I stand in the doorway, useless to everyone. I should've run for Mother and Father since Ichiro could at least do *something*.

"What's happened?" Dr. Goto's question reaches me back here in Aiko's room.

"They beat him!" The voice is male, but high and hysterical.

"There were six of them. I couldn't make out any faces because it was dark, and they ran off when they saw me. I thought he was dead at first, because he was just lying there."

"Peggy!" Dr. Goto barks down the hallway.

One of the nurses caring for my sister brushes past me. "Yes, doctor?"

"Get Mr. Tayama to a room and get him stabilized. I'll be in as soon as I'm done with the appendix."

The name is like a magnet, and I'm drawn the few steps down the hall to where I can see the hospital entrance. I don't recognize the hysterical man, and I wouldn't recognize the beaten man either if Dr. Goto hadn't used his name. But yes, it's Fred Tayama.

Number one on the death list.

It's beginning.

CHAPTER THIRTY-FOUR

Taichi

Sunday, December 6, 1942

News of Fred Tayama flies through the camp with the same speed and tenacity as the wind that whips down the Sierras. As I serve food and wipe tables at breakfast the following morning, it's all everyone is talking about.

That Fred was practically dead when he was found. That surely he would have died if he hadn't been discovered so soon.

Yet, oddly, Fred is more like a footnote to the story. Everyone seems much more interested in the fact that the only assailant Fred named to the police was Harry Ueno. And that Harry was taken from his home last night with no explanation to his wife or children, and sent to a jail outside of Manzanar.

"They're just looking for a way to get rid of Harry," one man says to another as he holds his plate out to me for toast. "The administration just wants Harry out of here because he accused them of stealing sugar. Fred probably didn't even say it was Harry."

Their voices drift away as they leave the line to find a table, and another conversation takes its place.

"I've no sympathy for Fred," one woman says to another. "He's the one who got us into this mess."

"Him *and* the JACL," the other agrees. "If they'd stuck up for us instead of kowtowing to the government, we would all be home now. Including Harry."

"Poor Harry."

George arrives behind me with a freshly cooked batch of scrambled eggs. "Crazy about Harry, huh؟"

I step back so he can pour them into the bowl I'm scooping from. "The whole situation is crazy."

"Harry would never do something like beat up Fred. Don't you agree؟"

I can't get the image of Fred's unconscious face out of my mind. Apparently he'd woken up at some point, if he had named one of his attackers. "But why would Fred have said it if it wasn't true؟"

"Dunno. To get Harry out of camp؟ Harry has been pretty vocal about his dislike of the JACL. That's like insulting Fred's wife, you know؟"

If Fred was going to lie about who his attacker was, it seems like he would have picked Joe Kurihara, the author of the death list. Joe had followers, sure. But he wasn't popular like Harry, who was a man of the people. Generous with sugar when he still had it, and willing to risk his neck by putting together a case against the administration. Though I also agree with George; Harry has never seemed prone to violence.

But while I'm thinking all this, the cook heads back to the kitchen.

". . . keeping my wife and kids at the apartment," one man is telling two others. "It's too dangerous out there today."

"I kept mine in yesterday too. I keep seeing young fellows making clubs. Have you seen that؟"

That's what James and I saw the Black Dragons doing. They weren't building furniture, they were making clubs.

"I have," I blurt before I can think better of it.

The man who brought up the clubs nods at me, and then says to all of us, "I have a friend who lives on nine. You know, where most of Terminal Island lives? He says his neighbor is this really strong pro-Axis guy. He's given speeches and stuff at some of these rallies. Anyway, he and Harry are buddies, and this guy was ranting and raving all over the block this morning about how it's time to take a stand. That we should unite and fight. That if we were to all descend on the police station, they wouldn't be able to hold us back. Crazy stuff like that. Everyone should stay inside today, or at least off block nine. It sounds like it could get real dangerous out there."

My heart has never beat so loudly before. "What was the guy's name? Was it Joe Kurihara? Or Raymond Yamishi?"

"I don't know. That sounds right."

Before he can say anything else, I fly out of the kitchen, pulling my apron off over my head just before I burst out the mess hall door. All this crazy death list stuff is starting and no one is here to persuade the Caucasian staff to take action.

My heart ricochets around my chest as I sprint to the administration building.

When I throw open the door, the secretary who dismissed me just weeks ago jumps up from her chair. "Boy, what are you doing?"

I charge past her desk, but halt in the hallway when I realize Mr. Campbell's office is dark. I fix my eyes on the next door, the office that very recently was changed from Roy Nash to RALPH MERRITT, CAMP DIRECTOR.

"You can't go back there! You have to have an appointment to see Mr. Merritt. Boy!"

Mr. Merritt is doing something that involves a folder full of typewritten papers, but he closes it when I barge into his office. Behind his round glasses, his eyes widen, and he leaps to his feet. "What's the meaning of this?"

"Pardon my intrusion, sir, but this can't wait. Are you aware that you are losing control of this camp?"

"Boy, you can*not* be in Mr. Merritt's office." The secretary puts her fists on her hips and glares at me as if this will be enough to make me tuck tail and run. As if, being Japanese, I'm not used to being glared at by Caucasians wherever I go. "We will call the police to come remove you, if necessary."

Mr. Merritt holds up a hand to calm his secretary. "Ms. Hatfield, let's allow the young man a few minutes to explain his statement. What's your name, son?"

"My name is Taichi Hamasaki. I'm an American citizen, and those in the camp who support Japan have taken matters into their own hands, and nobody seems willing to stop them."

Mr. Merritt adjusts his glasses. "If you're referring to the assault of Mr. Tayama, we've taken the perpetrator into custody. He was transported to the closest town jail overnight."

"Sir, I saw Mr. Tayama, and that's not the work of one man. The man who intervened said *six* men ran off—"

"Mr. Tayama only named one, so that's all I've been able to arrest. Mr. Hamasaki, I understand your concerns, and I promise you we're doing everything—"

"Mr. Merritt, sir, I know you're new to Manzanar. Harry Ueno is beloved, and people are angry about his arrest. They're . . . organizing."

Organizing sounds like a lame word. I should have picked something stronger.

"We are dealing with the assault of Mr. Tayama in a swift and orderly fashion. Justice will be served. You can trust that."

Why would I trust that? I haven't experienced an ounce of justice in the last year.

"The rumor is that they're getting a mob together. That they're making weapons. Some residents are staying in their barracks today because they're so afraid."

Mr. Merritt fixes me with a patronizing smile. "Manzanar is just like every other small town in America. There's always rumors flying about. If we chased every rumor we heard, we'd never—"

"These aren't common rumors. There's a death list. *I'm* on it. My uncle is on it."

"Son, you have my word that I'm doing everything in my power to calm the situation. I assure you that you're perfectly safe within camp."

"You assure me." My tone comes out twisted with sarcasm. "What exactly is being done to keep families like mine safe?"

The patronizing smile hardens into a grimace. "The most helpful thing you can do for the community is to remain calm as we investigate this situation. Now, Mr. Hamasaki, I need you to leave so I can get back to work. As you've said, there's a lot going on today."

I stalk out of his office. I tried to follow due process—something our government seems to have conveniently forgotten about—and it got me nowhere. Maybe Aiko is right. Maybe I've often confused doing what I'm told as doing the right thing.

Because I don't care what Mr. Merritt says—Manzanar is *not* a safe place today.

"I can't believe how many people are here." James cranes his neck to survey the size of the crowd. "How many do you think there are? Fifteen hundred? Two thousand?"

"Quiet, I'm listening."

Raymond Yamishi is the current speaker up on the oil tank in block twenty-two. He's yelling into a loudspeaker that they've somehow obtained, but it's still hard to hear him with how far back we are. There are ten others up there, but the only two I recognize are Raymond and Joe.

Cheers go up around the stage as my head still works through the Japanese.

"What'd he say?" James yells in my ear.

"I didn't completely understand the first thing. It sounds like they've picked five men to try and negotiate for Harry's release. And I think he said the Mess Hall Workers Union has resolved to go on strike if Harry isn't released today."

James rolls his eyes. "How will that work? Don't they want to eat too?"

"Shh."

"Nobody can hear me. And everyone back here is just a curious passerby. We're safely away from the frenzy."

"I don't think my mother would agree with that." Guilt bites at me as I look around. My mother doesn't want to leave Aiko—who's mostly sleeping, and should make a full recovery as her appendix thankfully had not yet burst—but she made it clear that I was expected to go nowhere except the barrack and to work. That I shouldn't leave block four today, not even for the post office.

She would be furious if she saw that I had not only ventured away from our block, but I was at one of the meetings led by the death list author.

Cheers go up again, along with a few cries in Japanese of, "Down with that dog!"

James looks to me again for the translation. "I caught hospital and Fred."

I swallow. "If Harry isn't released, they plan to storm the hospital and finish Fred off." My heart races as I think of Aiko, who's stuck there. Of my family who's coming and going all the time. "I'll have to warn everyone."

Raymond Yamishi's focus now swings to a spot in the crowd, and Joe yanks the loudspeaker from his hand. "No, stop!"

"I'm no rat!" The cry carries through the crowd, high and desperate. "I'm for Japan!"

"He's Tokie Slocum!" Another man yells. "He's spying for the FBI!"

Tokie Slocum. Number two on the death list. I push up on my toes, but we're too far back for me to see anything.

"What's going on?" James asks, trying to see too. "Why did he just say FBI?"

"I'm not Tokie!" The high and desperate cry again. "I swear I'm not! My name is Ronald Tatsuno, and I'm for Japan! I promise!"

"Leave him alone." Joe's voice booms over the loudspeaker again, and the crowd takes steps backward. "He's a friend."

"Taichi." James tugs at my sleeve. "Tell me what's going on."

"Some are saying he's Tokie Slocum. He's saying he's not."

"That's not Tokie," Joe yells from the stage, sounding panicked. "Stop beating him at once. I said"—he pitches his voice louder—"stop beating him! He's no rat! He's a friend!"

The scuffle halts, but the crowd has grown too restless to be content listening to speeches, and Joe seems to sense it. "Let us not lose track of who our enemy is. We, your elected Negotiating Committee, will go demand the return of Harry Ueno to this camp. Let us fight and fight to the finish!"

Many near the front hoist the crude clubs built of two-by-fours and jagged nails. The men leading the charge begin to climb down from the oil tank cover, and the crowd around us dissolves. James and I slip away to a spot where we can see how the mob progresses without chance of Raymond recognizing me. Fear screams through me when I think of those clubs and what nearly happened to the man they thought was Tokie Slocum.

James glances at his watch. "Somehow I have to get some sleep. I work tonight."

I grimace. "I don't think you'll be bored."

"No, I don't think so either." He chuckles drily. "But, you know me. I like to be in the middle of the action."

"Not *this* kind of action, though." I gesture to where the men are gathered around Joe, who appears to be doling out instructions.

"I still can't believe you barged in on the new camp director this morning. I would have loved to have seen his face."

I groan. "It was stupid of me. If I'd acted more rationally, maybe he would have paid attention to what I was saying."

"I think the only way he would have paid attention is if your face was white."

The group of men follow Joe in the direction of the police station, cheering in a way that makes me feel like I was just struck with an icy blast.

"They could go to the hospital next. I'm going to tell my family and Dr. Goto. Want to come?"

James shakes his head. "I'm going to follow these guys and see what happens."

I give James a horrified look. "No. Not alone."

"They don't care about me. And I'll stay out of the fray, I promise. I just want to see how it goes at the police office, and then I'll go home to sleep. I'll check on Lillian. The Yonedas too."

I close my eyes. Ted would be a wreck if he knew what was going on today. "Good idea. Mrs. Yoneda might be at the net factory, if you can't find her at home."

All that remains of the mob is the extra dust in the air. They wouldn't attack the factory, would they? It's all women who work there. Sure, Raymond and his group might throw rocks sometimes, but they wouldn't do anything else now that their focus is on getting Harry back . . . Right?

"Knock on my door when you get back to the block, okay?" James says, and he heads in the direction that the mob departed. Slow enough that he won't catch up to them.

I turn and run toward the hospital. As I do, I notice children peeking out at me from the windows of their barracks. Children who have been confined inside today so they won't get caught in the crossfire.

Dr. Goto is appreciative of the information and commends my bravery for delivering it.

My mother does not. I've never seen her glare with such intensity. "Did I not tell you to stay on our block?"

"You did. And I'm sorry, but—"

"You've always been my good boy, Taichi. You should not be putting yourself at risk."

"Based on what I heard, anyone sitting here at the hospital is at risk. Where are the others?"

"They're at the barrack." Mother pauses, then asks in a voice of stiff resignation, "Do you think that's the safest place for them to be?"

I think of the energy of the crowd, and the effort it took

for even Joe to convince the attackers to leave not-Tokie alone. "No. I think the safest place would be a different barrack. If they want to find Uncle Fuji or me, that's the first place they'll try."

"Yes." Mother rubs at her knuckles. "Yes, that's true. Though if we go elsewhere, we could endanger that family too."

Aiko groans and shifts in the bed. Her eyes flutter open. "Hey." Her voice sounds like sandpaper on rough wood. She coughs, and then winces.

"Here, Aiko." Mother helps her to take a sip of water.

"Nice to see you awake," I say. "How do you feel?"

"Groggy." Aiko's gaze slips to me again. "Thank you for getting me to the hospital so fast."

Her words are a little slurred, and her eyes are already closed again.

"That was Ichiro. He carried you most of the way."

"Did he see me throwing up?"

I smile. It's so nice to hear her sound like herself. "No," I lie.

"Okay, good." Aiko is quiet for a moment. "Have I missed any big news?"

Mother and I look at each other.

"No," Mother finally says, but it doesn't matter. Aiko is asleep again.

CHAPTER THIRTY-FIVE

Evalina

As I pedal away from the train station, I have a niggling uncertainty that I'll be able to find the Hamasakis' house. I saw it when I was here for Diego's farewell, but that was months ago.

I push away the doubts and pedal on. Tomorrow I'll join others in lighting candles and stilling myself to remember what we lost as a country, but this evening is just for me. For me to remember what I personally lost a year ago when the bombs fell.

I pedal past the restaurant that once had a sign saying WE DON'T SERVE JAPS! They've removed it. Probably because there are no Japanese patrons to dine there anyway. Still, I think of the look on Taichi's face that time we drove by. The clenched jaw. The resigned face. His, "It's fine, Evalina."

My vision blurs. Always trying to reassure me, even when he was the one under attack. *Especially* when he was the one under attack.

My uncertainties, it turns out, are unmerited. I steer to Taichi's house with no trouble. As though all those times I have visited in my heart have stamped a map in my head.

The ranch house looks small with all the fields stretching around it. Down the road, I can see the Medinas' home, and I think about the worry happening behind their walls. I close my eyes, draw up Diego's smiling face in my mind, and pray for his strength and safety.

I push my bicycle behind the toolshed and climb up an oak tree that Taichi and Aiko might've climbed as children. My bobby socks snag on a branch, but otherwise I climb proficiently considering my pleated skirt.

I settle onto a branch, rest my back against the trunk, and stare at the house. My heart is heavy, but my eyes remain dry for some reason. If Pearl Harbor and the evacuation had never happened, would Taichi be here, or would he have been at school with me? Would we have told our parents by now?

What are they doing in the camps tomorrow to recognize the anniversary of Pearl Harbor? I had asked Taichi in one of my letters, but of course he never responded. *Now* tears build in my eyes. I thought I would feel closer to Taichi here, but I don't. Really, being at the house just makes it that much more obvious how far away he is. And it's getting cold.

I wipe my eyes and swing a leg down only to hear the crunching gravel beneath the tires of an approaching vehicle.

I tuck my leg back up and peer through the leaves as a black car pulls up alongside the house. Even with the doors closed, I can hear the raucous laughter distinct to a group of teenage boys.

My heartbeat thunders in my ears as the doors swing out and five boys emerge. One of them drains the contents of a bottle, considers it a moment, and then throws it at the house. I jump when it shatters but manage to not yelp.

The boys laugh and send up a chorus of, "Nice one, Danny."

Another boy finishes his and throws it too. More laughter follows. My stomach is as tight as a fist, and I'm not sure my heart has ever beaten so loudly.

The one called Danny opens up the trunk of the car. I can't make out the contents in the graying light, but I'm still pierced with dread when he says, "All right, boys. Let's have some fun."

Taichi

Again a handful of men clamber on top of the oil tank cover in block twenty-two, including Joe and Raymond, and several others who I saw this afternoon but don't know by name. The ever-growing crowd members speak amongst themselves in hushed, excited tones. At this afternoon's meeting, the energy had felt like a rally or an upbeat assembly back at school. But this feels more like the tense moments before a big game, when you're about to take the field with your team.

I look at my wristwatch. It's nearly six.

When I met up with James earlier this afternoon, he'd still been at Lillian's.

"No big speeches made at the police station, which is good," he said. "I wouldn't have been able to understand them anyway. The only thing of note that happened is that Joe guy climbed on top of one of the vehicles—"

"He didn't." Lillian put a hand to her mouth.

"I think he was just trying to be heard," James said. "There were no loudspeakers this time."

"You probably didn't hear what he said, I guess?" I asked.

"I pretended I couldn't hear and asked a nearby woman. According to her, Joe said some terms had been agreed to for

Harry's release, and one included the crowd dispersing and no more mob demonstrations. And that if Harry hadn't been released to Manzanar by six tonight, they were going to . . ." He glanced at Lillian. "Do away with all the traitors in the camp."

Even the euphemism landed hard among the three of us.

"How did the crowd react?" Lillian asked, keeping her voice calm and light, but her hand moved absently over her round stomach.

"There was some grumbling, but they dispersed. Sounds like they'll gather again around six. Same place as earlier, Taichi. I'll try to be there."

But James must have finally been able to sleep, because there's no sign of him now. Unless he's here, but I can't spot him among the crowd, which has quickly swelled to be much bigger than the post-lunch meeting. There are over two thousand, I'm sure. And that's not counting those like me, who linger close enough to hear, but too far away to be absorbed by the mob.

My heartbeat slips into a fervent run as Joe Kurihara fiddles with the loudspeaker. Maybe he'll announce that Harry was released. Maybe this is where my faith in the administration will be restored.

There's a shrill moment of feedback and then Joe's voice projects across the crowd. "I am happy to say that Mr. Harry Ueno has been returned to Manzanar."

Relief seeps through me. A cheer goes up in the crowd, and the tense energy that had hung over the block seems to pop like a balloon. I applaud along with them.

"Those of us who negotiated with Mr. Merritt this afternoon have seen Harry with our own eyes. We spoke with him at the camp jail for about ten to fifteen minutes, and we therefore request to be relieved from further committee responsibilities."

Several boos rise from up front in the crowd, and the tension inflates just as quickly as it had evaporated.

"Harry should be at home!" one man yells. "Not in jail!"

"Bring Harry home!"

Joe raises his hands, as if to calm the crowd. "Harry is back in Manzanar. Those are the terms we agreed to—"

"Bring Harry home!" The crowd chants. "Bring Harry home!"

"We will bring Harry home," Joe shouts into the microphone. "We will! But let us continue our negotiations for his unconditional release tomorrow."

Joe continues to shout, but the crowd drowns him out. Some hold up homemade clubs, and others broken bottles.

My heart twists with fear as part of the group begins to march off in the direction of the jail, continuing to chant, "Bring Harry home! Bring Harry home!"

Joe and some of the others from the afternoon's meeting scramble off the platform, rushing to get ahead of the angry mob.

"Perhaps the administration thinks we will not kill the traitors of Manzanar, as we said we would should they not release Harry." Raymond's voice, pitched low and dark, makes me want to run and hide in my barrack. "After all, *they* never do what they say they will do."

Cheers of outraged agreement go up in the remaining crowd. A chant of, "Kill the dogs!" rises into the air.

Raymond allows the crowd several moments of building frenzy as he withdraws a piece of folded paper from his pocket. "We will show them that we know how to keep our promises. We will finish the work we began last night. We will go to the hospital, and we will find Fred Tayama."

The ground seems to tremble as the mob stomps and cheers. I feel as though my blood has turned to ice.

"And then we will take care of the others on our list. I will now read to you the list of traitors. The list of the condemned." Raymond clears his throat. "Tokie Slocum." He allows a beat before moving on. "Karl Yoneda. Ted Kamei. Koji Ariyoshi. James Oda. Togo Tanaka." The list stretches on in a dark, hypnotizing kind of way. Even though I know it's coming, my heart still thunders in my chest when he says, "Fuji and Taichi Hamasaki."

Raymond folds the list and puts it back in his pocket. Those in the crowd start calling out other names. "Aoki Taisedo is a rat!" one yells. Another calls out, "Dale Nunotani spies for the FBI! Block seven!"

And then a voice yells out, "Koko Ogawa!"

Koko Ogawa . . . Like Rose Ogawa. Koko must be her newly returned father. Do they have any idea that they're potentially in danger?

The volume of the crowd grows as more and more names are pitched toward the stage. After a few minutes, Raymond draws the microphone close. "I will lead a group to the hospital to take care of Fred Tayama once and for all. Tonight we will see Harry Ueno released, or we will die trying!"

I've never personally heard a battle cry, but that's what I think of when the loud, ferocious yell goes up from the crowd. There are chants of, "Down with the dogs!" and choruses of "Kimigayo," the Japanese national anthem, as a large portion of the mob moves northwest toward the hospital. Others head in the opposite direction, to join those who left for the police station.

My heart yanks toward the hospital, toward Aiko. The mob seems to be taking a direct route through the orchard, and even though I would have to skirt around them, if I ran at top speed, I could probably make it in time to warn the hospital staff.

Of course, I warned them earlier. But I don't think the

Ogawa family has any idea that their patriarch's name was mentioned tonight. The hospital has a strong leader in Dr. Goto; I must go to block nine to the Ogawas'.

Dinner hasn't been over very long, but I don't see a single person out in either of the blocks I cut through on my way to Rose's. I pound on her door, hoping I've remembered the address correctly.

A man on the other side calls, "Who is it?"

Not in a kind way, but rather like a man who anticipates unwanted visitors.

"My name is Taichi Hamasaki. I'm looking for the Ogawa family."

"He's a friend, Papa." Rose's voice rings clear through the gaps in the walls. "You can open the door."

The door unlatches and creaks open, and a gaunt man with thinning gray hair peers out at me. Rose stands behind him, smiling in a relieved sort of way. Her mother, younger brothers, and toddler sister are huddled by the heater.

"Sorry," Rose says. "It's a little scary out there today."

"That's why I'm here. A meeting just broke up where they read the death list. Mr. Ogawa, your name was shouted out in the crowd as a suggestion—an addition."

Mr. Ogawa takes the news without a flinch, but Rose's eyes widen, and Mrs. Ogawa leaves her place by the fire to draw closer to the conversation.

"It was a long list," I say. "I don't know that they're coming, but I think you should find somewhere else to stay for the night."

Mrs. Ogawa's chin sets, like Rose's did when I tried to leave her on the dance floor. "There's nowhere safer in Manzanar than block nine. Those of us from Terminal Island look out for each other."

"I hope you're right, ma'am." Because Joe Kurihara is from Terminal Island.

"Mother *is* right." Rose nudges her way to the front. "Taichi, if you're on that list, you shouldn't be out on your own. You should stay here with us."

I shake my head. "I need to make sure Ted Kamei's and Karl Yoneda's families have left their apartments. They're numbers three and four."

Rose's eyes search my face as her father drifts away from the cold, back to the heater. "After that, you should come here. You're just one person. You can't save everyone when you're up against a mob like that."

Those thoughts have been like vultures all day long, taunting me. What good do I think I can do against a large, angry mob of men? The truth is I don't know, and that maybe I can't do anything. But I won't find out if I just cower in my barrack with my bat.

"I know," I say, already backing down the steps. "But I have to at least try."

Evalina

For an unnecessary amount of time, the boys just pull items from the trunk—a few baseball bats, a can of paint, paint brushes so old their bristles jut in various directions. I can scarcely breathe, I'm so nervous.

But then they just stand by the house, holding the brushes and bats, laughing and chatting. Occasionally they look to the house, and then away from it. None of them seem to know how to get started.

Maybe they won't.

Danny has the bat slung over his shoulder, and his gaze is the one that is drawn to the house the most often. My breath catches every time I see him eyeing the place, and I frantically pray that they'll lose their nerve, that they'll realize this is stupid and just leave.

My heart plummets to my toes when Danny steps away from the pack and toward the house. Toward a window. He draws the bat off his shoulder, and the other boys fall silent as they watch.

My fingers ache from gripping the branch, and I've grown lightheaded from the rapid pace of my breathing.

Danny assumes a batting position. "This is for murdering my uncle, you filthy Japs."

Please no, please no, please no, please . . .

Danny swings, and the window shatters.

"No!" I hear myself scream. I clap my hands over my mouth, as if that will pull the sound back in, but nothing can be done.

All five of them turn in my direction.

I try not to move. Try not to breathe.

"Did you guys hear that?" one says to the others.

They stand unmoving, trying to hear me, and I stay frozen, trying not to be heard. My heart beats so loudly, I can't tell if they're making noise or not.

Danny glances at the Hamasakis' house, and then back in my direction, as if debating which to pursue. He shoulders his bat and takes several slow steps my way.

"There's no car or nothing," one of the boys says.

They've huddled together, though I'm not sure they realize it. Only Danny actively scans their surroundings.

"Let's just go," another from the group says, taking a step toward the car.

A breeze kicks up, and before I can somehow stop it, my skirt flaps. Fear slicks my throat as the moving fabric catches Danny's eye. As Danny's gaze travels up, up, up, until it connects with mine.

For a moment, we stare at each other.

Then Danny grins broadly, and my stomach clenches like I've eaten something spoiled.

"Hey, boys," he calls. "There's a kitty cat up in that tree."

My arms itch to pull me higher, to get further away from Danny's smile and the boys who are drawing closer. But that's silly. They could easily climb up after me, and then what would I do?

"Where did you come from, kitty cat?" Danny stands beneath me, the bat on his shoulder. His voice is good-natured, but his eyes tell a different story. "What are you doing hanging out in trees?"

I glance at the Medinas' house. There's a light on inside. If I ran, could I make it?

"Danny . . ." one of the boys says. While his voice holds caution, I can't imagine them doing anything more than suggesting Danny leave me alone. Danny clearly leads this pack.

Danny leans against the tree and calls up to me, "Come on down, kitty."

I scowl at him. I don't know him, but I can see this boy needs more people in his life who stand up to him. "Stop calling me that."

"She speaks!" His laugh is loud and showy. "If you don't want me to call you that, tell me your name."

If I grabbed that branch behind me, I would have a clear drop to the ground. It's higher than I'd like, but I think I could do it without injuring myself. And without giving these boys a view of my underpants.

"Instead, why don't you just leave me alone?"

"Why don't you come down here so we can talk about why you're spying on us?"

I've known guys like him, including Gia's Lorenzo. They're all charm until you put a toe out of line. And they're always at their worst when shamed in front of their followers.

I glance at the group of boys, who shift uneasily, their thumbs hooked in the pockets of their baggy jeans.

"I can talk fine from here, thanks." I adjust my footing so I can push off for that branch sooner. My legs feel like they're made of the fresh noodles we serve at Alessandro's.

"You know what I was just remembering, boys?" Danny's smile is like the edge of a razor. He looks to his group, and then back up at me. "There used to be a rumor going around that Taichi had himself a white girlfriend."

I feel my lungs expand with a sharp breath. I keep steady eye contact with Danny. The longer I look at him, the more pointed his stare becomes.

"Is that who you are, kitty cat?" Danny pitches his voice soft as he watches me. If he jumped, he could reach my foot. Grab hold of it. Instead, he twists the bat resting on his shoulder, spits in the dirt, and glares up at me. "Tell me. Are you that Jap's girlfriend?"

The self-preserving word *no* sits on my tongue, tasting sour. But it's true, isn't it? Only in my heart am I Taichi's girlfriend, because he called it off nearly six months ago. He could be seeing another girl in Manzanar, for all I know.

I open my mouth, try to say no.

But even though there are so many ways that it's true, it feels like a lie, and my denial of Taichi won't come out.

I glance from Danny's face to the bat. Danny sees me do so, and his grin returns, slick with spite. "You should see me swing this."

"I already did." The words taste like fire. "I think if you played on Taichi's baseball team, you'd be nothing more than a benchwarmer."

He jumps, grabbing for my foot.

I push back, take hold of the branch behind me, and drop to the ground. My knees groan in protest, but there's no time to pay attention to them. Danny's face is red, his eyes cold fury.

"Get back here, you Jap lover!" he bellows, his footsteps loud behind me as I run for the Medinas' house.

CHAPTER THIRTY-SIX

Evalina

I run.

I run with everything that's in me, making the wind whistle in my ears and my heart gallop. Or maybe that's the sound of Danny's footsteps right on my heels. I don't know, because I'm not turning around.

My eyes are bleary from the wind, so I don't see Mr. Medina until he's coming down his porch steps, jogging toward me. We have only met a few times, and I fear for a moment he won't recognize me out of context like this, but as he draws nearer, he puffs, "Miss Cassano. What is going on?"

Only then do I feel comfortable turning around to see what has happened. The car doors close one right after the other, the engine fires up, and dust puffs up from the car's tires as whoever is driving peels away.

"Those boys—" I can hardly get out a word with my labored breathing, and the stitch in my side that feels like a knife in my ribs. "They broke . . . a window."

"Wait to talk until you catch your breath."

The world is tilting, and I collapse onto the gravel. "One was . . . named Danny."

"I know all about those boys, Miss Cassano. I've already

called the sheriff. Called as soon as they pulled up. We thought there might be trouble at the Hamasakis' the next couple of days." Mr. Medina gives me an assessing look. "I couldn't figure out what was up in the tree that had the Nielsen kid so interested. You sit up in that tree often?"

"No, sir. I just . . ." I take a gulp. "I just wanted to remember. That's all."

"I don't know what you said to that Nielsen kid, but I thought he would start foaming at the mouth. Sure glad his friends tackled him." He removes his hat and scratches at his rumpled, graying hair. "If he's anything like his father, his bark is worse than his bite. But still. It can be a nasty bark."

The trembling that had been confined to my legs and arms now spreads to my whole body. What would Danny have done if he'd gotten ahold of me?

The screen door creaks on its hinges as Mrs. Medina comes out on the porch. "Everything okay?"

Before Mr. Medina can answer her, the sound of crunching gravel interrupts. The sheriff's car comes into view. Mr. Medina speaks in Spanish to his wife, and the only word I catch is my last name.

She goes back inside the house, and he says to me, "The sheriff will be interested in what you saw, but don't worry. I'm having Mrs. Medina call your father."

My father.

"She's calling my father?" I echo, but Mr. Medina is already striding toward the road as the sheriff pulls into the Hamasakis' driveway.

I stand on shaky legs and retie my trench coat.

I guess the time has come—like it or not—to tell my parents everything.

Taichi

As I'm cutting through block three, I find two young boys standing outside the laundry room, peering around the corner.

I slow to a stop. "You need to go home, fellas. It's dangerous out here."

One of them looks up at me with frightened eyes. "They're tearing up Mr. Slocum's place. Why are they doing that?"

I move to stand beside them and look around the building's edge. There are a few men standing around outside the open door of a barrack. Through the gaping doorway, I see men thrashing about inside. The clang and crash of destruction rings through the cold air, but it's the laughter and delight of the men that really chills me.

"Did they get Tokie?"

"No." The older of the two shivers in his thin coat. "He was already gone when they arrived. I don't know where he went."

I don't want to find out what will happen if Lillian and Ted's parents, or Mrs. Yoneda and Tommy are still at home when these men finish here.

"Which apartment is yours?" I ask the boys, and I make sure they're inside with the door closed before I slip down the firebreak.

The sounds of smashing glass and vengeful laughter become a ghost behind me. As I curl around the corner toward four, James hisses, "Taichi!"

Relief sings through me when I see it's not just James, but Lillian and Ted's parents as well.

"Thank God. I was just coming to check on you. What about Mrs. Yoneda?"

"She and Tommy already left. There's a group of them on block four." Lillian's voice is husky with fear. "Twenty or thirty of them."

"They're tearing up Tokie's place right now. It's good that you got out. Where are you going?"

All three of them grip suitcases. "The administration office. That's where Elaine Yoneda said she was going. I requested police protection, but no one ever showed up."

"We should go this way"—I point—"or we'll run into the group on three. Lillian, let me take your bag."

"We've seen a few police out," James murmurs as we move along the shadows. "I'm eager to get to the station and find out what's being done. What happened at the meeting?"

I give a truncated version of the out-of-control meeting, the list being read, and the groups splitting.

"I think the police station is going to be nuts." I look down another block as we pass by and find it deserted. "About half of them went to the station and the rest to the hospital."

Lillian's eyes are wide. "But didn't you say Aiko is there?"

"They only want Fred Tayama." I ignore that itchy fear that's been growing in my chest ever since I chose to go to Rose's instead of to the hospital. "I told Dr. Goto this afternoon about the threat, so they'll be prepared. My family is safe there. I'm sure of it."

Lillian keeps looking at me like all my family just died, and I turn away. The edges of Evalina's letters dig at my skin, and after seeing how the men ripped apart Tokie's place, I'm glad I removed them from under my mattress.

For once I'm grateful for the searchlights crisscrossing through camp. Even a block away from the police station, we can hear the noise of the mob.

At the administration office, James pulls open the door, and I pass Lillian's suitcase back to her. Mr. and Mrs. Kamei bow and say hurried thank yous.

"Thank you for taking care of me." Lillian's voice is stiff as she withholds tears. "Ted would thank you too."

"You're safe now, Lillian," James says in that authoritative way he has.

James and I watch the door of the office close behind her, and then we turn away. If only the same could be said for us.

We stare toward the streetlamps, which illuminate the crowd gathered in front of the building where James needs to go.

"You could come to the hospital with me," I offer. It's on the opposite corner of Manzanar, and I'm not looking forward to a solo walk through the dark camp.

James tilts his head. "Is that . . . singing?"

I listen for a moment. "Yes. 'Kimigayo,' I think. Some of them were singing it back at the meeting."

James starts moving closer, and I follow. Sometimes my mother would hum "Kimigayo" when she cooked, gardened, or missed her childhood, but I've certainly never heard it sung *this* way before. The words rise up in a haunting, ominous kind of fog.

"We shouldn't go any closer," I say.

"I have to get to work, though."

But that's not the only reason that compels James. Crowds are a flame that draws his inner moth.

In addition to the military police in the guard towers, there are more on the ground than I've seen in the entire evacuation. A whole line of them stands along the police station—at least a hundred—their faces hard and stoic. For the first time, I understand why they feel their presence is necessary. Why, maybe, they think they needed to set up those machine guns on either end of the police station.

There are hundreds of Japanese Americans crowded around the station. "Kimigayo" has faded away, and there's a restless energy pulsing. Every part of me wants to run. Wants to get as far from here as I can.

"James, no one will care if you don't show up for work."

James pushes onto his tiptoes. "*I* care."

"This crowd will kill you if they think you're headed into this building. And that's if the MPs don't get you first. Don't be stupid."

"I'm wearing my uniform. They won't hurt me." James nudges a man lingering on the fringe of the crowd. "Do you know what's going on here? What are we waiting for?"

"I don't know very much," the man says. "Two men are in the police station trying to get Harry released to go home. The captain came out just a bit ago telling everyone to go back to their barracks, but everyone wants to know what's going to happen." He gasps. "That young man is going to get himself shot."

I follow his gaze and gasp too. One of the Black Dragons has turned his behind to an MP in front of the station. He slaps his exposed buttock several times, laughing and taunting. The MP doesn't even flinch.

James gives me a look. "See? I'll be fine."

I ignore him and ask the man, "Do you know who's in there with the police?"

"I only recognized Joe Kurihara." He frowns and points to the other side of the crowd. "I had been standing over there, but then a large group arrived. They had been terrorizing the hospital, and they were too rowdy for me."

Terrorizing the hospital. The awful phrase sticks in my head.

James swallows. "Did they kill Fred?"

"No. It sounded like he escaped somehow."

"I have to go find my family," I say in a low voice to James. "It's dangerous here. Come with me."

"I'll go around the back way, and I'll be fine once I get inside. There's Yosuke." James waves his hand frantically. "Yosuke!"

Yosuke had been edging his way around the crowd and turns at the sound of his name. "Oh, good. We can go together. I think if we head in the back door, we'll be safe."

"I agree." James waves over his shoulder at me. "I'll come by your place tomorrow morning to see how your family is, okay?"

I barely get out the word, "Okay," when James breaks into a jog to catch up with Yosuke.

I want to sprint away from here to the hospital, but it seems dangerous to run while I'm still near the mob.

As I walk briskly away, several of the MPs guarding the door begin to shout at the crowd. "Back up! Everybody back up!"

The authority in their voices makes me break into a jog. I've just reached the edge of the closest block when I hear screams behind me. "Tear gas! They've thrown tear gas!"

I turn. My heart sinks to my feet at the sight of the fog rising up over the crowd, oddly reminiscent of my bay-side Saturday mornings with Evalina. No longer is the mob one sentient being, like at the rally after dinner, but rather like a vase being dropped to the floor and splintering in all directions.

There's a mass of people moving toward me, and I tuck

myself around the corner of a barrack. Did James and Yosuke make it in okay?

Pop, pop—the distinct cracks of a firing gun fill the air, and I hear myself screaming. Why is someone shooting? What's happening?

All around me, men yelp with fright as they run through the block.

Pop, pop. Pop, pop. More shots. I squeeze my eyes shut. My body slides along the tar paper to the ground. Did people try to climb the fence?

After a few minutes, the stampede of people thins and then stops. When I stand, my knees are trembling so much, I'm not sure I'll be able to walk. I peer around the corner, back toward the police station.

Bodies.

The streetlight that once illuminated an angry mob now reveals one still body. No, three. It's hard to tell with the harsh shadows.

I didn't know your heart could beat right in your ears like this. Or that you can hear your own blood roaring through your veins.

I was there in the mob. I walked away, but men slower to do so were killed.

One of the men is moving, and my heart leaps with hope. I run toward the twitching man, only to be blasted by the full glare of a searchlight and a deep voice on a loudspeaker. "Stop right there!"

I instinctively hold up my hands. The MPs are just silhouettes against the lights. So are their submachine guns.

"Don't shoot!" I hold my hands up higher. My eyes water from the hovering tear gas. "I only want to help the ones who are injured!"

"We've already called for medical help. Clear the area."

"Please, let me help!"

"Authorized personnel only. Move along, or we'll be forced to arrest you."

One of the Manzanar police cars pulls up, and out climbs George Fukasawa, who I've played baseball with before. "George!"

He looks from me, to the bodies, and up to the MPs. His face is as stricken as mine feels.

"I think some of them are alive. They wouldn't let me help."

"Yeah, come on over by the car, Taichi. You don't need to see any of this up close." George looks at his partner as he gets out of the vehicle. "Let's figure out who's injured so we can give the doc a head's up."

The squad car is warm, and I lean against it, as if it can penetrate the icy cold that's taken over my body.

George's partner crouches next to the man I had seen moving. I'm close enough to hear him speak in a soothing voice about how nurses are on their way. That he'll be taken care of soon.

George crouches over a long form. His mouth makes the shape of an O, and he presses his fingers to the man's neck. He waits, and the searchlight glints on the tears that have filled his eyes. He looks up at me. "It's James Kanito. He's . . ."

George doesn't finish, but he doesn't need to. I can see the horrible, unchangeable truth all over his face.

CHAPTER THIRTY-SEVEN

Evalina

As Mr. Medina and I pick up shards of glass from the ground, Daddy pulls up in the Espositos' car, Mama in the seat beside him. Their faces are unreadable as they get out, as though they agreed beforehand that they would reveal no emotion when they arrived.

What had Mrs. Medina told them, anyway?

Mama immediately comes to me, her hands cupping my face. "You okay?"

I lean into her touch. To my surprise, my eyes pool. "Yes." I choke on the word.

Daddy's arm slips around my shoulders, and when he rests it there, it feels like the weight of guilt.

"I really am fine." I wipe at my eyes with the sleeve of my coat. "I don't know why I'm crying."

"Could you please tell us what happened?" Mama asks. "Mrs. Medina told us you stopped some boys from vandalizing the Hamasakis' house, that the sheriff was here, and we should come too."

"I only kind of stopped them." I gesture to the house. "They broke a window."

"The damage would've been much worse without you, Miss Cassano." Mr. Medina dumps a handful of broken glass into the trashcan we borrowed from under the Hamasakis'

325

sink. It wasn't exactly the way I imagined seeing inside Taichi's house for the first time.

Mr. Medina rests his hands on his hips. "Brave girl you've got here, Alessandro. I was getting washed up when I saw a group of boys from town pull up. I knew there was going to be trouble when I saw who one of the boys was. Before the evacuation, his whole family had been pretty outspoken about their dislike for the Hamasakis." Mr. Medina makes a sour face. "I knew I could run the boys off on my own, but I called the sheriff right away. I hoped maybe he could catch them in the act. Of course, had I realized Miss Cassano was sitting up in the tree, I would've gone over right away."

Mama and Daddy both turn their gazes to me. I swallow and stare at my oxfords.

Mr. Medina goes on in agonizing detail about Danny making a grab for me, and how I shocked everyone by leaping out of the tree and running "like a deer."

"You should've seen her," Mr. Medina says with a gruff laugh. "She looked like she swings out of trees every day, she was so graceful. And boy, am I glad that Danny kid is slow. He was chasing her with a baseball bat, but one of his friends caught up quickly and tackled him. The boys high-tailed it out of here after that."

A beat of silence falls.

Daddy recovers first. "Well, that's our Evalina. A unique mix of fire and grace."

I keep my gaze directed down while the adults finish up their conversation, and then we load my bicycle into the back of the Espositos' car. I tell Mr. Medina thank you, and with trepidation, climb into the back seat.

I should speak first.

It would be the responsible thing to do.

Daddy backs out of Taichi's driveway. "Is heading back through town the fastest way to Berkeley?"

"Or you can just take me to the train station."

"I think we could use the extra time to talk, don't you?"

Fear digs into my heart.

Daddy looks at me in the rearview mirror. "It sounds like you were very brave this evening."

"I was just too angry to stay quiet."

"That counts as bravery, I think."

Even without seeing Daddy's face, I can tell he's smiling.

Another silence falls. I swallow and smooth my skirt over my dusty knees. I should just open my mouth and say it. *I've been keeping something from you for a long time now.*

"How fortunate that you were there to stop those boys." Mama's statement asks an unspoken question: Why *were* you there, Evalina?

I look at my lap. "I've been keeping something from you both. Something rather important. Taichi and I . . ." What are we now? What is the truth? "We're not just friends."

The car is quiet. I make myself look up. Mama has turned to look at me over the passenger seat. "Honey, we know."

"You do? Since when?"

Mama looks at Daddy. "When did you first figure it out, Alessandro?"

Daddy shrugs. "Well, I first suspected when suddenly she was at the restaurant for every produce delivery." He glances at me in the rearview mirror. "You were so snappy if you missed one. And on the few occasions that happened, Taichi would be looking all around the kitchen for you."

"You were well before me, then," Mama says. "I didn't really *know* until Taichi showed up at the house to tell you he was being evacuated. Oh, Evalina, the look of fear on your face when you saw him. If it hadn't been such a terrible cause for a visit, it would have been funny."

I swallow. "But when I say we're not just friends, I don't mean that we just like each other. I mean . . . we've been seeing each other. For a while now."

Mama looks at me, her face soft. "We know what you mean, Evalina."

"But neither of you said anything."

"Well, neither did you."

"I thought you would be mad."

Mama and Daddy exchange looks. Mama is the one who speaks. "We certainly hoped that it was more of a passing fancy than anything else. I think I said that to you when we left Manzanar. But that has nothing to do with Taichi, and everything to do with how challenging marriage is even when you've been raised in the same neighborhood with the same values."

Mama doesn't want to say it, but I will: "And when you're the same skin color."

"Yes." Mama draws out the word. "There are uniquely hard times ahead of you and Taichi if you marry. You know that."

I'm quiet. "Yes, I do. But I also don't know how to *not* love him."

Mama and Daddy look at each other again. I thought I might feel awkward saying love, but instead I feel freer. Lighter.

Daddy speaks this time. "If anyone I know is brave enough to handle what lies ahead, it's you, my Evalina. Though, I don't understand how you can be brave enough to choose political science as your major or challenge ignorant strangers at Yosemite, yet be too scared to tell us the truth about Taichi."

"Because she would be fighting for herself." Mama turns to face me again. "You have always excelled at fighting for others. But if you want to have the strength to continue to do so, you must value yourself enough to fight your own battles too."

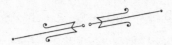

Back at my dormitory, feeling like I've been gone for days instead of hours, the room of silver mailboxes beckons me. I bite my lower lip. I haven't checked mine the last few days because I had grown so tired of being disappointed. But given the evening I've had, it's not like an empty mailbox is going to bring me much lower.

I pull out the key and open the door. My breath catches at the sight of a thick envelope. Of my name printed in Taichi's neat script.

I open it right there.

Taichi

Monday, December 7, 1942

Dark is the night at this hour. The searchlights don't reach this corner of the hospital. Or maybe the lights are turned off, or focused on a different part of camp. Even the moon has hidden its face tonight.

The at-capacity hospital room is finally quiet now that everyone has been sewn up or bandaged and is resting. I'm the only one awake in here. The only one waiting for the sunrise to come, for the dawn of December seventh.

Last year, it seemed impossible to think that another

day could feel as dark as that Sunday. But now I struggle to imagine how I could ever feel light or happy again.

Words swirl in my head, but they're the same words that have been swirling since last night.

James is dead. He was just trying to go to work. He was just trying to do the right thing. They shot him. James is dead. One of those shots I heard, it killed James. He was just trying to do what was right. He wasn't even part of the angry mob, and he got shot.

It's just me here with Aiko. Everyone else in our family is in the administration building with the other families on the death list, waiting to find out what will happen now. Fred Tayama is there too, having survived by hiding underneath an orthopedic bed while the mob was searching for him.

According to the nurse's gossip, Joe Kurihara, Raymond Yamishi, and many of the others trying to get Harry released have all been rounded up. Nobody seems to know where they are now.

Manzanar is quiet. But at too high a cost.

All day yesterday the hospital had been fairly empty, but now every bed is full of both those who were beaten up by the mob and those who were part of the mob. All of whom are being treated within feet of each other.

But not James. Because James is dead.

I rest my head on the edge of Aiko's bed, dizzy with fatigue and homesickness and sadness. I want to sleep in my own bed, walk land that belongs to us, eat a home-cooked meal, and see Evalina again. I put my hand inside my pocket and rest it on Evalina's photograph.

I snap up when Aiko's hand brushes against my hair. My neck is tight and aching from the way I had slept.

"I think I fell asleep for a minute."

My sister takes one of her pillows and moves it to the edge

of her bed, where it's easier for me to rest my head. "I think that would be good for you."

Out the hospital window, Mount Williamson turns a becoming shade of gold as the rising sun reflects on its peak. The day has dawned, and it has done so without James.

I lie there, think about James, and cry silently.

But not silently enough, because Aiko's hand rests on my head. "When I lost the baby," her voice is graveled from disuse, "I never thought I was going to feel happy ever again. Which is strange because it's not like I had even wanted to be pregnant or wanted to marry Dennis. He had broken up with me when I said I was going to have it. I felt like I had done the right thing, and then . . ."

She smooths my hair the same way Mother does when she's comforting me. I can feel Aiko's tears damp on the pillow alongside mine. "Taichi, sometimes we do the right thing, and life kicks us in the teeth just as hard as if we'd done the wrong."

Evalina

Tuesday, December 8, 1942

I run for the dormitory, not caring who thinks I look unladylike or strange. Grace's words, the ones she'd greeted me with at breakfast, reverberate with each footfall. "Father says to call him right away. He says it's about Taichi."

I keep telling myself it could be *good* news about Taichi. Maybe Mr. Bishop has finally worked out details for their release. Though would he have gone to the trouble of telephoning Grace and asking her to have me call him *right away* if it was good news?

My fingers tremble so much that I pinch the tips of them when trying to close the door. I fumble the dime into the slot and spin the dial.

After being transferred by Mr. Bishop's secretary and waiting for what feels like endless minutes—though it can't be *too* long because I haven't even put in a second dime—Mr. Bishop comes on the line.

"What's happened? Is Taichi okay?"

"As far as I know, yes. But when I spoke to Mr. Heath, the man in charge of relocations, he told me there was a riot at Manzanar on Sunday."

I gasp, my head a mess of all those stories about death lists and garbage trucks from Taichi's letter. "A riot?"

"Yes. He told me it was stirred up by a small group of men who were pro-Japan, and they targeted those who are vocally pro-America or for cooperating with the administration. The families who were in danger in camp are being moved to a facility in Death Valley. The Hamasakis are one of the families on that list."

I realize I'm squeezing the telephone, as if this will cause more details to pour out. "I don't understand how Taichi could have been in such danger."

"I know. I don't understand the details yet either, but I knew you would want to know. The Manzanar administration isn't quite sure what to do from here. If they should release the families from Death Valley, just not to locations within the military zone, or if they should send them to another camp until they get this figured out. There's a lot still up in the air."

Poor Taichi. He had already been destroyed by the news of Diego being presumed MIA, and now this.

"Thank you for letting me know, Mr. Bishop. I appreciate it."

"For whatever its worth, Mr. Heath thinks getting the Hamasakis released to Stafford—where my son lives—could eventually work. He just isn't sure if it will be days or weeks or months."

"I hope it's days."

"I hope so too, Evalina. And you'll need to talk this over with your parents, of course, but my family is going to Stafford over Christmas this year. You are welcome to come with us if there's a reason to. Again, if it's okay with your parents."

"Thank you. I guess we'll just have to wait and see."

Mr. Bishop sighs. "Yes. I guess so."

Taichi

December 20, 1942

When I awake, we're still on the bus. Kansas still stretches on, flat and snow-covered with a pearl gray sky for as far as I can see.

"Oh, good," Aiko says. "You're awake. We're supposed to arrive in a few minutes."

I rub at my bleary eyes. "Okay," I say through a yawn, and then I let my head rest against the cold, hard window.

Once again, I've been loaded on a bus and told where I'm going. Stafford, Kansas, with several other Japanese American families. Once more, I had to pack all my belongings into bags that are no more than I can carry, though I never really unpacked them at Death Valley, so at least it was easier this time.

And at least at Death Valley, everyone was saying goodbye. Aunt Chiyu and Uncle Fuji had been too nervous to come with us and live in predominately Caucasian communities, so they had chosen to be sent to one of the other camps in Wyoming. Lillian, her newborn son, and Ted's parents were going there as well. Mrs. Yoneda and Tommy were being permitted to move back to her parents' house in Los Angeles, so long as she promised to check in with the WRA about Tommy once a month.

A few other families had chosen to go to Wyoming as well, but most of us were being sent to various farms in the Midwest. Or for a lucky few who were the right age and could afford it, to a university.

I've desired a life outside the fence since April, but now that I have it, I find that I understand my aunt and uncle's fears. In Colorado Springs, our bus had stopped so we could get some food, only the restaurant refused to serve us. We were only able to eat because a Caucasian man saw and went in to place an order for us. I had never felt so ashamed while eating a hamburger. There had been another incident in Garden City when I tried to buy a piece of fruit at a filling station.

I'm jolted out of my thoughts by the bus stopping, and then turning off.

We're here.

Aiko stands, and an envelope flutters out of her pocket and onto my lap. She snatches it up before I have a chance to react.

I stand too, relishing how it feels to stretch my legs. "What was that?"

"Nothing." Aiko's smile is bashful. "Just a letter I received from Ichiro before we left Death Valley."

On a better day I would've smiled and teased my sister. Instead I say, "Anything interesting?"

"Mostly news about people we both know at the hospital. Not much that would be of interest to you. Though he did say that James Kanito had a very well-attended service. Even a lot of the administration came."

I snort as we start moving down the aisle. "I'm sure the Kanito family really appreciated their presence."

"Obviously it doesn't make up for what happened." Aiko's voice and expression are both tender. "But isn't it better that they came? Don't you think it hopefully shows that they won't just ignore complaints anymore?"

Since we're stepping off the bus, I don't feel like I have to answer her. Of course I'm glad James's service was well-attended, but I'm also not so naïve anymore to actually think—

Evalina.

I can't seem to move. It's really her. She's really standing at a bus station in Stafford, Kansas, shivering in the cold, and watching me with delight on her face.

When she opens her mouth to call to me, her jaw trembles. "I promised that when you got off the bus, I would be here."

I drop my bag and run to her.

Evalina

December 25, 1942

As soon as breakfast is over, I pull on boots to guard my feet from the snow and tie on my coat that's always been sufficient in California, but that the Kansas wind seems to laugh at as it blows right through.

I march down the road with exaggerated steps to warm myself until I arrive at the flaking, white house. Before I can knock, Taichi whips open the door—his handsome face still catching me off guard after being without it for so long—and pulls me inside. The wood-burning stove has their humble workers' house so warm, I don't hesitate when Taichi takes my coat off my shoulders.

"Thank you," I murmur. "Merry Christmas."

"Merry Christmas, Evalina."

Even after five days, I still feel a strange shyness in our first few minutes together. Both his parents and Aiko are always here, and they're always very friendly, but the newness still leaves me feeling awkward. If my mother were here, she would warn me that I'm being a pest, coming over here every day. Taichi assures me I'm not.

"Where are your gloves?" Taichi presses my hands between the two of his, which makes my heart feel as though it just burst into flames.

"I couldn't find them."

"You should have waited to come over until you found them. I like all of your fingers. I would rather you not lose any."

I laugh, and some of the embarrassment slips away. "Merry Christmas, Mr. and Mrs. Hamasaki."

They look up from their morning tea. "Merry Christmas, Evalina."

The house is so small, there isn't really anywhere we can go and have privacy. With the snow, we can't even go outside. But the Hamasakis are used to close quarters, and his family is respectful about letting Taichi and me talk as if they are not present.

We settle on the couch by the stove. Taichi's fingers clasp mine.

"How was Christmas morning at the Bishops?"

"Fine. They're a nice family."

"They seem like it. They've done a lot for us." Taichi smiles, but it's strained. Being sent somewhere else that he didn't get to choose has cost him in pride. I hadn't thought about that, but I could see it soon after arriving. He didn't just want out of Manzanar, he wanted to be free on his own terms.

"What will your parents be doing this morning?" Taichi asks.

"I don't know, really." My stomach squirms with guilt, even though Mama and Daddy had blessed the trip. "It'll be a quiet Christmas for them."

He squeezes my hand, perhaps seeing my sadness. "Maybe the three of you can celebrate next week."

I try not to, seeing as his parents are about ten feet away at the kitchen table, but my tears well and fall before I can do a thing to stop them. In five days, I will say goodbye to Taichi yet again, get on a train with the Bishops, and go back to San Francisco.

"I just wish you could come with me," I whisper.

I cover my face, feeling sharp humiliation. On the very first day, after Taichi got over the shock of me being there to pick him up from the bus station, we had vowed that we wouldn't waste our time whining about how little time we had.

"I'm sorry." I wipe at my tears with the sleeve of my sweater. "I know we said we wouldn't do this."

"I wish I could go with you too. Or that you could stay here."

"Maybe I could." My heart inflates at the thought. "They have universities here just like they do in California. What does it matter if I go to school here or there?"

"No, Evalina." Taichi's tone is gentle, but the words sting all the same. "That's foolish when we don't know that . . ." He swallows.

"You don't know that what?"

Taichi looks at me and takes a deep breath. "We've heard talk that enlistment might soon be open for the Nisei."

My response falls out involuntarily, no more than a whisper, "No."

Taichi is quiet for a moment. "How can I not, Evalina? If I want places like Manzanar to become just a bad memory, or Diego to be released if he really is in a POW camp, how can I not do my part?"

Given everything that's happened to him in this last year, how can he be willing to fight for America?

Taichi leans forward until his forehead is matched with mine. "I don't like it any more than you do, but you need to go back home. You need to study hard and get your law degree. And then someday we'll be battling together. Side by side."

"You can't guarantee that."

"No," he says quietly. "But I think the chance of it happening is worth fighting for."

I swallow. "Me too."

"But not now." He leans back. "Right now, we get to rest and enjoy being together. And you get to open your Christmas present. Don't look at me like that. It's not much."

"Still. I didn't expect anything at all."

"That's why it was so fun." Taichi grins and hands me a box. "Merry Christmas, Evalina."

I slide the top off the box and burst out laughing. "It's an orange." I pull it from the box and hold it out to him. "You gave me an orange."

"They had them at a gas station we stopped at on our way. I tried to buy it because it made me think of you, but they wouldn't let me." Taichi's face flickers again, showing his bruised pride. "Not until the guard said that we were on our way to help with cattle for the war effort. Then they seemed okay with it."

My blood pressure rises. "You should've bought it and thrown it at them."

Taichi laughs. "I thought about it, because I assumed that's what you would tell me to do. But then I decided that I would much rather eat it and think about you."

"So, why didn't you?"

"Because I slept instead, and when I woke up again, we were practically here. Now I get to enjoy it *with* you."

I pierce the peel with my thumb. "Mrs. Ling thinks oranges are lucky for that reason. That they're shareable."

I hand half to Taichi, and his fingertips brush mine.

He smiles. "This is the luckiest orange I've ever eaten, then."

In a few days, this will all just be a memory. And if Taichi really does enlist, who knows how long it will be before we see each other again.

But there will be plenty of days ahead for sadness and fighting. Today, I will instead choose to be brave by feeling the joy offered to me in this moment.

Epilogue

December 7, 1950

Somewhere outside of Mojave, James is lulled to sleep by the rhythm of the highway, and I follow close behind him.

I awaken when the car begins churning gravel under its tires. I blink, momentarily blinded by the glare of the afternoon sun on the snow.

"Good morning, Sleeping Beauty."

From the driver's seat, Taichi smiles at me.

I push myself upright. "How long did I sleep?" I can tell from how groggy I am, it was no catnap.

"Over an hour. James is still out."

"I'm so sorry. I shouldn't have slept that long."

He gives me a long look. "You've nothing to apologize for. I'm dragging you and James all the way out here—"

"You know I wanted to come too."

"Well." Taichi turns and looks out the rental car window. "We are here."

Now that my eyes have adjusted, I realize there isn't much to see. Where are all the buildings?

"You're sure this is it?"

"I drove by it once and had to turn around, but look." Taichi points.

Now I see the sign. MANZANAR WAR RELOCATION CENTER. Beyond it, the rickety remains of a guard stand. The fence is still there too, just none of the ugly barracks that I remember from my one and only visit to this place.

A gust of wind rocks the car and sends several tumbleweeds careening past. We both turn and look at James, who sleeps undisturbed across the back seat of the car.

Taichi reaches over and rests a hand on my round stomach. "It's hard to believe that this time next year, there will be two kids back there."

I settle my hand on top of his, and for a few minutes we just sit there. Staying in our mostly-happy present instead of slipping into the heartache of years gone by. Taichi lingers a suspiciously long time. He's stalling.

"Do you think the car can handle the old road?" I ask. "We could drive it while James sleeps."

Taichi holds my gaze, and the look on his face is reminiscent of when we were seventeen. Shame mixed with fear.

And just like when we were seventeen, there's only so much I can do to alleviate what he's feeling. I squeeze his hands. "It will be fine."

His mouth quirks. "Normally that's my line."

But with his jaw set, Taichi shifts into drive, and the car eases forward and through the dilapidated gates of Manzanar.

When we knew we would be in California to visit family and friends, Taichi had written to his friend from camp, Ted, to ask if he'd ever gone back to Manzanar. Ted said he hadn't, but heard there wasn't much there anymore. Veterans from the war had lived in the former staff housing for some time, but otherwise all that remained was the cemetery, the orchard, and the high school, which had been built after Taichi's time. After the war ended and the camps emptied, the government had sold whatever they could.

"Maybe it's senseless," Taichi had said to me, pacing the small kitchen of our near North side home in Chicago. "But I just want to see it again. I want to choose to go there, and I want to choose to leave."

"Then let's go," I had said. "We will make it work."

That had sounded fine in Chicago, but now as pain etches Taichi's face, I wonder if I should have talked him out of it. Maybe in a few years . . . what? When will the pain of the evacuation ever not feel fresh and raw? Seeing Manzanar again for the first time never would have been easy.

We tacked the trip onto our visits in southern California. First we'd stayed with Tony, Mary, and their kids, and then Diego and his wife, who just welcomed baby number three. As our James and their oldest played tag in the yard, Diego had winked at me. "Didn't I tell you we would get here someday?"

Something about it made my eyes go misty, a mix of sadness and gratitude that he and Taichi had both come back from war safe and whole. Diego still struggles with blue periods, understandable after his three weeks in a POW camp before a prisoner exchange. But his wife, a sweet former war nurse, said Diego's sad times seemed less severe than they once did.

From here, we'll head to San Francisco to visit Mama and Daddy. I will also get to meet Gia's new husband and baby, which I'm looking forward to. She mourned Lorenzo and his death so bitterly that for a time her parents had raised Lorenzo Junior, but Gia's strength and stubbornness finally served her well when she determined to break free of her grief. A year ago, she married a bookstore manager, who my mother says looks at Gia as though she hung the moon. They welcomed their first child just before Thanksgiving.

And I'll have a whole week to soak up time at home with Mama and Daddy. Plus they'll come to Chicago in a few months when the baby is born. Five years ago, when we told them we intended to settle in Chicago where Taichi's family had all found jobs after the war, I thought they might be mad. Good lawyer that I was, I had armed myself with all the arguments about how Taichi had job opportunities in Chicago, and we didn't face the prejudice in the Midwest that we did in California.

Instead, Mama had laughed about me somehow finding my way back to my roots. "Maybe you will be able to argue some of my nephews out of jail."

No matter how many times I explain that civil rights attorneys don't handle criminal cases like that, they never seem to understand. But they *do* always seem very proud.

Taichi points out the window, drawing me back to the present. "We played baseball over there. You'd never know it now."

The car bumps violently over the neglected road, and James sits up, rubbing his eyes. "Time to get up?"

"Perfect timing, buddy," Taichi says over his shoulder. "We're getting out of the car."

He stops at a tall, white obelisk with Japanese writing. The stone looks as though it's a monument of some kind.

"What does it say?" I ask as Taichi rummages in the back for our coats.

"This wasn't here when I was." Taichi studies it a moment as I put on my coat. "I think it says *soul consoling tower.*"

Together we get out of the car, a gust of wind assaulting us and drawing tears to my eyes. How in heaven's name did all those residents endure the wind whipping through the gaps of their homes? James buries his head against my shoulder as I follow Taichi out to the cemetery.

Though he never said this was why we came, I'm not at all surprised that this is where he drove to first, and that he walks along the stones until he finds the one for James Kanito. Taichi tucks his hands deep into the pockets of his wool coat. I lean against him, silent.

Not until we married did I realize how haunted Taichi had been by the death of James Kanito. On our honeymoon, he asked me if we were to have a boy, could we please name him James? Even after everything Taichi experienced while away at war with the 442nd Regimental Combat Team, when he had nightmares it was always James's name that I heard.

"Nineteen." Taichi speaks the word as though it tastes bitter. "A senseless waste."

The wind stops, and James squirms to get down. He wanders aimlessly near us, singing a convoluted version of the ABCs.

Taichi fits an arm around my shoulders. "How will we ever explain this place to him?"

I watch James pick up a rock, his silky black hair slipping forward. I wish I could freeze him at this age. When he doesn't know racism or hate. When he doesn't notice what an oddity he is, half-Japanese and half-Italian.

"We'll find a way," I say as I lean into him. "We always do."

About the History

The first time I ever really thought about the incarceration of Japanese Americans was at a family dinner with my nana, a native Californian. She was fifteen when Pearl Harbor was bombed, and she told me how there had been a Japanese family down the street who was sent to the camps. "They didn't mind going," she said. "They liked it there."

Nana was in her late eighties at this time, so I didn't argue. Even though I didn't know much about the evacuation, I was unsettled enough by her statement that I found myself thinking about it often. How could she truly believe that they didn't mind? That they liked it there?

As I did the research to write *Within These Lines*, I learned how she could believe it. Because that's what the general population was told. They were shown (posed) photographs of Japanese American families enjoying camp life. Maybe they even heard stories about how the residents had everything in the camps from Boy Scouts to three "free" meals a day. These weren't like Hitler's death camps.

If you wanted to believe it wasn't so bad for the 120,000 Japanese American families forced out of their homes and imprisoned in places that eroded their dignity, culture, and family life, it was very easy to do.

While I like to think I would have been an Evalina, I know

more than likely that's not true. History storyteller Dan Carlin talks about how dangerous it is to judge those who have come before us from our 20/20 hindsight, and he applied this statement specifically to the incarceration of Japanese Americans. That when modern Americans talk about WWII, we ask why so few Germans stood up to Hitler. Carlin makes the point that for Germans, speaking out had deadly consequences. In America even when it wouldn't have been deadly, and perhaps there would have been no real consequence at all, very few spoke out on behalf of the Japanese Americans.

But their history has been preserved for us to learn from. Thanks to the bravery of so many who have spoken out about the incarceration, and to those who have been wise enough to document it, there is an amazing amount of history recorded and available to us. I deeply admire that our country eventually formally admitted the mistakes made with a public apology in 1988, and that instead of steamrolling a place like Manzanar, the former concentration camp has been turned into a national historic site that we can all visit.

I struggled to narrow my focus for this book. There were so many stories from all the camps and all the families that I longed to tell. If this is a subject that has captured your interest, there are many books available for you to read. The ones that moved me the most were *Farewell to Manzanar* by Jeanne Wakatsuki Houston and James D. Houston, *Dear Miss Breed* by Joanne Oppenheim, and *Looking Like the Enemy* by Mary Matsuda Gruenewald.

In my blend of history and fiction, I had to take multiple liberties that I would like to address.

For the Hamasaki family, who is a fictional family, I struggled with where they should be sent. The evacuation was very hasty and disorganized, so sometimes newspapers said that a group had gone to one assembly center when really, they'd been sent to another. The first group that left San Francisco reportedly went to Santa Anita Assembly Center. As mentioned in the story, these were meant to be temporary housing locations, and were on converted fairgrounds or racetracks.

Originally when I wrote this story, I had the Hamasaki family going to Santa Anita because I wanted to talk about the hard emotions of temporarily being housed in horse stalls. But the result was a muddled story, and there was no room to give attention to the arc of the complicated events at Manzanar. So while it would have been much more likely that a family in the Hamasakis' situation would have gone to Santa Anita, for the sake of effective and clear storytelling, I sent them directly to Manzanar.

The more I dug into Manzanar's complex history, the more confused I became by the various viewpoints. Fortunately, many personal stories have been preserved about camp life and the events that culminated in the riot. But just like us, each person involved had their own beliefs on what really happened, so trying to nail down the "real story" is impossible. I did my best to stick with facts, but ultimately this is a work of fiction being told from the perspective of a character who never existed.

At the riot, in addition to several who were hospitalized for injuries, two young men were killed. Both happened to go by different nicknames for James. Instead of fictionalizing one of their real stories, I created James Kanito as a way to recognize the loss of life that took place.

Similarly, while the Black Dragons are a real gang that existed at Manzanar, Raymond Yamishi was not a real person. I did include several real people in the book, including Joe Kurihara, Harry Ueno, the Yoneda family, Dr. Goto, and those mentioned on the death list. My purpose in doing this was to realistically frame Taichi's world, not to put words into the mouths of real people.

I am more thankful than words can express to Patricia Biggs of Manzanar National Historic Site who read *Within These Lines* to help with accuracy. Not only is she deeply knowledgeable about Manzanar history, she is also generous with her time, opinions, and resources. Any mistakes that remain in the book are my fault.

I'm also grateful to Holly Frey and Tracy V. Wilson of the *Stuff You Missed in History Class* podcast, whose teaching on Executive Order 9066 sparked the idea for Evalina and Taichi.

The Lost Girl of Astor Street

By Stephanie Morrill

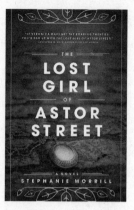

When her best friend vanishes without so much as a goodbye, eighteen-year-old Piper Sail takes on the role of amateur sleuth in an attempt to solve the mystery of Lydia's disappearance. Given that Piper's tendency has always been to butt heads with high society's expectations of her, it's no surprise that she doesn't give a second thought to searching for answers to Lydia's abduction from their privileged neighborhood.

As Piper discovers that those answers might stem from the corruption strangling 1924 Chicago—and quite possibly lead back to the doors of her affluent neighborhood—she must decide how deep she's willing to dig, how much she should reveal, and if she's willing to risk her life of privilege for the sake of the truth.

Perfect for fans of Libba Bray and Anna Godbersen, Stephanie Morrill's atmospheric jazz-age mystery will take readers from the glitzy homes of the elite to the dark underbelly of 1920s Chicago.